until
FOREVER
ends

ANNABELLE McCORMACK

Published by Annabelle McCormack

Editor by Marion Archer

Cover by Kari March Designs (ebook, paperback, hardcover)

Patrick Knowles (special edition paperback)

www.annabellemccormack.com

Hey Mamas: This is for you.
For those moments of loneliness.
When you would give your left arm for a nap.
For each time you feel crushing mom guilt.
Breathe.
And remember, taking care of yourself IS taking care of your kids. You wouldn't load them into a car that hasn't been taken care of, right? Mamas need to be taken care of, too.
So read the book.
Do the thing that makes you feel like YOU.

until FOREVER ends

PROLOGUE

April 1968

THE FAMILIAR BEAT of *I Think We're Alone Now* by Tommy James and the Shondells carried over the field, and Bernadette Durand lay back in the grass under the shade of the peach tree, covered in flower petals. Mom must have brought the record player outside for the party, which had started in her absence.

She couldn't will herself to get up.

With her long, dark hair cascading like a waterfall over her face and shoulders, she could almost block out the noise of everything but her heartbeat.

Forget that this was the worst day of her life.

Soft, familiar lips pressed to hers, and her eyes flew open. Blue eyes hovered above her, locked with hers.

He came looking for me.

Tears filled her eyes as she returned Peter's kiss, her heart lurching painfully in her chest. She lifted her hands around his freshly shaven face, tasting the familiar peppermint of his Doublemint gum, and her tears flowed down the corners of her eyes and pooled in her ears.

"I came for my girl."

Peter broke away and wiped her tears, helping her sit.

Then she got a good look at him.

He'd dressed in his Army uniform.

I should have expected it.

A lump rose in her throat. "Peter Yardley, I told you I didn't want to see you like this."

"And I told you I wanted to see you at my goodbye party. Come on, B. You couldn't even come for five minutes?"

Five minutes of what? Torturing herself? Him?

For the three years since they'd graduated from high school, this had been her constant fear. She'd begged him to go to college. Begged him to go to Canada. And he'd kept telling her luck was on his side. Their side.

"I'm a lucky sort of guy."

Until he'd taken matters into his own hands and enlisted rather than wait to be drafted.

How could he do this after what had happened to Robbie? Her brother had been captured a year earlier. *And we still don't know where he is.* How could her mother throw a party for Peter?

"Please." She sniffled, crying more freely now. "Please don't do this. Don't go. Just don't go."

She'd never even heard of Vietnam until a few years earlier. Now, the word threw a dark shadow into her heart, making her want to scream.

Peter said he couldn't live with himself if he sat on the side-lines anymore. *Not after Robbie.*

"B, I'll be fine. And when I come home, we'll get married. I'll make you proud, I promise."

"But I'm already proud of you." She flung her arms around his neck. "Please stay with me."

He held her tightly as she nestled her face into the crook of his neck. The first time they'd made love had been right here, under this tree, and she'd snuck out of her house in the middle of the night to meet him.

And now, it might be the last place she ever saw him. The last moment when he was hers.

"I love you, B. Nothing is going to change that. I'll be back before you blink."

She wiped her cheeks with her hands. "If you go, I won't be here. I'm going to Paris to go live with my mom's cousin. I won't stay a single day in Brandywood if you're not here. *I can't.*"

This time, it wasn't a vague threat. The thought of walking the streets of Brandywood without him was too overwhelming. They'd daydreamed of what they could build here in town together. She couldn't bear the thought of it without him.

If he was leaving, then she was going to leave, too.

He kissed her again, gently, then said, "I promise you this— I'm marrying you right here, someday. You'll see."

CHAPTER ONE

Travis

THE TROUBLE STARTED when Travis Wagner believed Hannah didn't want to do anything for Valentine's Day.

Why couldn't—for once—a woman actually just tell him what the hell she wanted to do for the over-commercialized, ridiculously priced, biggest guilt-trip holiday of all?

Want to go to a hotel and get room service and have sex all night?

Sounds good.

Hoping for a bouquet of red roses that costs quadruple what it usually does?

Just tell me so I can order.

Up for dinner with sardine-like table seating so the night can be extra uncomfortable?

Noted. I need a heads-up so I can make a reservation four weeks out.

But *nope.*

Hannah said she wanted to do *nothing.*

"Valentine's Day is stupid." Her *exact* words. *"I don't want to do anything."*

. . . except it was a *lie.*

And I was stupid enough to believe her.

As Travis drove through the streets of Brandywood with a frosty Hannah beside him, sweat beaded on the back of his neck. He'd called all the restaurants in a thirty-mile radius—which was not that many, given that Brandywood was a small town smack dab in the middle of the mountains of Western Maryland.

Not a reservation to be found.

In fact, the only possibility had come when the hostess at Yardley's told him that the high-tops on the bar side were first come, first serve, so if he could snag a table, it was his.

So he'd offered the hostess a free auto tune-up if she held a high-top for him, and by some miracle, she'd agreed. *Hallelujah.*

. . . *except it's Yardley's.*

Wagners didn't venture into Peter Yardley's famed restaurant, even if it was one of the town's favorite places. Travis's family would be furious with him for being spotted there, and given his father's recent escalation of the Wagner-Yardley feud, Travis might just get kicked out of Yardley's.

But what choice do I have?

He snuck Hannah a glance. She'd crossed her arms, her foot impatiently tapping on the floor mat of his restored Chevy Stingray.

They'd been dating for six months now, the longest relationship Travis had been in for

. . . well, *ever.* And even though they'd had a bumpy start, things had been going well for the past couple of months.

I don't want Valentine's Day to screw me over.

He should have known she didn't actually *mean* she didn't want to do anything, right? That was the joke. *Nothing never means nothing.* But how could he have? She'd been adamant. Sworn up and down how dumb and meaningless the holiday was.

. . . only to blow up at him over the phone an hour ago.

"I can't believe you didn't even buy me flowers, let alone plan a date."

Travis raked his fingers through his short hair, his chest unusually tight.

He shouldn't have even called Yardley's, except he'd been desperate.

. . . and it's not like it would be the first time I've gone against my family's wishes.

Pushing his pride low, he gritted his teeth, then pulled into the garage of his shop. Parking on Main Street was a nightmare tonight, and considering he lived and worked a five-minute walk from Yardley's, this was the best option. Besides, if Hannah cooled off, they might end up coming back here anyway.

She gave him a confused look as he killed the engine. "I thought you said you were picking me up to take me to dinner." Then her face brightened. "Unless . . . did you make me dinner?"

Riiiiiight. Yup. That would have been the next best thing.

He shifted uncomfortably in his seat, scanning her wide brown eyes. "Unfortunately, my stove is still broken." It was the truth, but dammit, if he'd thought of it, he could have gone up to his grandmother's café and whipped something up in the kitchen there. It was why he hadn't bothered fixing or replacing the stove for the past three months. He ate breakfast at his grandmother's or at Jen's place, made sandwiches for lunch, and then went back to the café for dinner—or went out with Hannah.

"Oh." Hannah's pretty face fell.

"I figured we could park here and walk." He was trying to avoid telling Hannah he hadn't made *any* plans even though she'd accused him of it. Instead, he'd said, *"Actually, I'm on my way to pick you up."* And then he'd hung up the phone and panicked.

The florist had been closed already, so he'd been forced to fly up to his best friend's farm and beg Ben for some flowers from the greenhouse. Then he'd swung by Jen's bakery and grabbed a box of chocolates—and once again, his two closest friends had saved his ass. He'd showered and changed in five minutes flat, then been out the door to pick Hannah up.

Hopefully, the hostess had managed to hold a high-top at Yardley's by now.

Who am I kidding? They don't clear out at eight on a normal Friday night, let alone a holiday.

He swung open the door to his car, then walked around for Hannah. She accepted his hand when he held it out for her, but when he leaned down to kiss her, she tilted her face, leaving him with a mouthful of air.

Ooof.

Why is she so mad, anyway?

He got her the flowers and the chocolates and the things she said she hated. Sure, he hadn't texted her *"Happy Valentine's Day"* until right before he'd called her this evening, but he'd been slammed all day doing paperwork for insurance claims, and Hannah frequently didn't text him until after work.

They exited the garage, and he reached for her hand. She gave him a limp fish handhold, not looking at him. "What's wrong?" He squeezed her hand.

Hannah tossed her long brown curls over her shoulder.

After a minute, she said tersely, "It just feels like you weren't that interested in trying to make our first Valentine's Day that significant."

For fuck's sake.

Irritation simmered low in his gut. Keeping his eyes level with the shops on Main Street, he couldn't help but notice the explosion of pink and red hearts that glared at him from all the store windows. Brandywood wasn't known for doing anything halfway, and decorating for each holiday majorly factored into that.

It probably wouldn't help him where Hannah was concerned.

He slowed as they got closer to Yardley's, which was brightly lit and warmed by outdoor string lights and heaters. Peter Yardley had made a lot of improvements to the property since he'd become a national homemaking sensation—Brandywood's biggest celebrity.

Travis's heart tugged as he thought about his grandmother's café, which had long been the town rival for the best food in town. The same magazine that had discovered Peter Yardley had given Nana a column, but that hadn't brought her the level of fame and collaborations it had Peter.

Hell, the man even has a TV show. So while Peter's business had surged with popularity—and resulted in the opening of his enormous Country Depot on Main Street and brought him wealth and throngs of tourists to the town—Nana was still working to make a living.

I shouldn't be here.

Still, he pushed the door open and moved inside.

He hadn't gone far when Hannah dropped his hand.

She stopped near the doors of the cozy foyer, a few feet from the hostess station. The crowded foyer brimmed with couples of all ages waiting to be seated, and—if Travis didn't know any better—they were all staring at him.

Because they know who you are. Where you are.

Tears shone in Hannah's eyes. Did she realize how hard he was trying here?

"What the hell, Travis?"

She wasn't quiet, and the foyer guests averted their gazes. Also leaned closer.

He quirked a brow at her. With a shake of her head, she turned and stormed out of the restaurant.

Travis followed her out into the cold February night. "Hannah, what? What is it?"

She whirled around. "Yardley's? You brought me to fucking *Yardley's?*"

"I—" Travis rubbed the back of his neck, heat rising on his cheeks. She was a lot shorter than he was—maybe by a foot—but stretched to her full length, and her anger poured from the tips of her fancy black shoes to the top of her head. "I know it's not as expensive as you might have expected, but I'm trying. This was the only place I could get a last-minute table."

Her dark eyes flashed. "Are you kidding me right now? So you were lying to me when you said you had plans?"

Why did she have to be so loud? He took her hand. "Can we go talk about this privately?"

She snatched her hand away. "I can't believe you. I thought this was going somewhere. My God, I am such an idiot."

Huh?

In a lower voice, with as much composure as he could muster, he managed, "You said you didn't want to celebrate Valentine's Day. That you didn't want to do anything."

"No, no." She lifted a hand. "What I *said* is that if you had to ask what I wanted to do, then it would be nothing."

"No, that is not what you said—"

"Don't tell me what I fucking said, Travis. And honestly, it doesn't make a difference. Because clearly, I don't mean enough to you to make plans to celebrate Valentine's Day, but then, to add insult to injury, you bring me to *Yardley's of all fucking places?*"

Her voice screeched, and Travis stepped back, hoping the people on the other side of the wooden door to the foyer couldn't hear.

"It's not a bad restaurant. I mean, not that I know from experience, but everyone else seems to—"

"Did you forget about my dad's complaint to the town council? About the *gelato?*" She said the word as though it were poison.

Oh.

Oh holy shit.

Fuuuuck.

Yes, yes, he had forgotten. Because he was so busy thinking about his own family's drama with the Yardleys that he'd forgotten about Fred Strickland's ice cream shop.

For years, Stricklands' Ice Cream had claimed they had an exclusive deal with the town to be the only ice cream shop on Main. Then Peter's Country Depot had opened and offered gelato, which Peter claimed was substantially different enough to be allowed.

And now that Travis's dad was trying to get Peter Yardley's store booted from Main Street, Fred Strickland had become a huge supporter of the proposal.

He could read the look on Hannah's face that this was the far bigger issue right now.

While they'd never really discussed the Wagner-Yardley feud, it had never occurred to Travis that part of his appeal might be that he was on the Wagner side of things.

"I—"

Hannah shook her head. "I can't believe you would even come here. Tonight, of all nights."

He stared at her, trying to figure out what to say to make this right.

Then the part of his brain that got him in trouble, the one that made him the least "Wagner out of the family"—as his sister Grace had so bluntly put it—clicked on. "They're just people. It's just a restaurant. A giant fissure isn't going to open in the center of town if we walk in. We just proved that." He reached for both her hands, a hint of a smile at the corners of his lips.

Humor usually helped their arguments.

But this time, Hannah didn't crack a smile. She pulled her hands away as though he'd stung her. "If that's what you think, then this whole relationship has been a huge fucking mistake."

Travis's eyebrows came together. "What?"

"You heard me. This is over. Don't bother to offer to drive me home. I'll call a friend. Because I can't stand the sight of you right now." Hannah turned and stormed down the sidewalk.

Travis followed her. "Wait, you're breaking up with me?"

"Not a moment too soon, apparently."

Come again? "Over the Yardleys?"

"Over your fucking disloyalty. Please." Hannah stopped and glared at him. "Get the hell away from me, Travis. I'm serious. This thing between us is over. Go back to Yardley's since that's apparently where you want to be tonight." She started forward again.

Her immaturity had never seemed so obvious. She was twenty-two—four years younger than him—which he'd told Ben didn't really feel like a gap. But now, somehow, it did.

Disloyalty?

Because of Fred Strickland getting his panties in a twist over ice cream?

He could handle going to Yardley's *for her sake* when his family had legitimate issues with the Yardley family over the years, so yeah, fuck that.

Maybe it was self-preservation.

Maybe it was the fact that he'd just spent the evening trying to bend over backward for her, and she'd been ungrateful.

"Grow up, Hannah," he finally snapped, not following her any farther.

She tossed him a venomous look over her shoulder. "I'll be sure to let everyone know where you stand on things tomorrow at the town council meeting."

Then she pulled out her phone and dialed someone, leaving him standing there.

Travis clenched his jaw. The town council meeting. Where his father would push forward the proposal to vote Peter Yardley's Country Depot off Main Street.

It won't be a good look for me if Hannah says something.

But, then again, he didn't exactly agree with his father on this.

If he was going to be thrown under the bus, he may as well get a beer first.

Turning back toward Yardley's, he headed inside, straight to the bar.

CHAPTER TWO

Lindsay

THREE MONTHS of being in charge had changed her brother into a total, unmitigated *asshole*.

Lindsay Yardley crossed her arms in disbelief as she stared at Logan, furious he'd pulled her from the bar during one of the busiest nights of the year. "You really called me back here for *this bullshit?*"

Logan's eyes, a similar blue-gray as her own, simmered with displeasure. "Hey. I might be your brother, but I'm still your boss. Watch it."

She rocked her weight back onto one heel of her tennis shoes, her fury building. "Or what, Logan? You'll fire me? Even you can't do that, and you know it."

"I can when you're stealing. Which you are." He clasped his hands together, leaning forward at his desk.

His desk.

Pops's desk.

God, she'd never missed her grandfather managing the restaurant and bar more than she did at this moment. The office used to be a place of comfort for her—she'd often come to do her homework here while she was in high school. Quieter than the library, with better food, and Pops to spoil her.

But then he'd gone and become a celebrity, with his own television series, a camera crew that followed him around, another enormous store, and way too much to do for a seventy-six-year-old. He hadn't wanted to give up bartending or managing the restaurant, but Mom and Dad had practically threatened a coup after Pops's cardiologist had told him he needed to take it easy last fall.

Enter Logan.

"Pops never had a problem with me comping drinks. Do you have any idea how many drinks that man gave away a night? Actually . . . no, you don't. Because you never tended bar here. Meanwhile, it's been my part-time job since I was in college."

"Well, Pops isn't running things anymore. And if you're right, then it's no wonder the bar was having trouble before he hit it big. You're giving away the product people are coming here to buy, Linds. Explain how that makes any sense."

She puffed out a long sigh from her cheeks. "Because," she said through gritted teeth, "they buy more of it. Plus, they keep coming back here and don't go somewhere else because they now have a favorite bartender."

"I don't buy it. And you know what? It doesn't matter. We aren't doing that anymore. You can comp five drinks a night. That's it."

Five? She gave away five drinks an hour—if not more.

This was ridiculous. Just one more thing Logan could hold over her. One more way he could prove what amazing things his master's in business would do for him and the restaurant—and how more qualified he was than Lindsay to be in charge.

Not that it makes a difference. No one in her family had even considered her for the position.

To them, she was "little Linds", youngest of the five Yardley children, preschool teacher, and most likely to get along with everyone.

Decidedly *not* the future face of Yardley Enterprises.

And that was fine. *Sort of.* They were right. She wanted nothing to do with business meetings, corporate sponsorships, and camera crews.

But now that the restaurant was in Logan's hands, she couldn't help wondering why she hadn't put up a bigger fight to have *some* say in the way they would run it.

Before she could think of any reasonable response to Logan's demands on her, a tap on the door sounded, followed by her other brother, Jake, cracking it open.

"Got a second?" Jake asked, poking his head in.

Logan raised his chin. "What's up?"

Jake smirked. "You'll never guess who just sat down at the bar." Before Logan could answer, Jake said, "Travis Wagner."

Lindsay's heart squeezed.

Travis is here?

Logan stood, the legs of his chair scraping against the floorboards. His face darkened. "What the hell is he doing here?"

Good question.

In all the time Lindsay had worked at her grandfather's bar, she'd never witnessed any Wagner come in here, which was unsurprising. She didn't know what made this worse—that one had finally made an appearance or that it was Travis.

Logan might go out there and make this ugly.

And tonight, of all nights, was not a night to make a scene. Not with the big vote at the council tomorrow morning.

"Not sure. But apparently he showed up with Hannah Strickland—and get this—she dumped him in a yelling match outside the door." Jake couldn't have looked more delighted at what must have been a humiliating for Travis. Lindsay had to restrain herself from speaking. "Want me to get rid of him?"

She should step in.

Lindsay cleared her throat. "Will you two just let it go? He's a paying customer, right? We're all about the bottom line now, apparently. I'll give him a few drinks and gently nudge him out the door."

Logan and Jake both shot her quizzical looks, and she hooked her thumbs into the belt loops of her jeans. "He's Jen's *other* best friend. Please. For her sake—and mine by extension—don't make a scene." They both loved Jen Cavanaugh. If anything could stay them, that might just do the trick.

Logan set his hands on his desk and leaned toward her. "You make it clear he's not welcome to come back, or I will."

Forcing a smile, Lindsay nodded, then pushed past Jake. Her cheeks burned as she fled into the hallway, her stomach churning. Logan had every right to be mad, especially given the hell that Travis's dad, Todd Wagner, was causing for their family.

She made a pit stop at the bathroom, pausing in front of the sink to splash some cold water onto her red face. *I can't take working for Logan much longer.* But the money was good, and she'd been bartending for so long.

Of all nights, why did Travis have to pick tonight to show up at the bar?

She scanned her own reflection and then loosened her honey-blond hair down from the ponytail she wore before gathering it up more neatly once again. She didn't have any reason to be nervous. Travis wasn't here to see her, and it sounded like he'd just endured a humiliating breakup.

On Valentine's Day. Yikes.

Jitters fluttered through her fingers. She'd avoided him for a good six months now, even skipping Jen's Christmas party a couple of months ago because she'd known Travis was going with Hannah.

She hadn't been jealous, of course. That would take being emotionally involved, which wasn't what she and Travis had ever shared.

But being around him always made her feel like their little secret was vulnerable to exposure.

Lindsay dried her hands, then left the bathroom, heading straight to the bar. Luis, who'd picked up an extra shift tonight to help, gave her an exasperated look as she scooted past him. "Where you been? It's chaos out here."

"Sorry. The *boss* wanted to talk to me about comping drinks." Lindsay rolled her eyes.

Luis grinned. "He worried they're going to tip you too well?"

Ugh. Yet another reason to not like Logan's new policy. She made such good money on tips.

"Can you help me make six Cosmos? The single ladies' club over there just asked for another round." Luis nodded at the corner of the bar.

Lindsay looked in the direction he'd indicated and spotted Travis seated at the very end of the bar. He wasn't talking to anyone and held his beer glass in both hands, staring down at it.

He looked miserable.

Ouch. Her heart tugged.

Even Travis Wagner didn't deserve to be feeling like shit on Valentine's Day.

She went to the cranberry juice dispenser, tearing her gaze away from Travis.

He looked good tonight, too. Dark hair, short and messy,

shaven. He'd always looked a bit more like a James Dean rebel beatnik than the typical jeans and flannel that Brandywood seemed to serve up so well. But built. Clearly, more than mechanic work went into that body—and she knew from first-hand experience.

. . . and that's enough of that.

She didn't need to go down that line of thought tonight.

She worked on the cocktails, then set them on a tray for a server to take. There wasn't time to think about Travis right now. The bar was just as busy with the people celebrating Valentine's Day as with the haters and the lonely folks who just wanted a drink on a Friday night.

Once Travis finished his beer, she'd close out his tab—if he had one—and the receipt would be a nudge to get going.

. . . except forty minutes later, Travis still sat there, staring at the same beer.

He'd pulled out his phone at some point, but that was it.

Not a sip.

Sighing, Lindsay went over to the shelf and grabbed a bottle of Patrón and a shot glass.

Setting it in front of Travis, she poured him a shot and set it down with a lime wedge. His eyes met hers as though it surprised him she'd finally come over. "What's that for?"

"You. Because clearly whatever light beer you ordered isn't cutting it tonight."

Travis scowled. "Maybe I don't feel like drinking alone." He pushed the shot back toward her.

She held his gaze, then grabbed another shot glass. After setting it down, she poured herself a shot. "Cheers." She lifted the glass, raising her brow.

Travis didn't move for a minute, then he took the glass. "I don't even know what the hell I'm doing here, you know?"

"Neither do I. But drinking seems like a good excuse." She

winked, then downed the shot, the liquid burning her throat. She grabbed the lime wedge and popped it into her mouth, biting down.

Travis followed suit a moment later.

Now that he'd had his drink, he could leave.

But Travis nudged the glass toward her. "Another round?"

"Maybe for you. You have a heartbreak to heal." She poured another shot and winked. "I can't afford to get drunk on the job." She turned to go.

"She said she didn't even want to celebrate Valentine's Day."

Hannah?

Lindsay turned back to him with a smirk. "And you believed her?"

"I didn't have any reason not to."

Now she smiled more broadly. "You stupid, stupid man. Rule number one. Never believe any woman who says not to make her feel special on a romantic holiday."

Travis frowned at his tequila. "Yeah, well, it's a little late for that. Laugh it up."

Lindsay bit her lip. She shouldn't make fun of him. No matter what had happened between him and Hannah, no one deserved to be dumped publicly. She'd worked too long at this job and had seen too many private issues aired in humiliating manners. Alcohol had a way of doing that.

She hesitated, then poured herself another shot. "One more. Just because you need this tonight." She downed it and then nodded at him to do the same.

"I don't need your pity, Lindsay." Travis's eyes narrowed, but he took the shot, then pushed the glass away. "You don't have to pretend we're friends because I got dumped at the doorstep of your freaking restaurant. And I didn't drink the beer because I'm pretty sure your brother spat in my glass before he poured it."

It sounded like something Jake might do.

"So you just sat here at the bar instead?"

"Why not?" Travis shrugged. "I've got nowhere else to be tonight. And if that's how Jake's going to play it, I may as well occupy a paying seat." Bitterness tinged his voice.

Lindsay sighed and snatched the beer away. Dumping it, she grabbed a fresh glass and poured a new one. Setting it down in front of him, she said, "Here. On the house. But my advice is to drink it and go. Spitting in your glass is one of the more innocuous things my brothers will do, and you know it."

As she backed away from the bar top, she felt as though she'd slammed into a solid wall. She startled, then turned to see Logan standing there, his expression dark.

"Giving drinks away again, Linds?" he hissed, displeasure written on his face.

She shrank back. How long had he been standing there?

"You asked me to get rid of him," she managed in a low voice, hoping Travis wouldn't overhear. The last thing she needed was to be humiliated by her brother in front of him.

"Yeah. Forty minutes ago. Not give him shots of Patrón and beer for free."

"There a problem?" Travis's voice was clear, and she looked over her shoulder at him. Travis stood, his eyes dark.

"Travis was just leaving, Logan. Leave it alone, will you?" She gave Travis a firm look, hoping he could read her eyes. *Just go, you idiot.*

"Actually, I wasn't. And I have no problem paying for my drinks. Even the one Jake spat in." Travis edged closer to the bar and pulled his wallet out, then set a credit card on the surface.

Logan reached past Lindsay and lifted the edge of the card

with his thumb and forefinger. Flicking it off the bar, it spun through the air toward the floor. "I'm not interested in your money, asshole. Get out of my bar."

Travis's eyes glittered darkly, but his face was a hard mask. He didn't budge.

"Logan, please." Lindsay set her hand on his forearm, giving him a pleading look. "People are staring." The bar had started to empty out. The one thing about Valentine's Day was that the romantics all had somewhere to be and the depressed only got more depressed. But the Brandywood locals who remained all watched with curiosity. No doubt everyone in town would know about this confrontation before sunrise.

"Well?" Logan spoke over the top of her head.

Travis didn't move for another full minute. Then at last, he leaned down and retrieved his credit card. Slipping it back into his pocket, he made his way out of the bar.

Lindsay watched him leave, a mixture of regret and relief in her chest. She glared at Logan. "That was a dick move."

"You. In my office. *Again.*" Logan didn't look at her, then left with a scowl.

Oh hell no.

Her eyes prickled, stinging with sudden tears. How dare he treat her like a petulant child?

"Get out of my bar," Logan had told Travis.

His bar.

Like she, Jake, Maddie, and Naomi didn't have as much right to this bar as he did. Just because he was the eldest.

Swallowing back her tears, she sidled up to Luis. "You think you can handle the rest of the night?" She hoped her eyes weren't red.

"Wha—" Luis scanned her face, a divot showing between his eyebrows. Then he nodded. "Sure. You take off if you need to."

She gave him a thin-lipped smile, then peeled off her apron, stashing it under the register. Hurrying past Luis, she started for the exit. As she walked, she grabbed a bottle of Patrón and turned toward Luis. "Tell Logan to take this out of my pay."

Luis gave her a wink, and she scooted out of the bar, heading toward the back of the restaurant.

She passed Logan's closed office door, her throat clenching. He could wait there for her all fucking night.

Pushing open the back door, she stepped out into the icy winter air and shivered. She'd left her coat inside but didn't feel like returning for it.

Pausing by the back, she sucked in a deep breath, letting the air cool her burning face. She didn't want to go home. Logan would talk with Mom and Dad, and she'd have to deal with this whole thing before she ate breakfast tomorrow. Maybe she'd walk to Pops's house and spend the night there. He never locked the back door anyway and wouldn't care if she crashed there.

She hadn't gone far when she spotted a dark figure leaning against the wall in the brick alleyway between the restaurant and the pottery shop next door, Slip and Grog.

Travis.

Her heart gave a thump.

Her grip tightened on the bottle of Patrón. What was he still doing here? Hoping to confront Logan?

She strode up to him. "Do you have a death wish tonight?"

Travis lifted his gaze toward her. She knew his eyes were unique hazel, as though they couldn't decide what they wanted to be, but right now, she saw nothing but dark. "Maybe." Then he raised a brow at the tequila. "You still trying to follow me around and ply me with alcohol?"

She grinned and rolled her eyes. "Yeah, because we both know how well that went for us last time. Maybe I just needed a good drink after dealing with my asshole brothers." She uncapped it and took a swig for effect. *Careful now.* She was already feeling the effects of the last two shots.

Travis left his spot against the wall and came closer to her. His fingertips skimmed the back of hers as he took the bottle and lifted it. "Was last time really so bad?" He swallowed back a mouthful of tequila.

She breathed out, the alcohol making her lips tingle.

Or maybe it was the way his hand had brushed hers.

She leaned back against the alley wall, then took the bottle back. "It's going to take a lot more tequila for that to happen again, Travis."

He shrugged, stepping closer to her. "I don't have any plans. What about you?"

His palm curved over her hip, and her breath hitched.

He's Travis.

Your brothers hate him.

You're heading to Pops's house.

Tequila really wasn't her friend.

CHAPTER THREE

A GIANT, slobbery dog tongue swiped across Lindsay's face, snapping her awake.

What the hell?

A soft exhale from the other side of the bed made the synapses of her sluggish brain fire.

Oh shit.

Lindsay rubbed her eyes, tugging the crust from the corners, trying to think as she rolled over. The dog, a black lab named Ratchet, set his chin on the mattress, staring up at her with soulful eyes while his tail wagged.

A few drinks? Was that all it had taken?

She hadn't been completely drunk.

But it had been enough.

The room was still in darkness, the curtains of the room-darkening variety. Getting to the bedroom had been a tangle of clothes and bumping up against furniture in the dark, though, and she'd never stayed here during the day long enough to really see his room.

She wasn't wearing any clothes, was she? She checked under the sheets.

Nope.

Of all the men in this freaking town, why did Travis Wagner have to come to the bar last night?

She smiled to herself as she remembered the night before.

It was so good.

It always was.

Sex with Travis was incredible.

Addictive.

And completely, totally a mistake.

Again.

I can't believe I did this again.

Each time this had happened, they'd discussed that it was stupid. Besides the fact that they barely tolerated each other and their families would kill them, they should have some self-control by now, right? One-night stands—no matter how steamy—had never been Lindsay's idea of the best way to handle a ridiculous sexual attraction or fill a lonely void . . . or whatever drove them back to this again.

One thing was for certain, she wasn't about to let Travis see her naked in the daylight, no matter what they'd done last night.

She slipped out of the bed, looking around for her clothes.

Ratchet chose that moment to bound toward her again and made a play bow.

"No," Lindsay hissed in a low voice, pointing toward the open door. "Go back out there."

When Ratchet didn't budge, Lindsay grabbed one of Travis's shoes and tossed it out the door. "Fetch!" It banged into the wall, and she winced, glancing back toward the bed. Travis didn't move.

Whew.

But neither had Ratchet, who stood in front of her with his tail wagging.

Screw it. I need my clothes. She dropped to the floor and located her phone on the wooden floorboards by her jeans. She tugged it out and flipped the flashlight on, shining it over the scattered clothes.

This is so embarrassing.

She'd thought she was over this stuff. Gone almost a year without one of these ridiculous hookups.

You're not a hormone-raging teenager anymore, Linds. Get a grip.

But now here she was, crawling around butt-naked Travis's apartment bedroom, trying to find her underwear, even more humiliated than she'd been when Travis had come into the bar the night before, and—

"Good morning to you, too."

Dammit.

Lindsay grabbed the first thing near her and pulled it over her head. It turned out to be Travis's work shirt—*man, it smells good.* Like a soft combination of fabric softener, a rugged men's cologne, and the scent of Travis's shop.

She scrambled to her feet. "Hey." She pushed a strand of hair behind her ear, hoping she didn't look like the mess she felt.

Travis chuckled and propped himself up on his elbows, showing off bare arms that were equal parts ropey, thickly built with tanned muscle and tattooed skin. "Leaving already?" He stretched back, then pushed some pillows behind his head, leaning up against the headboard.

"I just remembered I left some laundry on." She found her lacy red bra dangling from the lamp on his dresser and hurried over to snatch it.

"Hilarious. And here I thought you might be up for round four—or is it five? Are we counting the alleyway?"

The alleyway. Man, they'd been reckless. "Don't you think I've already stayed long enough?"

Travis shrugged. "I can think of worse ways to spend the night." He grinned, clearly amused by her discomfort.

"In all seriousness, we both know it shouldn't have happened." She put the clasps of her bra together and then stepped into it, pulling it on under the long T-shirt. Attempting to be modest in front of Travis was sort of ridiculous since he'd obviously seen her naked just a few hours ago. But she may as well try to salvage whatever last scrap of dignity she had here.

Travis wasn't entirely wrong. The showdown at the restaurant—both Travis's with Hannah and hers with Logan—had made for volatile emotions and irritation. Sex had made all that go away for a few hours. Not that using each other as scratching posts was dignified or fixed anything.

Locating the rest of her clothes, she pulled them on and then swept her hair into a ponytail. Travis still watched her from the bed wordlessly, and she turned back toward him with a grimace. "Why do you keep looking at me?"

He smirked and pushed aside the sheets, and she averted her gaze. His chuckle followed. "Can't stand to look at me now?" He strode up beside her, then plucked his boxer briefs from the bookcase at her side. She pressed her lips together, focusing on the spines of the books on the shelves, the memory of peeling those briefs off with her teeth searing through her.

Travis grabbed a fresh pair of briefs from his dresser, and she saw him pull them on from the corner of her eye. Not that he wasn't good-looking. He *was delicious.* Like a fucking forbidden piece of chocolate when she was on a diet. *Maybe fucking forbidden isn't the right term.* Fucking seemed to be the one thing they didn't completely rule out between them.

Her cell phone rang in her hand. Her sister, Maddie. Lindsay held a finger up to Travis in warning, then answered. "Hey."

"Hey, where are you?" Maddie sounded like she was speaking in a crowded room.

Lindsay furrowed her brow, then winced. *Crap. The town meeting.* Her gaze shot to Travis, her chest tightening. If her sister only knew where Lindsay was, she would murder her.

"Uh . . . I'm on my way. Sorry. Late night."

"Where the hell did you spend the night? Logan says you walked off your shift without permission. He's really pissed at you right now."

Maddie wasn't the type to take sides usually. She was solidly the middle child who got along with everyone. But the word "*permission*" hit Lindsay in the gut. "Logan was being an ass. If he wants to treat me like an employee and not his sister, he's going to get the attitude I would give a boss if they were acting like a self-righteous prick."

She could practically hear Maddie's eye roll. "Whatever. Just get down here. Dad is counting on your vote. It's going to be a tight one. Fucking Wagners have called in every favor they have, and this place is packed."

Lindsay hung up, hoping Travis hadn't overheard and thankful Maddie hadn't pressed her on where she was. She clicked off her phone screen, avoiding Travis's gaze. "I have to go. The town meeting starts in ten minutes. Could you drop me off somewhere within walking distance this time?"

Travis raised a dark brow. "Or we could just walk in together. We're twenty-six, Linds. Even if someone else in Brandywood suspected what happened last night, we could handle it. It's not like we're dating. The idea of a Yardley and a Wagner hooking up won't trigger a nuclear meltdown. We're two consenting adults."

Her jaw dropped. "Um, Logan almost punched you just for coming into the bar. Do you have any idea what he would do to you if he found out we were together last night? Jake, too."

Travis crossed his arms. "I'm not afraid of your brothers."

"Well, my family might disown *me*. Not to mention the fact that you and your girlfriend just broke up last night. You know how that makes me look? I'll be slut-shamed and called a total traitor—which I pretty much am."

"That's ridiculous. You're not a traitor. Or a slut."

"Yeah, well, hopping into bed with you whenever I've had something to drink won't help anyone's perception of me. And stop looking at me that way. This is done. You're done thinking of me sexually."

"So I should probably return that sex tape we made at Halloween a few years ago?" He smirked.

What. The. Hell.

She gasped. "You still have that thing? My God, Travis! Yes, give it to me. What if someone—like a girlfriend of yours— saw that?"

"You can't tell it's you. That hot witch costume made it impossible."

She outstretched her hand, tingles of pleasure running down her spine. She couldn't believe he'd kept it after all this time. *Did he still watch it?* "Give it to me now."

Travis sighed and went into his closet. Pulling a shoebox down from the top shelf, he rummaged through it and pulled out a thumb drive. He brought it over to her and held it out. "This isn't a war."

Lindsay snatched the thumb drive from him. She was going to burn this thing.

Maybe watch it first, then burn it.

Ack. No. Definitely just burn it.

. . . after a quick watch.

Just to make sure I'm not recognizable.

Thank God Travis couldn't see her inner struggle.

That's it. I need to cut off this thing between us once and for all. Then she settled her weight onto her back foot. "Is your dad going to drop his campaign to have my grandfather's store kicked off Main Street?"

Rolling his eyes, Travis grabbed a pair of jeans from the dresser, which triggered Ratchet into hopping up from his space in the corner of the room. The dog's tail wagged excitedly as though pants signified his daily outing. "Your grandfather's store is a public nuisance. There's no parking anywhere anymore. Buses are pulling into our streets—which aren't meant to handle public transport like that—and stopping traffic for minutes while unloading their tourists."

"Riiight. So that's a no, then." So typical of a Wagner—only looking at the negatives rather than the influx of tourism money that her grandfather had single-handedly brought into town.

Travis cocked his head. "Okay, fine then. Is your sister going to drop her lawsuit that Bunny's didn't disclose an allergen and almost killed a kid at her daughter's birthday party?"

Lindsay narrowed her eyes. "Not funny. That little girl ended up in the hospital for four days, Travis." Naomi wouldn't lie about something so serious.

"Yeah, well, it wasn't the cookies. My grandmother is careful about shit like that. Unlike your family who doesn't care two licks about how their behavior affects others."

And there it is.

Why we agreed to stop hooking up.

Why this doesn't work, no matter how good the sex is.

Why this was another colossal mistake.

People in Brandywood laughed about the infamous Yardley-Wagner feud, but Lindsay guessed that was mostly because most people didn't understand how much their families really hated each other. She'd grown up living and breathing it. Hearing her father grumble about the Wagners was a regular discussion in her home.

No one knew how the whole thing started, but the feud had lasted several generations. What the people in town knew? How much worse it had gotten when Travis's grandmother, Bunny, married into the Wagner family.

So even if the folks from Brandywood didn't take it seriously, Lindsay knew from the inside how much their families did. Her parents and siblings would be furious if they ever found out she'd hooked up with Travis. *Multiple times. Over the past ten years.* But she wouldn't think about that.

Lindsay gritted her teeth, then grabbed her bag from the floor. No more Patrón if Travis Wagner was within a five-mile radius. That needed to be her new motto.

For a split second, her gaze flitted to the bed, and she remembered how soft that mattress was as Travis pushed her into it face-first, holding her hips from behind.

Nope. Not going to even imagine it.

She turned and gave Travis a hard look. "This stops today. No more. I'm serious this time. Now, are you going to drop me off or not?"

It was sad that they even had a way of handling the morning after. Travis's job as a mechanic who lived above his shop meant she could easily sneak into the closed garage and his car stored there. She'd ride in the back seat, hidden under a blanket, and they'd drive to an isolated spot and she'd get out. Then she'd walk, if needed, or get a rideshare.

Travis pulled his shirt over his head, yanking it down. He seemed as irritated as she was. "You got it, sweetheart."

"Don't call me that." She started out of the bedroom door, Travis steps behind her.

Ratchet bounded past them both, making circles around their feet.

"Linds, I'm not your freaking enemy. Look, we had a good night together, given how badly things started for us both. It was fun. I'm not asking for it to happen again either, but for once, can we just not make this a thing where we decide all future decisions two seconds after we wake up?"

She glanced back at him as he scrambled over toward the kitchen table and grabbed a dog food scoop. Popping open a plastic bucket of food beside the table, he leaned down, then picked up the dog bowl next to it and served Ratchet his breakfast. Plastic buckets and scoops and furniture that looked like a mismatched hodgepodge he'd picked up at various yard sales—he had the quintessential bachelor pad.

No wonder Hannah dumped him. How could anyone see a future with Travis Wagner?

Ouch. *That was mean.*

Why am I so mad at him, anyway?

But she wasn't. She was mad at herself. She knew her foils, and Travis was one of them. No matter how many times she'd tried to tell herself one more night wasn't a big deal, the older she got, the more *one more night* just seemed to affirm that she couldn't get her shit together or be responsible—just like her family seemed to think.

Logan had been the natural first choice for running Pops's restaurant because—unlike her—he looked great on paper. He had that business degree, and people respected him and thought he could run things. Her family seemed to think all she was capable of was mixing cocktails and singing the *ABC's* with her preschool students. And her dating life was nonexistent because she lacked time and was incredibly picky. She kept making the same damned mistakes and Travis was one of them.

I thought I'd be settled by now. Content.

"I'm really not trying to be harsh. You're right. It was fun. It always is fun. Yet we always regret it, don't we? I'm just speeding up the process where we say never again because you're also right about us being twenty-six. I want to be taken seriously. My friends have serious jobs, own their own businesses, and are married and having babies or engaged—both of which aren't even on my horizon, thanks to the terrible dating pool in town. I don't have the luxury of screwing around anymore. And I don't think this arrangement is what you're looking for either, is it?"

Travis's features softened. From the little he'd revealed last night, Hannah had hurt him. He'd never had a reputation as a playboy and was just as well liked in town as Lindsay was, thanks to their families.

"No, I'm looking for something more long-term."

"Right. So why beat around the bush? This has to end." The soft crunching of Ratchet gobbling down his food filled the tense silence. Amazing how easy it was to be matter-of-fact with him. Maybe because they'd hooked up so many times over the years, and there wasn't that mystery and tension there.

Sex. No strings attached. Funny how people said it didn't work with your friends. It almost weirdly worked with her enemy. He had as much to lose from people finding out the truth as she did, so they made sure that information never got out. Only Jen knew about it, and even then, Lindsay had only told her about it the first time when they were sixteen.

Travis didn't respond and palmed his keys from a bowl on the kitchen counter that also held a spotted banana, a few randomly sized batteries, and a wrench. "Shall we?"

"Don't you need to take the dog out first?"

Travis shook his head. "He'll let himself out back when he

needs to go." He gestured toward the back stairwell that led to his shop.

She went ahead of him, her heart unusually heavy as she clamored down the metal steps into the garage. The scents of car oil, grease, and gasoline hung heavily in the space, reminding Lindsay of the time she'd spent in Travis's arms the night before.

Not that he'd smelled like that last night. Though that one time a couple of years ago they had hooked up in the garage. She gripped the railing, closing her eyes. She didn't want to hate herself for this. So what if she sometimes hooked up with a single, consenting hot guy?

No doubt about it, Travis Wagner was hot. He was cut with broad shoulders, and in the summer, he tanned like a Greek god. If she was honest, part of her pickiness with the men in town resulted from her comparing them to Travis.

Then again, hooking up with a guy she didn't particularly like wasn't exactly a net positive.

Gritting her teeth, she went toward Travis's refurbished 1960s Chevy Corvette Stingray. *Great.* She'd forgotten that he'd been driving this thing around. A two-seater. Fortunately, he had the cover on it since it was winter. Where was she supposed to ride? The floor of that passenger seat looked cramped.

Still . . . wow. He'd done an incredible job restoring it. Her grandfather had even commented on how he wished he could talk Travis into selling it or restoring one for him.

"People might see me in this thing," Lindsay said, glancing at him as he arrived at the driver's seat. "How am I supposed to sit on the floor?"

Travis grinned. "Let me get you a moving blanket to sit under. Unless you'd prefer the trunk?"

"You would try to shove me in the trunk of your car."

"Only if I happened to bring a shovel with me, too." Travis went to the trunk and pulled out a folded blue moving blanket.

"Hilarious. You ever try digging a hole in the winter? I'm confident you'd be caught."

She leaned in and spotted a bouquet and a box of chocolates on the seat.

And then she felt truly horrible.

He'd clearly bought them for Hannah, maybe even driven her in the car before the whole debacle at the restaurant.

She winced and grabbed them, holding them out to him. "Someone forget these?"

Travis's expression didn't change as he took them quietly, then dumped them in a garbage can.

That's sad, too.

Lindsay climbed into the tight space and sat in the passenger seat. Travis took the driver's seat and then unfolded the blanket. He draped it over her a moment later, and she shook her head. *The ride of shame. Humiliating.*

The garage door opened, then Travis started the engine with a roar. She'd never really thought about how loud these old cars were, or maybe it was exacerbated by the blanket, but she wished she could see Travis drive it. It seemed like a fun car to take a drive in.

Just not under these circumstances.

The seat floor seemed to vibrate as they exited the garage, and she leaned back, trying to think through the dull headache. She needed water, coffee, breakfast, and sleep. Not necessarily in that order. *Also a toothbrush.*

Instead, she was heading to a damn community meeting because her dad would be furious if she missed the vote.

"Do you have any gum?"

"Yeah, I do. But it might look a little weird if I'm seen handing a pack of gum to the chair beside me."

The fact that Travis thought about things like that—that he understood her own paranoia—was also why these hookups had worked. *He really is one of the good ones.* Regardless, his hand slipped under the blanket a minute later, his palm grazing her thigh as he dropped a stick of gum onto her lap.

She took it from him and popped it in her mouth, trying to think. This meeting wouldn't be a fun one for either of them. His dad, a councilman for the town, had forced a vote on the issue about her grandfather's store. And even though Travis had made it clear he supported his dad's actions, any town meeting where the Yardley-Wagner feud was at the center of the agenda was usually uncomfortable and felt slightly . . . wrong. It was hard to put her finger on it, but it felt as though the town's best interests sometimes got overlooked because of the feud. How was that good for Brandywood?

They rolled to a stop a few minutes later, and Travis leaned across her and opened the door.

"Is it safe?" Lindsay asked.

"Would I have stopped if it wasn't?"

True. Lindsay pulled the blanket off her head, feeling flushed. He'd stopped near the woods just outside of Main Street. Fortunately, with Brandywood being a sleepy little town in the mountains, there was no shortage of woods with no one around.

She climbed out, feeling like she should say something else, but was unsure of what to say.

What more is there to say, really?

Thanks?

This was fun, let's not do it again?

Her hand hesitated on the door handle. "Travis . . ."

He gave her an expectant look, his features not betraying what he might think or feel.

"I just want to say . . ." Lindsay swallowed hard, her brain scrambling. She shouldn't linger here. That defeated the purpose of a drop-off. At last, she managed, "Hopefully, our families will behave at the meeting, but if they don't, I'm sorry in advance."

Now, why the hell did I say that? His dad is trying to force my grandfather to move his store!

Travis's eyes registered a faint look of surprise.

But before he could answer, the chime of a bicycle sounded, and Brian Pearson—one of her grandfather's best friends—pedaled past them on his bike, whistling a low tune, then kept going, not looking at them.

Lindsay's heart gave a hard thump.

She exchanged a look with Travis. Between the Stingray and her being completely visible, there wasn't a chance Brian didn't know who she'd been talking to.

Oh fuck.

CHAPTER FOUR

SOMETHING ABOUT LEAVING Lindsay on the side of the road had never quite sat right with Travis. It went against everything his father had ever taught him about how to treat women, but that was what she had always insisted on. Travis's gaze flicked toward the rearview mirror, and he caught sight of her, already marching along the side of the road toward Main Street.

She'd freaked out after Brian Pearson had gone by, and her expression made him smile as he drove out of sight. Out of the two of them, she cared more about people finding out about their occasional hookups. But he had the advantage. Lindsay was gorgeous, and all his friends would get it, even if his family wouldn't be thrilled.

Then again, she was right. Logan or Jake might kill him for touching her.

Still, he couldn't help thinking about the fact that, while sex left him in a good mood, Lindsay's reaction this morning had already worn him out. The whole thing at Yardley's last night—starting with Hannah and ending with Logan throwing him out—only made him loathe this stupid feud even more.

All of it was ridiculous.

But what the hell was he supposed to do about it?

Show up to the goddamn community meeting, cast a vote to please his family, then go back to his car shop and try to stay out of it, that was what.

He sighed, pulling into the parking lot at the top lot on Main, near his grandmother's café. He'd disappointed his family enough already when he'd refused to take over the "family business." Going to culinary school out of high school had done nothing but get their hopes up. He still held down the fort at the café whenever his grandmother went out of town, though, which meant that his family thought he'd come to his senses someday.

Maybe it was time to just realize that despite how little investment he felt in the Wagner-Yardley feud, the least he could do was stay away from Lindsay Yardley. He felt like crap anyway after Hannah had dumped him, so hooking up with Lindsay had done nothing for his self-esteem.

He hadn't expected a forever relationship with Hannah, but her reaction had still stung. And then there was Lindsay. Despite the morning-after discomfort, they always had such an incredible connection during sex. *Something I may never have with Lindsay again.*

He ran his hands over the smooth leather of the steering wheel, closing his eyes as he let the rumble of the engine lull his thoughts. Maybe that was why he had always preferred cars to everything else: even when everyone else looked at them as heaps of scrap, they were generally fixable. A little love and attention and know-how went a long way.

Engines were easy. People were not.

Killing the engine, he pushed open the door. The meeting would have started by now in the town hall. Whoever had planned it for the day after Valentine's Day had a sense of chaotic evil—half the people there would be angry or miserable, the other half feeling pretty good about their lives. Just the sort of feeling necessary to make for a contentious meeting.

Travis crossed the street, hurrying toward the town hall. The meeting had been scheduled for eight in the morning because the organizers rightly felt that Main Street grew too crowded with tourists toward the middle of the day and evenings, making it impossible for most concerned business owners to attend.

He went in a side door and headed down the corridor to the main gathering space. When the hall had been built one hundred years ago, the people in town hadn't anticipated how much room they might need eventually. The space fit about one hundred chairs—but now it was standing room only, with the aisles and back rows crowded.

Travis found an open spot close to his friend Ben, grandson of Brian, who had just seen Lindsay and Travis together. Brian appeared to be sitting with the older contingent of the towns-folk, right next to Millie Price, and didn't seem to notice Travis slipping in.

He didn't see Lindsay anywhere.

"You made it after all," Ben whispered as Travis squeezed in beside him.

Travis grunted a response and crossed his arms. "Anything important yet?"

Ben made a face. "Poor Mrs. Wong was dragged into the Strickland-Yardley ice cream debate. Someone brought up that the Wongs have been serving ice cream at their deli for years without a problem, and now Fred Strickland is acting like this is the first time he's ever heard about it. By the way, what the hell happened with Hannah? The news that she dumped you in front of Yardley's last night is everywhere. Didn't you get my text?"

Travis winced. His gaze flicked toward the Stricklands, and he spotted Hannah beside her father. Her words from the night before haunted him.

"Your fucking disloyalty . . ."

If she only knew what I did after she dumped me.

He felt a bit bad about that part. Having sex with Lindsay made it seem like he didn't care about either woman. But a part of him had wanted to put a nail in that coffin Hannah had created. There would be no going back now, not after that. Not that he wanted to go back. Hannah's behavior last night had been eye-opening.

He tore his gaze from her, not wanting to be caught staring, then addressed Ben's question about Hannah. "I overslept. Didn't see my phone. But let's just say she made a big deal about me not doing something for Valentine's."

"The flowers didn't help, huh?"

"Nope."

Travis didn't want to discuss it here, where even the slightest whisper could be heard and misinterpreted. He focused his attention on the center of the room. Bill MacKintosh, the mayor, was directing a question from his podium to Mrs. Wong. The older Chinese woman trembled in her seat.

"How long have you been serving ice cream, Mrs. Wong?" Bill peered over the rims of his glasses.

For Pete's sake. Everyone in town knew the Wongs served ice cream in their deli. It was some of the best.

"Five years," Mrs. Wong answered in a small voice.

Fred Strickland threw his hands up in frustration as though he'd just learned the fact. "This is outrageous. Exactly what happens when you let one person break the rules." He gave Peter Yardley a wicked side-eye.

"Except in this case, wouldn't it have been Mrs. Wong who broke the rules first and not my father?" Larry Yardley asked. Lindsay's father sat with the entire Yardley clan, who appeared to have arrived early to sit in the front by Peter. The four Yardley siblings were all in a row, Naomi's husband sitting beside her. Lindsay's absence from the group stood out.

Strickland reddened. "That's not the point—"

"It absolutely is the point." Larry stood, his metal folding chair scraping back against the marble floor as he did. "This is a witch trial meant solely to get back at my father."

"You going to get in my face, Yardley?"

Interesting how the Stricklands, including Hannah, were sitting beside the Wagners. Travis tried not to look at his ex, the sight of her making him feel a bit nauseated with anger and guilt. He shouldn't have ever stayed with her as long as he had.

An agitated feeling rose through Travis's spine, choking his throat. Then he spotted Lindsay sneaking in through the side door. *Wonder if anyone else will notice she's wearing the same thing as last night.*

Damn but those jeans hugged that perfect ass.

He didn't regret one moment he'd spent with that woman, no matter what she felt about it. But this inane feud and forces outside their control had always complicated anything between them. What if they'd been born one town over with different last names?

Maybe then Lindsay could have admitted that their connection was more than physical.

. . . just the way I know there could be something more if she didn't stop it.

Last names. What a fucking joke. The most ridiculous thing of all to stop two people who might care about each other from being together.

And he was sick of it. Sick of the way everyone in this town made issues about such trivial things.

As the hubbub grew, the mayor banged a gavel against the podium, like a judge at a trial. "Hold on now, hold on."

Something inside Travis seemed to snap.

Travis cupped his hands around his mouth. "Maybe it's not ice cream. Maybe the Wongs sell frozen custard. Ask her if she uses eggs in the recipe."

Ben practically cackled beside him. "Ah damn, man, getting yourself involved?"

The room drew to a hush, and all eyes seemed to turn toward him. *Shit, this was stupid. Should've kept my mouth shut.*

"What's that now?" Bill MacKintosh asked.

Travis shrugged, trying to play off the fact that his heart had slammed into his ribs. "Well, gelato is fundamentally different from ice cream. So is sorbet and frozen custard. Everyone knows how rich and creamy the Wongs' ice cream is. Maybe it's custard."

Fred Strickland's eyes seemed to bulge from his face. Hannah raised her eyebrows at Travis, as though stunned that he would say something that might take the Yardley side.

Actually, Travis's entire family was looking at him like that —especially his sister, Grace.

Shit and double shit.

MacKintosh looked back toward Carol Wong. "Do you use eggs in your ice cream recipe?"

"Eggs?" Carol Wong repeated as though she'd suddenly forgotten what the word even meant. She turned and muttered something to her husband in Chinese, and her husband put a soothing hand on her wrist.

"Yes, Mrs. Wong. Eggs. If your ice cream, as Mr. Wagner has suggested, has eggs and can be considered frozen custard, that's important for the council to know."

Does MacKintosh know how asinine this all sounds?

Mrs. Wong shot Travis a faltering look. He gave her a quick nod.

"He's leading the witness!" Fred Strickland shouted.

"Mrs. Wong isn't on trial, asshole." Travis gave Fred a lethal look. "And this isn't a fucking courtroom." *So maybe I'm displacing my anger with Hannah a bit.*

Mouths dropped open, a murmur going among some of the rapt audience.

At least that could be the excuse he used when his family lambasted him later.

"Whoa, whoa, Wagner." MacKintosh banged his gavel again. "This isn't a courtroom, but if I hear that sort of language again, you'll be asked to leave. There are kids present."

What sort of idiots brought their kids to a town meeting? Lindsay's family, that was who. Her niece was sitting beside Naomi, staring right at him. *That'll do nothing to warm them to me.*

Peter Yardley stood. "Bill, I think we've given Mrs. Wong enough of a shakedown. Her recipe is her proprietary business. Bunny Wagner and I may not agree on everything, but I think I can get her to agree on the fact that neither of us would like it if the town council demanded we give up the ingredients to our best-selling products." He appealed to Bunny, his blue eyes seeming to beg for her agreement.

Everyone turned to look at Travis's grandmother, who wore her gray hair in her trademark bun. Her normally pleasantly plump face was devoid of a smile, her lips drawn to a thin line. After a moment, she gave a slight nod. "I agree."

The tense air in the town hall dissipated. Relief flooded Mrs. Wong's face, and she offered Travis a grateful nod.

It was funny how Peter Yardley played the town patriarch to his grandmother's matriarchy despite being on opposite sides of the feud. Maybe because they'd both lost their spouses over twenty years earlier at the same time—a fatal car accident that had only widened the gap between the two families.

"Ice cream or custard or whatever it is aside, the reason this meeting was called today was to vote on the motion that Todd Wagner brought before the council at the last meeting—the petition to relocate Yardley's Country Depot to a more suitable location away from Main Street. Since the petition passed the required signature threshold for a vote, that's what we'll be doing today." Bill MacKintosh removed his glasses and cleaned them with a folded tissue in his pocket. "Unless there are any other arguments that either of the involved parties would like to make to the town."

Peter Yardley, who had never retaken his seat, held up a hand. The town hall went dead silent. "I would just like to point out that several business owners on Main Street have come to me personally and told me how grateful they are for the Depot. How much foot traffic it has brought to their businesses. How they've doubled and even tripled their incomes since the Depot opened three years ago. But they're afraid to vote in favor of keeping it on Main because of fear of retribution from the opposing side. Some even felt coerced into signing that petition Todd Wagner passed around."

I wouldn't put it past Dad to put pressure on people. The thought made Travis feel equal amounts of frustration and sadness.

"Oh, come on now." Travis's dad shook his head, disgust written plainly on his face. "No one coerced anyone to do anything." Out of all the Wagner siblings, Travis was the one who resembled his father the most, a fact that didn't entirely amuse Travis now.

Harassing old ladies over ice cream recipes and booting businesses from Main Street—weren't they all better than this?

This was a Pandora's box Travis wasn't sure his father understood how dangerous it was to open.

Peter's face was grave. "I'm just repeating what I heard."

"Then why don't we put it to a vote here? See what the town has to say about your Depot?"

"I agree." Bill MacKintosh banged his gavel.

Maybe he really wants to be a judge after all.

"All in favor of keeping the Depot on Main Street, raise your hands."

About half of the hands in the town hall went up, and the count started immediately. Travis rolled his eyes, leaning back against the wall as he scanned the room. Anyone who didn't want to vote and get caught in the argument was noticeably absent—most of the families who got along with both the Wagners and Yardleys weren't there, including the Klines and Doyles.

Travis's friend, Jen, and her husband, Jason Cavanaugh, had shown up and they had their hands up to vote with Peter Yardley—which didn't surprise Travis. Jen's bakery provided most of the baked goods for Peter's Depot and his restaurant. Jen was so beloved in town, though, that he doubted even his own parents would be miffed with her lack of support.

As the official count continued, Travis shot Ben a look. "Thank God they didn't invest in that voting software you suggested last year. Just think—we might all have to be at work now."

Ben grinned. "Yeah, what do I know? I'm just a farm boy. Then again, it is Saturday. They're not in a hurry."

Travis grumbled. "Some of us don't get Saturdays off." Not that he had anything lined up for the day. *But that's a worry for later . . .*

At last, it was time for the counter-vote. As arms shot up,

Travis kept his own arms crossed, a niggling feeling of annoyance in his mind. *I should have just skipped this.*

But his family would have given him hell for it.

As though they had telepathy, he caught his sister and older brother staring at him from beside his dad. Grace had a hard look on her face, and she raised her brows as though to say, *"Aren't you going to raise your hand, moron?"*

All right, so maybe she wouldn't say moron, but Travis heard it loudly enough in his head.

By now, Grace's look had attracted attention. His whole family stared now, including his grandmother.

And that was really the only person who made his heart throb. He met his grandmother's blue eyes. She wasn't close enough for him to read the subtleties of her expression, but he swallowed hard, wishing she'd just put a stop to this herself by voting against this.

But her hand was up.

It would always be up when it came to something against the Yardleys.

Travis sighed, then raised his hand to join his family in the vote. Especially after what had happened last night with Hannah, and then him going into Yardley's, he'd be the talk of the town if he abstained from voting.

When the count ended, Bill MacKintosh banged his gavel again. "All right. Well." He scratched his head as the room grew silent. "It appears we have a bit of a problem. We're tied, sixty-two to sixty-two."

Fantastic.

If I'd just stayed home, this would be over.

And he never would've heard the last of it. One hundred twenty-three other people had shown up, making it the largest town hall meeting Travis could remember.

The two divided sides of Brandywood stared each other

down, and Ben rubbed his hands together. "This should get interesting," he muttered.

As various people started talking at once, all of them proposing ideas, Bill MacKintosh fought for control once again. Then Brian Pearson stood beside Peter Yardley and started toward Bill.

"Oh, what's Pops doing now?" Ben jerked his chin toward his grandfather.

Travis didn't know quite how to look at the man. He hadn't been as freaked out by Brian as Lindsay had been, but something about him going toward a microphone made him want to squirm.

That feeling grew stronger as he whispered something to Bill MacKintosh, who nodded and stepped to the side, allowing Brian toward the podium.

The microphone squeaked as Brian raised it. "Listen up, folks. At the end of the day, we all know why we're here. But enough people seem to have a legitimate problem with the Country Depot that the Yardleys can't dismiss the Wagners' attempt to drive them from Main Street without thought and consideration. But since the Wagners and Yardleys are the originators of this mess, I think we should let them come together and solve it. I propose making a committee. Give them a month to find a solution that leaves everyone satisfied."

"I volunteer for the committee." Fred Strickland raised a hand.

"Sit down, Fred, you're misunderstanding me. Like I said, the Wagners and Yardleys should solve this."

"So who do you suggest should head this committee?" Travis's dad asked, looking unamused at the old man.

Then Brian smiled, and his eyes found Travis's. "Travis Wagner and Lindsay Yardley."

CHAPTER FIVE

LINDSAY SLOUCHED DOWN on the stool at the counter of Jen's bakery, almost banging her head into her latte. "This is a nightmare."

"Having to work on a town committee or who you're working with? I'm not sure who will be more fun for you to spend time with—Travis or Brian Pearson." Jen chuckled from the other side of the counter, then grimaced, setting her hand on her burgeoning belly. "Ugh, someone should have reminded me how laughing and pregnancy don't go together at the end."

"Or warned you not to work while this pregnant with twins." Lindsay laid her cheek against the menu that had been beside her plate. "I thought they weren't going to let you go this far because of what happened last time." When Jen had been pregnant with her firstborn, Colby, seven years earlier, she'd had preeclampsia that had almost killed her. It had terrified Lindsay, fearing she'd lose her best friend.

Jen shrugged, appearing unconcerned. "My doctor seems to think I'm doing fine. Jason wants me to slow down, but I just wanted to get through Valentine's Day orders. Now that the weekend is almost over, I can probably start cutting back." She reached into the glass case beside her and pulled out a few chocolate-covered strawberries. Setting them on a plate, she put them in front of Lindsay. "But we weren't talking about me. What's up?"

Bleh. The committee thing. MacKintosh had not only accepted Brian Pearson's proposal, but he'd put the man *on* the committee with her and Travis. Maybe that was karma for him trying to meddle. No one in Brandywood liked being assigned to committees. On the other hand, it meant she had to work with Brian and Travis.

In some ways, she worried more about the old man than Travis. He was clearly up to something.

Then again, being around Travis, especially when they'd just hooked up, was problematic. She couldn't take the usual route of avoiding him as much as humanly possible.

"Ugh . . . nothing." Lindsay avoided Jen's gaze. Maybe she shouldn't have brought it up. Talking about Travis didn't seem like the smartest move, especially with her best friend. "It's no big deal."

The chances of Jen not seeing right through me?

Jen smirked. "Right."

Nonexistent.

"All right, fine." Lindsay looked around, but thankfully, Sweet Escapes was pretty empty right now. "It's Travis. I-I can't work with him. That would be awful. I have to get out of this."

Jen unlocked her cell phone and opened her online orders. Studying them, she bit her lip, then looked back at Lindsay as she grabbed a cupcake box from behind the counter. "I'm not sure you *can* get out of it. Last year, when they voted Jason into the zoning committee, he tried to resign because of a conflict of interest, and they told him it was in the town bylaws or charter or something like that. Town committees are a nonvoluntary, obligatory position for anyone of legal age and voted into them. MacKintosh gave Jason a whole lecture on civic duty."

"I'll civic duty him. You know how many of this town's preschoolers I'm in charge of? I can't be divided in my attention from them." Lindsay sat straighter. "Maybe I can get some of my parents to write in on my behalf, saying they would be concerned if—"

"Come on, Linds. It's not that big a deal. It's Travis. You guys have known each other since you were born." Jen gave her a knowing look and leaned closer, lowering her voice. "You've even slept together."

Lindsay cringed, heat crawling into her cheeks. "Yeah . . . that's sort of the problem."

Lindsay and Jen were closer than most sisters were. Hell, she was closer to Jen than she was to her own sisters. As the youngest and with Jake being right above her, Lindsay had grown up with the disadvantage that she wasn't as close in age as Naomi and Maddie. She had just been their annoying little sister. Not that it had mattered because Jen had been her best friend since before kindergarten. *She knows most of my deepest, darkest secrets.*

But she's also best friends with Travis.

Jen quirked a blond brow. "You're going to let a meaningless hookup in high school get in the way of working with him? You guys were both in my wedding party. You see each other at my house. It's been, like, ten years."

Lindsay scrunched her nose. *Here goes nothing.*

"Actually, we hooked up last night." She hid her face again, not wanting to see Jen's eyes.

She waited for Jen's response, and when it didn't come, she finally peeked from between her fingers.

Jen stared at her, mouth open. "Uhhh . . . what? Didn't Hannah just break up with him last night?"

Now, the blood really flushed Lindsay's face hot. "He came into the bar afterward, and I was working. Logan was being a dickwad and kicked him out of there, and I left and took a bottle of tequila with me, and then I bumped into Travis and . . . well, you know."

"No, I do not know." Jen pushed her cupcake box to the side and came out from behind the counter, taking the open stool beside her. "Was it just a hookup? The start of something? I can't believe you've been in my bakery for a whole two hours, and you're just now telling me this." Jen grabbed her phone. "And Travis, that son of a bitch, I can't believe he didn't say anything either—"

"You can't tell him I told you! You're not allowed to know. No one can know about this." Lindsay's eyes widened, and she set her hand on Jen's.

Jen gave her a confused look. "I'm not allowed to know?"

"That's not what I mean. I mean, it's not anything. And we agreed not to tell anyone, including you, and it's never going to happen again."

"You weren't planning on telling me something so monumental?" Jen searched her face.

Please don't hate me.

"Okay, don't kill me. But this isn't the first time this has happened." She drew her hand back from Jen's.

Jen flipped her long blond ponytail over her shoulder, then stood, holding a hand to her forehead. "I don't even know what to say right now." She took a few steps away, then came back. "Are you two secretly dating? I thought you didn't even like Travis. Is this why Hannah dumped him?"

Lindsay shook her head. "No, I had nothing to do with that. And I don't like him. He annoys the crap out of me. But . . . I don't know." Lindsay shrugged. "I guess I . . ."

"How many times?"

Lindsay looked up at Jen's inquisitive face. "How many times have we hooked up?"

Jen nodded.

"Six . . . or seven?" *Maybe more. Probably more.*

"*Six or seven!*" Jen's words seemed to reverberate from the walls, and she looked at the kitchen to make sure her assistants hadn't come to listen in. She sat and lowered her voice again. "Seven! Lindsay! And you didn't tell me?"

"I was so . . . it was nothing. It *is* nothing. Look, just because we're physically compatible doesn't mean anything."

"This from my friend who preaches about not swinging from monkey bars, and always wearing a seat belt and bicycle helmet and *condoms.*"

"Hey, you have no idea how many injuries I have personally witnessed from kids falling off playground equipment."

"Lindsay Anne Wagner. And here I thought you were this little rule follower. And you gave me an earful when I first got together with Jason with no intention of dating long-term. The whole time, you're really a closet nympho. I *never* pegged you as the one-night stand type."

Lindsay covered her face with her hands, cooling her cheeks with them. "I'm not. I swear. I don't know what it is— but every time it's been something. Like last night, I was so freaking mad at Logan for being such a jerk about the restaurant. And Travis was just . . . there, available, and the man clearly knows how to use his hands—"

"Obviously. He's kept you coming back for seven rounds. Good *Lord*, Lindsay, were you ever planning on telling me this had happened?"

Fortunately, Jen didn't appear to be hurt. A smile lit her eyes, her expression amused. That brought some relief, even though Lindsay almost hated to be the one who had the sorry task of convincing her that her two best friends were, in fact, not ever getting together. "No, but seriously, because it's nothing and never happening again. I don't want that. You're right. I'm not a one-night stand girl. I was just lonely, and it was stupid. And Travis doesn't want it either."

Jen rolled her eyes. "Yeah, I'm sure."

"I'm serious. We were both talking this morning about how it's time. Time to move forward. Date the person we're meant to be with." Lindsay picked up one of the chocolate-covered strawberries.

Okay, so maybe I was the one who was more vocal about that, but Travis clearly agreed . . . didn't he?

Jen didn't look convinced either, so Lindsay quickly added, "But *not date each other.*"

"Why, because of the family stuff? So what? Your families will just have to get over it."

"Not all of us have moms as understanding and patient as your mom. Or perfect as your dad." *And that's an understatement.* Jen's parents were so wonderful that Lindsay had often wished Betty and Bob Kline could have adopted her. As much as Lindsay loved her parents, she didn't feel particularly close with either of them.

She lifted a strawberry and bit into it. *Oh my God, how does she make everything taste so good?* "These are incredible, by the way."

"They're Jason's favorite treat." Jen's blue eyes twinkled, her face lighting up. "He got this shipment of strawberries from some special farm he found in California just for Valentine's Day, so they'd be extra yummy."

Lindsay's heart tugged in her chest. "See? That's what I

want. What you have with Jason. You guys are like the perfect little family with your two boys and two girls on the way and the way he dotes on you."

"You could have that with Trav—"

"Jen, you're not hearing me." Lindsay polished off the strawberry. "Travis is hot. But that's it. We made the silly mistake of sleeping together as horny teenagers, so we know just how sexually compatible we were. But that's it. That's all it ever has and is going to be. You saw how he was back there in that meeting, being obnoxious about the poor Wongs and voting with his family to shut my grandfather's Depot down."

Jen frowned. "I didn't get that about the Wong thing. I think he was honestly trying to help out there."

"Oh, come on." The sound of Travis's voice as he'd stepped in had made her stomach sour. "He was clearly making fun of the fact that my grandfather claimed gelato was different from ice cream. Which it is. He was stirring shit. If he had any respect or feelings for me at all, he would just keep his mouth shut at those meetings rather than inserting himself into the clan wars."

Jen's expression was dubious. "Well, if he was, it backfired. But I can see why you might feel that way."

Is she patronizing me? "Trust me when I tell you, I know what I'm talking about. Anyway, more importantly, *I* don't want him."

"All right already." Jen laughed, then went back around the counter. "If I don't get this cupcake order ready for Mrs. French, she might have my head when she gets here." She tapped her phone open again, then pulled on a pair of clean gloves. "If you're not into Travis, that's fine. I won't push. God knows the last thing I want is for two of the people I love most in the world not to be able to be in the same room together."

"See? Even more reason for Travis and I not to risk

anything." Lindsay winked, placated by Jen's ability to drop the subject.

"But that still doesn't solve your problem about working with Travis for the next thirty days on the committee."

Lindsay gave her a wry smile. "So now you agree that it's a problem?"

"Definitely." Jen pulled a tray of cupcakes from out of the case. "You're both going to be attacking the Depot issue with way too much baggage, and it could get messy. Brian Pearson couldn't have picked two worse people for the job."

Lindsay lifted another strawberry, her gut churning. "Brian Pearson saw Travis dropping me off on the side of the road right before the meeting this morning. I think he was trying to get a reaction out of us or figure out what was happening, so he suggested we should be on the committee. Only it blew up in his face, and now I'm stuck having to be around Brian, too."

"How does Brian know Travis was dropping you off?" Jen tilted her chin. "Did he see you get out of the car?"

"No, I was already out of it."

"Okay, so for all he knows, maybe Travis just stopped to talk to you. I think your guilt is clouding your opinion."

That's true. Why didn't I think of that?

"A Wagner stop to talk to a Yardley, though? He had to have been suspicious."

"Or he saw that you two aren't completely hateful to each other and maybe hopes you could work together nicely to solve this thing."

Lindsay polished off another strawberry, then pushed the plate back. "I can't solve this thing, though. No one can. The Wagners aren't going to be happy until my family leaves Brandywood, no matter how bad it is for the people who benefit from what my family has built."

"I don't think all of the Wagners feel that way." Jen finished counting the cupcakes, then folded the top over the box and sealed it with a sticker. She pulled out a Sharpie to write the name on the side.

"You're just saying that because you love Bunny and Travis." Lindsay shook her head. She'd spent most of her life avoiding the topic of the Wagners with her best friend. Even though she could talk about the issue with her more than others, she still had to be sensitive to the fact that Jen's loyalties were divided. Not to mention the fact that the Wagners loved Jen, so much so that Lindsay had never felt unwelcome at Bunny's when Jen had worked there, and she'd gone to hang out with her.

"Partially. But also because it's gotten awful in the last couple of years. It was all sort of funny small-town lore when Bunny and Peter used to argue at town hall meetings. But petitioning for businesses to move and lawsuits? It's a lot."

"I know." Lindsay felt suddenly drained. "My dad says that tourists have even started to leave negative reviews for the Depot after their buses have been forced to relocate or other business owners have talked badly about my grandfather to them."

Jen gave her a sympathetic look. "That's awful. But you know, you should give Travis a chance"—she held up her hands—"I don't mean romantically. I mean about working with him. As someone who knows you both, there aren't two people who I think are more capable of putting aside their own interests and doing what's best for the town."

Lindsay gave a dry laugh. "You don't have to butter me up. Because you're not getting in my pants if that's what you're going for. I'm done with being easy."

Winking, Jen blew her a kiss. "You know you couldn't resist me." She ran her hands over the length of her belly.

Lindsay's guffaw felt like a dose of medicine to her heart. "I love you, crazy lady." Then she took out her phone. "I do have one more favor to ask, though."

"What's that?"

She tried not to think about how nervous this all made her —and how ridiculous this question was, given what had transpired the night before. "Can you give me Travis's phone number?"

CHAPTER SIX

Travis stepped out of the steam-filled bathroom with his towel wrapped around his waist. Normally, his evening would just be getting started at this time of night—sleep usually evaded him until at least midnight. But, thanks to Lindsay, he'd barely slept the night before.

Also, thanks to Lindsay, he'd nursed a mild headache all day from the tequila he'd downed. He preferred an ice-cold beer any day, and it had been her idea to do shots.

He pulled on some pajama pants, then shoved Ratchet to the side of his king-sized bed. Damn dog thought the bed was all his. He scowled as Ratchet offered not an ounce of cooperation in moving. "You take advantage of sleeping on the bed for now, but once there's a woman back in my life, I'm moving you to the floor. Permanently."

Ratchet offered a loud snore.

Propping some pillows against the headboard of the small space he'd cleared on the bed, Travis sat, feeling the familiar pressure of anxiety against his chest.

Strangely, Lindsay's words were at the forefront of his mind.

"I'm really not trying to be harsh. You're right. It was fun. It always is fun. Yet we always regret it, don't we? I want to be taken seriously. My friends have serious jobs, own their own businesses, and are either married and having babies or engaged. And I don't think this arrangement is what you're looking for either, is it?"

Travis had a serious job but still wasn't taken seriously, even by Lindsay. *We did have fun, Linds.* But as soon as it was over, she wanted to run out the door.

It wasn't just the women in this town getting to him—work was unusually slow. He'd spent the afternoon in an empty garage, tinkering on his own car to keep busy during business hours. Because except for an oil change in the afternoon, *nothing.*

Over a month of this.

And for a mechanic who had cornered the market on car repairs in the small town of Brandywood, that was concerning.

Slow was one thing . . .

. . . but I'm pretty sure this is something else.

The thought was unsettling, especially since he had bills to pay, and they all hit at the beginning of the month. February was short, which meant he didn't have a lot of time to turn this thing around.

But what was he supposed to do? He didn't have the luxury of offering sales and promotions like other businesses in town did.

Of course there's always Peter Yardley's offer to pay me whatever I want to restore an old car for him. Travis's family would see it as one more betrayal—but business was business, wasn't it?

Yeah, right.

As though he'd been able to intuit Travis's stress, Ratchet took that moment to lay his head on Travis's leg. He looked up at him with big, mournful, dark eyes.

Between Valentine's Day with Hannah, having sex with Lindsay, and then the way he'd hesitated at the meeting today in front of his family, he wasn't exactly making smart decisions lately.

What was it Lindsay had said today?

"I don't have the luxury of screwing around anymore."

Screwing around wasn't what he wanted either.

Or was it?

He'd tried to be a good guy. Never cheated on a woman. Always opened doors and got along with parents.

Yet here he was.

Dumped without a second thought.

And even if sleeping with Lindsay had oddly made him feel better, Hannah's actions had hurt. He hadn't deserved that—had he? Was he really the asshole she'd made him out to be?

Maybe. Logan Yardley sure seemed to think so. And Travis knew what he'd been doing when he'd gone up to Lindsay when she walked out of the bar.

But what he and Lindsay had went far outside of a few hookups. He'd never had the courage to say anything—she seemed prepared to shoot him down—but *what if?*

His phone buzzed on the bedside table, and he palmed it. A message from Jen had come through.

Jen: *Hey, Lindsay asked me for your digits. You better be nice to her with this Depot bullcrap.*

Travis smiled. Jen didn't mince words, especially not about how she felt about her friends.

Travis: *Who says I'm not nice to her?*

Jen: *Then be extra nice.*

Before Travis could type another reply, a text from an unknown number showed up on his screen.

Unknown: *Hi, it's Lindsay. Jen gave me your number.*

Travis stared at the text, his mouth drawing to a line.

So they were texting now? This morning, she'd bolted. He wasn't entirely sure how to proceed, so he went with the standard.

Travis: *Hey, what's up?*

Lindsay: *I just thought we should have each other's numbers for the committee thing.*

Travis smirked. Funny how awkward she could be about normal with him, given their history. Even her texts seemed . . . strained?

Travis: *And here I thought you just wanted booty calls on demand.*

Lindsay didn't respond for a minute, but three dots appeared to indicate she was typing. From the amount of time she spent, it seemed like he was going to get several paragraphs back, but instead, all he got was:

Lindsay: *You wish.*

He chuckled. *Maybe I do wish.*

Travis's thumbs hovered over the screen, then he tapped out another message.

Travis: *You're always welcome to stop on by.*

There. That was as close as he could come right now to telling her he wouldn't mind their encounters becoming something more—even if it was physical. Enemies with benefits wasn't really a thing, but they could make it one.

Maybe random hookups with a beautiful woman like Lindsay weren't the negative thing he'd been raised to believe. He'd been trying so hard for a relationship . . . maybe he just needed to relax. Not make any commitments for a while.

He didn't feel the same pressure as Lindsay to "settle

down" and have kids. Twenty-six was far too young to be doing that, as far as he was concerned.

Lindsay: *Don't be an ass. What happened last night was a huge mistake. It can't happen again. Ever. Especially if we're forced to work together. I'm serious, so please don't make this more awkward than it needs to be.*

Travis swiped the message away, then almost clicked his phone off without responding.

"A huge mistake," he muttered. That was how she'd always seen this. *That's how she'll always see this.*

So much for telling her he wanted more.

Travis: *Sounds good.*

What had been the point of her messages anyway? To further his frustration? Make sure he knew there wasn't a chance in hell he'd ever get to be with her?

His doorbell rang, and he clicked open his phone app to see his sister standing at the door, her arms crossed.

Great.

"I'm not home," he said through the speaker.

Grace looked right at the camera. "I know that one. Open up." Then she lifted a bag. "I brought cream of crab soup from Nana."

Would she still be mad from this morning if she was bringing crab soup?

With a sigh, Travis got up, then got dressed. He made his way to the living room, Ratchet at his heels, and went to the front door, opening it.

Grace breezed past him, then looked down for a doormat. "What happened to the doormat I got you?"

"Ratchet ate it."

He was convinced the dog had been bred with a goat as he'd made his way through countless shoes, couch cushions, pillows, bedspreads, and even a light bulb once—which had necessitated a long and expensive trip to the vet.

He'd replaced most of the ruined furniture with cheap stuff while he tried working on Ratchet's chewing habit and had learned to be careful about putting most things away.

Grace raised a brow at him, then shook her head. She kicked her boots off instead and then went toward the kitchen. "That was quite the performance at the town council meeting this morning." She plopped the bag on the counter, then went to the cabinet and opened it. "Where did the bowls go?"

Travis shoved his hands into his pockets, following her. "To the right of the kitchen sink. Hannah decided it would be fun to rearrange the kitchen." He cleared his throat. "Look, I know you're mad—"

"I'm not mad." Grace didn't look at him as she found two bowls and pulled them down. "Dad's mad. I'm . . . concerned."

"There's no reason to be concerned." Travis leaned against the counter. When he'd first rented the shop and the apartment above it four years earlier, he'd appreciated the sleek open concept, which had been made to look industrial. Now it just felt bleak and sparse. None of the coziness that Wagners were famous for.

"Hannah told me all about your breakup." Grace opened a couple of drawers until she found spoons, then served the soup.

"I know. I know. You liked her, and—"

"I didn't like her. She was a bitch. And the way she dumped you was disgusting. I told her that myself." Grace met his gaze, smiling. "You should have seen the look on her face. She came sidling up to me like she was going to try to tarnish my baby brother's image to me, and I kicked her to the curb."

Travis felt a slight lump in his throat. *That's Grace.* He shouldn't be surprised. His family was all fiercely loyal. And

Grace and Travis had always been as close as siblings could be, especially since it was just the two of them. "Well, thanks."

"But"—she held out the bowl of soup—"that doesn't mean I'm not concerned. You took her to Yardley's? Seriously? And then Annie from the bookstore told me Logan Yardley kicked you out of the bar there not too long afterward."

Travis took the bowl of soup, then pulled up a stool to the counter.

She slid a package of crackers to him and took a seat beside him. "So you going to tell me what's going on with you?"

"Nothing's going on." Travis shrugged. "I . . ." He sighed. "Hannah said she didn't want to do anything for Valentine's Day, and I believed her. Then when I figured out she hadn't been telling the truth, I scrambled to make last-minute plans. I wasn't even thinking about the Stricklands' stupid ice cream war with the Yardleys."

"Are you sure maybe a part of you wasn't intentionally trying to sabotage that relationship? You all had been up and down for a while."

And then there's this side of Grace. The armchair psychologist who wants to figure out everything that's wrong with my life when she has her own problems she's avoiding.

He swallowed some soup, remembering with that first bite how lucky he was to have a grandmother who could cook like his did. A cup of her soup always made things better, even when he didn't realize how much he might need one.

"Does it really matter? I dodged a bullet. She did me a favor, really." Even if it made his gut clench to think about it.

"Yeah, well, I still don't like it. Her dumping you, *or* what led to it. Logan Yardley would beat the shit out of you without you giving him a reason to. And the Yardley brothers are particularly infuriated right now. The other day, a tour bus double parked me into the art studio for an hour—driver nowhere to be seen. When he finally turned up, the bus driver told me Jake Yardley had told him to park there."

"You ever think that maybe they've got a reason to be mad? I mean, how would you like it if their dad was getting half the town to gather pitchforks and kick your studio off Main?"

"But that's the thing." Grace tossed her long, dark ponytail over her shoulder, the pink and blue tips showing. "It's not just Dad. The Depot is causing all sorts of problems to a lot of people. That's why the petition got so much support."

"I think we're inviting more trouble than it's worth, Grace. I'm sorry. I'm not going to apologize for that." He hunched his shoulders, bracing himself for her lecture.

"Travis, don't take this the wrong way." Grace sighed and leaned back in her seat. "You haven't been happy for a long time now. And all of it started the minute you decided to strike out on your own, showing how different you are from the rest of us. There's nothing *wrong* with being different. But you know you're not happy with this 'Wagner 2.0' schtick, either. And I think Hannah only made it worse." She rubbed her temples. "Got any beer?"

Wagner 2.0.

That was the problem. Like his parents, Grace thought he just wanted to do things differently, when that wasn't the point. He didn't want the same things they did. Didn't see things the same way. "I'm not a rebellious teenager anymore."

A beer did sound good.

Travis slid out of his seat and went to open the fridge. His hand bumped against the bottle of Patrón Lindsay had left in his fridge the night before, and he smirked.

That was what he needed in his life. What he'd had last night for a few fleeting hours.

Fun.

Maybe not with Lindsay, since she was making it *very* clear that it wouldn't ever happen again, just in general.

Funny how right now I'm smarting more over Lindsay not wanting anything than I am Hannah.

Because Lindsay had always been that girl. The one he thought of that *what-if* with.

But she thought of their night together as "a huge mistake."

And he couldn't even let himself hope she'd change her mind.

"You know, Gracie, maybe I am trying to put a square peg in a round hole." He uncapped a beer and handed it to her.

Relief filled her face, as though she'd finally gotten through to him. "Really?"

"Yeah. Really. I think maybe a settled life of monogamy might not be my style. Maybe what I really need is to go out there and see what life is like on the other side. Date around. Not make a commitment to anyone."

"Wait—what?" Grace gave him a double take. "That's not what I meant."

"No, I'm serious. It's a good plan. I think it's what I need. Sex shouldn't have to be so complicated. I think I'm ready to stop worrying about happily ever after and just think more about happy endings." Despite being earnest, he barely got the words out with a straight face.

Grace held her hands up. "Stop. I don't want to think about that."

"Says the woman who gave me a box of condoms when I was sixteen."

"That's just good sense." Grace took a spoonful of soup. "I didn't mean to imply you're not happy because you're not sleeping around."

"I spent the past few months of my life trying to make a woman happy—which, really, is like an oxymoron. They tell you they're fine when they're not, they say they don't know what they want to eat and then reject every idea you give . . . God, Grace . . . three weeks ago, Ben and I hung out. Played video games. Hannah had said, 'go have fun.' Then she's texting me the whole time, making me feel guilty for going. What's that about? Why do women do that shit? I don't need—nor want—that. It's like they hook you on those first few dates, acting all sexy and enticing because they haven't put out yet and want you to think they're fun and interesting. Then you finally have sex, and things are still good because those first few days of sex are amazing. So you get together and, bam"—he pounded his fist into the palm of his opposite hand—"next thing you know, you're spending Saturday afternoons wandering around Target, and it's been weeks since you slept together."

Grace laughed, taking a swig of beer. "What's your point?"

Why did he get the feeling she was making fun of him? "My point is I don't want that. I want to stay stuck at that fun and interesting part." He didn't sit, the idea oddly energizing him.

"The part where—according to you—women are pretending?"

"Yeah. I mean. No. I don't want the pretending. But if I can't figure out how to get a woman who doesn't pretend, then fuck it. I just want those first few hot hookups. Then we can part as highly satisfied former lovers and move on before the miserable part starts. Preferably with a woman who doesn't wake up the next morning and think our hookup was a giant mistake."

Clearly, Lindsay's words had hurt him more than he realized.

Grace rolled her eyes. "Wow, this sounds like such original

thinking. So refreshing and—you're right—not at all like a rebellious teenager. Or an asshole."

"So I'll be the ass everyone seems to think I am. I'm not afraid to admit I enjoy sex. That puts me in good company with basically the entire male population of the planet." He stopped his rant, trying to think of a more coherent argument. Lindsay's face flashed through his mind.

Never again. Even if those hadn't been her precise words, that was the sum of it.

More quietly, Travis said, "I can't keep hoping and praying some dream girl comes to her senses and decides I'm worth her time." *Not when she's adamant it's never going to happen.* "And if a dream girl isn't an option, then what's the harm of enjoying myself with no strings attached?"

She finished her soup and stood, carrying her bowl to the sink. "It's never going to work."

"And why's that?" Travis crossed his arms.

"Because deep down, you're a good guy, Travis. Actually, not even that deep down. Think about it. You were willing to step foot into Yardley's to make Valentine's nice for Hannah. But maybe the problem is that you *don't* actually worry about what you want enough. When was the last time you spoke up for yourself in a relationship? Have you ever tried telling a woman you don't want to go to Target or that they're not being fair to you?"

Fair?

Who says any of this is about fair?

He pictured Lindsay in his T-shirt that morning, looking so beautiful, her hair messy from their night together. And all he'd wanted was to pull her right back into that bed.

That was what he wanted. *Simple. Uncomplicated.*

Of course, with anyone other than Lindsay Yardley, since her last name made things complicated for a different reason.

"Nah. I'm pretty sure it's not me. It's them." Travis shrugged, trying to convince himself of it. "And if I'm wrong, then what's the big deal? I have some hot dates? Yeah, that sounds terrible. Ben was telling me about this hookup app he uses occasionally. If it works for Ben, I'm pretty sure it would work for me."

"You know what?" Grace held her hands up in surrender. "Do what you want. You're a grown-ass adult. Eventually, you'll figure out that what you really wanted was the right woman instead of sex with strangers, and I'll be here to tell you I told you so."

He chuckled, then sipped his beer. "Gee thanks, sis."

"Don't worry, I'm letting you off easy. Because Dad told me to tell you that he's really pissed at you. He wants to talk with you to strategize your work on the committee with Lindsay Yardley but said you've avoided his calls all day."

"And that's why I avoided his calls all day." Travis gave her a pointed look. "The whole point is that I'm supposed to handle this with Lindsay. Not be Dad's voice by proxy."

Grace came toward him, then set her hand on his forearm. "I'm not telling you this because Dad said so, but because, as your sister, I don't want to see things get further strained between you and him. But this is a huge opportunity, and you've got to get it right, Travis. But be careful around Lindsay Yardley. Of all of them, she's the one I'd worry about the most. She puts on a good front, but at the end of the day, she's just like all the other Yardleys—she'll smile prettily while she stabs you in the back. Just . . . watch out."

CHAPTER SEVEN

April 1970

Dear Bernadette,

I GOT *the news from Mom.*

I don't know what to say, B. I wish I did. I wish I could be there to hold you. I knew it wasn't possible when I joined, but I swear I kept hoping that someday I'd be in the middle of this jungle and we'd find him. Crazy of me, maybe, but crazier things have happened.

Every time I think about him, I remember that first summer when I fell in love with you. I'd always known Robbie's sister was pretty, but there you were, sitting at that lemonade stand, and I couldn't take my eyes off you.

Did I ever tell you I spent every nickel I made from my paper route on lemonade that summer?

He knew. He wouldn't stop teasing me about it. And maybe some brothers would have told me to scram, but not Robbie. He was so proud. Excited that we'd be brothers someday, too.

God, I miss him.

I miss you.

I wish you would write to me. Do you read my letters? I hope you do. I'll keep sending them.

I wish I were there with you, under our peach tree.

I wish I were there for you. I'm sorry I'm not. I'm so sorry, B.

I love you always,

Peter

CHAPTER EIGHT

Lindsay stepped into the automatic doors of the senior center, shifting apprehensively. She'd barely had time to go home and change after work, which felt more like a necessity than a basic desire. In her first few weeks of working as a preschool teacher, she'd had to fight the urge to burn all her clothes at the end of the day. She still caught more colds than most of her friends did, but she'd become a lot more used to having random things she didn't want to know about encrusted into her jeans at the end of her workday.

But still. She hadn't seen Travis since Saturday, and that was four days ago. Neither had she worked up the courage to text him again.

Which meant that when Brian Pearson had left her a voice-mail telling her he'd set up a meeting with Travis at the senior center at six, she'd felt obligated to drop everything and go, or risk missing out on a seat at the table.

Travis was already there. She'd seen his car in the parking lot, and now she spotted him standing in the lobby, wearing jeans and a worn brown leather bomber jacket as he stared at his phone.

Because, of course.

I look like a mess, and he looks like he just walked off the runway.

His eyes met hers as the lobby doors closed behind her, and her heart skipped a beat.

This is fine.

It's just Travis.

You can handle being around him on a regular basis.

For goodness' sake, it wasn't that long ago when she'd had to see him every day in school.

Be confident.

Calm.

She started toward him, thankful she'd brushed her hair rather than just tossing it up into a messy bun, and held his eye contact. She lifted her chin, about to toss her hair over her shoulder and say *hey* . . .

. . . WHAM.

A sharp pain exploded across her forehead and nose, her head colliding with something hard, followed by her upper body.

She fell back, dizzy spots in her field of vision as she flattened to the floor. She held her nose, her brain still not fully comprehending what had happened. "Ow!"

The sound of running footsteps met her ears as she blinked up at the recessed lights of the lobby. "You okay?" Travis knelt beside her.

She blinked at him, then her eyes shifted toward the door, which was now open.

Shit.

Heat rose on her cheeks. "I—" Her gaze shifted to the silver button in the lobby, which needed to be pressed for the door to open automatically. She hadn't seen it.

I walked into a freaking door.

Travis scanned her face, then helped her sit. "Did you break anything?"

"Nope. No. Besides my pride, I'm good." Her nose and forehead hurt like hell, but she wasn't about to tell him that. Embarrassment crawled up the back of her neck as she relived the moment.

Oh my God.

Did I really just walk into a door?

"I-I—didn't see—"

"Well, obviously." Travis laughed. He helped her stand. "Do you need ice? You're getting a bruise on that forehead."

Her face was burning. "No, I'm good. I just wanted to inspect the glass. Make sure it was still solid." *I can't believe I did that.*

Travis gave her a skeptical look, then helped her through the door into the actual lobby. He continued holding her elbow. "Let's just get you some ice anyway."

She winced. "Why are you being so nice?"

"I'm not, don't worry." Travis smirked. "I fully plan on uploading the video somewhere in a few minutes, letting it go viral."

Her eyes widened, and he chuckled. "Just kidding, I didn't get it on video."

"Hmm, not sure I can believe you. You seem to like keeping scandalous videos of me." *Oh God. Now why did I bring that up?* She let him lead her, unsteady and eager to change the subject. "They should really post something. Imagine if that happened to a senior citizen."

"There is a sign. Plus the logo for the senior center on the glass."

She looked over her shoulder toward the door. *Damn, he's right.*

That was so much worse. He'd distracted her so much she hadn't paid attention. "Maybe I need to get my eyesight checked." *Ouch, my forehead does hurt.* She felt over the bruised skin gingerly. A painful lump rose there.

Travis left her on a bench in the lobby and soon returned with a bag of ice.

She thanked him and leaned back against the bench, icing her forehead. *Dammit, Travis.* She didn't want him being so sweet to her. It made it harder for her to pretend they were simply unwitting partners and nothing more.

The silence between them grew uncomfortable, and Travis rubbed the back of his neck and looked around the empty lobby. "Where the hell is Mr. Pearson?"

"Mr. Pearson? That's cute." She'd always just thought of him as Brian. He worked as a security guard in a lot of random places around town—one of those Brandywood figures everyone was used to seeing everywhere. And he was friends with everyone, including her grandfather.

The two of us should be able to shut down this Wagner nonsense once and for all.

"He's Ben's grandfather. I've been calling him Mr. Pearson since I was two years old. He's practically family."

Lindsay grimaced.

Well, there is that slight problem. She'd nearly forgotten how close Travis was to the Pearsons. He and Ben had been friends their entire lives.

As though he'd sensed he was being talked about, Brian chose that moment to come down the opposite hallway toward them. "Well, look who it is." He held his arms out in a greeting, his thin frame still appearing spry.

He stopped in front of them. "You know, it's the darndest

thing. I completely forgot about bingo night tonight. So why don't we take our meeting over to the hall? I've got to call the bingo numbers."

"I don't know if a bingo hall is going to be the best place for us to talk about this," Lindsay said, furrowing her brow. That was a mistake, though, because moving her forehead at all resulted in a sharp pang in her skin.

"I have to agree," Travis said, shoving his hands into his back pockets. "We can always meet another night. I have a date at seven thirty."

A date?

Lindsay tried not to give him an interested look.

That was fast.

No wonder he looked so good tonight. He'd put effort into it because he was going out after this.

"No, no, no, no. It won't take long. Why don't you all head over to the caf and grab a table? It's the meatloaf special tonight —pretty tasty, actually. Grab me a slice before it's gone, and I'll be there in no time," Brian said.

Before either of them could respond, Brian turned and sauntered away in the direction he'd come from.

Lindsay and Travis stared at his receding figure. "The 'caf'?" she repeated.

"Fantastic." Travis checked his watch. "How long does bingo usually take?"

"I have no idea. I might like crocheting and knitting, but I don't usually spend my Wednesday nights at the senior center." She regretted the words instantly as Travis gave her a quizzical look.

"You knit?"

Her cheeks weren't going to get any redder tonight, so she just shrugged. "Sometimes." *Better just wrap this up.* Besides, it wouldn't be *that* bad if Travis couldn't talk with Brian. She could give him her ideas first that way. "But why don't you go on ahead? You don't want to miss your date hanging around here. Who knows how long Brian will be."

Travis scanned her face, then his eyes grew distrustful. "Are you just trying to get rid of me so you can butter up Mr. Pearson and get him on your side?"

Damn. "Travis Wagner, how dare you accuse me of such a thing? One would think you don't trust me at all."

"One would be right." Travis scratched his clean-shaven jaw and looked back at the door. "I guess we can go to the cafeteria and wait for a few minutes."

"'The caf"—as Brian had put it—had conjured ideas of a hospital-like cafeteria for Lindsay since she'd never been there. Instead, it was more like a restaurant with seat-yourself tables and proper servers who appeared to be local high school and college kids.

One of them brought Lindsay and Travis menus shortly after they sat, and Lindsay's stomach growled. She hadn't eaten anything since her tuna fish sandwich at lunchtime, which had been at eleven. Setting the ice pack to the side, she peeked at the offerings. The dinner food scents were mouthwatering.

But they weren't here to eat dinner together. Travis didn't even pick up the menu.

Because he has a date soon.

"Not getting anything?" Lindsay burned with curiosity—and disappointment. That he would already have a date after a breakup *and* a hookup went against what she thought she knew of Travis. *And it's hard not to take it sort of personally.*

Not that I have any right to do that.

Travis's gaze flickered over the menu, and he shifted as though uncomfortable with the topic. "No, I'm good."

Then a more worrisome thought occurred to her. What if he was having dinner with Hannah?

Would he really do that? Get back together with his ex-girlfriend after sleeping with Lindsay?

Would it be like that episode from *Friends*? *"We were on a break!" Travis would tell Hannah.*

Or, worse still, would he not tell her at all?

Oh God, if this is like Friends, *then I'm that girl from the copy place.*

Cringing, Lindsay reached for the glass of water the server had poured and took a sip.

But they *were* on a break.

She never would have slept with Travis if he'd still been dating Hannah.

Was there a window of being too close to a breakup that was just a no-go zone? And hell, had she completely betrayed all of womankind by going there?

Shit. No!

For the first time ever, she had to admit, Ross from *Friends* was right. A break was a break, wasn't it?

"Look," she started, her mind spiraling as she blurted quickly, "I know it's none of my business, but if you're seeing Hannah tonight, could you please not mention anything about us? And not just for my sake. I mean, definitely for my sake because we agreed not to talk about it. Which, by the way, don't kill me, but I sort of told Jen about us. But that's beside the point. It's more about you. Hannah doesn't really need to know anything. I mean, no harm, no foul, right? You weren't trying to hurt her, and you all were on a break. *I'm* definitely not going to tell her. And Jen won't either—because you know Jen won't say anything. But it won't help to get it off your chest, I promise. And it's really not like cheating . . ."

She lapsed into silence and squirmed, then lifted the bag of ice to her head. "I must have hit my head harder than I thought."

Travis stared at her, blinking, a small divot appearing between his brows as though he was trying to process everything she'd spewed. Then, at last, he said in a low voice, "I'm not seeing Hannah tonight. Or any other night."

A warm, strange feeling of relief flooded her. She tried not to ease into the sigh that wanted to fill her chest and nodded. "Oh. Good."

Good?

What the hell, Lindsay?

What are you saying?

The server chose that moment to return. The girl couldn't have been older than a senior in high school. But from the way she focused all her attention on Travis, it was clear she found him attractive. "Did you all decide what you want tonight?"

"Nothing for me, but can I get the meatloaf special to go? It's for a friend who's at bingo." Travis gave the server an easy smile, then glanced at Lindsay.

Lindsay blinked, suddenly unable to form coherent words.

The server gave her an expectant look, and Lindsay managed, "Nothing for me."

The girl frowned as though to say, *why the hell are you two here if neither of you are going to eat anything?* Except Travis *had* ordered something, even if it wasn't for him.

Dammit, Travis. He always found a way to come off looking so suave.

As the server walked away, Lindsay glanced at the menu beside her. She could have just about killed for a burger right now. But with her luck, she'd probably wind up with a ketchup stain down her shirtfront.

"You told Jen about us?" Travis met her gaze with a piercing look.

Shit.

She put her hands in her lap and shifted back into her chair. "It may have come up."

"I thought we agreed not to tell anyone. Including and especially Jen." Travis's face burned with displeasure.

She bit her lip. She was the one who had specified that Jen shouldn't find out, so why was he making such a big deal of it? "It came up. I was talking to her about working with you and how it might be complicated, and I don't know, she didn't seem like the worst confidant."

"That's convenient, Linds. You forget that you're not the only person who has a relationship with Jen. She means as much to me as she does to you. Or is this just one more attempt to get someone on your side? Because that's pretty damn low."

"Hey." Lindsay plunked the ice down on the table. "That's unfair. First of all, we both know where Jen stands on this issue with the Depot. She'll be the first one to stand up for my grandfather because she's not the sort of person to benefit from someone's help and kindness and then turn around and kick them when they're successful."

A muscle in Travis's jaw seemed to clench. "I wouldn't know. Can't say that anyone in my family has experienced that same sort of kindness from your grandfather."

His anger was clearly spilling over from him being irritated with her for having told Jen anything. "And *second of all,*" Lindsay said, ignoring his comment, "I would never tell her that to try to win some sort of sympathy or sabotage your friendship. When have I ever tried to sabotage your friendship with Jen? Never. So don't even start with me."

He sipped his water, then looked away. "You should have asked me first."

"I didn't have your phone number."

"Now we both know that's a lie."

"I asked Jen for your number *after* I told her. So ha. Not a lie. I win this round, Wagner."

Ha?

Even Travis cracked a smile. Shaking his head, he pulled his phone out and tapped it open.

The transition was odd, and when he lapsed into silence, she tried to avoid peeking at his phone. "You keeping score or something?"

"No, I'm just telling the girl I'm going out with tonight that I might be a bit late. We're supposed to be meeting in Londontown."

Two towns over? She was too curious not to nudge open the window of conversation he'd cracked a bit further. "How'd you meet her?"

"WinkMe. It's a dating app."

A dating app already? "Wow, you're really ready to find someone else, huh?" Maybe he really didn't like being alone.

"Not exactly." Travis flipped his phone face down onto the table. "It's more of a casual meetup thing."

Lindsay gave him a curious look, then pulled out her own phone. Looking up the app, she furrowed her brows, a strange pressure in her chest. "A hookup app?"

Travis shrugged, his expression giving little away.

"I didn't know you were into that sort of thing" didn't quite sound right coming from her, given how many times they had casually hooked up. But it did surprise her. And that odd feeling near her heart was definitely disappointment, wasn't it?

Travis cleared his throat. "I just signed up for it."

She gave him a thin-lipped smile. "I mean, whatever you do is your business."

What else could she say?

She wasn't in a position to judge him, and they weren't

friends, so she wouldn't offer him advice—especially unsolicited.

But Travis had told her in the past he'd never done the hookup thing with anyone but her. And maybe that was it. Maybe she was just smarting at the realization that if he could be so casual about sex with her, he could be that way with anyone.

Great, now I'm glorifying our stupidity into something special.

He's a guy. Guys can have sex without emotional attachment, right? At least that's what they say.

Travis's voice dropped lower, and he leaned forward on his forearms. "I wasn't expecting to connect with anyone on the app this soon, but this girl said she was free tonight and—"

Was that guilt in his expression?

"You don't owe me an explanation, Travis. I wasn't trying to pry. Or make you feel like you needed to justify it to me. I mean, I'm definitely not in a position to judge you about something like that given our history."

Travis studied his phone. "Otherwise known as huge mistakes. Right?"

Huge mistakes? She was almost offended until she realized he was repeating her own words back to her.

Did I hurt his feelings with that?

"I didn't mean it like that."

He held her gaze. "Just that it never should have happened? And will never happen again? That we don't have the luxury of screwing around anymore?"

Again, more of her own words. *Wow, was I really that harsh?*

"Well, I assume you don't want to screw around. You've always been a relationship guy, and I can't offer you that."

Travis looked away. "Yeah, well, I just . . . need something different. A break from relationships for a while."

Lindsay focused on the dining room. There weren't a lot of people here, despite the senior center being one of the most popular places for the senior population in Brandywood to spend time. They called it The Nest, which didn't make much sense and sounded oddly salacious for some reason.

Maybe they were all at bingo right now.

In some ways, she didn't know if she would prefer or dislike for there to be more people here. Being seen alone with Travis in a public setting was disconcerting enough.

"Like I said, Travis. It's your business. I think it would probably be smart for us to stay on task with the committee stuff. We don't need to complicate this by bringing our personal lives into it."

"Right." Travis scooted forward some. "Should we wait for Mr. Pearson, or should we talk about some of the basics?"

"We can talk about the basics. I had a thought the other day that I think is really important." Her stomach growled, and she wished she'd ordered something, even if it was just a plate of french fries. Maybe when the server came back, she would.

"What's that?"

Lindsay leveled her chin at him. "I think we need to agree not to discuss this with our families. Like at all. This whole mess will only be more complicated to navigate if we have to deal with everyone's list of demands and have a bunch of opinions to consider."

This close to him, she couldn't help but catch a whiff of his aftershave or cologne or whatever the hell it was that made him smell so good. His scent made her want to lean closer. Like it or not, Travis had a way of drawing her in magnetically.

You need to watch yourself around him. Now more than ever.

Travis's eyes were intense. "That's easy enough to say. What assurance would I have that if I agree to that, you'd actually keep your end of the bargain?"

"Well, I guess you'd have to trust me." She held out her hand toward him. "We can shake on it."

Travis let out a muffled snort. "Trust isn't exactly what's kept our families in each other's radar. And you just admitted that the one thing we agreed to in the past—that I *trusted* you not to share—you went ahead and shared anyway."

She lowered her hand. "Seriously? You're going to have the audacity to be mad at me over that?"

Travis kept his face blank. "Not mad. Worried. Frustrated. But not mad." He sank back in his chair and crossed his arms. "Fine, you want to leave our families out of this? I think that's fair. But I'm serious. I don't want to find out later that I've been telling my family I won't talk about things with them, and in the meantime, Logan and Jake have been pulling the strings on you like a puppet. You're the soft side of the Yardleys, and they know how to exploit that."

His words made a pang of sadness go through her. *Is that what he thinks of me?* She blinked back the sudden tears, her eyes prickling. "You really think I'm that easily manipulated and gutless?"

No wonder no one took her seriously.

The soft side.

Travis frowned. "I-I didn't mean it in a bad way."

"Really?" She pushed a strand of hair behind her ear, trying to keep her tears at bay. "Because it sure came off like you think it's a bad thing. Something to take advantage of. And don't worry, it's not just you. My own family treats me like 'little Lindsay'—incapable of actually running the bar that I've been working at while Logan was in business school. But does he know the regulars? How Mr. Stephanopoulos comes in every

Thursday and has a gin and tonic poured for his friend Eddie, who died in the war? Or that Missy Blake doesn't ever have enough money to cover her BLT, or Gene Watts can't read the menu anymore, even though he pretends he can? My grandfather didn't care if I gave Missy the BLT on the house, but Logan acts like it's a crime. He's forgotten the people in this town while he's been away at school."

Then she shook her head bitterly, sniffing as she looked down. A few stubborn tears slipped onto her cheeks anyway. *Why did I tell him all that?* "Sorry. I'm just a little raw right now."

Travis's eyebrows were set in a deep frown. He was silent for a few beats, then said, "For the record, I think you're the best of your entire family. So when I said you're soft, it's not an insult. It just means you care more. And that's something exploitable." Then he reached and brushed a tear away with a swipe of his thumb. "And I think you'd be amazing at running the bar. Have you *asked* your grandfather if he'd consider you for the job?"

Her cheek tingled where he'd touched her, as though only those nerve endings of her skin still worked. She shrugged, unable to meet his gaze. *He's just saying that to make me feel better.* "What difference does it make? It's a done deal. Pops is too busy anyway, and my parents don't want anyone to stress him out further. His health hasn't been very good recently."

"Well, you should ask. It may not help, but it can't really do any harm, can it? I don't see how it would stress him out."

"It doesn't matter." She hated that Travis had seen her so vulnerable. It was only further proof that she was "soft." *He* could take advantage of her if she wasn't careful. "Why don't we just wait until Brian comes back, and then we can figure out what else we need to discuss tonight?"

Travis looked at his phone and grimaced. "Dammit, I told

him it would have to be a short meeting tonight. What the hell is taking him so long?"

Lindsay looked around for the server, who wasn't anywhere to be seen. "Um, I mean, if you need to get going, go ahead. You've got a hot date, after all."

"You sure?" Travis moved his seat back as though he was ready to bolt.

"Yeah, definitely. I'm tired. I wasn't expecting this meeting in the first place, and I'm sort of starving." She sighed, a blue feeling settling in on her. "You should go."

He watched her closely, hesitating. After a moment, he settled back into his seat. "You know what? I think I'll just reschedule."

She frowned. "You sure? Won't your date be mad?"

Travis shrugged. "Yeah, well, that's the beauty of this arrangement, right? There's no emotion either way."

Somehow, Lindsay doubted that, but she nodded, relieved he wasn't leaving. The thought of him going to meet someone for a hookup had left her unsettled. *Why is that? I was fine when he had a girlfriend.*

Of course, if she were honest, she'd also admit that going out of her way to avoid Travis while he'd been dating Hannah wasn't exactly being "fine" with it.

She would chalk this one up to having smacked her head so hard. She'd been a clumsy mess tonight. "Well, thank you. I'm still not entirely sure I didn't give myself a concussion when I got here."

"I think there's a very good chance you gave yourself a concussion." Travis's eyes lifted to the bump on her forehead. "You should keep icing it. Why don't we get you something to eat? I'm pretty hungry." He signaled a passing server. "Could we get Leah back here to take an order?"

The server nodded and then hurried away.

"Leah?" Lindsay asked with faint surprise.

"Leah Rodgers—our server. She's one of my grandmother's neighbors."

Funny how that worked. Between the two of them, they could probably name at least one member of many Brandywood families. Because, like it or not, their own families were the backbone of this town. They'd been here forever, and everyone knew them.

A shadow passed over the table, and they both looked up expectantly for Leah. Except it wasn't her—it was Millie Price, Jen's grandmother-in-law.

"As I live and breathe." Millie offered an amused look, setting her hands on her hips. "Never would've thought I'd see the day where you two would be in here having dinner together."

For some reason, her words made Lindsay feel like twitching with discomfort. "We're here for committee—"

"Oh, I know, sugar pie. I know. But still—" Millie shook her white curls. "Took me back to when I was about your own age. It's like seeing Peter and Bernadette all over again. Of course, she wasn't a Wagner then." She took an anxious gasp and grabbed Travis's hand. "Oh, don't tell her I said anything, please. I'm just an old, senile woman. What do I know?"

Travis blinked at her. "Tell her what?"

Millie gave him a faltering smile. "Exactly, dear. Exactly."

Millie left just as quickly as she'd come, her absence like a void whooshing between them.

Peter and Bernadette?

What the hell was that all about?

Lindsay hesitated, then looked at Travis, who frowned in the direction Millie had gone. "Who's Bernadette?"

"My grandmother. Bunny is her nickname, but she and Millie have been friends since they were kids."

Huh. This whole time, Lindsay had never thought to question that Bunny Wagner's name was anything other than "Bunny." But, come to think of it, who named their kid that?

But Peter and Bernadette? "Did she mean my grandfather?" She scanned Travis's face.

His expression was dark. "I think so."

Lindsay rubbed her forehead. This whole evening had gone sideways from the start. "What was she talking about?"

"I don't know. You know Millie. She's not the most reliable source of information." Travis scowled. "But I'm going to find out."

CHAPTER NINE

Travis killed his car's engine, hesitating as he sat in his parents' driveway. He'd purposely waited until late morning to drive over here, not just because of his unsettling evening the night before. Instead of a date in Londontown with Ashley, the girl he'd been talking to on WinkMe, he'd ended up having a meatloaf special with Lindsay at the senior center. Brian Pearson had failed to reappear—until, finally, around eight, they'd gone looking for him and learned that bingo had ended an hour earlier.

But that wasn't what bothered him.

Nor was it the fact that Lindsay had hit her head so hard he'd insisted on driving her home. He should have insisted she went home long before that, if he was honest, and he hated that she made it so hard for him to treat her like he'd treat anyone else.

As he stared at the front door, thoughts of Lindsay reminded him that he hadn't been disappointed that the date with Ashley had fallen through. He'd contemplated canceling it almost as soon as he'd set it up. Staying with Lindsay was preferable in every way. Not that she would have chosen dinner with him at The Nest if Brian hadn't forced it to happen.

And that's what I have to keep reminding myself. Picking Lindsay won't end well for me in the long run.

At any rate, his inability to stop himself from spending more time with Lindsay than necessary wasn't the issue right now.

He couldn't stop thinking about what Millie Price had said when she'd stopped by their table. The implication was that she sensed something romantic between him and Lindsay, which was worrisome enough.

And she also implied that Nana was once involved with Peter Yardley.

He pushed open the heavy door to his car and stepped outside. The morning had been icy, and it appeared his father had salted the driveway before he'd gone to work. Travis's boots crunched against the ice as he made his way up to the house, his mind churning. He'd thought about going directly to Nana and asking her about Millie's cryptic statement, but then there was the way Millie had grabbed his hand and pleaded with him not to.

Much as he wanted to learn what Millie had referred to, he didn't want to hurt the old lady either. She had a "tough old bird" exterior, but he knew from Jen that she'd also had a hard life. If Millie didn't want him to say anything to his grand-mother, he'd have to respect that—for now.

But the next best person to ask wasn't exactly the most pleased with him, either. Travis had gone out of his way to avoid Dad the last few days, especially after Grace's warning that his father was angry.

So . . . *Mom it is.*

His parents never locked the front door, so he turned the

knob and went inside. The familiar scent of home—something like cinnamon apple mixed with cedar—wafted toward him, and he held on to the doorknob for a moment longer than necessary. A wave of nostalgia and sadness encircled his heart.

Gone were the days when he'd felt like he could find refuge here whenever he wanted. Hell, he even waited until Dad was at work to visit Mom.

"Mom?" He started down the hallway toward the kitchen.

Before he could reach the doorway, she poked her head out. She was dressed in workout clothes and held a cup of coffee in one hand. "Travis!" She gave him a warm smile, then came toward him. "Sorry you caught me looking like such a mess. I just got back from the gym."

He kissed her cheek. "You could never be a mess, Mom." He meant it, too. His mom was always put together, even in gym clothes. She'd worked as a secretary for his father's pediatric practice for years but recently decided she'd had enough and retired to work part-time with Grace at the art studio. And while his neat and tidy mom sometimes clashed with Grace's carefree artistic sensibilities, he'd also been amazed at how much further Grace's business had gone with Mom helping run the administrative part. Mom was everything Grace had needed to counterbalance her B-type tendencies.

"Want a cup of coffee? I just made a pot." She tilted her head back toward the kitchen.

"Sure." Travis stuffed his hands into his pockets, following her. Mom made the best coffee—partially, she'd admitted before—because she'd faced such stiff competition from her mother-in-law when it came to all domestic affairs. She'd made the decision to master a few things well early on in her marriage. So while Mom didn't cook or bake too often, what she did do in the kitchen tended to be amazing.

"Dad's at work." Mom headed toward the coffee maker without looking back at Travis. "If you were looking for him."

"I wasn't," Travis said in a flat tone.

Mom glanced at him out of the corner of her eye. "I figured. But what can I say? I'm your mom. I keep on hoping something will end this hostility between you two."

"I actually don't even want him to know I stopped by. I just had a few questions for you." Travis settled back against the counter. He grabbed the sugar bowl as she poured him a cup.

Mom frowned, then set the cup on the counter beside him. "What's it going to take for you and your father to talk to each other? This can't go on, Travis."

"Dad and I are both fine with the way things are. He's too busy torching his enemies while I try to do my best to stay the hell out of his way." Travis spooned some sugar into the cup and replaced the bowl, then went to the fridge for some half-and-half. He didn't see it and frowned, picking up a bottle of sugar-free oat milk creamer. "No wonder Dad's been extra cranky. You making him use this in his morning coffee?"

Mom laughed and swatted him in the arm. "It's good. You should try it. And it's good for you."

He rolled his eyes and replaced it, then grabbed a milk container instead. "This is what happens to empty nesters. They forget all the things they need to entice their kids to come home—all while complaining about it."

"Fine, I'll add half-and-half back to my grocery list. But you know what'll happen? It'll spoil waiting for you. Just like the last one did." Mom pouted and sipped at her own coffee. "I'm not trying to guilt you. You know that's never been my strategy. But I am starting to worry if I'll ever see my husband and son in the same room again."

"Then talk to your husband. Because this all started a long time before the town meeting on Saturday and our fight after

Christmas. It's a lifelong pattern of me, predictably, falling short of his expectations and him holding me to impossible double standards. Hell, Mom, he didn't even come to my basketball games in high school because I quit baseball."

"Travis." Mom gave him a firm look. "You can complain all you want about your side of things to other people, but I'm your mother. I see the full picture better than you'd expect. And you know you've always gone out of your way to do the exact opposite of what your father wants, even if it's not what you want. You'd cut off your nose to spite your face so long as Dad isn't getting his way."

Travis gritted his teeth, unwilling to continue the argument. Maybe she had a point. *And maybe she doesn't.* But the fact remained: Dad wasn't in the business of compromise either.

He checked his watch. "Pleasant as this has been, I don't have a whole lot of time before I have to return to the shop. I have Johnny watching things at the moment, but I don't like to leave him in charge for too long." He sipped the coffee. *Damn, I miss this.* Mom's coffee had a way of hitting right even without the half-and-half.

Mom sighed and curled both hands around her coffee cup. "All right, all right. I'll stop. I'm sorry. I know I get carried away. How are you? What brings you so urgently here this morning?"

Steam rose from the top of his cup, curling in the sunlight coming in through the kitchen window. The whole kitchen was an eclectic mix of French country and Tuscan village—the clash of his parents' sensibilities. Either way, it was warm and inviting, unlike his own sterile apartment.

"Want to sit down?" Travis nodded toward the small round kitchen table.

Mom looked at him curiously, and they went toward it together. As Travis stretched back into his seat, he couldn't help but remember the half-billion times his parents had begged him not to lean on the two back legs of the chairs in the kitchen when he'd been growing up. One by one, he'd broken them, and it appeared Mom had finally upgraded to new ones that weren't reinforced with wood blocks.

Old habits, though. He had to force himself to keep the front legs of the chair on the floorboards.

"So, uh, I'm not really sure what to ask. But . . . this just stays between us, okay?"

A look of concern crossed Mom's face. "What is it, honey?"

He sipped his coffee. "It's not about me, don't worry. It's just that I met with Lindsay Wagner and Brian Pearson last night at the senior center to talk about the committee, and while Lindsay and I waited for Brian, Millie Price stopped to talk to us." He shifted in his seat, not wanting to give her the full context. "Millie said something about Nana having been romantically involved with Peter Yardley. Then she got nervous and begged me not to say anything."

"She did not." Mom's eyes widened, both with alarm and anger. She looked away, staring down at her coffee cup, her jaw setting.

Uh-oh.

Her reaction seemed odd.

"What's she talking about?"

Mom was silent for a few more beats, and when she looked up, she appeared more composed. "Millie is . . . well, you know Millie. She's old. She doesn't always get things right."

He blinked at her. *She's not being honest.*

Wow.

That was rare.

Mom was usually the one person besides Grace he could count on to be honest.

Which meant that when she wasn't telling the truth, it was usually obvious to him.

"You're not telling me something." Travis frowned. "You want to try that one again?"

Mom released a long, protracted sigh. "Travis, sweetheart, this is really something you'll have to talk to your dad about. I'm sorry. I know that's not what you want to hear, but when you're a parent, you'll understand. Sometimes one parent has to agree to let the other handle certain topics."

What the fuck.

He felt sick.

She just won't tell me.

"So there is something to what Millie said." Travis ducked his chin.

"That's not what I said." Mom stood abruptly.

Surprise rose in his chest, tension knotting in his gut. Mom was acting nervous. "So what is this? Some big family secret I'm not supposed to know about?"

"Travis!" Mom's face flushed. She smoothed her hands over her dark hair. "You know your father. He's as difficult and stubborn as you. Now, I would love to continue talking about this, but I can't. I have half a mind to go to Millie Price and ream her out about this, but I'm not going to do that either. So please, I'm begging you, if you want answers, talk to your father."

He was clearly not going to get the truth out of her.

Which meant there was just one person left to ask: his grandmother.

Travis stared at Mom, then stood slowly. He inhaled a deep sigh through his nose. "You know what, I really don't need to know that badly. But I should get going. Thanks for the coffee, Mom."

He offered her a kiss on the cheek before leaving, not wanting to walk away with things so tense between them.

As he was about to climb into his car, Mom hurried out behind him. "Wait!" She reached the door, an anxious expression in her dark eyes. "You have to promise me you won't go to Nana's and pester her about this."

Travis raised a brow. "Mom—"

"Promise me. I'm begging you. This is a can of worms you really don't want to open, sweetheart. But especially not with her."

Just what was Mom hiding?

"You know all you're doing is telling me Millie wasn't so far off base."

"Promise me, Travis. Your father would be furious. And that's the last thing your relationship with him needs right now. Please."

He'd never been especially good at telling Mom no, particularly when she pleaded with him. But this felt like an unfair promise. He deserved to know if his family was hiding something from him.

"I won't go to Nana," Travis said, and Mom's face relaxed, "yet. But I'm going to get some answers. And that's something you and Dad will have to deal with."

CHAPTER TEN

"You trying to sprout a horn?" Maddie asked as Lindsay sat down at the farmhouse-style table on the back patio.

Lindsay grimaced and reflexively touched the tender spot on her forehead where she'd slammed into the door the day before. "Didn't use enough concealer, huh?"

"What'd you do, honey?" Mom asked from her perch beside the outdoor pizza grill. Ever since almost everyone had left home, Mom had instituted family pizza night on the third Thursday of the month.

And if there was one thing you didn't do, it was mess with Susan Yardley's family traditions.

So even though it meant Naomi now came with her husband, Jeremy, and their two young daughters, and everyone else came from their apartments or houses around town, all five Yardley kids were always in attendance unless they were out of town.

Not that it was hard for Lindsay to do.

She lived at home. While for the rest of her siblings, moving out had somehow meant that they'd grown closer to their parents, Lindsay still had the strain of trying to maintain a private life as an adult in her parents' house. She wasn't particularly close to Mom or Dad, which meant drawing firm lines where she needed. But they tended to know necessary things, like her schedule, and could ensure she wasn't working that Thursday at the restaurant.

Which was why Lindsay was so nervous about *this* particular pizza night.

She sat, then realized her mom still watched her expectantly from beside the grill, pizza peel in hand. "What was that?"

"She wanted to know what you did to your forehead," Pops said, coming outside from the back door with a glass of wine in each hand. He handed one to Lindsay with a wink. "Only the finest of white zinfandel for my sweetest grandbaby."

"Hey, what are we, chopped liver?" Naomi asked, tucking the blanket around her baby Olivia. "Do we really have to keep doing this outside in the middle of February, Mom? It's freezing out here for the kids."

"It builds character," Logan said from the other side of the patio, where he, Jake, and Jeremy were seated on the oversized outdoor furniture with Naomi's three-year-old, Emily, cuddling next to them.

"That's easy for you two to say." Maddie shivered at the table. "You're under blankets, you wusses."

"Hey, we're taking care of children here," Jake said, tugging the blanket up closer to Emily's chin. With a grin, he leaned over and tucked it under his own bearded chin, and Emily gave a delighted laugh.

"Here, let me bring you girls some more heat." Dad tilted one of the outdoor heaters to the side and pushed it closer to Naomi and the baby at the table. He swerved around the strung patio lights that Mom had insisted on four summers ago, having learned his lesson the hard way that moving the outdoor heaters without watching the lights could be disastrous. "Don't want my grandbaby to be cold, after all."

"She's fine, Larry," Jeremy said, sipping a steaming hot cocoa. "Naomi's just been on this kick where she thinks the girls should be watching the world from our windows."

"She's eight months old, Jer." Naomi shook her head at him. "Most of the time, she watches from the side of my chest on this baby carrier."

Lindsay sipped her wine as Pops settled onto the bench beside her. She was tempted to nestle against her grandfather's arm, just sit back and enjoy the bickering and banter that came with being part of a large, tight-knit family like this.

If she could just let herself relax some, she'd admit that she didn't really begrudge her mother's attempts to maintain family closeness. This was what she loved the most about her family. Nights like these, moments when they could forget about all the stuff that was going on outside their front door, like it had been when they were young kids all playing and arguing nonstop.

Time had changed so much and so little.

And she didn't want to stir the pot any further.

Mom crossed the patio, a pizza steaming on the peel. She slid it off onto a large wooden cutting board waiting on the table, then gave Lindsay a direct look in the eye. "So are you going to tell us what happened?"

"Kind of impossible to get a word in edgewise sometimes," Lindsay said, grabbing a pizza cutter. With the mouthwatering scent of the crust and tomatoes mixed with the smoky wood burning from the nearby firepit, she tried to keep her stomach from growling. "I walked into a door at the senior center."

Maddie gave a cackle. "You what?"

"Oh, don't laugh at her," Mom chided in a protective, *don't mess with my baby* sort of way. "That looks like quite a nasty bump, sweetie. When did you do that?"

"Last night. I wasn't paying attention. The first set of doors was automatic, and I didn't realize the second set had one of those buttons you push to open it." *Not to mention, I was distracted by Travis.*

"That's one technique for going through a door," Logan teased.

"Don't worry, Linds, when I can't figure out how a door handle works, I usually try to knock it down headfirst, too," Jake chimed in.

"Har, har, very funny, you two." Lindsay rolled her eyes at them but couldn't help smiling at their antics. "I think I gave myself a concussion, but sure, let's just laugh it up."

"A concussion? Did you go see the doctor?" Mom asked.

"What were you doing at the senior center in the first place?" Naomi slid into the open seat beside her.

"No, I didn't go to the doctor. Hand me your plate, will you, Pops? This one has spinach and feta." They shared a common love of spinach and feta pizza. As he held it out toward her, she went on, keeping her gaze down. "Speaking of which, I ran into Millie Price, Pops. She said something about how she used to see you and Bunny Wagner wandering around town together when you were young."

There. I asked. She'd promised Travis she'd ask, and this was the neatest way to put it without opening too many questions.

Pops snorted. "Oh, did she?" He gave a chuckle and bit into his pizza. "When I was in my younger days, I used to try to date all the ladies. What can I say?" He gave a wink. "I was a ladies' man. Of course, she was a Durand then."

Maddie rolled her eyes. "Of course you were. And now we all know where Jake gets it from."

Jake lifted his hand. "Air high-five, Pops."

Dad shook his head at Pops, frowning.

Naomi gave Lindsay another look. "So you went to the senior center to hang out with Millie Price?"

She would be the sister not to let this go.

"No." Lindsay cleared her throat. She'd been hoping to avoid this. "I had to meet with Brian and Travis for the committee thing."

If they hadn't been watching her before, all eyes went to her now, and Lindsay shifted under the weight of their curiosity. Silence in her family was never good, even for a short period.

Dad turned the heater up some, then sat across from her. "And what did he have to suggest? Lousy bastard."

Lindsay winced. "I'm assuming you're not talking about Brian?"

"No, though maybe I should be. Don't know what the hell he was thinking getting involved like this. He owes Dad too much to stick his nose in things like he did."

"I didn't see it that way at all, Larry." Pops winked at Lindsay, then lifted the slice of pizza she'd given him. "This smells delicious. As usual, Susan. Thank you."

"Was he on Dad's side at all during the committee meeting?" Dad asked, leaning forward in his seat.

Lindsay had the feeling the grilling was about to begin, and she shifted, wishing she hadn't brought it up. "I don't want to discuss the committee meeting, Dad." Or how Brian hadn't shown up and Travis had driven her home. Luckily, her parents hadn't seen him drop her off even though she didn't doubt one of the neighbors might have seen. Travis's car was certainly loud enough for it.

"What do you mean you don't want to talk about it? That's

our family's livelihood you're talking about." Dad's eyes flashed with displeasure.

And he's right. Everyone in her family had gone all-in with Pops's business venture a few years earlier. He'd wanted to keep as many jobs as possible in the family, so they all had roles. Maddie and Naomi ran the Country Depot—and did a fantastic job of it—and Mom helped coordinate Pops's filming schedule. Logan and Jake were at the restaurant, but Jake also occasionally worked with Dad at Pops's home office on marketing and social media, while Dad handled all contracts with his law background. Dad still kept his law office, but he devoted at least a couple of hours a day to Yardley Enterprises.

"It's all right. She doesn't have to talk about it." Pops patted her forearm. "It's fine. Let's all just enjoy dinner."

"That's not really fair to the rest of us." Logan stood and approached the group at the table. "She holds all our fates until Dad can get a legal challenge going to this whole thing. The very least she can do is talk about it."

"Shocking. Logan wants to tell me how I should do things," Lindsay muttered loudly.

"Maybe if you acted like you gave a damn about what we care about, I wouldn't feel the need to." Logan narrowed his eyes at her. "The Wagners won't like it very much once they realize what it's like to have someone putting the squeeze on their businesses, mark my words."

"I agree with Peter," Mom said, going back toward the pizza grill. "Let's not talk about business over dinner."

"No, I think Logan is right. Lindsay has a big responsibility to the family now. It's important for us to know what we might be up against in this whole process." Dad's gaze was focused on Lindsay with laser-like attention, reminding her that Dad could sometimes forget he was at a family dinner and, instead, act like he was in a courtroom.

"Well, I agreed not to discuss it with my family," Lindsay said in a matter-of-fact way, meeting his intrusive gaze head-on.

"See? That's that. Let the girl eat her pizza." Pops nudged her with his elbow and gave her a wink.

She smiled at him. He meant well. He always did. Pops was protective and sweet, and if she was honest, she was probably his favorite granddaughter. They'd always shared a special relationship, and he'd always babied her.

But maybe that was part of the problem. If Pops himself felt the need to shelter and protect her, to baby her and fight her battles, it wouldn't help her at all in the long run when it came to how her family saw her.

"Maddie, can you get me a slice of cheese for Emily?" Jeremy asked. "She devoured that last one."

Lindsay watched Maddie as she stood with a piece of pizza. She was only four years older than Lindsay, but it was old enough that she'd been out of college and able to jump into a role at the Depot when it had opened. Lindsay had missed everything by being too young.

And now her contribution to the family businesses was to work at the bar. *And for what? To cop my brother's caustic anger?*

"I'm quitting," she blurted out loud without even really thinking.

Gazes focused on her again. "You're quitting the committee?" Dad asked. "I didn't think that was possible."

"No." Lindsay took a large mouthful of wine and swallowed. *Thank God Pops brought this to me.* "I'm quitting bartending. Sorry. Random, I know. I was going to make a whole announcement out of it, but I guess that doesn't matter now."

"You're quitting your job at the bar?" Logan watched her with curiosity.

"Yeah and, actually, I've decided to move out, too. I went and looked at an apartment a couple of months ago and didn't move forward with it, but I think I'm ready to now." She avoided looking at Mom specifically, who had cried the last time Lindsay had mentioned being interested in her own place.

Naomi frowned at her. "Talk about a non sequitur."

"It's not, actually." Lindsay drew in a deep breath. "You all still see me as the baby of the family. I'm on this committee, but no one trusts me to represent our family. Logan doesn't trust me to know what I'm doing at the bar." Pops lifted his head sharply at Logan. "And I'm ready. I need to prove to all of you that I can do this on my own. That I'm not going to let the Wagners just run the Depot off Main. But it starts with all of you seeing me as a grown-up who can handle herself."

And now I'll go throw up somewhere.

Especially because she didn't really have an apartment to go to—she'd never moved in her life.

Her family watched her as though she really *had* sprouted a horn on her head.

"What do you mean Logan doesn't trust you at the bar?" Pops questioned in a gentle voice.

"That's ridiculous," Logan scoffed, crossing his arms. "All of this is. I know you don't like some of the changes I'm making, Linds, but I need you there. And that's with you even walking out on the job in the middle of the Valentine's Day rush. You think you could do that at any other job and not even get a slap on the wrist?"

"Well then, maybe you shouldn't have threatened to beat up a customer and throw him out of the bar."

Logan gave a bitter laugh. "Ask Pops if he ever had to throw a customer out of his bar."

"What's this?" Dad turned toward Logan, displeasure on his face.

"Travis Wagner. The prick had the nerve to sit down at our bar the other night. That's what she's so upset over."

"Prick!" Emily repeated from her seat, and Jeremy gave a bark of laughter.

Naomi glared at Logan. "Language."

Logan shook his head at Lindsay. "You've always had a soft spot for the Wagners because of Jen Kline."

"Cavanaugh," Lindsay corrected sharply. Even if she continued to think of Jen by her maiden name, it was still somewhere she could make a little winning dig against Logan.

"Whatever," Logan grunted. "Even Jen has been outspoken in telling them they should back off about this. Meanwhile, Travis Wagner has the nerve to come traipsing into the bar the night before his father tries to get the Depot kicked off Main, and you're in a huff because I kicked him out?"

"It wasn't just that you kicked him out." Lindsay stood, no longer wanting to eat. "It's the way you talked to me in front of him. And the fact that you accused me of stealing from the bar by comping a few drinks, instead of trusting me to know how to bartend. I'm not your employee—"

"Actually, you are."

Ouch.

"Well, not anymore." Lindsay crossed her arms. "Because I'm done. I'm not going to work at the bar as long as you're running the place."

"And this is how you're going to prove how mature and responsible you are?" Logan's eyes blazed. "All you're doing is showing that you can't handle something as huge as this committee is. You can't even handle *your boss* telling you not to give away drinks. You say you want not to be treated and seen as the baby, but then you go and throw a tantrum when you don't get what you want."

Tantrum?

The fact was, she did want to stomp her foot. Or punch him. The latter would be preferable.

And she really, really did *not* want to cry right now, but tears pricked her eyes anyway.

"I'm not throwing a tantrum," she said in a low voice. "I'm just telling you I'm quitting, Logan. And that I'm not going to satisfy the family's curiosity by telling them everything about this committee. It'll be a lot easier to make decisions without everyone's voices in my head. And I deserve the chance to prove I can do this."

"And if you can't? What then?"

She felt everyone staring at her again, now with the added guilt of having ruined a perfectly lovely pizza and family dinner night.

But why was Logan allowed to yell at her, and no one backed her up? Why weren't her mom and dad supporting her? *Why wasn't Pops? He's always backed me at the bar.*

Even Maddie and Jake, who usually felt the need to insert jokes at tense moments, suddenly seemed to have singular concentration on the plates in front of them.

Unless . . . *they all agree with him.*

She shrugged. "Failing isn't an option to me, Logan. But you're going to have to trust that I won't."

Then she left the table and hurried into the house before the tears stinging her eyes could slip out and give her away.

CHAPTER ELEVEN

Travis had waited until Sweet Escapes had almost closed before he went inside, which meant that Jen was wiping down the counter when he went in. "Hey," she said with a smile, her blond ponytail bobbing behind her as she worked. "What brings you in here so late?"

"Couldn't sleep. Can I get a warm milk and cookie to go?" Travis said with a grin.

"You know you can always get a cookie. Though you don't really need mine." She gave him a pointed look. "I remember back in high school when you used to make *me* cookies when I was having a bad day."

"My stove's still broken," Travis said with a shrug and went behind the counter. He grabbed the rag and bottle of cleaning solution from her. "Sit down. I'll take care of this while you prop those feet up. You should be home resting by now."

"Sure you haven't fixed it on purpose?" Jen gave him a side hug and a grateful look, then practically waddled toward a chair.

"I'm positive I haven't fixed it on purpose. Why do I need

to when I have the best cooks and bakers I know within walking distance of my home?" Travis started wiping counters, grateful for the familiar task. He and Jen had become especially close in high school when they'd both worked at his grandmother's café.

Of course, Jen had gone on to become Nana's protégé and then opened up her own bakery in time. Not that Nana minded—she didn't have the energy to make everything these days—and had started taking orders from Jen for some baked goods.

Deep down, Travis wondered if his grandmother wouldn't have been thrilled to have Jen take over the café since Travis didn't want it. A missed opportunity in some ways. Of course, Jen was happy baking all day and not doing the rest of the menu from the café, so maybe it hadn't entirely been a perfect match. But it sure would have saved Travis some guilt.

"So what really brings you here so late? Other than a very Molly Wagner-like desire to clean?"

Travis smiled. Jen had spent enough time at his parents' house to know what a neat freak his mother was. Then his smile faded, and he gave her an ironic look. "Actually, my mother brings me here. Or what she isn't telling me, anyway."

"What isn't she telling you?"

"It's about something Millie said." He straightened, looking over the counter at Jen. How many of their late-night and best conversations had taken place like this, but at the café, with the sweet scent of coffee and pastries hanging in the air? He'd never had a sweet tooth—he could take one bite of most pastries and consider it enough—but it was comfort food, nonetheless. Especially the process of making it. "I don't have to tell you about the secret details of my history with Lindsay because I know she already told you—"

"I was wondering when you were going to bring it up." Jen

stood and stretched with both hands at her back, coming back toward him.

"No, you sit. I can do this."

"Standing helps right now. One of the babies has her foot in my ribs." She scrunched her nose. She placed her hands on the opposite side of the counter but didn't attempt to continue cleaning. *Smart woman.* "I think the only thing I really had left to do was clean the espresso machine."

"Got it." He went toward it and started gathering the dirty components. "So you're not mad at me for not telling you about Lindsay?"

Jen laughed. "Mad isn't exactly how I would put it. I'm not quite sure what to say. Except that I think you're playing with fire, Travis. Lindsay might think it's all no big deal, like she says—though I'm not sure I buy it—but you? You've always had feelings for Lindsay. And don't you dare try to deny it to me. *Then* I'll be mad."

I am not going to make a pregnant woman mad.

The problem was, Travis had been pushing his deeper attraction to Lindsay away for years. *How can I not be attracted to her? She's loyal, funny, gorgeous, sexy as hell, and I've often wondered—what if.* But if Travis knew one thing with absolute certainty, it was that Lindsay would never see him as potential dating material. Family feud aside.

"Feelings that don't go anywhere for years are easy to ignore."

"Yeah. Right."

He took the machine components over to the sink by the coffee station. "I'm serious."

"Mm-hmm. I totally believe you. Especially because something *did* come of them—you slept with her. Multiple times."

Turning the faucet on, Travis sighed. "That's not really important right now. Because, especially now that we're working together, we've agreed it will never happen again. And it doesn't matter what I want because she's been more than clear she considers our hookups mistakes. So I'm moving on. I'm not going to continue moping over any woman who doesn't want me—that's just pathetic."

"Spoken like someone great at putting up fronts." Jen poked her finger at her belly and spoke to it. "Put that foot back on your own side." She grinned at Travis. "Go on."

Seeing Jen talking to her belly was always strangely weird and cute. She had that ability to light up a room, though, so even when she was doing something that Travis didn't quite get or saying something he didn't want to hear, she was impossible to be irritated with. "So anyway, we went to the senior center last night to meet up with Brian Pearson—"

"As one does."

"—and ran into Millie. And then Millie said something about how seeing Lindsay and me together reminded her of my grandmother and Peter Yardley when they were young."

Jen grimaced. "Millie has never been the most tactful person, has she?"

"Yeah, well, that's the problem. Millie is tactless, but that doesn't mean she's dishonest. And to make it worse, she asked me not to say anything to my grandmother about it—she looked legitimately worried, too. So I asked my mom instead. And rather than give me an honest and clear answer, Mom freaked out, told me that if I wanted to know anything, I had to ask my dad, and then begged me to promise her I wouldn't go to my grandmother, too."

Jen gave a deep frown. "You know, this isn't the first time that Millie's implied to me that the tension between Bunny and Peter is romantic in nature. I always just laughed it off because she's got an outrageous delivery with a lot of things, but . . . you think there's something to it?"

Travis concentrated on cleaning the espresso machine parts, his jaw clenching and unclenching.

I completely think there's something to it.

And . . . what's more, my family has gone out of their way to hide it.

He lifted his gaze to Jen. "Would you be willing to ask Millie some more about it? Discreetly, of course. If she knows I'm the one probing, she might just be worried enough not to say anything. But she trusts you. Or better yet, get Jason to do it. He's got a good poker face."

"Are you implying I don't?" Jen set her hands on her hips. "Ouch, but okay. I'll do your little favor. But you're going to owe me something."

"What?" Travis asked with a chuckle.

"I haven't decided yet." She raised her chin and gave a sly smile.

Why does it seem like she already knows what favor she will ask me?

He narrowed his gaze at her. "If your plan is to try to make something with Lindsay happen, that's off the table."

She laughed. "A favor is a favor, Mr. Wagner. And apparently, this not only means a lot to you, but I might be one of the only people who can help you learn what you want to know."

"Or I could just go to Jason directly."

"Not anymore. I'll warn him you're coming and tell him to come right back to me."

Travis was about to answer when the bells on the door rang as it opened. He glanced over his shoulder, then frowned.

Lindsay.

And she looked upset.

Lindsay glanced from Jen to Travis, her eyes red and face blotchy. "I'm so sorry to drop in so late . . ."

Jen rushed toward her. "What happened?"

Travis shut the water off and set the tamper he'd been washing on a clean cloth. Then he dried his hands on a paper towel and left the area behind the counter, concern creeping into his chest.

"I"—Lindsay took a hesitant glance at Travis, then continued—"I was at family pizza night, and I quit my job at the bar, and then I told my mom I was moving out. And then Logan just spewed all this crap at me, and everyone was just sort of making me feel like they were on his side, so I went inside and packed a couple of suitcases and left. I mean, I just left. Like I actually have some place to go. I told my mom I was going to take my stuff to my new place. But I don't have a new place. I have nowhere I can stay—"

"You can stay with me." Jen put her hands on Lindsay's shoulders and gave her a firm look.

"I know." Lindsay drew in a broken breath. "But that's the thing. I'm trying to prove to them how I can be responsible and stand on my own two feet. How I can be responsible," she repeated, then shook her head. She broke away from Jen and walked dazedly toward a chair, sitting down in it with a defeated look. "I don't have enough money for an apartment without the job at the bar. The preschool is pocket change compared to the money I make bartending."

Travis watched from beside the counter, feeling oddly useless and out of place. He gave Jen a taut smile and then mouthed, "I should go."

"No, stay. You don't have to go because of me." Lindsay looked right at him. "We've shared a best friend for a good ten years. We can make it work."

"You should stay with me." Jen sat across from Lindsay. "But if you don't want to, there's always the Redding Cabins—"

"Laura told me a month ago they were booked solid

through the rest of the year," Lindsay said with a shake of her head.

"Well, what about Dan and Avery? I don't think the Serendipity gets booked out as far as the cabins."

Travis grimaced. "A B&B on a weekend near Valentine's Day? I seriously doubt they have vacancies."

Both women gave him a look, and he held out his hands. "Just giving my two cents."

"Well, I can text Dan and ask." Jen scooted closer toward Lindsay and reached for her hand. "And if not, will you consider staying with Jason and me? I can have the guest room ready in less than twenty minutes."

"You could stay with me," Travis offered, feeling completely unhelpful. *Now why'd you go and say that?* He wasn't used to being the insensitive prick around women, but this was Lindsay, after all.

Lindsay wiped her eyes. "No. I don't think either option would work but thank you. All it takes is one person saying one word to Logan and he'll just use it against me. I need my own apartment. But if I can't have that, I need something off the grid where I can figure out a plan until I can get my own apartment and my family can't judge me."

"Linds, I really get your need to stand on your own two feet, but that's crazy talk. What you *need* is a place to stay that has a bed and is safe and where you can have the love and support of your friends—"

An idea bubbled up in Travis's head, sparked by the *off the grid* talk. And before he could stop himself, word vomit spewed out once again, "You could always use my family's hunting cabin."

Now Jen full-out glared at him. "You know, Trav, maybe you *should* go. Your place and the hunting cabin? What are you going to offer next? For Linds to stay with Bunny?"

Travis grinned. "That's not a half-bad idea. Nana has a spare room, and no one would ever think of looking for Lindsay there. Good food, too."

"Except she might poison that food when I'm not looking," Lindsay replied with a wry laugh.

"I'm offended on her behalf. She's fed you more than once at the café, and you've lived to tell the tale." Travis crossed his arms.

"That's because there were too many witnesses."

"Neither here nor there." Jen shook her head at them both. "Bunny isn't a serious option. Neither is the hunting cabin."

"Why not? It has electricity and running water. And no one goes there. Ever. We've been trying to convince my grandmother to sell it for twenty years, but she can't let it go because my grandpa loved it so much."

"Because it's in the middle of the woods, Travis. No woman should have to stay by herself in the middle of the woods."

"I can lend her Ratchet," Travis said with a shrug. Lindsay was strangely quiet, as though she was considering the option.

"No." Then Jen set her hand on her stomach and wrinkled her nose as though she was uncomfortable. "No. That's it. She's not going to the hunting cabin. She's coming home with me. Even if Logan finds out about it, she can just say her apartment wasn't ready yet or something. It's not up for discussion. You're upsetting the babies, so stop it."

Lindsay sighed and then sank back into her chair. "Fine, but only for a night or two. I seriously can't stay there for long."

"Well, since my work here appears to be done, I'll just leave you ladies to it, then." Travis tipped an invisible hat at them. "Have a good night."

He started forward when Jen gripped the table in front of her, suddenly. "Whoa, what was that?"

"What was what?" Lindsay frowned at her.

"Nothing." Jen blinked, then raised a hand to her temple. "I just got a little dizzy, and my vision blurred. It happens sometimes."

Travis exchanged a look with Lindsay, his heart squeezing. Slick fear broke out on his neck, a memory from a much darker time surfacing.

They'd both almost lost Jen once when Colby was born. One of the worst experiences of Travis's entire life.

Whipping out his phone, Travis typed in "symptoms of preeclampsia" and started reading. "Wait, you said you had a pain in your ribs?"

"The baby's foot—" Jen said, her face looking pale.

Travis didn't wait for her to finish and started dialing 911. "Linds, call Jason. I'm calling an ambulance."

Lindsay's eyes widened with alarm, and she moved closer to Jen, gripping her hand as the emergency operator answered Travis. "I need an ambulance at Sweet Escapes on Main. I've got a pregnant lady here who is showing signs of preeclampsia and needs to get to the hospital right away."

Jen started to wilt just then, and Lindsay caught her. "Travis, help me!"

Travis's breath hitched, and he shook his head. "Screw it. I'm driving her myself." He hung up, then bolted toward Jen, picking her up with both arms. "Grab her keys and lock up," he instructed Lindsay.

"I'm coming with you. Where are your keys, Jen?" Lindsay stood and rushed toward the counter.

"Behind the register," Jen said weakly against Travis's chest.

Lindsay found them a moment later. Travis was already at the door. Lindsay held it open, and he pushed his way out, carrying Jen into the cold air and onto the sidewalk.

"Where's your car?" Travis asked, glancing back at Lindsay.

He'd left his at the shop, which was only about a five-minute walk, but five minutes too many.

"I had to park in the annex parking lot," Lindsay said with a frown. "There wasn't anything open on or near Main Street."

"Fuck!" Travis swerved on his heel, looking from side to side as panic clawed at him.

Main Street was so crowded that he couldn't easily drive Jen without walking five or ten minutes to a car.

This never would have happened a few years ago before the goddamn Depot. There had always been parking on Main, except during major holiday events and parades.

Seemingly out of nowhere, the telltale blue and white of a police cruiser shone on their faces, a siren piercing his hearing. Sweat broke out on Travis's forehead as the cruiser double parked in front of the bakery. Then Jen's brother, Dan Kline, climbed out from the driver's seat.

"What happened?" Dan asked at Travis's side moments later. "I heard something come through on the scanner."

"She just sort of faded. I think it's preeclampsia."

Dan took her from Travis immediately. "I'll get her to the hospital."

He didn't wait for them to follow, leaving Travis and Lindsay standing there, shoulder to shoulder.

Travis watched as Dan settled Jen into the back of the cruiser, then hurried around to the driver's side. His hands trembled, his gut twisting.

"Oh my God." Lindsay covered her mouth, her cheeks wet with tears.

This never would have happened if one of them had been able to park near the bakery.

Travis swallowed hard, unreasonable anger at Lindsay spiraling out of nowhere.

It's not her fault.

But her family wasn't willing to see how much harm the amount of traffic in town was causing.

It's not her fault.

But Jen lost valuable seconds just now.

It's not her fault. She's just as worried as you are.

Jen, who was loving and kind, and always generous. They had both come to whine to her tonight. What if they hadn't been there?

Oh God, did we set her over the edge with our stupidity?

Travis tried to breathe, his chest tight. "Do you want to come to the hospital with me?" he asked at last, the words deep and low in his throat. "My car is at my place."

Lindsay nodded, unable to speak, and they started toward his shop.

For once, Lindsay didn't seem to care who saw them together.

CHAPTER TWELVE

The smell of something delicious woke Lindsay from a deep sleep, and she blinked, the corners of her eyes feeling dry and crusty. *Gross.*

She wiped her eyes and rolled over, the room familiar and unfamiliar at the same time . . .

Then she sat straighter, the events of the previous night coming back to her.

Jen. The hospital.

The babies.

Travis.

The whole thing had been a flurry of emotions and activity. Jason had been there by the time they'd arrived at the hospital. Jen's mom had gone to their house to watch Colby, and Jason's younger son, Blake, was at Amanda's for the evening.

But since Colby was technically Jason's nephew, and Jason had no longer been married to his ex when Blake was born, in some ways the twins were a new experience for Jason as far as pregnancy went. And the panic in Jason's face had been clear enough.

So Travis and Lindsay had stayed at the hospital at Jason's side, along with Dan and Jen's father, while they prepped Jen for an emergency C-section. Eventually, around three in the morning, two healthy baby girls—Ava and Nora—had been born. Jen was okay but needed rest. Jen's other brother, Warren, had come to the hospital at that point, and Travis had suggested they go get some rest.

Which meant that the best and easier option for Lindsay to spend the night was at Travis's.

Travis had offered to let her use the bed and had taken the couch. She'd fallen asleep like a rock when her head hit the pillow, only waking to call out of work a couple of hours later when her alarm had gone off. Then she'd gone right back to sleep, which Travis's blackout curtains helped with.

Bacon. That has to be bacon.

Ugh, I don't feel good.

She checked her phone. Almost noon.

Maybe food will help.

Her nose felt a bit stuffy though, her throat scratchy as she climbed out of the bed. On their way back from the hospital, they'd swung by the annex parking lot and picked up her suitcases from her car, so at least she had clothes.

She didn't feel well at all.

Probably from the lack of sleep.

Rubbing her eyes, she made her way to the hallway bathroom and found that Travis had laid out a towel for her. She washed and dried her face, tied her hair into a messy ponytail, then went back to the bedroom and slipped on a pair of sweatpants and thick woolen socks.

Zipping her suitcase back up, she picked up her phone and swiped open to the pictures of Ava and Nora once again.

Her heart melted at the sight of the two newborns.

Wow. I can't believe Jen is a mom to four kids.

That was crazy to think about. She tapped out a quick text to Jen.

Lindsay: *Just wanted to tell you that you make the cutest babies on the planet. Again.*

Though she had expected Jen to be sleeping, a message came back immediately.

Jen: *They can't wait to meet their aunt Lindsay! Love you so much. I'm so sorry I couldn't set up the room for you. Did you go back home?*

Lindsay glanced around her and bit her lip.

Lindsay: *Not exactly. I spent the night at Travis's apartment.*

She started a text explaining the circumstances when the phone rang in her hand.

"Spill," Jen said before even saying hello. "Did you guys hook up again?"

"No, no, no," Lindsay croaked, then set a hand over her throat. *Wow, I didn't realize my voice was so raspy.* "I just crashed here."

"Whoa, you don't sound good. You okay?"

"I think I caught something at school. Again. But I probably won't be able to come see you and the girls until I'm better." Disappointment tinged her voice.

"I totally get it. So, no news about Travis, then?"

Dammit.

She didn't want to get Jen excited and let her down. "No, it wasn't anything like that. He was a perfect gentleman. Stayed on the couch. Our hookup days are over. He's moved on to a hookup app and one-night stands with strangers."

"He did not." Jen sounded outraged. "Are you kidding?"

"I'm not." Lindsay held back a smile. If Jen didn't know better, Jen was offended on her behalf . . . which was sort of great, if she was honest. "Just ask him. He had a date set up for

Wednesday that he only didn't go on because bingo ran too long."

"Bingo? Uhhh . . . there's clearly more in that statement I need to unpack."

"Not a big deal. Brian set up a meeting at the senior center but then ran off to do bingo. Travis has probably already rescheduled the date by now."

"I bet he doesn't. He was probably glad to cancel it. I want to talk more about this, but my nurse just arrived to take my vitals." In a hushed whisper, she added, "I swear they don't leave me alone for more than ten minutes. Keep me updated on the Travis situation."

Lindsay hung up, feeling lighter. Jen somehow always made her feel better, even if she wasn't physically present. She didn't want Jen to get her hopes up about a relationship between her two friends—which she needed to be more mindful of. Jen was oddly in the middle of this. Making things awkward with Travis had the potential to impact Jen, too.

Lindsay tiptoed to the bedroom door and cracked it quietly.

The door flew open as though someone had been waiting on the other side, hitting into the wall with a bang. Ratchet nearly jumped on her, tail wagging eagerly, his front paws on her chest. A swipe of his warm tongue wet her chin, and Lindsay laughed, trying to get him down.

"Ratchet!" Travis's stern voice came closer, and she glanced beyond the dog to see him come into view, a strip of bacon in one hand. "Sit."

Ratchet sat immediately, his gaze locked on the bacon. Travis broke it in half and gave it to him. "You'll get the other half when you go lie down." Ratchet bolted for a big, round bed just inside the bedroom door and lay down eagerly.

Travis tossed him the other half of the bacon and gave her an apologetic look. "Sorry about that. Hope he wasn't scratching at your door. He's been trying to all morning, and I got a little distracted taking a waffle off the iron."

"You made waffles?" *Wow.* She couldn't even remember the last time she'd had waffles.

Travis nodded. "My options were a bit limited as my stove is broken. But I have a waffle iron and a griddle pan, so I made Belgian waffles, scrambled eggs, and bacon. Want some? I also have coffee and juice."

The corners of Lindsay's mouth tipped in a smile. Leave it to Travis to make a full breakfast. He really was a Wagner.

She swallowed, a painful lump in her throat reminding her of how she wasn't feeling that amazing. "Juice would be nice. I mean, so would everything else, too. You didn't have to go to all that trouble for me. What about your work?"

Travis frowned. "Things have been a bit slow lately. Johnny Miller is down there watching things if anyone comes in, though." He tilted his head back toward the kitchen. "Come on."

She followed him down the hallway into the main living space, then sat at the stools at the kitchen counter. Ratchet was already back again, and this time, he sat at Lindsay's feet as though waiting for her to feed him, two big bubbles of drool at the corners of his mouth.

Travis shook his head at the dog as he brought Lindsay a glass of orange juice. "Dude, where are your manners?" He grabbed a napkin, then wiped his mouth. "If you want, I can crate him."

Lindsay frowned. "Crate him?"

Travis gave her a chagrined expression. "Yeah, he used to annoy the shit out of Hannah, so I crated him a lot when she was over."

Seriously? Why had Travis tolerated that?

"He's fine." Lindsay leaned down and rubbed the top of

Ratchet's head. "More than fine. He's just a hungry, happy guy, aren't you?" Ratchet's tail started to wag happily. She grinned at Travis. "You never have to crate him on my behalf. That's just stupid."

Relief crossed Travis's face. "All right. Thanks."

Travis's reaction made her sad for him—and Ratchet. It made her wonder about his own insecurities, though. He clearly loved Ratchet. Had he really wanted to make Hannah so happy that he'd been willing to put what he wanted so low on the priority list?

And if that's the case, what else does that affect?

Lindsay sipped the juice, then scrunched her nose, the acid hitting the rawness of her throat a bit harder than she'd expected.

"Not good?" Travis asked with a frown. He crossed back into the kitchen, checking on the waffle iron. He flipped and opened it to reveal a perfect golden waffle.

"No, I mean, the juice is great. I just woke up with a bit of a sore throat this morning. It's been a long week. My defenses are probably down. Not to mention the fact that I spend most days getting sneezed and coughed on."

"You not enjoying preschool anymore?" Travis asked as he picked up a plate. "Butter and syrup? Or are you more of a scoop of vanilla ice cream and strawberries type of girl? I think I also have whipped cream."

Lindsay's lips parted with surprise. "Is this your normal breakfast? I usually just crack open a box of Frosted Flakes. I'm good with anything. Probably not ice cream, though."

Travis shrugged. "Cereal at my house was only for rare occasions, like when we were traveling and the hotel breakfast included it. Grace and I used to act like getting one of those tiny boxes was the world's biggest treat. But my dad grew up with my grandmother making real breakfasts."

Travis set a plate in front of her with a waffle topped with syrup and whipped cream, with strawberries making it look photo-worthy. Then he gave her another plate with perfect scrambled eggs and crispy bacon.

"This is amazing." She'd never had any guy make breakfast for her, let alone one that had often been at the end of her glares and grumbles. "Thank you."

"I cook when I'm stressed," Travis explained, making himself a plate. "In high school, every time I had a big midterm or something, my parents would wake up to find brownies or chocolate chip cookies or macarons on the counter. Sometimes I'd spend the whole night in the kitchen." He sat down beside her, a wolfish grin on his face. "I probably should have spent that time studying instead."

That was both adorable and something she didn't want to think more about. He wasn't supposed to have humanizing traits like this. It would be so much easier if she didn't get to know him better. Part of why it had worked for them to share Jen's friendship—at least for Lindsay—was that Jen knew not to discuss Travis with her.

"No wonder Jen liked to go to hang out at your house."

Travis shrugged. "You grew up with a family in the restaurant business. You probably know what it's like."

"Eh." Lindsay dug her fork into the waffle and cut a small piece. The instant it hit her mouth, she nearly closed her eyes.

This is the best damn waffle I've ever had.

Gah. *Why?*

Why does he have to be so good at everything he does?

"This is incredible, by the way." She hadn't realized how hungry she was and even though her throat hurt, she couldn't not eat this. "Anyway, yeah, no. I mean, food was always a big part of parties and special events, but otherwise not really. Plus, Mom and Dad aren't known for their cooking, and Pops was always at the restaurant. My mom got really into grilling pizza a few years back, though."

"Grilled pizza is amazing. Once you start grilling, you can't really go back to the oven, can you?"

"Mm-hmm." She didn't want to be the only one sharing so much, though. "So why are you stressed?"

Travis focused his gaze downward, and she studied him. He'd always been quiet in school—that guy who everyone felt like they knew but not because he was overly social. "There's just a lot going on right now."

Not a lot to go on with that.

How sad is it that I'm just realizing how little I actually know him?

Did that make her terrible? She'd slept with him. In a strange way, it didn't even seem like the two of them in the mental images that came back to her. Like it wasn't either of them who'd been there.

The unrestrained versions of two restrained individuals.

Individuals who might have been something more if not for a family feud that didn't make sense when they were together.

And then there was the fact that Jen considered Travis one of her best friends. *Jen thinks so highly of him, and she only likes good people.*

"Yeah, I hear you. I need to figure out how I'm going to make up for the loss of income from the bar and where to stay tonight. Maybe my grandfather will take me in and not tell anyone else, but he's the last person I want to think of me as weak since it's his business empire that needs running." Lindsay shook her head as though trying to clear the thoughts from her mind.

She wrinkled her nose. *Ugh.* The food was so good, but with each bite she took, she seemed to feel worse. "What about you? Going into work today?"

"Eventually. I have a few things I need to sort, and then I'll probably go check on Jen."

"I want to go, too, but if I caught something at the school, I don't want to pass it on to her. And the twins." *I can't believe the twins are here. And they are so, so adorable.*

"Makes sense." Travis stretched his shoulders back. "And then I rescheduled that date from the other night to tonight, so I have to come home and get ready and be in Londontown at six."

So much for not rescheduling that date. He seemed eager to go on it, actually.

The thought wasn't a pleasant one, but instead struck her with a cold, brutal edge that made her stiffen. What if he brought the girl back here tonight? It had only been a week since they'd tumbled into his own living room.

Lindsay blinked down at the surface where her plate was.

This counter.

He'd lifted her onto it . . .

Oh God, don't think about that right now.

"That sounds fun. You should probably leave early. You know, traffic and all." She kept her voice as light and even as possible, her heart giving a strange little dip that echoed how hallow and sick her stomach felt.

"Yeah, speaking of which, I keep thinking about how hard it was to get Jen out of Main Street last night," Travis said in a flat tone.

Lindsay bit her lip. She could tell how much that had upset him last night.

It upset me, too.

Not just because of how dangerous it had been for Jen. What would they have done if Dan hadn't shown up? Or if Jen's brother didn't happen to be the cop on duty? They'd have to have waited for the ambulance, but sometimes minutes made a difference in an emergency. She should know, with all her training with the preschool.

"I know Brian's not here, but we should probably actually make a plan to deal with the issue the town gave to us." Lindsay frowned. Her stomach churned painfully, her appetite dwindling despite the delicious meal Travis had made.

"The Depot is making our town into a circus. I don't think I even realized the extent of it until last night. It's too much for the infrastructure of Brandywood to handle."

Lindsay looked up at him sharply, defensiveness rising in the rigidity of her spine. "Now you sound like your dad."

But is he wrong?

"You saw what happened, Lindsay. What if it was someone having a heart attack? Or a hit-and-run? Out-of-towners get a little crazy over parking spaces out there."

She set a hand over her throat, the sick feeling she'd awoken with growing stronger. "Don't take this the wrong way, Travis, because breakfast was delicious, but I think I'm going to be sick."

Then she bolted away from the counter, nausea clawing at her.

Oh no.

She hated throwing up. So much.

But she found her way to the bathroom and got there just in time.

After she'd finished, she curled up on the tile floor, her stomachache stronger now, and squeezed her eyes shut.

A tap on the door followed. "You okay?" Travis asked from the other side.

"No, I think I might have something," she groaned, her gut feeling unsettled.

Ugh, why, of all places, did this have to happen here?

She didn't care if Travis hated her or if they didn't get along or any of the family rivalry nonsense because, at the end of the day, he clearly had seen her as sexy.

This was anything but.

The door creaked a bit as though Travis had leaned against it. "You want a glass of water?"

"Yes. But I don't want you to see me like this." Lindsay opened her eyes and stared at the cabinet under Travis's sink. The bathroom mat smelled clean, and the floor was surprisingly spotless. Men usually kept their bathrooms so gross, but Travis didn't appear to. In fact, it was much neater than hers was at home.

Home.

Oh God. What did I do?

Now she would have to return, tail between her legs, apologize to her parents, and look like a brat in front of everyone. She couldn't stay with Jen now—she was in the hospital, and it would be weird to crash with Jason and the boys. And when Jen got out, she wasn't exactly going to be able to entertain houseguests. Especially not sick ones.

A glass clinked, and Travis said, "I put a glass of water out here. Anything else you need?"

"A pillow," she mumbled, squeezing her eyes shut again. Maybe she hadn't slept so long because she'd just been tired. Maybe her body had been trying to stay unconscious.

She waited until it sounded like Travis was gone, then she crawled over toward the door to get the water. Reaching up for the knob, she unlocked the door, then pulled it open.

Travis, sitting on the other side with his back to the adjacent wall, raised his brow at her. "Hi there."

"Ooof," she grunted, then reached for the glass. "I didn't know you were still there."

He gave a low chuckle. "I've never had anyone react so positively to my cooking. I wanted to make sure I wasn't going to get sued later for accidental poisoning." Then he got a devilish gleam in his eyes. "And you were worried about my grandmother."

She groaned but smiled. "You're hilarious." She sipped on the water, but it didn't feel good or refreshing, mostly like a way to clear the terrible taste in her mouth. She grimaced, not wanting any more of it.

"No, I mean it. Here I am trying to extend an olive branch, and—*boom*—my hand just got a little too close to the ipecac syrup when I reached for maple."

He can be funnier than I give him credit for. "I probably got it from one of the kids at school. Jessie Mercer threw up on me during craft time on Tuesday."

"I really hope Jessie is a kid." Travis held out a hand toward her. "Why don't we get you back to bed? I can get you a sick bucket or something."

Back to his bed? As tempting as the thought was, she couldn't possibly impose on Travis today. The fact that she'd ended up here after everything last night had been a purely last-minute decision when she hadn't had a lot of options and had been too exhausted to consider anything else.

"I can't take up your bed. I just can lay on the couch for a few until I'm feeling better."

"The couch isn't super comfortable," Travis said, helping her stand. He reached for the glass of water he'd brought her. "Trust me, I know. My back is still asking me what the fuck I did last night."

She swayed, and Travis's arm swept against her back, supporting her.

Just as he'd done for Jen last night when he'd lifted her, no questions asked.

In her panic at Jen's collapse, Lindsay hadn't needed to be resourceful or strong because Travis had been there. He'd come in like a sexy cowboy to rescue the damsel in distress with a clear head and the strong arms to sweep Jen up like—

The palm of Travis's hand brushed up against her forehead, pushing back her hair as he lay it flat against her skin. "You're burning up, Linds."

"You could have saved my dignity and just told me I'm hot." She laughed in a semi-delirious, *this-sounds-so-much-funnier-in-my-own-head* sort of way.

Travis leaned her against him and helped her through the short hallway toward his bedroom door. "You know I think you're hot." He led her into the room and set her on the edge of the bed.

He does?

Lindsay blinked up at him as she slid into the bed, then rolled back onto the pillow. "Really? Even right now?"

He tucked her into the bed, then set the water on the nightstand. "Even right now, sick lady. I'll go get you that sick bucket. If you need anything else, I'll be here. Probably hiding the evidence of my poisoning and burning my kitchen utensils in shame. Get some sleep."

Lindsay closed her eyes and swallowed, then contorted her face at the rawness of her throat. Sleep did sound like a good idea.

A bounce on the bed made her open one eye as Ratchet jumped up on the bed, then lay down. "Ratchet! Come on, boy, get down."

"No, let him stay," Lindsay said as the dog lay his head on the pillow beside hers. She curled into him, feeling the comfort of his presence.

"You sure?"

"Mm-hmm. He's a good boy." She stroked Ratchet's soft fur by his ears, closing her eyes again.

The door creaked as Travis started out. "Thank you," she mumbled after him.

"Like I said, I'll be here. Anything you need, just let me know."

As the door closed, Lindsay took a few slow breaths. She shouldn't be here, given their past, what they'd agreed to—and how badly things had gone with her family last night.

But why did it feel so right?

CHAPTER THIRTEEN

Lindsay being sick had made it impossible for Travis to go visit Jen, so he was surprised when a knock in the afternoon revealed Jason Cavanaugh on his doorstep.

Travis hesitated. Inviting Jason in would be an invitation for him to find out Lindsay was here—and while there was nothing untoward about it, and Travis trusted Jason, it also felt like a careless risk.

On the other hand, staying outside on a freezing cold day would be equally suspicious. It couldn't be more than twenty degrees out there. Lindsay hadn't stirred for the last hour or so.

Travis held the door open for Jason. "Hey, didn't expect to see you here. Come on in."

Jason's eyes were veined red from exhaustion, a five o'clock shadow on his normally clean-shaven face. He gave Travis a weary nod, then moved inside. "Hope I'm not intruding. I tried the shop, but the sign said you were closed for the day."

"Yeah." Travis tried not to think about the anxiety that circled in his chest at the thought. "Business was slow, so I told

Johnny to go home for the day. I'm only running on two hours of sleep anyway."

Jason nodded absentmindedly, his gaze sweeping over the interior of Travis's apartment. Despite his friendship with Jason through Jen, a part of him couldn't help but feel self-conscious at the yard sale hodgepodge in his living room. Jason was insanely wealthy, a fact that didn't always jar with the way he and Jen lived their lives. Not that they didn't do the occasional luxurious splurge, but they had a normal-sized, single-family home in a regular neighborhood. And while Jen had recently upgraded to a minivan in preparation for their larger family, Jason had moved from his sports car to a Land Rover—not cheap, but definitely not as expensive as Travis imagined Jason could afford.

After a moment of awkward silence, Jason shifted, stuffing his hands into the back pockets of his jeans. "I just . . . I needed to come and thank you. Jen . . ." He cleared his throat, his eyes growing glassy. "She's my whole world, and I don't know what I would have done if you and Lindsay hadn't been there to help her last night. When I think about how she would have been alone if you two hadn't stopped in . . ." Jason put a fist in front of his mouth, overcome with emotion.

Travis set a hand on his shoulder. "But she wasn't alone. So don't think about that. And she's doing better now?" He raised his brows.

"Yeah, she's perking up. And the girls are just beautiful." He laughed sardonically. "Doctors don't think they're even going to need to stay in the NICU for long. Don't know how we're going to manage with twins, but that's another story."

"That's amazing. You're going to be fine. You're a great dad." He meant it, too. Travis couldn't imagine how horrible Jason must feel now given the circumstances of Jen's delivery, and he probably needed the reassurance, considering he didn't have any family outside of Millie.

"Yeah, I don't know." Jason sighed. "Listen, I need to find a way to thank you better for what you did for Jen. But in the meantime, I have a problem I need to solve, and I think you might be able to help."

"What's that?" Travis waved him out of the foyer to sit on the couch. "Can I get you a cup of coffee or something?"

Wow, I do sound like my mom sometimes.

"No, I'm good. I can't stay long." Jason sank into the couch, and Travis felt that self-consciousness creep back as he saw Jason frown.

Damn lumpy couch. Sure, it had only cost him fifty bucks, which had helped ease his pain when Ratchet had chewed on one of the cushions, and he'd had to flip it.

But it didn't really help when company, however rare, came over.

"Smells good in here," Jason said, glancing at the kitchen. The counter was a mess of tools and cooking supplies. Travis had spent about three hours fiddling with the stove—which now worked—and then started making chicken soup. He hadn't had time to clean up, though.

"I'm making soup." Travis sat across from him on a papasan chair. "What can I help with?"

"Jen was in the process of trying to make a long-term plan for her maternity leave when this all happened for the bakery. And I know she was trying to work up the courage to ask you—see if you'd be interested—but now the whole timeline has been pushed forward."

Travis had a sinking feeling he knew what was coming next.

"Would you be interested in helping put in some hours at the bakery for a couple of months? We'd work around your schedule and any time you have available. But there's no one Jen trusts or thinks more highly of—other than your grandmother—to help keep the quality of the bakery products up while she's out."

"I'll do your little favor. But you're going to owe me something," Jen had said last night when he'd asked her to help him find out more from Millie.

Travis's jaw flexed. Was this what Jen had in mind? Had she planned on asking him to do this all along?

And how can I say no?

But saying yes felt equally complicated. Sure, he filled in for his grandmother at the café occasionally. And things were slow right now at the shop.

I need the money.

But taking time away from the shop didn't bode well for business, either.

Travis smoothed the flat sides of his palms over the rough fabric on the knees of his jeans. "Can I give you an answer tomorrow? I'd have to figure some things out."

Jason nodded, his expression sympathetic. "That's completely reasonable. Sleep on it. I know you have a lot going on right now with that committee thing, too. How's that going, by the way?"

"That's mostly been talk and taking up space in my head instead of actual time—not much has come of it yet." Travis met Jason's gaze. "But if you have any ideas for a good real estate location to suggest the Depot be moved, I'd love to pick your brain. You know what's around here better than most."

"As a transplant, I take that as a compliment." Jason smiled lazily. He'd spent so much time investing in local real estate and flipping properties with Garrett Doyle that it was hard to remember a time before Jason had arrived in Brandywood even though it had only been about four years.

He leaned forward on the couch. "Truth is, though, I'm not sure I think moving the Depot from Main Street is the best thing for Brandywood."

Travis shouldn't have been surprised. Jen was a vocal supporter of the Depot's presence and had told Travis how much foot traffic it brought her bakery. But the news disappointed him regardless.

"I've always been a bit more in the middle of the issue. Until last night." Travis frowned at Jason. "When I realized how parking and traffic made emergencies like the one Jen had so dangerous. This town wasn't built to be a big tourist stop. And maybe I don't know if that's taking away from its charm or whatever else is being said, but I do know that the people of Brandywood who have been here for generations didn't get a say in the way the decisions of one man would affect the whole town."

Jason nodded. "And that makes sense. All of it. But just because one man changed things doesn't mean they're bad changes. Real estate prices have never been better, for example."

"Unless you're a young family just starting out. A few years ago, they could have afforded a home in the area more easily. Now some of them are having to look elsewhere," Travis said flatly. He didn't have to think hard about the arguments against the Depot—his father had been spouting them for a while.

And even when Dad doesn't think I'm listening, I am.

Before Jason could respond, the door to Travis's bedroom opened and Lindsay shuffled out, a blanket wrapped around her shoulders.

Shit.

If Travis had any hope she might notice Jason and quietly slip back inside the room, that hope was soon deflated as

Ratchet bounded out of the room, yipping and tail wagging at the new company.

Jason lifted his head sharply as Ratchet bounded toward him, then focused his attention on catching the dog's front paws as he jumped on Jason. "Whoa, hi to you, too." Jason smiled and patted his head before setting his paws on the floor. His eyes collided with Lindsay, and her face paled before she rushed into the bathroom, shutting the door behind her.

Oh God.

Jason gave him a curious look.

Lindsay knew Jason as well as—if not better than—Travis did. For her not to greet him had to look suspicious.

He shouldn't care what Jason thought. Truth be told, Jen had probably already told Jason about Travis and Lindsay hooking up occasionally—Jen had told him she told Jason everything.

But, for once, that wasn't why Lindsay had spent the night, and Travis felt the need to set the story straight.

Travis stood abruptly. "She's not feeling so well. She spent the night because we got back so late."

As though taking it as his cue that he should leave, Jason also rose. "It's really none of my business."

"Yeah, no, I know, but—" Travis rubbed the back of his neck, glancing at the closed bathroom door. "I think she's got some sort of stomach bug. Actually, it might not be a great idea for you to hang out and risk getting it. That's why I didn't come back to the hospital this afternoon."

Jason nodded. "Sounds good." He started for the door. "Just let me know about the bakery. And thanks again. For everything."

Jason was gone before Travis could really process what had just happened.

Did he think I was kicking him out?

Given their uncomfortable conversation about the Depot, he hoped not.

Travis stared at the closed door, then hurried over toward the bathroom. Ratchet had parked himself in front of the door as if he was now Lindsay's guardian.

Damn dog. Where was the loyalty?

But given the way Lindsay had looked earlier, Travis doubted she was much better. "You doing okay?"

"Did Jason leave?" Lindsay croaked, opening the door. Her voice was raspy. "What did you tell him?" Her hand automatically went to Ratchet, who stood and stuck his head through to get to her, whining pathetically.

I really should have paid more attention to Ratchet's dislike of Hannah, especially considering how he loves Lindsay.

"Well, first, I went into graphic detail about all the hot sex in the kitchen this morning . . ."

She rolled her eyes, a smile on her lips. "Shut up."

He chuckled. "What do you think I told him? You crashed here last night and were sick. He had to go, though. Also probably didn't want to take the plague back to his wife and newborn daughters."

"I'm so worried about that. You don't think I passed anything on to Jen, do you?"

"You were barely around her." He scanned her face. "You want some chicken soup? I swear I went easy on the poison this time."

"Ugh, I'm not sure my stomach can handle anything yet." Then she limped toward the couch, wrapping the blanket tighter on her shoulders. Ratchet was at her heels and bounced happily as he walked. She sat, then gave him a mystified expression. "Did you stuff these cushions with rocks?"

"Only the finest of Maryland granite. Actually, the couch cushions are where I store all my work tools inside the house."

He squatted beside her. "Honestly, though, I'm not trying to kick you out of the living room, but I wasn't kidding when I told you the bedroom is more comfortable."

"Yeah, apparently not. No wonder we skipped the couch and went right to the kitchen counter last week. And here I was thinking you were being creative." Lindsay stood and looked down at Ratchet. "I think I have a shadow."

"He really likes you," Travis said, and Ratchet's tail wagged.

She hugged the blanket around her. "What can I say? I'm really likable."

Yeah, you are.

The thought came out before Travis could neatly tuck it away in the back of his mind where it would be safe.

Goddammit.

"Ratchet has only the finest of taste. Yesterday, he tried to befriend a raccoon during our walk in the woods. He also was really interested in all the many pellet 'treats' the deer had left everywhere."

Lindsay scrunched her face. "That's disgusting." Her shoulders shook with laughter, though, as she started back to the bedroom. She didn't invite him to come with her, but he followed regardless.

Something about watching Lindsay plop down comfortably on his bed affected him in a way he didn't know how to quite interpret. "Is there anything I can get you?"

She looked at him, then felt her own forehead. "I think I still have a fever. You have any Tylenol?"

"I think so, yeah."

"You think?" She lay her cheek on the pillow, curling her knees up. "Who doesn't have Tylenol? Is your dad a bachelor?" she asked Ratchet, who hopped up on the bed with her. "Does he have lumpy cushions and no medicine?"

He wanted to bring up the fact that, up until a week ago, he'd had a girlfriend, but that didn't seem the best of examples. Hannah had hated his apartment and complained about it frequently. Not that he'd cared enough to change anything about it for her.

"I mean, I definitely have some. Some cold medicine. I just have to go find it."

At the store. Which is only a short walk away.

He started back toward the door.

"You don't have to grab it yet." Lindsay settled back against the pillows, then looked around. He didn't have a lot of places to sit in his room, just a wooden chair, which was where he sat, straddling the seat and facing the back of the chair.

She gave him a curious look as he set his arms on the top of the chair frame. "Is that the chair you built in high school shop class?"

He was impressed she remembered. "I didn't know you knew that. We barely had any classes together—and definitely not shop."

"You told me that one time when I came over," she confessed. "But you were always good with your hands, so I wasn't surprised." Then a blush crept into her cheeks. "I didn't mean—" She tore her gaze away. "I mean, not like it sounded. Or how you think it sounded."

"Or how you think I think it sounded." Travis lifted a wry brow. *Which, to be honest, was how it had sounded, but she doesn't need to know that.* But he decided to spare her and change the subject. "How are you feeling?"

She sighed, sniffling as she reached for the tissue box he'd left for her earlier. "Like death. I have like every cold and flu symptom on the planet all at once. You might not want to hang out here long, actually. I might infect you."

He laughed a bit, shrugging his shoulders. "I don't get sick often." It was the truth, a fact that Grace often begrudged him. Colds would often rage through his family in his childhood, and he'd be the only one left standing. "Probably spent too much time eating dirt and playing in the woods as a kid."

"It's weird, isn't it?" Lindsay leveled her chin at him. "How we grew up a stone's throw away from each other. Always knew each other. Even shared a best friend. Yet because everyone told us we couldn't be friends, we don't know that much about each other. I never pictured you as the outdoorsy type. Maybe because of the baking and car stuff."

Her words gave him pause, his back going more rigid.

If they crossed the line from former casual lovers who acknowledged they were also enemies and became former casual lovers who knew each other better . . . what else would change? Yet he liked talking to Lindsay. Liked having her here. Wondered if she needed the conversation at that moment.

Like I do.

Then cautiously, he said, "Can you really be from Brandywood and not be outdoorsy? Plus, you forget Ben Pearson and I are good friends. I spent ninety-five percent of my free time wandering around his farm, getting into trouble."

She blew her nose. "You never got into trouble. You were like this Goody Two-shoes who didn't ever even go to detention for talking."

"I started a forest fire."

"What?" Lindsay's jaw dropped open.

His posture relaxed some. "When I was eight. Ben and I did. Not a big one. And his grandfather helped us get it out before it got too bad. But Ben's dad was so mad he ended up making us muck stalls for a month straight. Didn't tell my parents, though."

And outside of Grace, no one else knows that story. At least from my lips.

"So you're like this secret pyro, too? Should I start looking up all the unsolved mysteries in Brandywood and see what else you did?"

"Not exactly a secret pyro. Ben's grandfather had this old copy of the *Alchemist's Cookbook* so we filched it and tried all sorts of stuff. Some of it literally blew up in our faces. Ben's dad also took that away from us after the fire."

As he probably should have.

He cleared his throat and continued, "But nah, there's nothing else I'm hiding. Except for a scandalous few trysts with Lindsay Yardley." He winked at her.

She lifted the sheet over her face. "We can't talk about that. That's so weird."

Now, he threw his head back and laughed. "So we can fuck but not talk about fucking?"

"Oh my God, Travis, if you say that again, I will kick you out of your own bedroom." She peeked out from behind the sheet, her face crimson.

Seeing her so embarrassed about their past, when she'd had absolutely no embarrassment about while they'd been together, was also sort of . . . *cute.*

"But where will you stay tonight? You're sort of at my mercy here."

She gaped at him, her eyes twinkling. "Are you threatening to kick me out into a cold February night when I'm sick and homeless?" Then she sighed, her demeanor growing more serious. "Seriously, though, I wasn't thinking you had to put me up for another night, by the way. I was just planning on going home."

But he didn't want her to leave.

Especially not with the sadness that had filled her face when she said that.

"You don't have to do that." He met her eyes. "*Seriously*, as you put it. You're welcome to stay."

The laugh she gave was bitter and tired. "I really can't, though, Travis. It's not a good idea."

"Who's going to know? I'm not going to tell anyone. And I doubt Jason will. Stay. You need a place to sleep while you're sick, and I've got the world's least comfortable couch to sleep on in the meantime." He winked, his expression otherwise serious.

"Talk about guilt. I can't possibly put you out of your bedroom knowing that."

"It's good for me," he said with a shrug. "Gives me time to think about who I must have hurt in a past life and do penance."

A snicker broke out from her throat. "You're ridiculous, Trav."

The nickname, however rarely she used it, made his heart feel like a spool unwinding. *Stop.*

"Just stop fighting me on this. Stay." Then he leaned forward, setting his chin on his forearms. "But, if you don't mind me asking, did something happen with your family? Besides the whole wanting to be responsible and show them you're independent thing?"

She turned onto her side, tucking her cheek under her hands. "No, I mean, I don't think it was deliberate. My grandfather had to have some stents put in last fall, and the cardiologist said it was time to slow down. So Logan took over the restaurant."

Much as Travis didn't want to show his dislike for that son of a bitch and make this conversation awkward, he felt a muscle in his cheek twitch. "I knew about that. Not about the stents, though. I'm sorry." She'd mentioned Peter Yardley's health wasn't that great the other night at the senior center. He hadn't realized it was so serious.

"It was the best decision for Pops. He needs to rest. But . . ." She sniffed and reached for a tissue, her expression growing tearful. "Forget it, I'm being dumb. Anyway, you heard most of it the other night. And, honestly, it's not even Logan running the restaurant that bothers me. It's the fact that I was never even in the running. And then yesterday, Logan went off on me in front of everyone . . . and no one said a word. It's why I couldn't stand to stay there any longer."

"Have any of them reached out at all?"

She shrugged. "My mom has called me a few times. And Maddie texted. But I ignored them. I'm not ready to talk to either of them."

As a tear slid down her cheek, Travis slid from the chair. "Scoot over," he told her, sitting on the edge of the bed.

She looked both hesitant and surprised but did as he said, her eyes red. "I'm going to get you sick," she protested as he slid his arm under her, setting her cheek against his chest.

"It's fine." He stretched his legs out on the bed, smoothing his palm over her shoulder. "You look miserable right now. I can't just leave you lying on the bed alone without comforting you." Then in a more exaggerated way, a line that she wouldn't recognize as coming from his father, he added, "It's not the Wagner way."

She still felt warm. He should probably get that Tylenol soon, and then he could try to get some soup to her after she'd slept a bit more. But she closed her eyes, relaxing against him. For a few minutes, he listened to the soft sound of her breathing, feeling the hammering of his own heart as he let himself be near her.

I like this. Trusting friendship. Holding someone when they need it. He knew it wasn't just "the Wagner way." It was *his* way.

Like it or not, he liked Lindsay Yardley.

And with every step he took toward admitting it—both to himself and to her—he felt more uncertain about how he'd be received by his own family.

"In a weird way," he said in a low tone, "I have the exact opposite situation going on with my family. My dad is barely talking to me right now because he's so mad that I won't commit to taking over the café."

"That can't be fun to have your dad not talking to you."

He leaned his head back, resting it against the headboard, his chin tilted up. "It's not. We were never the picture of a father-and-son relationship. I think after my grandfather died when I was six, he just sort of spiraled into depression for a while. But he didn't treat me like I was his biggest failure, which I'm pretty sure is how he sees me."

"That's stupid. It's not like he had any interest in taking over the café. He's a doctor." Lindsay didn't bother moving her cheek from his chest, making her voice sound flat and muffled. "So you're not allowed to have your own dreams? Does he guilt Grace, too?"

"No. And I told him that around Christmas, which resulted in our biggest fight to date. The problem, though, is that I went to culinary school and then changed my mind about doing anything in cooking or pastry arts after I finished. I still owe him some money for the training, and what's worse, he got his hopes up."

"And I'm sure it doesn't help that my family is doing everything to carry on my grandfather's rival business."

Yeah, there's definitely that. But she didn't say it in a mean way. A simple observation of facts.

"I doubt Nana getting old someday was even remotely on his mind when he was choosing medical school. But that still doesn't mean it should all be put on my shoulders. I appreciate what she's built, but I don't want it. And he won't forgive me for it."

She was silent for a beat, then released a slow sigh. "I'm sorry, Travis, I didn't know. We really do have the exact opposite problem."

He didn't respond, and they settled into comfortable silence. His thumb stroked her shoulder gently, and he tried not to think about how good it felt to have her nestled against him, even if she was sick.

You're being reckless. You keep shifting those goalposts. Letting her get under your skin in the sort of way that will leave you hurt.

At the end of the day, she still doesn't want you.

"What time is it even?" She lifted her phone from the nightstand, then frowned at him. "Don't you have a date in a couple of hours?"

His hand tightened reflexively around her shoulder.

Shiiiiiiit. His date.

He'd meant to text Ashley to reschedule earlier but then got so involved with fixing the damned stove and making soup that he'd forgotten.

He glanced at his watch, and his stomach dropped. He was supposed to be there in an hour. Disentangling himself from her, he stood.

Hoping Lindsay couldn't read his expression, he gave her a smooth smile. "She canceled. I guess that bug you have is going around. I should go get you that Tylenol."

Travis started for the bedroom door when Lindsay croaked out in a raspy voice, "By the way, what did Jason want? Is everything okay with Jen? She hasn't answered my last few texts, but I don't want to bother her."

Ugh, I almost let that go completely out of my mind, too.

Looking over his shoulder, Travis hesitated. Then he

turned and leaned against the doorframe. "Jen's doing good. Probably resting. He wanted to offer me a job. Helping run Sweet Escapes while Jen is on maternity leave."

"Oh, wow. That's nice." Lindsay studied his face, as though wondering if she should comment on the fact that he'd just said he didn't want to have anything to do with taking over his own grandmother's business. Instead, she asked, "Does he have a job for me? I hear the ex-bartender from Yardley's is a fabulous catch."

Too bad Lindsay isn't a pastry chef. Then they wouldn't have to ask for my help at all.

"I'm sure they could use some help. And if not at Sweet Escapes, they would probably welcome your help with the babies. Why don't you ask Jason?"

Lindsay gave a tired murmur. "Maybe I will."

He slipped out of the room as she was lying back down. After fetching his phone from among the tools on the counter, he swiped it open.

He had a message from Ashley.

He clicked it open, and a pair of perfect female breasts lit up his screen.

Ashley: *Really looking forward to getting to know you better, hot stuff.*

He groaned.

I'm going to look like such an ass if I send a message canceling in response.

He closed the message, letting out a slow breath through puffed cheeks.

Fuck.

He wasn't about to leave Lindsay sick and alone in his apartment.

He didn't *want* to leave Lindsay.

Not that Ashley wasn't alluring. *Yet I still don't want to go.*

The truth was, Ashley was no one. He didn't know her beyond some messages on the WinkMe app and some texts they'd exchanged. Never anything this sexy, but that was the whole point of a hookup app, wasn't it? The expectation was clear.

He rubbed his jaw. Was there any good way to put this text to her?

Hey, I'd love to fuck you, but instead, I'm going to need to cancel and help watch over the sick girl in my apartment.

That conversation practically formulated in his head immediately.

Ashley: *What? You're canceling on me to watch a sick girl? Who is she?*

Travis: *Don't worry, we're not even friends. We just occasionally hook up. She means nothing to me.*

Yet that fake conversation was all wrong, too. Because he didn't want to fuck Ashley. And Lindsay wasn't just some random stranger he'd hooked up with occasionally. He'd known her his whole life—a portion of which he'd spent avoiding thinking about her more than necessary. And if something happened to Lindsay . . .

He let out another slow breath.

I wouldn't be happy about it, that's for sure.

But what to do about Ashley?

Fuck, the whole point of this is supposed to be easy and fun. No emotions. How the hell does Ben do this?

Or was something wrong with Travis that he'd pick the girl who'd told him he didn't stand a snowball's chance in hell over the one trying to sext him?

He could practically hear Grace's voice in his head. *"It's never going to work . . ."*

What if he devastated this girl? Made her think that he'd

thought there was something wrong with the picture she'd sent? He didn't want to do that either.

Feeling as though a peach pit was stuck in his throat, he opened his phone and typed:

Travis: *Hey, you're gorgeous. I'd love to get to know you better. But I've had something come up—a friend had to go to the ER last night with preeclampsia, and things have been sort of a mess since. I'm so sorry. Can I take another rain check?*

He looked down at the long message, feeling a bit like an idiot. It was a far cry from the short messages he was used to sending, but he didn't want to come off as an ass either.

Setting his jaw, he clicked the send button.

The "Read" message showed up right away, then three dots to show Ashley was responding.

Ashley: *Cool. Sounds good.*

Travis stared at the message, then a chuckle of hilarity bubbled up in his throat.

That's it?

All that agonizing for that?

Not that she'd given two shits about his friend with preeclampsia, but then again, this wasn't a girlfriend who knew and cared about him.

Because she doesn't care.

She's not interested in your world.

He frowned, feeling oddly dissatisfied with himself.

Grace would be gloating right now.

"Deep down, you're a good guy, Travis . . . you were willing to step foot into Yardley's to make Valentine's nice for Hannah. But maybe the problem is that you don't actually worry about what you want enough. When was the last time you spoke up for yourself in a relationship?"

He shoved the phone into the pocket of his jeans and then

reached for his jacket, not wanting to overthink it. Right now, he needed to go get medicine for Lindsay.

CHAPTER FOURTEEN

"How'd the date go?" Ben's voice carried from the other side of the garage, and Travis blinked away at the brake pad on Ben's truck.

"Didn't happen. Hey, when's the last time you rotated your tires? Your brake pads are wearing thin."

Ben rubbed the back of his neck, squinting. "I got a little busy last year. Didn't get around to it."

"Or the year before that?" Travis smirked.

"Maybe so." Ben grinned. "They say never to lie to your mechanic."

"Is that what they say?" Travis rolled the tire over to him and pressed his thumbnail into the shallow treads. "You're probably due for new tires, too. I can order them for you if you want."

"Just do whatever you need to do. I trust you." Ben crossed his arms. "So what happened to that girl? I thought you said you were going on Wednesday."

"I was, but I canceled because your grandfather called a last-minute committee meeting."

Ben grimaced. "Shit, man, I didn't know that. I wonder why he did that. I told him you had a WinkMe date on Wednesday."

Travis cocked a brow. "You told your grandfather about the hookup app?"

"No, well, not on purpose. He was asking about what had happened with Hannah, and I told him, and then he said he hoped you had better sense than to go for someone like her again." Ben drew a sharp breath as though he'd said more in that sentence than he had for days. "So I told him about WinkMe."

Travis studied Ben as he set the tire down on the concrete floor. He waved Ben over toward his desk and then turned the computer monitor on. Why would Brian Pearson set up a meeting if he knew about Travis's plans?

Unless he was trying to interfere.

Travis pushed the thought away. That was ridiculous. Brian wasn't exactly devious.

"So you gonna see that girl another time?" Ben crossed his arms.

"Nah." Travis typed the make and model of Ben's truck into his computer keyboard. "I don't think so. I might not be cut out for WinkMe."

Ben looked surprised. "You giving up already?"

"Yeah, I don't think it's my style."

Ben smirked. "You know, I didn't suggest it because I thought you'd be into one-night stands. I know you like your his-and-her towels."

Travis didn't take his eyes from the screen and wrote down a few numbers on a slip of paper. He wasn't sure he wanted to have this conversation, but Ben rarely went this personal, either. They tended to sit at the bar or play video games together in companionable silence most of the time, which had driven Hannah crazy.

"Why did you suggest it then?"

"Because you need to go outside your comfort zone. Look for spectacular. The girls you date have engagement rings on their brain. The groom is secondary to the wedding they want. But once you're in it with them, you stop looking out for yourself."

Travis gave him a narrowed-eye look. "You been talking to Grace?"

Ben chuckled. "No. But I'm right, aren't I? She said it, too, I bet."

"And I'm supposed to find what I want on a hookup app?" Travis slid an estimate over toward Ben. "It's eight hundred thirty-four for the tires."

"Who says a relationship can't start with sex? You shouldn't give up yet." Ben had a determined look in his eyes. "You can order the tires."

"Actually, I can't." Travis's gut clenched as he glanced back at the screen. Ben was used to Travis ordering parts and then paying him back later when they came in. But he didn't have the money right now to pay for it upfront. He'd been scraping from the bottom of the barrel, and nearly a thousand dollars in tires just wasn't something he could manage. "Things have been slow lately. Can you pay for them up front?"

It wasn't an abnormal request. With most of his other customers, Travis asked for payment when he ordered parts—he'd been left holding spare parts he didn't need on a couple of occasions when people didn't come back. But something about having to ask Ben pay first felt humiliating. Like he couldn't help his friend.

Like I'm failing.

Shit, I really need to make some money. Fast.

Jason and Jen's offer came to mind immediately.

Ben took out his wallet. "Yeah, sure." He handed Travis his debit card.

The shuffle of a footstep sounded as a figure stepped into the garage, and Travis glanced up.

Dad.

What the hell was he doing here?

Travis's shoulders tensed, and he nodded at him. "Hey, what's up?"

"That's the way you greet your father?" Dad asked skeptically, his hands in the pockets of his long peacoat. He smiled at Ben. "Hello, Benjamin. Good to see you."

Oh God, don't start.

"Hi, Mr. Wagner." Ben went forward and held out his hand to shake his father's. "It's been a while."

"Certainly has. You're doing quite well for yourself, though. Always impressive to see you around town, making deliveries to everyone. Sydney from Bloom's Basket was raving about you on Valentine's Day. Telling me how much you'd helped her out."

"Thank you, sir."

Travis looked at the computer again as he entered Ben's card number into the system. He knew his father well enough. His effusive praise of Ben's accomplishments wouldn't be so out of the ordinary if they didn't serve a double purpose—to highlight his lack of pride in Travis.

Dad cleared his throat as though to capture Travis's attention again. "Travis, I was hoping we might have a conversation in private. Can we go upstairs to your apartment?"

Upstairs?

Travis almost laughed.

They could go up there, but Lindsay was up there. He'd left her sleeping earlier that morning when Ben had called and asked about getting his tires rotated. Who knew if she was still asleep, though. And he couldn't risk his father finding her there.

"Right now isn't a good time." Travis handed Ben's card back to him.

Dad's face colored, and he shifted uncomfortably, taking a quick glance at Ben. "You've been avoiding my calls, son."

"Because I don't want to talk about the committee or the Depot or your petition," Travis said in a flat tone. He looked his father square in the eye. "Those of us on the committee agreed not to discuss it with others."

Ben stepped back, clearly uncomfortable to be present for this.

His father gave a deep frown. "I just thought—" He stopped short, then shook his head. "Never mind. I don't know why I bother with you." He started for the open garage door again.

The part of Travis that had once tried to meet his father's expectations, that wasn't all right with his father's disapproval, seemed to pole vault to the front of his mind. "You thought what?"

Dad glanced back, and his dark eyes were unreadable. "I thought you stopped by the house the other day to discuss it."

Travis's disappointment was visceral. Hadn't he told his mother he didn't want her to mention to his father that he'd come by? She clearly hadn't told him why Travis had come, thankfully, but that she'd mentioned it at all felt like a betrayal.

Before Travis could say anything, though, Dad seemed to catch the look in his eyes. "I saw you on the doorbell camera."

"Oh." Travis's guard lowered somewhat, and he kneaded the knot of tension in his shoulder with his hand. He didn't want to kick Ben out of the garage to talk with his father about Nana and Peter Yardley right now. He wasn't even sure he *wanted* to bridge that topic with his father. He scrambled for another excuse to explain why he'd stopped by. Hopefully Mom would continue to safeguard the real reason. "Uh, actually, I came by to let you know that I'm going to be picking up some work at Jen's bakery now that she's on maternity leave."

So much for taking the time to think about it.

But the truth was, he was probably going to accept the offer. He couldn't let Jen and Jason down, and he needed the money. *A lot.*

And his father had just given him an easy way to announce it to the family.

Dad processed the information slowly, then gave a curt nod. "So you'll bake for your friend but not your grandmother. I got it."

Exactly.

Just as I assumed.

"Dad, you know I fill in for Nana whenever she goes out of town. This isn't me picking Jen over the family. And the truth is, Jen *is* family to me. You know that, too."

"Family is family." Dad glared at Travis. "But you've more than proven that you're willing to help others succeed while our family stays stagnant. Good to see you, Ben."

Dad left without a goodbye, and the air in the garage hung with the tension he'd left behind. Ben blew out a long breath through puffed cheeks. "Shit. I could'a left. Gone to get some coffee or something. Or you could have gone upstairs with your dad for a few minutes. I don't care about staying here alone."

Travis went back toward Ben's truck and grabbed the tire off the floor. "It's fine. I didn't want to take him up anyway."

"Why, you hiding a body up there?" Ben asked with a laugh.

If he only knew.

"If I were hiding a body, you'd be the first person I'd call to help me move it." Travis rolled the tire toward the back of the truck.

Ben gave him a curious look suddenly. "Speaking of bodies, where the hell is Ratchet? I thought that dog didn't leave your side in the garage."

"Uh—" Travis's eyes flicked toward the back stairwell. *He's found someone he prefers to shadow.*

Ben followed his gaze, then his eyes glinted. "Oh, you motherfucker. You *are* hiding someone up there. You did go on that date, didn't you?"

"No."

But Ben, being his friend from forever, gave a mischievous smile, then headed straight for the back stairwell.

Fuck.

"Ben," Travis called out in warning.

Ben whistled as he went up the stairs. Travis dropped the tire, then bolted behind him. By that point, though, Ben was already at the top of the stairs, his hand on the knob.

"Wait, hold on—"

Ben opened the door and stepped through, Travis steps behind him.

Oh fuck, this isn't good.

Maybe Lindsay would still be in bed.

But she wasn't. She was sitting, her legs crisscrossed on the couch, a pile of tissues beside her as she knitted. The TV was on, and a blanket was draped over her shoulders. Ratchet was beside her but bounded up from his place, eager to greet the new arrival.

Lindsay looked up, and her face froze.

Ben stopped short, and Travis slammed into his back. "What the—"

Lindsay scrambled up from the couch. "Ben."

Ben's eyes filled with confusion, and he looked from Travis to Lindsay. "What?"

"Um—" Travis closed the door, then gave Ratchet an obligatory rub. "It's not what it looks like."

Ben guffawed. "I'm not sure I know what the hell it looks like." He ran his fingers through his scalp. "Other than the fact that I missed the invitation to the senior convention. Are you knitting?" He squinted at Lindsay.

"I'll have you know knitting is becoming popular again," Lindsay said hoarsely, crossing her arms.

Travis smiled at her. Even though she wore an oversized sweatshirt and leggings and her hair was thrown up in a messy ponytail, she looked . . . *perfect*.

Just the sight I wish I could walk in from work to.

He blanked his expression and grabbed Ratchet's collar to stop him from pawing at Ben. "Lindsay ended up crashing here after Jen went to the hospital. And then she woke up with the flu or something yesterday so she stayed again."

"Sure. Makes sense." He crossed his arms and Travis wasn't entirely sure Ben believed him.

For several beats, the only sound that bridged the awkward encounter was Ratchet's panting as he tried to wiggle out from Travis's grasp. "Uh—" Lindsay looked back at her knitting and gathered it. "I should go. Thanks for the soup, Travis. I finally had some this morning and it was great. Just what I needed."

"No, no. You're sick." Ben studied Travis's profile. "I'll go." He winked at Lindsay. "I was just being nosy. Nice seeing you, Lindsay." He edged past Travis and started down the stairwell again.

Travis held Lindsay's anxious gaze. "I'm gonna go talk to him."

Lindsay nodded quickly.

He pointed at the couch. "Don't go anywhere. I'm not

expecting you to leave." Then he hurried behind Ben and this time, Ratchet followed him.

Ben was already near the bottom step by the time Travis got outside. "Hold on, wait up." Travis jogged down the stairs toward him.

Ben turned and gave him a wary look. "Now I know why you quit the dating app."

"No, it's not like that—"

Ben set a hand on his shoulder. "Travis, I love you like a brother. So don't take this the wrong way when I tell you—you're in over your fucking head."

"We're not together," Travis said emphatically. No way in hell he'd admit to Ben that he'd ever slept with Lindsay. And Ben needed to understand just how far off-base he was.

Ben chuckled, lowering his hand. "You're practically making house with her. Chicken soup? When was the last time you made me chicken soup because I had the sniffles? And let's not try to pretend I haven't been aware of your lifelong crush on that woman. I'd say good for you, man, because you deserve to get what you want, but in this case, it's like that Greek idiot who tried to fly too close to the sun—"

"Icharus."

"Whatever. Getting what you want here isn't going to end well for you. You're going to crash and burn, just like Ichabod."

"Icharus. Ichabod was from the *Legend of Sleepy Hollow*." He should just keep his mouth shut, but he couldn't help himself for some reason.

"Nerd. Look." Ben shrugged. "You can't try to convince me you two are friends or something. I know you. And I know her. The only reason she's up there is because there's something else going on. Otherwise, she would've stayed with anyone else in this town. She's only up there because she's into you. Congratulations. You got what you wanted."

Explaining to Ben that he couldn't be further from the truth was pointless. And it would require more detail than Travis cared to go into. Travis shoved his hands into his pockets, too tense to argue.

It didn't matter anyway. Ben wouldn't say anything. He always had Travis's back.

And when Travis stopped trying to argue, a knowing smile turned the corners of Ben's lip up. "Why don't I leave you to your lady? I'll swing by for the truck later."

"Yeah, I'll text you when I have the tire rotation done." Defeat filled Travis as Ben shook his head and gave another chuckle, before heading out the door.

Well, shit.

Yet.

". . . she would've stayed with anyone else in this town. She's only up there because she's into you."

Was it possible that Lindsay wasn't as cool to him as she'd said? Ben was usually fairly good at reading people.

He glanced down at Ratchet and squatted in front of him. *Hell, Ratchet's pretty good at judging people, too.*

"What do you think, buddy? Should I give it another shot? See if she wants to spend time with me?"

Ratchet's tail wagged.

And for all the tension Travis had felt minutes earlier—between his father's searing disappointment in him and stress about money and Ben finding Lindsay there—that all seemed to dissipate as the slightest kernel of hope planted in his chest.

Maybe.

Maybe had never sounded so good.

CHAPTER FIFTEEN

"Where the hell are you?"

Jake's voice had a worried sound to it, and Lindsay shifted under the covers onto her back. She'd been lying on her side, scrolling real estate locations in Brandywood mindlessly on her phone for too long anyway. "I'm sick." She sniffled, then rubbed her scratchy eyes.

The truth was, she was feeling much better. The stomach part of this bug had gone away after Friday, and Travis had spent the day feeding her chicken soup and crackers and watching a *Lord of the Rings* marathon with her the day before after learning she had a quiet fantasy obsession that she didn't tell almost anyone about.

And when he'd suggested she spend the night again, she hadn't had to pretend to fight him. He wasn't insisting on coming into the room, after all—poor guy was still sleeping on that terrible couch—and it bought her time to deal with all the things she had going on.

Somehow Ben finding her there had felt oddly . . . *okay.* Like she and Travis could bridge some of the animosity that existed between their families. To have two of their friends know that they could be cordial to each other made the whole issue of the committee—which they'd managed to avoid discussing—felt somehow manageable.

"Okay, but that's not what I asked." Jake's voice brought her back to reality. "Where are you? You went totally MIA after Thursday, and then Mom says you haven't answered your phone at all the last couple of days. Maddie and Naomi said you ignored their texts. And Logan says your car has been sitting in the annex lot at least since Friday morning."

"I texted Mom. Told her I was crashing at a friend's house." Lindsay shoved the covers to the side and crawled out of the warm bed. Thank goodness she'd had her suitcases with her. It had made staying at Travis's place easier than expected.

As she did, Ratchet hopped out of the bed, where he'd been sleeping beside her again, and gave a big shake, his dog tag clinking.

"What friend? Was that a dog?"

She ignored the question about the dog, her shoulders tensing. "Jen."

"Really? Mom says Betty Kline told her Jen had the babies on Friday morning. You're staying with Jason and Colby?"

God, it's annoying how quickly news travels in this town.

"Yup," she squeaked out, wanting to throw the phone.

"Jason said you weren't staying there. Mom asked." Jake's voice was flat.

Shit.

Normally, she'd expect this sort of drilling from Naomi or Logan. They were the oldest, so they always played mini-Mom and mini-Dad, especially to Lindsay. But Jake had always been the one she was closest to out of all her siblings. *But I'm not feeling that right now.*

"It's a friend you don't know," she managed, certain Jake wouldn't believe her.

"Try me. I know a lot of people in this town."

"Well, you don't know him. He's from Londontown."

A pause on the other end. "You're crashing with some random guy? What happened to the apartment you were supposedly moving into?" Jake cleared his throat. "Are you sleeping with this *friend*? Is he there right now?"

She laughed. "No. I told you, he's just a friend. But I didn't want to tell you because I *knew* you'd think it was something else. Please don't tell Mom and Dad. I'll come up with a good excuse. I really have been sick all weekend."

She glanced at the time on her phone. Just after seven. Jake really must be worried if he was calling her this early on a Sunday morning.

Yet, no mention of why she'd been upset and left in the first place.

She understood her family were worried, but it still irritated her that no one had jumped to her defense on Thursday night. No one had really said much about Logan's tirade, and Lindsay would be lying if that didn't sting.

"And the apartment?"

"My lease doesn't start until a few weeks." The lies were beginning to feel unmanageable, and she felt gross telling them, so she said quickly, "Listen, I should get going. But I'm fine. I'm alive and well, so tell everyone to call off the search party."

"You don't sound sick—"

Lindsay ended the call before Jake could finish, then tossed the phone on the bed and knelt in front of her suitcase.

The phone dinged with a text message—no doubt from Jake—and curiousity won over and she picked up.

Jake: *Don't even try to pretend you're not busy banging some guy. ;) I'll keep your little secret, kid.*

Before she could worry about the fact that Jen was probably too busy to deal with her issues right now, Lindsay dialed her quickly. Jen picked up immediately.

"Hey, I was thinking about you. Jas, can you take Nora from me? She's done."

Of course. She's busy. "I can call back."

"No, no. I was just nursing the twins. It's a bit of a crap-shoot, but I have a second. Hold on . . ."

The soft murmur of voices in the background sounded, and then Jen said again, "I'm all yours. Well, partially, Ava's still latched on. She's a hungry monkey."

"I can't even imagine." Lindsay sank onto the floor beside her suitcase, looking for an outfit for the day.

"She's the cutest thing ever. She sounds like a goat, I swear. She's got this like bleat that makes me laugh. But anyway, what's up? Feeling any better?"

"Yeah, so much better. Travis—" Lindsay stopped short. She hadn't meant to tell Jen about her extended stay with Travis yet but, then again, this was what she needed her best friend for.

"You're still with Travis?" Jen's voice didn't give away what she thought about that piece of news.

"Yeah."

Jen cleared her throat. "Platonically?"

"Yes, Mom."

"I'm just asking. So are you guys . . . friends now?"

"No." Lindsay ran her fingertips over the rough fabric of a pair of jeans. "We're nothing. Not friends. Not romantic. Just . . . I don't know. I know we can't be friends. But he's been sweet, and I was sick, and it was . . . *nice* having someone to hang out with. But there's nothing between us, friendship-wise or otherwise."

"Lindsay, I'm not trying to take sides because I care so much about you both, but don't mess with his head. Travis is a good guy. He has always been. And he might not see you staying there the same way you're talking about it. If you truly have no interest in any sort of relationship with him—and I'm going to be honest, friendship isn't the likeliest thing, given your history—then don't stay there with him anymore. He could get hurt. You both could."

Was Jen implying that Travis had feelings for her?

They'd been lovers, sure, but he'd never said he wanted something more. Even if he seemed less worried about people finding out about their hookups, it had never been, *"Hey, Lindsay, I'd like to date you. I want to be with you."* It had always just been, *"So what if people know we slept together?"* And even then, he wasn't always so blasé about it as that. He occasionally freaked out about anyone knowing—like when she'd told Jen about it.

"Travis doesn't feel that way about me," she finally told Jen in a flat tone.

One of the babies started to wail, and Lindsay sucked in a shaky breath. "You should go. Talk soon?"

"Yeah, definitely. Love you, babe. Be careful."

Lindsay hung up and stared at the blinking time on the phone. She wished she could just ask Jen what she'd meant. But Jen would feel obligated to protect Travis. Talking about him was a difficult topic to navigate.

I really can't continue to stay here.

Appealing as it was to not have to look for her own place, this had been a temporary emergency thing. Travis was barely her friend.

At least, that was what she'd thought when this long weekend had started.

But then he'd made her waffles.

Gotten her medicine and water.

Made her soup.

Watched movies with her.

Ugh.

Why in the hell did Hannah Strickland dump him?

She felt a surge of anger for him. Travis was a lot of things and among them was being a sweet guy. Thoughtful.

Any girl would be lucky to have him.

And that's about enough thinking about that.

She was getting too close, too involved.

They'd successfully navigated the last couple of days without talking much about their families or the committee or the issue at the heart of it in the first place.

But as soon as that became front and center to their relationship again, they'd be on opposite corners. She couldn't let her judgment be clouded by his likability.

She frowned as she pulled a robe from her suitcase. She needed a shower. If she could tiptoe into the hallway and get into the bathroom, maybe she could take one before Travis even woke up.

Changing out of her pajamas into the robe, she put her dirty clothes away, then set out an outfit to change into. She turned toward Ratchet, who followed. She didn't want him going into the living room and waking up Travis. "Sit," she said, holding up a hand.

He sat dutifully, staring up at her.

"You stay here. I'll be right back."

Then she left the room, closing the door in front of his face.

She made her way down the hallway as quietly as possible. She'd showered in the middle of the afternoon yesterday, but somehow being sick always made her want to take twice as many showers as usual. Sidling up to the closed bathroom door, she set her hand on the knob to turn it gently.

The knob turned in her hand, and a thick wall of steam whooshed out as Travis smacked right into her.

They both gave startled cries, and Lindsay smacked back against the doorframe. Travis's hand shot out to steady her.

Disoriented, Lindsay blinked in the dim light of the hallway at Travis. Beads of water from the shower were still on the smooth, hard muscles of his shoulders and chest, his dark hair damp. He wore only a towel around his waist, slung so low that her eyes followed the outline of his ab muscles as they made a V down . . .

Crap.

Her eyes lifted to his. "What are you doing?" she asked, stepping back and finding there was nowhere to go. She was already leaning against the doorframe.

"Taking a shower." He cocked a brow at her. "Get a good look?" Shamelessly, his own gaze dipped to the front of her robe, which plunged low, exposing a generous amount of cleavage.

"I wasn't looking at your dick," she blurted out, then cringed. Swallowing hard, she met his eyes. "I mean, you know I wasn't because you're wearing a towel. I just—I just was surprised to see you so disrobed."

He stepped closer, his lips at her ear. "Ironic, coming from someone who is clearly not wearing anything under that robe."

She shivered at the feel of his breath against her ear, her own breath hitching. He was close enough now that she could feel the warmth of his body radiating from his skin. And, *God, he smells good,* the masculine scent of his body wash clinging to his skin. He'd shaved, too, and she felt the urge to trail her fingertips against that strong jaw.

"Who says I'm not?" Lindsay managed at last, raising her chin in a dare. "I'm fully dressed under my robe. Except for pants." She wasn't, but a part of her wanted him to find out for himself.

This isn't a good idea. Abandon ship. Get off now.

Travis smirked, those full lips so close to her own that she wanted to lean forward and taste them.

You can't just kiss him. You've got a cold, Lindsay.

But Travis's hand skimmed her hip, gathering the fabric of her robe in his palm. She leaned back, her breath growing shallower as he stepped closer still, one knee pushing between her thighs, the dampness of the towel on her skin.

"Should we find out if you're lying?" Her heart pounded in her chest as he pushed his hand under the fabric, then traced his rough palm up against the outline of her thigh. His eyes locked with hers as he went higher on her hip, stopping at her waist, then back down again.

"I don't feel anything there." Then his hand smoothed back over her ass and she let out a shattered breath, her head falling back, feeling hypnotized by his touch.

I want him to touch me.

A pool of hot wetness had formed between her legs, her body feeling instantly alive.

He slid the other hand above the tie of her robe, and sparks of electric shocks shimmied their way up her skin as his palm cupped her bare breast. Then his thumb brushed up against her nipple, making a slow, soft circle. Heat rose in her face, and she felt herself losing control, her body wanting to mold itself to his touch.

"I win," he whispered, his lips at her ear again.

His breath was as heavy as her own, and she closed her eyes. All she had to do was reach out and grab him, let him know this was what she wanted, to be held and touched by him like this . . .

But I swore to myself I wouldn't do this again.

The dizzying temptation was overwhelming. His lips grazed her jaw, his hand daring back farther against her ass, cupping her, his fingertips dipping between her legs.

"We said we wouldn't," she managed, her body now begging for him to push those fingertips just a little farther inside her.

"We're awfully good at it, you know."

"Oh God." She closed her eyes, her hand edged to the top of his towel. He was hard against the flat of her palm.

As though he knew exactly what she wanted, two fingers pushed deep inside her, and she gasped. She wanted him so badly.

"You're so wet, baby," he whispered and rolled her nipple against his thumb and forefinger.

With her body on fire, she tried to think clearly. Having sex with him would solve nothing. They'd be right back where they started.

"We can't do this," she whispered.

His fingers withdrew immediately, his hand falling away from her breast. The absence of his touch was almost as big of a shock as him touching her had been, and her eyes flew open as he let out a shallow breath. "I'm sorry."

"No, I mean, I want to. I really do. I just—we can't. It's stupid, Travis. We know how this ends."

He drew a deep breath and stepped back, adjusting himself. "If you say so." He scanned her face, then moved past her into the hallway. "I should go get dressed."

She closed the bathroom door in a rush and turned on the lights. The mirror was still fogged up from his shower, and she was glad she couldn't see herself.

I hate this.

She sank back against the door, filled with longing and regret and closed her eyes.

How is it possible that something that feels so damn good is actually so bad? Now she was horny and frustrated.

A soft creak in the floorboard out in the hall made her smile, sadly. "Are you still on the other side of the door?"

"Maybe."

She imagined him there, leaning against the other side, separated by so much more than this damn door.

After a few more moments, he said, "For the record, I don't care what my family thinks. About who I sleep with, who I date, or anything else."

In other words, I'm the one getting in the way?

Was he saying he wanted more? That, if not for her dictate to stop, he'd be interested in . . . what? Sleeping together again? Or something else?

Did he care about more than he'd admitted?

Do I care about him?

Then her thoughts clouded with other ones. Jake calling her just minutes before, the reactions that Naomi, Logan, and Maddie would have. And Mom and Dad. Her family had never really loved the Wagners, but it had all gotten so much worse recently with Travis's dad trying to get rid of the Depot.

And if I can't solve things in a way that keeps the Depot on Main Street, what then?

They'll think I failed the family.

Add any type of relationship with Travis—casual or not—and her family might even think she'd betrayed them on purpose.

She took a few deep breaths, feeling more grounded now that there was space between them. With the sexual impulse ebbing away, it was easier to think clearly.

"I *do* care what my family thinks, Travis. I always have."

And like it or not, that wouldn't change soon.

She needed to get her act together, focus on bringing about the result her family wanted from her being on this committee, and stop screwing around with Travis Wagner.

It's time for me to leave.

CHAPTER SIXTEEN

April 1975

THE RAINSTORM HAD HIT without warning, and despite having an umbrella, Peter ducked under the awning of the Price Hardware Store, not wanting to get his pants legs soaked. Rain like this could happen any time of year, but it was always worse in April. A river running behind Main Street meant that sometimes flooding was terrible during this time of year, and the rain was falling so fast that it looked like a flash flood was possible.

He crossed his arms and was determined to wait out the heavy rain under the awning.

Then he saw her running across the street, her little boy in her arms.

Peter's throat clenched.

He'd gone out of his way to avoid her. Started going to a

new church. Avoided the side of town where she'd set up her café.

He hated that everyone called her Bunny now. Mostly because that son of a bitch, John Wagner, was the one who'd started it.

As though he gets a say.

The few times they crossed paths, they kept their heads down and didn't look or talk to each other.

But that's the way it went when you got a *Dear John* letter from your high school sweetheart.

Robbie's death had changed her. She couldn't look at him the same after that. She was angrier, hated the war more, hated that he'd gone there willingly when her brother had been drafted and forced to go.

Right now, he couldn't help but look at her. She'd been carrying a brown paper grocery bag, which had soaked through because of the rain. As he watched, the bottom fell out of the bag, and everything inside it tumbled into the gutter.

He was at her side a moment later, helping her collect things.

"Just leave it," she said as he reached for a bag of sugar. "It'll be ruined anyway."

The little boy at her side—Todd, she'd named him—shivered in the cold rain.

Peter picked up the boy and opened the umbrella, then walked them both back to the awning. After depositing them there, he returned to the site of the grocery bag and pulled off his blazer. He collected what he could, using his blazer like a sack, and brought it back to her.

"I think most of it will dry out just fine. You might lose some of the labels from the cans."

Bernadette gave him an awkward smile, her bright red lipstick making her look paler.

Gosh, she is still so pretty, though.

"Is this Todd?" Peter asked, winking at the boy.

She smiled and set her hands on his shoulders. "Yes. He's three." She met Peter's gaze. "And you have a little one, too, right?"

"Yes, he just turned three also. Lawrence."

And just like that, they ran out of things to say to each other.

Peter looked away. It was hard to remember a time when she'd been his every thought all the time.

Not that hard.

But he loved Marion. Sure, maybe it'd been a shotgun wedding, but that was in the past. It wasn't fair to her to think back on when Bernadette had been his world.

The fact that she'd married the man she knew he disliked the most in this town, though, made the sting of it hurt more.

"So . . . are you happy?" he finally blurted out, unable to think of anything else.

She gave him a horrified look. "What sort of a question is that?"

He shrugged. "It's not that deep. Just figured I would ask."

"I'm a married woman, Peter."

"And I'm a married man." He smirked. "Married people can still be unhappy."

She dug in her purse for a cigarette, then lit it with trembling fingers. "Well, it's not appropriate. Especially not in front of my son."

He hated to see her smoking. Sure, when they'd been kids, they might have tried a cigarette or two, but she'd never cared for it. John smoked, though. Like a chimney.

Guess that's another thing she picked up from him.

"Could've been my son if you'd just waited for another year," he finally muttered.

Why do I keep shoving my foot farther in my mouth?

She snapped a cold look at him. "You're outrageous." She looked away and tapped her foot as though trying to will the storm away. Then she leaned down toward Todd. "Darling, why don't you go into Mr. Price's shop? See if he'll give you a lollipop?"

The little boy scampered inside happily. She watched him go, then turned back toward Peter. "You knew how I felt about the war. Knew how much I didn't want you to go. And then you go and sign up? How could you possibly think I would want to have anything to do with you after that? It was over before you left Brandywood, Peter."

Ouch.

He winced.

"So you married John Wagner because I went to serve my country? I'm a patriot, B. Always was. You knew that about me, too."

"I married John Wagner because he loved me and wasn't over there fighting a war we never should have been in, in the first place."

He could practically hear the slogans being chanted as he'd returned from the war, greeted by angry protestors rather than as a hero.

Peter's grasp tightened around the bundle he'd made with his blazer. "So to spite me, then. And how's that working out for you? Because you don't look happy, Bernadette. You look tired and agitated and like you've got too much nicotine in your blood."

She pressed her lips together, gave him a pained look, and crushed out her cigarette against the brick wall.

Then a sob broke out, and she turned her face into his chest. "I think John's having an affair."

Peter hesitated.

What?

That goddamn son of a bitch.

His hand came down on her back gently, and he held her. *That rotten bastard. How the hell could he do that to Bernadette?*

"That's horrible, B. I'm sorry. You want me to take him to task for it?"

"You can't say a word. To anyone."

She cried for a few minutes longer while he held her, then the rain subsided. She pulled away, trying to put herself back together. "I should go after Todd."

Peter nodded and held out his blazer. "Take it. You can use it as a sack. Drop it by the restaurant I'm building later."

She took it from him, and she was gone.

Peter felt his gut twist as he reached for his umbrella. Then he noticed the bright red stain of lipstick against his shirt.

CHAPTER SEVENTEEN

THE DEPOT LOOMED in front of Lindsay, and she paused on the sidewalk, her fingers tightening on her purse strap. From here, she could see the appeal the building held for the people who came to visit. Before her grandfather had bought the Depot, it'd been a large antique mall that rented out rooms to different vendors. By the time Pops had taken it over, most of the vendors were no longer operating there. He'd planned a multimillion-dollar renovation, built a large annex parking lot behind it, fixed the employee parking lot, plus put in an outdoor patio space on the side and the top of the huge flat rooftop of the Depot.

The final result was truly beautiful.

Even the Wagners had attended the ribbon-cutting and grand opening.

The redesign of the old antique mall had been impeccable, with the old floor-to-ceiling windows giving anyone outside the view of everything they seemed to be missing out on. At Christmas, especially, something was magical about looking in at the customers, like watching a snow globe.

Lindsay could practically smell the sweet confections and apple cinnamon scents she knew Naomi diffused in the store.

She sighed, nerves fluttering in her stomach, the cold seeping in through her jacket. She'd had a long day at work already, and the sun was setting. Going to another job after work had long been a practice of hers, but this time it was different.

Pops, who had been giving her a room to sleep in, no questions asked, had suggested that she pick up some hours there since she'd quit the bar. And while it wasn't entirely what she wanted, working for her sisters sounded infinitely preferable to working for her brothers right now.

She felt weirdly adrift, especially after the weekend she'd spent with Travis. The proximity had forced a weird sense of friendship—maybe even something more—and now several days had gone without her hearing a word from him.

"He could get hurt. You both could." Jen's voice rang through her head, and she bit down on the soft flesh of her lower lip.

Had she hurt Travis by turning him down?

"I don't care what my family thinks."

His words had haunted her for days.

Of course, she couldn't really know if it was unusual for him not to contact her. They'd only just shared phone numbers, and it wasn't like he'd been texting and calling her tons before this and then stopped suddenly. He'd moved on to that hookup app fast enough—a sure sign that he wasn't hung up on her or Hannah or anyone else.

Inevitably, though, she was going to have to contact him. She'd been looking into ideas for the Depot problem on her own in the meantime and coming up with a plan she thought might work, but that required talking to the other committee members.

Maybe I'll call Brian. Have him set the meeting up again.

She shoved thoughts of Travis and the committee out of her brain and headed toward the door of the Depot.

The inside of the Country Depot was dazzling, aesthetic, and spacious. It offered home and garden goods, foodstuffs, a kids' section, books, and candy. There was a stage in the back, where her grandfather's cooking and home show was often filmed—though sometimes they filmed at his kitchen at home—and a small café that featured sandwiches, desserts from Sweet Escapes, and gelato.

Yes, there was some overlap with the items for sale in the Depot and other businesses on Main, but many of the Depot customers were tourists who wouldn't have otherwise come to Brandywood.

Naomi was at the register as Lindsay came into the store, and she waved her over with a tired look on her face. Her eyes moved over Lindsay's jeans and sweater. "Did you come straight from work?"

Lindsay nodded, peeling her coat away. "Should I store this in the employee workroom?"

"No, just keep it for now. I'm going to send you out on a mission in a minute." Naomi came out from behind the register and looked around until she found Maddie, who was serving a guest gelato. "You sure you don't need a few minutes to take a break? You look exhausted."

"Right back at you." Lindsay smirked.

"Yeah, well, I have a baby and a toddler. What's your excuse?" Then Naomi winced. "Did that sound as cringe-worthy as it did in my head? I'm sorry. I *am* exhausted. I hit about four o'clock in the afternoon every day, and it's a struggle not to go back to my office and take a nap on the couch." Then her eyes teared up. "I don't think I've gotten a solid night of sleep for three years straight."

"Aw, Naomi." Lindsay pulled her in for a strong hug. Her oldest sister wasn't the type to cry easily, so she must be truly fried.

Naomi yawned and wiped her eyes with the back of her forefinger, then returned Lindsay's hug. "I'm glad you're here. And that you're feeling better. You had all of us so worried all weekend." Then she lowered her voice, her eyes darting to Maddie. "Between you and me, Maddie's doing everything in her power to discover who you ran off with, so watch it. She thinks you have a secret boyfriend."

Naomi's words chilled her. There wasn't any way for Maddie to find out she'd been with Travis, was there?

Lindsay smiled sweetly at Naomi. "Well, I don't. It's just my friend Chad from when I was in college."

"I don't remember a Chad from Londontown." Naomi frowned.

That's because he doesn't exist.

"You were too busy getting married and being ridiculously happy with Jeremy to pay attention to my college friends," Lindsay countered with a shrug.

Naomi shrugged. "That's probably true. And now the honeymoon is over. Did I tell you we got into an argument over a blanket the other morning?"

Lindsay scanned her sister's face, worry crawling up her spine. "Are you and Jeremy having problems?"

"No. But this is the shit married couples argue about. He uses a blanket every night while watching TV. And every damn morning, I find the blanket in a lump on the couch. Then I fold it and put in the basket, where he finds it in the evening. I had to explain to him—for the two thousandth time—that the blanket doesn't magically refold itself. And I'm sick of it."

They argued over blankets? Lindsay raised a brow. "Why not just leave the blanket for him to fold?"

"Because he won't fold it. Plus, it's *supposed* to be folded when not in use." Naomi wagged a finger at her. "If it has a place, it needs to be put back in its place."

Lindsay smirked and started back toward the register. She set her purse behind it. "Now you sound like Mom."

"I do, don't I?" Naomi sank her forearms onto the counter. "I'm turning into Mom. I'm thirty-two, and I'm already my mother. Soon, I'll be demanding everyone come to pizza night at my house."

"You already dress your girls in matching outfits for the holidays."

"That's because they're so freaking cute, Linds."

Lindsay smiled, feeling unusually relieved to be here. *Who knew I needed some time with my big sister?*

As Maddie finished up with her customer, she came sailing over. "Did you ask her yet?" Maddie's eyes were sparkling.

"She says her secret boyfriend is some college friend named Chad."

Maddie narrowed her gaze at Lindsay. "Chad who?"

I really should have thought this all through before showing up here. "Chad Jones."

Maddie rolled her eyes. "Chad Jones? That's like the most generic name on the planet, Linds."

"Yeah, well, he's not my secret boyfriend. He's just a friend."

"Jake is trying to find out. And you know what happens when Jake gets his mind on something." Maddie looked mischievous. "So you better be telling the truth."

Yikes. Maddie was teasing, of course, but her siblings were busybodies with each other. She wouldn't put it past Jake to do some quiet digging to find out what Lindsay might be hiding. Lindsay reached for an apron that Naomi handed to her. It was a cute little blue pinstripe number with her name embroidered on it. She needed to change the subject, and fast, and there was only one thing she could think of to make the inquiries die for now.

"I do have something I want to talk to you guys about," Lindsay said, setting the apron on the counter in front of her rather than putting it on. She checked to make sure no customers were in earshot and went on. "I was really hurt on Thursday when you guys let Logan go on a tirade against me, and no one stepped in. I know I'm the youngest sibling, but I don't want to be treated like a baby. And maybe stomping my feet and asking for respect isn't going to get me anywhere, but letting Logan act like a dick and not saying anything isn't fair either, even if we're all used to him being a bosshole."

Maddie cackled. "A *bosshole*? Oh my God, I love that term. He is a bosshole. Like, I could not think of a more perfect term for him than that."

Naomi nudged her and then gave Lindsay a sympathetic squeeze on her forearm. "I'm sorry we didn't say more in front of Logan, Linds. It's just . . . it's a hard topic, the stuff that's happening with the Depot and the Wagner petition. Maddie and I have poured our blood, sweat, and tears into this place—both of us have taken turns sobbing in the back about that stupid petition—and we get a little emotional about it."

Maddie's face sobered, and she nodded. "It's true. And I'm sorry, too. I tried to text you, but then you didn't text me back. If it makes you feel better, after you left, we all gave Logan hell for what he said to you. Especially Pops and Mom. I mean, we all did, but Mom was really upset because she felt like Logan drove you out of the house. And you know how she is about that."

"But I don't." Lindsay searched Maddie's and Naomi's faces. Funny how much all her siblings looked alike. They all had the same honey-blond hair and blue-gray eyes, except

Naomi had dyed her hair to a lighter blond. Lindsay sighed, looking away from them. "Mom isn't as close to me as she is to you two."

"That's because you haven't moved out yet. She worries more about us not coming back, so she puts the extra effort in to make sure we don't leave her permanently," Maddie said with a pointed look.

Naomi affirmed her words with a quick nod. "I swear she calls me more now than she did when I was in college even. She also probably feels like she can catch up with you whenever she sees you around the house. She doesn't have to go out of her way to make lunch dates and girls' nights with you because you're there. It'll help now that you're moving out. Speaking of which, how's the apartment thing going? Do you need Jeremy and me to help you move stuff?"

Somewhat soothed by their apologies and how sweet they were being, Lindsay sighed. *It's better that I try to be as honest with them as possible. They're my sisters, after all. And I'm going to be working with them.*

"There's not actually an apartment yet. I'm sorry I lied. I told Mom and Dad I was going to stay with Pops in the meantime until it's ready, but I need to find a place." Then she made a face. "Well, first I have to figure out if I can afford a place. The money from the bar was most of my income."

Naomi slung her arm around Lindsay's shoulder. "We might not be the bar, but we are more than happy to hear your ideas. You're one of us now. How's it feel coming in from the Dark Side?"

Lindsay laughed, giving her an amused look. "I like fantasy, not sci-fi."

Maddie took a few steps away to grab an iPad from under the counter. "God, Naomi, quit being so old. She likes to fantasize about her lovers having wings, not lightsabers."

Cringing, Lindsay stepped back and pulled the apron over her head. "I am not discussing this with either of you."

"If you need a place to crash, you can always come sleep on my couch," Maddie said, then grimaced at the line forming over by the gelato. "I better go help Jane. But listen, I'm serious. If I didn't already have a roommate, you would be my first choice, but you can always sleep at my place. And maybe I should get rid of my roommate. Jake's a lot smellier than you are." She hurried away before Lindsay could answer.

Naomi handed her the iPad Maddie had gotten out. "Same goes for me. Jeremy and I are more than happy to take you in. But we don't have an extra room, and you'll also have to deal with *Bluey* and *Paw Patrol* at like six every morning."

"I'm good with Pops. It's cozy there. Plus, he spoils me." Warmth spread through her at the kindness of her sisters' words, though. They'd gone out of their way to make her feel better, and she appreciated it.

"Yeah, well, don't get too comfortable. Before you know it, you won't want to leave there." Naomi winked and pointed at the other iPads set up as registers. "Here, I'll show you the system and get you logged in with your own credentials."

As Lindsay followed her, a sense of peace settled over her. Maybe change was good for her. She wasn't good at change— didn't like it—but she rarely stomped her feet to try to get what she wanted until it was too late. Then she'd snap like she had the other night on pizza night and be completely out of sorts until she figured out how to pick up the pieces.

But this time, change felt oddly hopeful. And if she could get this part of her life sorted out, maybe the other things would start to fall into place, too.

CHAPTER EIGHTEEN

JASON OPENED the door before Travis could even ring the doorbell, and Travis smiled at the sight of one of the newborns in his arms, one little bare leg sticking out from a swaddle.

Jen's voice carried from further in the house. "Jas! Get Nora away from the front door. It's freezing, and you need to change that diaper! I'm still dealing with Ava."

Jason shook his head, his eyes filled with laughter, and he met Travis's gaze as he passed through the front door. "She's commanding the troops from the living room. Good to see you."

Travis heard the door close behind him and tucked the box of diapers he'd brought them under one arm. He didn't know whether to turn back toward Jason and greet the newborn or to go on toward Jen, but considering he didn't have free hands at the moment, he chose the latter.

Jen was on the couch, a pile of pillows around her, and about eight half-empty glasses of water on the side table beside her. Her blond hair was thrown up in a messy bun, and she had one newborn propped up on a pillow on her lap, changing her diaper.

She looked up with a grin. "You just missed an epic diaper blowout."

"Can't say I'm sorry." He laughed and set the diapers down beside her. "Is this the hungry one?"

"Oh my God, yes. I think that's why she nearly exploded." Jen wrinkled her nose and turned the newborn to face him. "Say hello to Uncle Travis, Ava. He likes food, too."

"Oh, please let that be the way you introduce me to everyone," Travis said in a flat, sarcastic tone and then laughed. But he bent and scooped up the diaper-wearing beauty, taking her blanket with him. Both babies had a shock of dark hair like Jason's, and Ava's eyes were open, showing off her bright blues. "She's beautiful."

"You don't have to lie. Newborns all look the same." Jen smiled as Jason returned to the room and sat on the plush rug with the other baby.

"Where are Colby and Blake?" Travis asked, glancing around the room. He knew Jen and the babies had just come home from the hospital the night before, after a week there.

"My mom has them. She wanted to give us the weekend off to adjust to the new routine with the girls." Jen stretched her shoulders back. She looked great, and considering the circumstances when Travis had last seen her, the relief he felt was huge. Even though Jason and Jen had both called to thank him, he still felt like he hadn't done enough that night.

"Your mom is a gem. Both your parents are." Travis sat down beside Jen and smiled at the baby. He was never quite sure what to do with newborns, who mostly seemed to give long, unbroken, slightly cross-eyed stares or sleep. "I don't want to intrude for long. I know you have a lot going on, but I thought it might be good for me to stop by and talk shop about the bakery."

He'd told Jason and Jen he'd take the job after that

confrontation with his dad, expecting to start at the bakery immediately. Instead, Jason had told him they'd decided to keep the bakery closed for the week until Jen was out of the hospital. Now that she was home, Travis would need to start, but he also imagined the businesses that relied on Jen for baked goods would be desperate to restock.

"I made a list." Jen eyed Jason as he changed Nora's diaper. "Uh, Jas, can you grab that yellow legal pad from the nightstand when you're done?" She looked back at Travis. "I wrote down everything you'll need to know, but honestly, I'm not worried about you. You know your way around the back. Feel free to bake or go in there whenever you can. I know you're making a huge sacrifice for me."

Guilt made its way to his stomach, simmering there. Normally, he'd tell Jen what a tight spot he was in and how her offer couldn't have come at a better time, but he also couldn't stop from hoping things would turn around at the garage. That he *would* be eventually so busy at work that he'd need to step away from helping Jen. Admitting that he was failing was painful.

"I'm happy to help," he said in a low voice, still looking at Ava. Maybe that way Jen wouldn't notice he wasn't completely being honest. He *was* happy to help her. But this wouldn't have been his first choice of *how* if it hadn't been necessary.

And, ultimately, it had only given his father one more reason to be upset with him. He might need to go talk to Nana soon, too. Give her a heads-up before she found out from someone else.

Jason stood and handed a newly diapered and swaddled Nora back to Jen, then headed out of the room.

Immediately, Jen turned toward Travis. "All right, now that he's gone, you need to spill. Lindsay hasn't told me much even though I tried to get it out of her. What the heck is going on with you two? She spends an entire weekend at your house with you taking care of her? What? And you *still* didn't tell me about that, either."

Lindsay. He should have expected Lindsay to fill Jen in on what had happened, even when he didn't want to talk about it.

Travis winced and rocked Ava on his knees. "There's nothing to talk about. Nothing is going on. She was sick. I took care of her. She went home. End of story."

"Travis Wagner, that is *not* the end of the story, and you know it. And you know I know it. So stop it. What happened?"

He released a long sigh. "Nothing, Jen. Nothing happened. Well, unless you include the part where I put myself out there and told her I didn't care what our families thought about us being together, and she shot me down. Then left."

Saying it out loud didn't make the sting of it hurt any less.

"Ouch. I'm so sorry." Jen set her hand on Travis's arm. "I really am, Trav. But, for what it's worth, I think you should keep trying. I know Lindsay cares about you, even if she won't admit it. And I might be the worst best friend in the world to insert myself in this because I really don't want to take sides, but Lindsay isn't great at fighting for what she wants. She's not like you. Going against the grain in her family is a big deal. You're fine with being the rebel. She's not. But that doesn't mean she doesn't care."

Travis sank back against the couch. *So this is what a comfortable couch feels like. I could sleep here, no problem.* "I can't say I blame her, Jen. It's exhausting being the one at odds with everyone in my family. I don't know how to make peace with that. And I don't want her family to ostracize her because she cares about me. That would be horrible."

"So you'd prefer a life without her?"

Travis glanced at her out of the corner of his eye. "I didn't say that."

"But you're willing to settle for it, so long as that's what she wants. But what about what you want, Travis? And what if what you want is what she wants, too? One of you just might have to be the stronger one willing to make that move."

He grunted. "I did. Hell, I've been trying for years. You think it's easy having the woman you care about wake up next to you in the morning and have her roll over and tell you, 'that was fun, let's never do it again'?"

"Are you meddling again?" Jason said from the hallway, and he returned a few seconds later and gave Jen a sharp look. He bent beside her, then kissed her forehead. "What did I tell you about meddling?"

Jen pouted. "But I love him. And I love her. And I want them both to be happy."

Jason shook his head and took both babies. "Does he look happy that you're grilling him about this?"

Travis almost laughed, not surprised that Jason knew exactly what they were talking about and with his response.

"It's fine," Travis said, relieved by both Jason's presence and that he'd taken the baby. He relaxed into the seat. "I just don't have good news on that front. What I want is only a small piece of the puzzle. I haven't even heard from Lindsay for days, including that committee issue we're supposed to be working on."

"Speaking of that, how's it going? Did you make any headway on it?" Jason asked with interest.

"Don't think I'm going to let you get away with changing the subject." Jen wagged her finger at him.

"Nothing is happening on that front either. Brian couldn't have suggested two people less willing to want to talk about anything important, including the Depot."

"Really?" Jason appeared intrigued. "Because Lindsay

emailed me the other day with some questions. I assumed you all were working on it together."

The news that Lindsay had been making plans on the committee issue surprised Travis, but maybe it shouldn't have. "She's not going to let the Depot be moved without a fight."

"No, especially not since she's working there now," Jen said in a soft voice.

Lindsay is working at the Depot?

Wow, I didn't expect that either.

In some ways, it felt like it had been more than five days since she'd left his place.

Because each moment without her feels like a lifetime.

The thought, from deep within his wounded heart, curled at the top of his lungs, burning the oxygen there.

How can I miss something—someone—I never had?

He clenched his jaw, trying to harden his thoughts to her.

No matter what Jen says, Lindsay has made what she wants clear—and it's not me.

I have to look out for myself.

"It sounds like I've got my work cut out for me, then."

If Lindsay's on the move with the matter, I better figure out a counterattack—and soon.

CHAPTER NINETEEN

Lindsay knew her parents' Saturday morning routine almost down to the second—and it was hard to believe that up until a week ago, she'd been a part of it. Dad never slept later than five, and Mom had the coffee maker set to brew a pot at six fifteen so it would be ready when she got up at six thirty. By then, Dad would have read the entire *Wall Street Journal* and eaten an instant oatmeal. Mom would put on her long purple fleece robe to come down, even if she was fully dressed already, and would usually make a remark about how cold it was in the kitchen—unless she'd gone to bed upset about something. Then her silence was a cue about how mad she still was.

Day in. Day out.

Her parents were predictable.

So as Lindsay turned the key on the back door that led to the kitchen, she knew exactly where her parents would be sitting when she entered. Mom would be at the kitchen table, in front of her laptop, and Dad would be at the counter, getting his cup of coffee together.

Except they weren't.

The lights were on. The newspaper was open at the table.

Mom's coffee pot was brimming with freshly brewed coffee.

But her parents were nowhere to be seen.

Lindsay frowned and closed the door behind her gently, then set the backpack she'd brought down by the door. "Mom?" She peeked around the corner. *Not here.* Maybe she'd decided to sleep in.

Neither of them was in the living room, so Lindsay called out again, "Dad?"

A small thud, the sound of water shutting off, sounded. "Lindsay?" She heard Mom's voice, as though from far away, and frowned as she came farther into the living room, toward the stairs.

A minute later, her mom arrived at the top of the stairs, her head wrapped in a towel, her normal purple robe on. "Lindsay. What a surprise." Mom hurried down the stairs, wearing a smile on her face. She set her hands on Lindsay's shoulders and kissed her cheek. "You should have told me you were coming. I would have made you breakfast." She guided Lindsay back toward the kitchen.

Lindsay gave her a curious look. "Where's Dad?"

"Oh, he'll be along shortly." Mom's eyes were bright, and she squeezed Lindsay's arm. Then Mom headed toward the coffee pot. "I'm so glad you came by, honey. I've been worried about you, but I've been trying to give you some space since you didn't want to take my calls. Naomi tells me you're doing really well at the Depot, though."

"It's fun. I didn't realize how nice working with Maddie and Naomi might be. I think I worried that there might be sisterly drama, but they're actually really easygoing."

"That's *good*, sweetie. I'm so happy for you. You should

have told me long ago how miserable Logan was making you. I would have had a word with him, you know."

Something about the way Mom was talking—almost *too* chipper and enthusiastic—made Lindsay frown. *What in the heck is going on?*

"Uh, well, I kinda wanted to handle it on my own." Lindsay looked over her shoulder again, feeling strangely awkward. She hadn't been out of the house that long. Hell, she'd been on vacations longer than this. But somehow everything seemed . . . different.

Her eyes narrowed on the kitchen curtains. The ones she'd made for her mom in high school—cherry print with a scalloped edge—were gone, replaced by something more modern and white. "Hey, what happened to the curtains I made?"

"Oh . . ." Mom patted the towel, then took it off her head and combed her fingers through her wet hair. "I took them to the cleaners. Put these up in the meantime."

Lindsay blinked at her. *Why do I get the feeling she's fibbing?*

Before Lindsay could respond, her dad came into the kitchen. "Hey, kiddo," he said with a wink. "Didn't know you were coming by this morning."

Lindsay turned toward him to say hello and froze.

Dad's hair was wet.

Oh my God.

Oh . . . oh, noooo.

Her parents. In the shower. *Together.*

She tried not to think about it, her cheeks growing warm.

Oh no, no, no.

She'd practically walked in on her parents.

By now, Mom was staring at her with understanding dawning on her face. "I think she figured it out, Larry."

"Ew, Mom—" Lindsay took a few steps back, unable to look either of them in the eye.

Mom shook her head at her father with a frown. "Now why the hell wouldn't you blow-dry your hair?" She came closer to Lindsay. "Honey, you have to understand, it's been a long time since Dad and I had the whole house to ourselves—"

"Okay, you know, I really don't want to know that." Lindsay held out her hands. Was that what was happening now that she was gone? No wonder they hadn't been calling to get her to come home.

They're probably happy I left.

This whole time, she'd been thinking she'd devastated her mother—even her siblings had said she'd been upset—but that wasn't the case at all. Mom was busy changing the curtains and showering with Dad.

Wow.

Too overwhelmed to process it, Lindsay turned toward her bag. "I can go. It's not a big deal."

"No, no, honey, stay." Mom rushed to her side, her eyes wide. "We're not trying to make you uncomfortable. Intimacy is a very normal part of any healthy marriage. And honestly—"

"Mom." Lindsay met her eyes. "Really. I'm good."

Dad cleared his throat, likely sensing that Mom was only making things worse. "Was there something you needed, sweetheart?"

"Uh—" Lindsay went over to the bag and slipped her laptop out of it. "Yeah, I just wanted you to look over the proposal I had made for the committee. Let me know what legal challenges might exist and anything I might need to tweak in order to make it something that would work for the town. My laptop is still connected to the wireless printer here, so I'll just send the file there, and you can look it over and let me know what you think."

Dad raised a brow. "Doesn't that go against the rules of not discussing things with your family?"

Lindsay sighed. "Who knows. The committee has . . . sort of fallen apart." *Or Travis and I have too much history between us to work together effectively.* A bit more conciliatory, she added, "So I've been working solo. And right now, I need my dad's legal advice."

Dad's eyes softened. "Of course. I'm happy to look it over."

"Thanks, Dad." Lindsay opened the laptop on the counter and pulled up the file. Dad came up behind her and looked over her shoulder, pulling his reading glasses out of his pocket.

He was quiet as she showed him the file briefly. "There are four sections—the plan, the budget, the fundraising, and the implementation. I tried to lay everything out as clearly as I could, but I'm sure I made a few mistakes along the way."

Then she hit print and turned back to her dad, hoping the printer would hurry so she could leave. "You don't need to tell me if it's a good plan or a bad plan or anything like that. I just need to know the legal challenges that might come from it."

Dad's eyes were warm. "You did all that by yourself? That's really impressive, Linds."

"Thanks, Dad." *It just took lots of late nights and heartache.*

But the compliment soothed her more than she thought it would.

After glancing at the printer queue to check if the file had fully transferred, she closed the laptop and shoved it away. "Just let me know what you think. As soon as you do, I'll call Brian Pearson and schedule a meeting so I can talk to him about it."

"I'll look it over today," Dad said, tucking his glasses away.

Lindsay said a quick goodbye to her parents, then hurried out of the house. Her cheeks were still hot with embarrassment.

She checked her watch. *It's not even seven in the morning, and I already feel like I need a drink.*

There was only one person she could talk about this with who would be awake at this hour on a Saturday and up for a drink.

Taking out her phone, she dialed Jake as she climbed into the car.

"Hey, monkey, what's happening?"

Lindsay couldn't help but smile at her brother's greeting. "I need you. You at the bar?"

"Yup. It's like you're a mind reader. I was about to call you. I'm just coming up with the new seasonal cocktails since our best bartender up and left us before I could make her do it. Hey, maybe you can help me."

Damn. That had been one of her favorite jobs at the bar. She'd been so proud of herself when Pops had put her in charge of it a few years earlier. He'd even paid for her to take a few mixology classes. Resisting the urge to go backward, she started the engine and backed out of the driveway. "I don't work there anymore, remember? But I'll be happy to taste test what you've created. I was going to force you to make me a Bloody Mary anyway."

"Rough night?"

"Rough *morning*. I just walked in on Mom and Dad." She paused, not wanting to elaborate.

Dead silence hung on the other side of the phone for a few minutes. "Like . . . in their bedroom?"

"No, they were in the shower together."

"No fucking way. You walked into the bathroom while the shower was running?"

"No-I—you know what? Let's skip past that part and just go straight to the part where you know why I'm distressed, and you soothe my ick by feeding me vodka and talking about something else. I'll be there in five."

Lindsay hung up and leaned back in her seat, gripping the steering wheel. A part of her didn't want to go back to the bar, except that, in some ways, it still felt like home to her. And she wasn't likely to run into Logan there, fortunately, because he rarely got to the restaurant on Saturday before noon since he stayed until 3 a.m. on Fridays and Saturdays to close.

Which meant she and Jake would have the place to themselves.

She sighed, a heavy feeling pressing in on her chest.

Until moments ago, she'd never really considered the option that she couldn't go back home. Not that Mom and Dad wouldn't let her stay again if she asked—they would. She'd just been under the illusion that they wanted her around still. That they weren't ready to be empty nesters.

But maybe . . . I was holding on to the idea of what they wanted.

She felt strangely untethered from the world she'd felt so comfortable in just a few months earlier. If anyone had asked her in the fall if she'd be quitting her job at the bar and moving out in the spring, she would have laughed.

But things were changing more quickly than she could adjust herself to.

"Everything is changing," she whispered as she pulled into the employee parking lot behind Yardley's Pub.

She went in through the back—she still had her key at least—and found Jake standing in front of a row of bottles and shakers with a notepad beside him.

"You know, I thought you might be calling to tell me about trouble of the Chad Jones variety, not Dad banging Mom. Thanks for that mental image I'll never be able to scrub from my brain."

Lindsay laughed and shook her head as she went to the other side of the bar and sat. "You and me both, bud." *Chad Jones drama would have been oddly preferable.*

Maybe because it would mean that Travis was still in her life in some meaningful way.

The thought made her heart ache, and she gritted her teeth. She didn't need to think about that right now.

Jake glanced up as he poured something out of a shaker, then set it in front of her with a wink. "Enjoy."

"Bottoms up?" She eyed it suspiciously. As far as she knew, Jake didn't know a single thing about mixology, but maybe Logan was too cheap to pay for someone with experience for this job.

"Just try it. I thought it was good." Jake set both hands on the bar, watching her expectantly.

"It doesn't have enough ice, to start."

With a glare, Jake scooped more ice into the glass so that it was practically spilling out, then pushed it forward.

"And your presentation sucks." Lindsay laughed and picked up the glass. "Where's the love? A cocktail should say, 'You know what? You deserve this little treat.' How do you think the divorcée out celebrating her first day of freedom from a cheating rat would feel about this drink? It should be 'time to live it up!' not 'my drink had as lousy of a time as I did!'"

Jake gave her a steely-eyed look, then plopped a lime wedge on the rim of her glass.

She sniffed it. "Did you just shake an aromatic cocktail?"

"Do you want free alcohol or not, lady?" Jake crossed his arms.

She laughed and slung back a sip. It was . . . *drinkable.* But not great. She gave Jake a little smile, and he hung his head with a shake.

Yet even though she'd only been teasing Jake, she felt more herself than she had in weeks.

Because I'm good at this.

She took another sip. "Here, hand me the notepad. I'm going to give you a few things to try. I can't promise they'll work without tasting them, but they'll be a good start."

"Lindsay, I will literally move you and anything you need into your apartment whenever you want, no questions asked. Assemble any furniture you need assembled." Jake took a few steps back and dropped to his knees. "*If* you spend a couple of hours helping me figure this shit out."

Lindsay gave him a wry grin. "And not tell Logan I did the job he'd assigned you to?"

"Yeah, basically. But only because you make it look so easy that I had no idea how hard it is." Jake lifted his hands, pleading. "Please?"

She sighed and pushed his mediocre cocktail away. Then she stood and came to the other side of the bar with him. "I'm not saving your ass next time, you know. And the next time Logan decides he wants to throw down in front of the family, you'll have my back, Jacob Yardley. I think I might have been madder at you than anyone for not taking my side that awful pizza night. And at least Maddie and Naomi apologized."

Jake pulled her into a bear hug unexpectedly. "I'm the world's worst brother. And I'm sorry. *And . . .* I promise I will find a way to make it up to you. Somehow. If it's possible to make it up to you."

Lindsay grumbled and shoved him away with a chuckle, feeling oddly gratified as she started pulling liquor bottles from the shelves.

Not just because of Jake's apology.

But because this was where she belonged.

As much as she enjoyed working with Maddie and Naomi, it didn't feel like this.

She fit here.

Now I just need to find a way to convince everyone else of that fact. Show them all that I'm fully capable of handling any challenge.

And for the first time in a long time, she felt oddly hopeful.

CHAPTER TWENTY

Brian Pearson was in the back of the barn, brushing down one of the horses with Ben as Travis approached. The rules of the Pearson farm included one that no one worked on Sunday, but Ben and his grandfather had never considered time spent with the animals as work since things like feeding couldn't be skipped, and anyway, they were "family."

Ben especially had an attachment to the animals—one Travis suspected he'd inherited from his grandfather—and on more than one occasion, Travis had arrived in time to hear Ben cooing at the goats or cuddling with a piglet.

Course, if Travis told anyone what a softy his friend was, Ben also had the ability to pummel him.

"Well, look who it is." Brian grinned over the top of the horse. "And here I was thinking you'd never come visit me."

Travis crossed his arms and leaned against one of the posts in the stall. "Says the man who called me to a bingo night under false pretenses. Don't think I don't know what you were doing."

"What was I doing?" Brian's eyes twinkled. He gave Ben an exaggerated wink. "That Lindsay Yardley's a mighty fine-looking young lady, Benny. You should ask her to dinner. Hear she likes meatloaf."

Ben chuckled. "Maybe I will."

Fucker. If Travis didn't know any better, he'd guess that Brian had put him and Lindsay together at dinner, then abandoned them. "If you're going to try to play matchmaker, *sir*, you might have to do a bit better than the goddamn senior center."

"I don't know. If I was a younger man, I'd do just about anything for a chance to plow—"

"And you've gone ahead and crossed the line, old man," Ben said with a curt look. Thank God Ben knew how to leave well enough alone. He hadn't brought up the topic of Lindsay at all after that awkward encounter the week before.

"I have no idea what you're talking about. I'm just an old farmer, kicked off duty by my upstart son and forced to scrounge for pennies by part-time guard work."

"I'll be sure to tell Dad." Ben set the brush in his hand down, then gave the Palomino beside him a pat. He shook his head toward Travis. "I swear we make him take his medication."

Travis forced a smile. Maybe if it hadn't been for Travis going on a limb and telling Lindsay more than he should have, it wouldn't have bothered Travis.

But he had said too much.

And he'd felt even dumber than ever.

Which was why he needed to be proactive about this whole committee thing.

Lindsay Yardley isn't your friend.

"I was thinking it might be a good day to go for a drive, Mr. Pearson. I know you've been interested in taking the Stingray for a spin."

The gaps in Brian's smile showed as he straightened, wiping his hands on his overalls. "So you've finally come to bribe me, have you? Butter me up, get me on your side for the committee?"

Travis fought to keep his poker face.

"No business on Sunday." Travis shoved his hands in the pockets of his jacket. "But it's supposed to snow later this week, and who knows when we'll have a good clear day like this again. If you're not interested, it can just be Ben and me."

"Now, hold on, hold on." Brian scratched the scruff of his jaw. "Don't be hasty. You have to give an old man a chance to think."

"You sure you really want Grandad driving your car?" Ben gave him a skeptical look. "He might wreck it before you leave the driveway."

"Speak for yourself. I'm the best damn driver in this town." Brian puffed his chest.

"Explains why the state took your license." Ben rolled his eyes.

Brian smacked him in the arm. "I told you not to tell anyone that."

"Grandad. Everyone in town knows that. They've all seen you riding that damn bicycle, tooting that little horn like you're driving a tractor trailer."

Brian glared at him, then gave Travis a steely-eyed look. "I'm gonna go get my coat. See you over by that Corvette."

Travis and Ben shared a laugh as he started toward the house. "Coming?" Travis asked, nodding in the direction Brian had gone.

"You kidding me? Between you and me, we've done some scary shit, but nothing's more terrifying than getting in a car with that man. You're taking your own life into your hands." Ben followed Travis as they headed out of the barn. "So since Grandad brought it up . . . how *did* things go with Lindsay?"

"They didn't." Travis kept his hands in his pockets. No way in hell he was getting into what had happened last weekend.

He didn't need someone else to tell him what a damn fool he was.

"Decided to go back to WinkMe?"

"Nah, not really." He drew a sharp breath as they moved out into the brutal cold. "Just turns out I'm probably going to be too busy for dating during the next month or so. I've got that fucking committee, and I just started moonlighting at the bakery while Jen's on maternity leave."

Ben gave him a skeptical look. "What about the shop?"

He had gone long enough without telling his friend. With a sigh, he said, "Business is dead right now. I don't know what's going on, but I need the money Jen is offering. Plus, I want to help."

"I'm sorry to hear that. About the shop."

Yeah, it sucked. He'd been so sure he could make it work—and the shop had done so well for four years that it had never occurred to him it could fail. He would have been in great shape, too, if he hadn't bought Mr. Ryerson's equipment and expanded into body work last summer when the old man had closed up shop. But now he was in debt and didn't have a clue where his former clients were taking their business.

And if he couldn't figure it out? Then what? Was he supposed to go back to a kitchen?

His father would love the irony in that.

Of course, he still didn't know how to break the news about working for Jen to his grandmother. He hated to disappoint her and was already doing his best to avoid her to keep from asking about what Millie had said to him.

But Nana wouldn't be mad at him, would she? He helped when she was out of town—why not fill in for the woman who made half of her baked goods? Helping Jen was a help to Nana.

Maybe I'll pass the idea to her like that. So I'm supporting her . .

They walked in silence until they arrived beside the Stingray, which was still warm from Travis's drive over here.

"So you really taking Grandad out to butter him up?" Ben asked, a glint in his eyes.

"Hell yeah." Travis's brows furrowed as he grew more serious. "After Jen had to be rushed to the hospital the other week, I realized how bad the traffic situation has gotten. If there are three of us on this committee, and your grandfather is supposed to be the balance to the scale, then I think he needs a little tipping in one direction. That Depot has to go."

"Lindsay's going to be pissed when she finds out."

"Lindsay is apparently making committee plans all on her own. I may already be too late when it comes to making a move here."

Ben searched his face. "Be careful, Travis. You don't ever think clearly when it comes to that woman. Letting your feelings cloud your judgment—for good or bad—might come back and bite you in the ass later."

———

BEN HADN'T BEEN KIDDING about Brian's driving, and as the Corvette skidded to a stop in the parking lot near Nana's café, Travis peeled his fingers away from the underside of his seat.

No way he stopped more than two centimeters away from that light pole.

He drew a deep breath, then turned toward Brian, who was still grinning.

"Don't think I've ever driven a hundred and twenty on a back road before."

"Just wanted to test how fast this baby could go." Brian gave a regretful shake of his head. "They just don't make these cars like they used to. Damn crap from overseas."

"You know the latest model of the Stingray can go up to one ninety-four."

"Still a piece of crap compared to this beauty." Brian ran his hand over the dash appreciatively. "Pete's going to shit his diaper when he hears I got to drive his dream car at top speed."

Travis couldn't help but guffaw at the thought of Peter Yardley in an adult diaper. "You can't tell him I let you drive this thing. He'll think I was trying to win you over to the Wagner side."

Brian winked. "Don't worry, bud. Pete knows you'll have to do a hell of a lot better than this to get me to make a biased decision. Come on. Let's go grab some grub over at Bunny's. I feel like I lost thirty years on that drive."

Before Travis could answer, Brian swung the door open and stepped out.

Damn if there isn't a skip to his step.

Travis followed him, dreading the thought of going into his grandmother's café and seeing her. Every time he imagined it, he'd started thinking about Millie's comment last week—and his mom's nervous response.

With Jen just out of the hospital, there was little chance she could help him anytime soon. This meant that if Travis wanted to find out the truth, he might have to break his promise to his mom and ask Nana. He'd go to Millie himself, but he knew her well enough to know she wouldn't tell him anything she didn't want to tell him.

But Brian wasn't kidding about feeling younger, and Travis had to pick up his pace. He caught up with him as they reached the sidewalk in front of Bunny's—then slowed.

Peter and Lindsay were sitting on a bench in front of the café.

Ah, fuck.

He didn't want to look at her, snow cap over her head in a big puffy coat and a backpack beside her, like she should be going skiing instead of sitting on Main. Had it been a full week since they'd seen each other? He'd done a good job of avoiding her, trying to stay away while he licked his wounds.

She shouldn't affect me.

But the thought of her in that robe made him suck in a shallow breath.

She can't see me here, especially with Brian.

To his dismay, though, Peter looked right at them, then stood.

Brian went up to Peter, a grin wide on his face. "You should have seen that puppy purr, Pete." He clapped Peter on the back. "Glad you could meet us for dinner."

Travis stopped in his tracks, his eyes narrowing at the back of Brian's head.

That son of a bitch.

Peter looked past Brian toward Travis. "You sure you don't want to sell me that car, Travis? I'll pay whatever you ask."

Travis felt heat rising on his neck, flushing his face. Lindsay stood beside her grandfather but had done him the favor of not meeting his gaze. "Yeah, pretty sure. But you'll be the first to know if I change my mind."

"Well, shall we?" Brian held the door open for Bunny's Café. He gave Travis a sly wink. "You don't mind that I invited Pete, do you?"

Peter went inside and Brian followed, leaving Lindsay and Travis still outside.

This isn't what I was hoping for.

"Listen." Travis rubbed his neck. "I—"

"No, I get it. Smart move." Lindsay's eyes flashed as she finally met his gaze. "We need to get this committee thing over with, anyway. I would have preferred to have a little more time to get myself together, but this works." She yanked the door for the café open, not bothering to hold it for Travis, and it banged shut in front of him.

He winced.

Did she think he'd been trying to meet with Brian in secret? Hadn't he been?

I should just abandon ship and leave now.

But he'd also created this mess.

Travis pushed his pride down, trying to pull out whatever semblance of calm, and went inside.

He hadn't wanted to see his grandmother, but the sight of her brought a strange sense of relief. She'd already come out from behind the counter and was at the table where Brian was sitting down with Peter and Lindsay. The café was seat yourself, and Brian appeared to have taken a table front and center by the large picture window.

In all the years Travis had worked or been coming to the café, he'd never seen Peter Yardley inside his grandmother's restaurant. Nana had her hands on her hips. "I have a bone to pick with you, Peter," Nana was saying as Travis stopped at the table.

Nana didn't turn toward Travis, but she grabbed his arm and tugged him closer to her, protectively. "There's a rumor going around that your grandson kicked Travis out of your bar on Valentine's Day. You and I had a deal about that sort of thing. Lindsay—and any other member of your family—has always been more than welcome here. Since when is that the way my boy gets treated?"

Oh God. While he appreciated his grandmother's loyalty, the noise in the café had dropped, and the guests were paying attention. He didn't need Nana treating him like a five-year-old, either. Especially not in front of Lindsay.

Peter frowned at Nana. "I had nothing to do with that. But I've already talked to Logan. He said Travis was drunk and harassing my granddaughter—"

"What?" Lindsay's eyes widened.

"I didn't say I believed him." Peter patted her hand. "I'm just saying that maybe there's more to the whole thing. Two sides of every story."

"Pops, Hannah dumped Travis that night, and—"

And that's enough of that.

"Logan's right. I was drinking too much. He was right to send me on home," Travis said. He didn't need Lindsay or his grandmother fighting his battles. Especially not while there were witnesses. "Now, why don't we all sit down?"

To his surprise, Nana pulled up a chair.

Peter looked over at her and raised a brow. Nana smiled sweetly. "I'm assuming this is about the Country Depot committee. I'm not about to be left out of the discussion."

"Who says we're doing that? Two old friends can't have dinner with their grandchildren?" Peter feigned innocence. A spark of his trademark humor showed in his eyes, and Travis's gaze darted to Lindsay, whose face was like a mask.

"Then Brian can go get Ben. This one is mine," Nana said, nodding toward Travis. "No matter how much he might have scampered around in Brian's barn as a kid."

Brian gave her a wide grin. "Has he taken you for a spin in that fine car of his? He's talented, this one. You should be proud."

"I am proud." Nana raised her chin and looked Travis in the eye. "I always have been." She wrinkled her nose at Peter. "And he doesn't have to go around bullying others to prove what a strong man he is."

Dammit.

"You know," Lindsay said before Travis could change the subject again. "It might be a good idea for us to talk to you all about the Depot. Get a gauge on your grievances, Bunny, and then find out from my grandfather if he has any suggestions to alleviate the problem."

"I agree completely. That's why I suggested we meet here when Lindsay called me earlier this afternoon," Brian said.

Huh?

Travis looked from Brian to Lindsay.

Lindsay's eyes were practically shining with the admission. *Two can play at this game,* she seemed to say.

If she was hoping he wouldn't say anything about it, she was wrong. "I didn't have any intention of purposely trying to talk about the Depot with Mr. Pearson while you weren't present," Travis said, narrowing his eyes.

"Bullshit." Lindsay leaned forward on her forearms. "You just have a raging need to spend time with octogenarians recently? Particularly ones who could help sway the decision we're supposed to make together?"

"There's only so much *togetherness* with you I can handle." Travis finally sat directly across from Lindsay. If Lindsay had been attempting to talk to Brian, too, then what did he have to feel bad about?

Lindsay held his gaze and gave him a warning look. "Next time, I'll try not to intrude."

"Maybe it's not the intrusion that's the problem. Maybe it's the timing of the exit."

Are we really having this discussion in front of our grandparents?

They both seemed to come to the same conclusion at the same time and tore their gazes away. Nana and Peter stared at them with slightly alarmed expressions.

Brian, on the other hand, appeared to be gloating.

"See what I mean?" Brian said with a twitch of a grin. "We all need to sit and discuss this together. It's the perfect group to solve Brandywood's biggest problem right now. I realized it the morning of the town council."

The morning of the council. When he'd seen Travis dropping Lindsay off in the woods.

Lindsay had been right to freak out about it.

Brian apparently seemed to understand exactly what that might be about. And he'd been on a mission ever since to use Lindsay and Travis's attraction to each other to bring about a peaceful solution for the Depot issue.

But he hadn't just gotten Lindsay and Travis here. This time, he'd dragged in their grandparents.

What does Brian know about our grandparents, though?

Millie knew something. But that made sense—she was good friends with Nana.

Just like Brian was with Peter.

Travis leaned toward Brian. "Did you send Millie Price to pay us a visit after bingo the other night?"

Brian had a self-satisfied look in his eyes. "Bingo. It's a funny word, isn't it?"

If Lindsay was keeping up like Travis was, she didn't show it. Then again, Travis was going out of his way to look her in the eye.

By now, Nana and Peter were exchanging looks. "Brian, what's going on? There seem to be several different conversations happening here at once," Nana chimed in.

Peter glanced around the table at all of them. "Look here. When I built that Depot, I had a vision of what Brandywood could be. Not that it hasn't always been a place we know and love, but it's never quite been on the map, has it? And now— look at things. The café has lines out the door at lunch, Jen

Cavanaugh can barely keep up with bakery orders, and my restaurant is up in profits at levels we've never seen before. Even Fred Strickland admits they have to get up two hours earlier than before to make waffle cones every morning just to keep up with supply. Business is good."

"But business isn't everything, Peter. You know that. A wedding party from out of town traipsed into Main just last week. Held up traffic and climbed boulder rock despite the signs. Damaged Mrs. Porter's gate around the post office. The groomsmen even left some pornography in Sylvia Jenkins Little Free Library," Nana said.

"Damn, why didn't anyone tell me?" Brian asked with a cackle.

"Actually, it was just a romance novel. And it was probably one of the bridesmaids, though you never know," Annie, who worked at the bookstore next door, piped in from the table beside them. "Mrs. Jenkins is the one who called it a porno. There are some detailed sex scenes, but it's a really good book— a fantasy where the protagonist . . ." Annie trailed off and ducked her head down, looking back at her open book as though she'd just realized she'd revealed her eavesdropping.

Annie's face was crimson.

"There's pornography in women's books now?" Brian asked with a gleam in his eyes. "And all this time, I've been saying I couldn't find anything to read."

"Sex is a very important part of character development," Nana said, sitting straighter. She raised her chin. "I love a good steamy novel. Write down the name of that book for me later, dear."

Travis almost choked on his own spit, then coughed.

Good for Nana, but that's also something I really didn't need to know.

Lindsay cleared her throat as though to redirect the conversation. "That's the thing, though. No one in my family wants to see Brandywood lose an ounce of its charm. It's a wonderful town, and we want to share it with others, but we also want to keep it for our own. And that includes keeping the Depot right where it is. My grandfather's dreams shouldn't be given any less consideration than others."

Travis didn't know whether to hug her for changing the subject or to give her an appreciative look for her business-like demeanor.

I like this side of her.

But . . . there aren't many sides of her I don't like.

Except the part of her that didn't want to be with him. And he needed to remember that before he let himself get carried away.

Lindsay directed her attention to Travis. "And we don't want it to be unsafe, either. Traffic is a problem. A big one. But I don't think the solution we need to come up with has to be an all-or-nothing situation."

She reached to her side and pulled a few spiral-bound packets out of her backpack, then passed them around the table. "I spent the last week trying to think of a few tenable solutions to handle the traffic. To begin with, I think we could have a few more parking lots built, but it might require getting the land for it, which could be complicated. But another solution I think might work is seeing if we could build a new tourism center away from Main. That way, things like tour buses can go directly there and then catch shuttles into Main Street to alleviate traffic."

Travis stared at her, and his jaw nearly dropped.

Wow.

She came prepared.

With spiral-bound presentation books.

And Grace was right. Lindsay could be a force to be reckoned with if she wanted to be. Her family was foolish for not taking her more seriously when it came to business. She was impressive.

Then again, Peter Yardley didn't appear not to be listening. He had a proud look on his face and squeezed her forearm.

"That's all lovely to dream about, Lindsay," Nana said. "But that could take years to build. The infrastructure isn't there. Not to mention the costs. Who's supposed to pay for this? The town?"

"I would be willing to put in the costs for up to fifty percent of it, considering the fact that the blame for the congestion is being put on my shoulders," Peter said congenially.

Holy crap. How much was Peter Yardley worth these days? He must not have any idea how much something like that would cost.

"Pops, that's way too much," Lindsay said, her eyes widening. "This isn't your fault. My suggestion would be a tourism center owned and operated by the town. I don't think anyone should have to pony up that much money for it. We can fundraise. Make it happen *as* a town."

"I think we need some food before we get into the semantics of all of this," Brian muttered, tapping his fingers on the tabletop. "I think my blood sugar is dropping. If only we could get someone who works here to help us out."

Nana laughed, fizzling some of the tension between them. "Brian Pearson, not everyone in town expects to be fed every hour on the hour. But, sure, I can have some food brought over. What're you in the mood for?"

More people had come into the café while they'd spoken, and Travis eyed them now. The tables were all full, so the newcomers started crowding the spaces between them.

Travis could just hear the gossip now. *Bunny Wagner and Peter Yardley are sitting together at a table in Bunny's Café.*

Probably for the first time ever.

That had to be what was happening because Travis's phone buzzed while a server came by and took their order.

Grace: *What's going on at Nana's?*

Travis: *I'm . . . not sure I really know.*

He'd gone into this afternoon feeling the need to do *something* about the Depot situation. Grab the bull by the horns. Stake his claim. Be persuasive and influential.

. . . or at least proactive.

But it appeared a much more worthy advocate had beat him at his own game.

Grace: *Annie said you're at the table right next to her with Nana.*

Travis gritted his teeth.

Travis: *I'm here, but it's complicated.*

"What do you think, Travis?" Lindsay said, pulling him back into the conversation.

He set his phone face down on the tabletop and looked up at her, his heart thudding. *For you, Linds, anything.* But he couldn't say that, could he? What Nana wanted mattered, and she was right here next to him, even trying to defend him to Peter Yardley over the whole incident with Logan.

He cleared his throat and turned his focus to being as business-like as he could. He might be a failing businessman, but at least for a while, he'd pretend he could be good at it.

"The way I see it, there's not a whole lot of sense in discussing the semantics unless we can even think of a feasible location for a tourist center. But I do have a slightly more worrisome question—what happens when Peter's show goes off the air or his brand fades? Brandywood can't be a destination for one person's business. It has to be a destination in and of itself."

From the look on Lindsay's face, it was clear that he'd thought of something she hadn't really considered.

"I don't think it's up to any of us to decide the plans of today based on hypotheticals that may be decades away," Lindsay said, her face flushing.

"No, I think it's a valid point," Nana said with a nod. "Let's face it. Peter's not getting any younger. Sure, people come because he's helped highlight Brandywood—but also to see him. And it's a fickle world out there. What's popular today might not be so popular tomorrow."

Lindsay rubbed her temple, thrown off guard. "As much as I understand that, I doubt the council wants us to come up with a solution for that. We aren't being asked to figure out a way to make Brandywood a tourist town."

"I think this one may have spent her childhood learning from her father. She talks like a lawyer," Brian said with a shake of his head.

Lindsay lifted the file she'd prepared. "Look, at the end of the day, we've been asked to come up with a plan that preserves what we love about Brandywood and Main Street but is also fair to the business that has brought success to so many people in this town. We're not in charge of enacting it. We just have to give the council an idea. And I think the sooner we do it, the better."

And then we can both go back to our merry lives, keeping our distance.

"Actually, dear, Peter and I haven't been asked to come up with anything," Nana said in a polite tone that made it clear she didn't appreciate the no-nonsense way she was dealing with the conversation. Then Nana smiled as the server approached with a tray of soups. "Here's Hélène with some sustenance, Brian."

"Holy smokes, is that steam coming from the server or the soup?" Brian muttered at Travis.

As she put the soups down, Travis glanced at the server to see what he was talking about. He didn't recognize her. She was gorgeous—maybe just a few years younger than him, with hair so blond that it was almost white. She turned to go.

"Oh, Hélène, wait," Nana said, setting a hand on Travis's arm. "This is my grandson Travis, the one I've been wanting you to meet."

"Oh hello, Travis. I'm very pleased to meet you," Hélène said with a soft accent and a dimpled smile.

"Hélène is the granddaughter of my friend from France whose family I stayed with when I was studying in Paris so many years ago. She's come to work with me for a few months."

Travis raised a brow. How had he not heard about this?

Hélène continued to smile at him. "Your grandmother is wonderful. I just love her."

"Where are you staying in town?" Travis asked, glancing at the soup she had set in front of him. *Cream of crab.* He hadn't ordered it, but he wasn't surprised that his grandmother had gotten one for him.

"With your grandmother, of course." Hélène gave a broader smile.

"You know, Travis, you should come by more often. And maybe take Hélène out for a spin. I'm sure she'd love to spend some time with someone her own age, instead of an old fuddy-duddy like me."

Was his grandmother trying to set him up on a date in the middle of all this?

The gleam in her eye seemed to indicate she was.

Travis felt Lindsay watching him and desperately wished he could take a time-out from this whole disastrous encounter.

He had absolutely no desire to go on a date with Hélène, no matter how pretty she was, and especially not have his grandmother set him up in front of Lindsay. He also didn't have a reasonable excuse to say no to Nana and didn't want to make

Hélène feel badly when Nana wasn't outright asking him to date her.

His brain felt oxygen-starved, and he blinked, trying to think of a response that would be inoffensive to everyone involved.

"That would be great. Maybe this week sometime."

"This week, I work every night but Wednesday," Hélène said, glancing at Nana. "We are working hard on learning the laminated doughs. But yes, I would love to."

"Wednesday it is, then." Nana patted his hand and smiled. "Travis knows all the fun spots where the young people spend time in town."

Travis didn't dare look at Lindsay. If he could bury his head in the bowl of soup, he would.

As Hélène left back toward the kitchen, Brian watched her appreciatively. "Got another Hélène back there for me, Bunny?" He winked at Peter, then looked at Travis. "If it doesn't work out with that one, send her my way, will you?"

"Brian Pearson, I may have to put up a sign saying '*No Leering Dirty Old Men*' on the outside of my café if you don't knock it off."

A flash of annoyance crossed Lindsay's face. "All right, Brian, don't you think that's enough being inappropriate?"

Travis sat back in his seat, intrigued by her reaction. Something had clearly gotten under Lindsay's skin. Had it been Hélène?

He wasn't sure how he felt about that.

But if it hadn't bothered Lindsay, that would have been much worse, wouldn't it have been? If she didn't like the thought of him going out on a date, then maybe what he'd felt last weekend hadn't been so one-sided.

Travis reached for the soda he also hadn't ordered and took a sip. "Why don't you walk us through your idea, Lindsay?"

Lindsay's gaze shifted to Peter, and he gave her an encouraging smile.

Had she run this plan by her grandfather beforehand?

A part of Travis felt a twinge of regret. This was why Lindsay had trouble with her family if he didn't know any better. Logan and Jake could be like sharks—just the scent of blood, and they would strike.

And Maddie and Naomi were known for their ability to handle themselves. In high school, a rumor floated around that one of the freshmen had tried to prank Maddie, and she'd given him so much hell for it that he'd climbed into a locker and hidden there until the end of the day.

If Lindsay showed any vulnerability to them, they'd take advantage of it.

Not that it makes a difference what I think. She doesn't want my help.

"So I was studying a map of Brandywood, and there are two places I think could easily work for the tourist center proposal. The first is Gulliver's Pass, which is great because the land has already been cleared, but I think utility access might be tricky based on where the lines run."

The more she talked about it, the more blown away he was with how much time she'd put into this.

"Getting the Gullivers to sell any part of their land is also tricky," Travis said with a frown.

"And then there's the old Durand farm . . ." Lindsay trailed off, biting her lip.

Nana's lips drew to a taut line. Her land. Where the family hunting cabin was. The farm was long gone, torn down years ago when it had become uninhabitable. But the fact that it had once been inhabited meant that many of the utilities had already been run out to the property.

Surprisingly, Peter was the one to speak up. "I think we've

probably had enough business talk for one meal." Peter lifted his spoon. "And seeing Brian eat so enthusiastically has me jealous."

Lindsay's face fell, and Travis felt his jaw clench.

But it wasn't his place to comfort her or encourage her to push harder.

Especially not when what she was asking would be something bound to only further enrage his father.

With the talk of business at an end, Nana got up. "Well, it's been fun, boys. But I should probably get to work."

Travis pushed back his chair and stood. "Hey, Nana, can I talk to you for a second? I'll be right back," he told the table.

He followed Nana back behind the glass counter. There were too many people here for him to even think of mentioning what Millie had said—anyone might overhear him. So he took Nana by the elbow and drew her closer to the coffee grinder. "I haven't had a lot of time to come by lately, but I wanted to let you know that I'll be working for Jen for a while. You know, while she's on maternity leave."

Nana met his eyes and gave a small nod. "I heard that, actually."

Is she upset?

He couldn't tell from her reaction.

Travis felt his ears growing hot. "I-I didn't want you to be mad—"

"Oh, Travis, I'm not mad." Nana squeezed his arm. "You remember when you were a little boy and your parents used to drop you and Gracie over by my house to spend the night? We'd make cookies and brownies and . . . gosh, I was just always so happy to see that *someone* loved what I loved. But I always used to ask you, 'you sure you want to make this? I don't want you to do it for my sake.'"

"I remember." He held her gaze, thinking back on those nights.

They'd been his favorite moments.

So what if he didn't always tell Nana that baking with her was sometimes just because it made him happy to see her happy?

Especially after Grandpa had died.

Doing things to make her happy always made sense.

"If baking for Jen is what you need to do, then bake for Jen. But I don't want you getting distracted from what Travis needs to do for Travis, either." Nana gave him a firm look, then raised a brow. "I hope Jen won't take advantage of you—I trust her not to—but you're also running a full-time business. Don't exhaust yourself, darling."

Oh.

That was her worry.

Because . . . *she knows me. She knows I sometimes can't say no to certain people, even if I should.*

She wasn't upset because he'd said he'd bake for Jen. She was just worried about him and his business.

He leaned down and pulled her into a tight hug. "Thanks, Nana."

CHAPTER TWENTY-ONE

April 1999

THE CHURCH HAD EMPTIED after the Easter service, and Bernadette hung back, wanting a moment before she headed back home to the chaos of hosting brunch. John had already gone ahead with Todd and Molly and the kids to the green behind the church for the Easter egg hunt, but she had a ham that needed to come out of the oven.

She sighed, feeling oddly peaceful. Easter had always been her favorite holiday, especially because she loved the food for it better than any other holiday—she'd take a rack of lamb and potatoes au gratin, deviled eggs, and carrot cake with cream cheese icing over almost all other holiday foods.

Heading out of the church, she stepped into the bright sun and went down the steps. As she reached the walkway, she paused to admire the daffodils—her favorite flower. She'd just bent to sniff them when a tiny hand gripped her skirt from behind to balance.

Bernadette looked over her shoulder at the tiny cherub in a pink frilly dress with nearly white-blond hair.

Larry Yardley's youngest daughter.

A few steps behind her was Peter.

Bernadette straightened quickly. Encountering him always felt strange. He wasn't a stranger—not really—though in some ways, he also *was. Goodness, has it already been thirty years since we were sweethearts?*

"Happy Easter, Peter," she said, offering a smile. "Is this your littlest granddaughter?"

"Yes, this is Lindsay," he said and gave the little girl an adoring gaze. She gave him a bright smile that featured four little teeth.

"She's beautiful." Bernadette clutched her purse in front of her. Funny how life had worked out. They'd each had only one son. Both of their sons had married quite young and were now working through professional schools. But in contrast to Todd, Larry Yardley seemed determined to have a large family. "You have a beautiful family. So many grandchildren."

Peter chuckled. "They're a handful. Bunch of rascals. But I'm very lucky."

His words brought back memories from years before. What was it he always said when they were younger?

"I'm a lucky sort of guy."

He was lucky.

Meanwhile, her luck had never been quite on par.

Decades of couple's therapy. Arguments. Lonely nights when she'd wondered *why God, why?* Wishing she could get out. But once she'd finally decided enough was enough, she'd learned she was trapped by the debts John had heaped upon them. He'd risked everything—even everything she'd built. She couldn't afford to leave.

So she stayed. It was easier once Todd was happily married and out of the house. She and John could sleep in separate bedrooms without him noticing. She felt like such a hypocrite. People in town called her a strong woman. A role model for young girls because she ran a successful business.

If they only knew how weak she felt.

"And how are you? Doing okay, Bernadette?"

She lifted her gaze and met Peter's. She could lie to him, but she was certain he'd know. But only her closest friends knew just how bad things were. "I'm fine, Peter, thank you."

The baby girl toddled forward, then gripped one of the daffodils. "Oh no, little bee, those are not for picking," Peter said with a light laugh, then bent to gather her in his arms. But the toddler had a firm grip on the daffodil, and it broke free from the plant with a long stem.

Peter straightened, holding the little girl at eye level with Bernadette. Lindsay held the flower out toward Bernadette, and Peter smiled. "I think she wants you to have it."

Little bee. Does he realize that he gave his little grand-daughter a very similar nickname to the one he used to have for me? Suddenly flustered, a sheen of tears came over her eyes. "Why thank you," she said, taking the outstretched daffodil.

"You know," Peter said, holding her gaze, "if you ever need anything or to talk to anyone, you know where to find me." He shifted awkwardly. "I hear rumors sometimes. That's the cross of running a pub."

"Oh, Peter." Bernadette sighed. She didn't doubt that there were whispers. "If it were that easy, I would. But one step through your pub door, and the whole town would know about it." All it would do was make more problems in her marriage.

"To hell with all that. Everyone needs someone they can

count on when things get rough. I know how things were with your parents, may they rest in peace. And with losing Robbie. All I'm saying is you can still count on me. Wagner or not."

"There you are," Marion said as she stepped out from around the corner. She paused her eyes, shifting between them. "Oh hello, Bernadette." She came over toward Peter and plucked Lindsay away. "Larry's been looking all over for this one. She's going to miss the egg hunt. Hurry up if you want to see it!"

"Happy Easter," Bernadette called after her as she walked away. She didn't quite know why, but she'd always felt that Marion didn't like her. Maybe it was the mutual dislike between their husbands. More than likely, it was the fact that they'd been schoolmates, and Marion had *always* been infatuated with Peter while he'd only had eyes for Bernadette.

But nearly thirty years of marriage to the man should have soothed Marion's jealousy, shouldn't it have?

She wished she could say something more to Peter, but a chastised look came over his face. "Remember what I said. And Happy Easter."

As he walked away, regret filled her heart. She pressed her lips together, trying not to remember a time when she *had* felt like she could go to Peter and pour out her heart to him. He'd been Robbie's best friend, so her parents had never worried about the time she'd spent with him. They might have minded more if they knew the kisses they'd snuck when no one was looking, but she wished she could be as bold as she'd been back then. Instead, life had flattened her, and she felt feeble.

She closed her eyes and brought the daffodil to her nose, taking a deep sniff. The sweet scent made her smile, and she lifted her hand to her heart, instantly more peaceful.

A footstep made her blink her eyes open, and she startled as Marion Yardley paused steps away from her. Her brow knitted as she searched Bernadette's face, then she scooted past her and bent to the sidewalk. "Baby dropped her shoe. Silly thing is always falling off."

"Oh—" Bernadette managed, but Marion had already turned and was hurrying away.

She recognized that look on Marion's face.

I know it because I've felt it deeply. The worry of what-if?

"Marion, wait," Bernadette said, hurrying behind her. She felt too old for this nonsense, but she owed Peter that much.

Marion stopped and turned stiffly. "I have to hurry back to the egg hunt."

"You married a good man, Marion. You have nothing to worry about," Bernadette said in a low voice, hoping it sounded as friendly as she meant it. Surely, Marion didn't think anything was going on between Peter and herself?

Marion's lips pursed. "It's not *him* I worry about," she said, her cheeks reddening. Then she continued forward.

Bernadette's heart fell. She should leave well enough alone. Who knew what difficulties couples hid between them? She'd obviously struck a nerve. *Damn.*

CHAPTER TWENTY-TWO

Lindsay handed the backpack to Emerson Bailey's mother as she opened the child safety gate to let her out of the classroom. "Emerson did great," Lindsay told her mom as the toddler grinned like she hadn't spent art time throwing a tantrum about not being able to do fingerpaints.

Not that she wouldn't have told Emerson's mother all about the tantrum if there was time. But most of the time, she had about ten seconds to greet each parent and say, "Here's your kid." Some parents wanted to get a more detailed rundown of the day, but it would also back up the line for the other parents waiting to pick up their children.

But as Emerson and her mother walked away, happily hand in hand, Lindsay couldn't help but wonder if the generic but generally dishonest responses to inquiries about general well-being started there.

After all, when she'd walked into school this morning and her boss and friend, Tierney Smith, had asked how she was this morning, Lindsay had replied, "I'm good. Feeling so much better after a few days off."

And physically, she was better. Whatever flu had smacked her down was long gone, work at the Depot was going great, and Pops had also spoiled her at his house.

Yet . . . she'd never felt like she couldn't go home before. Like she wasn't missed there. That made her feel a little *unsteady*.

She couldn't talk to Jen as often—who was often Lindsay's anchor—since she was so busy with the twins. They'd been texting, but she needed to hear her voice and get her point of view.

She had other friends, of course, but going to them with the issues on her mind was impossible. Only with Jen could Lindsay pour out her heart about her family and Travis and everything else.

Maybe I'll call her on the way to the Depot today.

After the last child had left, Lindsay started wiping the desks and chairs with bleach wipes, then flipped the chairs upside-down onto the tables. She picked up scraps of paper from the floor—somehow, every craft seemed to result in paper shards everywhere—then bent to pick up a few crushed Goldfish and Cheerios that had escaped during snack time.

She sank onto the circle time rug, her gaze wandering over the red heart crafts they'd done a week earlier. The head-shaped cutouts that they'd done for Presidents' Day were drying on the art racks, and she smiled sadly to herself.

All of this used to bring me so much satisfaction.

But at some point, singing the *Wheels on the Bus* and reading about llamas and pajamas and doing freeze-time dances with little friends had lost its luster. And not just because of her own career needs.

She was ready for *the next thing*.

Whether that was taking on a more active role in her family business.

Or starting to build a life separate from her parents.

Or dating the man she would eventually marry and have her family with.

But knowing she was ready for it wasn't the problem.

It was allowing herself to have what she wanted. She'd had a glimpse of that when she was working on making cocktails with Jake the other morning.

And she'd had a glimpse of it when she'd spent the weekend with Travis.

Because part of what I want . . . who I want . . . is Travis Wagner.

She hadn't been able to stop thinking about him the last couple of days since she'd seen him at Bunny's Café. Maybe it was that he always seemed so ready to move on and date other people whenever she told him no, or maybe it was the fact that they'd felt almost like friends for once, but each time she thought of him, her heart squeezed in her chest unhappily with regret and angst.

He'd barely been able to look at her during that awkward café dinner with their grandparents and Brian.

Barely talked to her.

And that was how it was supposed to be, wasn't it?

They'd mastered the art of avoidance.

Lindsay sighed, then stood. She'd been telling herself for years she didn't care about Travis. But why was it so much harder now to convince herself of that now?

She grabbed her coat and bag and headed out of the preschool for the day. As she hopped in the car, she dialed Jen, praying she'd pick up.

Jen answered after the second ring. "Oh my gosh, I needed to hear your voice so bad," Lindsay blurted out.

"Are you okay? Do you need to come over?" Jen sounded concerned.

"No, no." Lindsay caught a glimpse of herself in the rearview mirror, looking as frazzled as she felt. "I just . . ." What was she supposed to say? *I need my best friend, but my best friend has a bunch of babies that need her more, and I know I can't be selfish.* "You know what, it's nothing. I just miss you. How are the girls? And you? When can I bring you another meal?"

"Everyone here is great. And I'm feeling pretty good. Walking is getting easier by the day. And you know you can come anytime, with or without food. But don't think for a second I'm going to let you get away with telling me nothing is wrong. What's going on?"

Lindsay lifted her eyes and stared at herself in the rearview mirror again. She could admit the truth to Jen, couldn't she?

But then it made it real.

"You remember a week or so ago when you said not to mess with Travis because you thought he cared about me?"

"Yes . . ."

"Has he *told* you he has feelings for me?"

It wasn't fair of her to put Jen in this position, but she needed to know. Was she conflating everything?

There was a pause on the other end of the line. Then Jen said in a low voice, "Do you think Travis would tell you he didn't care what his family thought about the two of you being together if he hadn't given it a lot of thought beforehand?"

It wasn't a bad answer. It was just political. And they both knew discussing Travis was dangerous territory. But, for once, Lindsay felt selfish. She wanted *her* best friend in *her* corner. Sure, Travis and Jen had become best friends in high school, too, but Lindsay had been there first, as juvenile as it sounded.

Jen is mine? At least, I need her to be right now.

"That doesn't answer my question." Lindsay turned onto Main Street, wishing she could make the commute between the preschool and the Depot drag out further. "I feel like I'm drowning here, Jen. I miss you so much, and I feel like such a brat for even saying it. Everything with my family is messy and complicated, not being at the bar feels weird and awful, I'm barely speaking to Logan. And by the way, did I mention that my parents aren't so hung up on me being gone?"

She took a deep breath.

"And then there's Travis. I keep turning it over in my head. Why do I keep coming back to this? To these hookups with him? Why, if none of those times ever meant anything, well then why don't I just move on? He's had girlfriends. Joined hookup apps. God, Jen, his grandmother even set him up on a freaking blind date *in front of me*, two days ago, and he didn't bat an eyelash and said okay."

She was ranting now, but the words kept coming. "Why don't I just do that? Just move on? Date? Get a boyfriend? And every time we joke about how picky I am or a blind date goes wrong, it's like, haha, Lindsay isn't willing to settle for anything less than Prince Charming, but that's not it, is it? It's that I'm not willing to settle for anyone other than—"

"—anyone other than Travis Wagner," Jen filled in for her quietly.

Boom. There it is.

"Yes," Lindsay admitted in a whisper. She pulled into a parking space but continued to clutch onto the steering wheel.

"Lindsay. It doesn't take a genius to figure out you both have feelings for each other," Jen finally said. "I've been able to see it for years. Just a couple of minutes in shared company is usually enough. But that's where I have the advantage over most people. I'm one of the few people you'll both share company with."

"The only one."

"And your secret is safe with me. But that's the thing, hon.

Is keeping your family happy worth being miserable over? You might be missing out on the best thing in your life. Being with the right person brings joy like nothing else does."

Lindsay let go of the brake, and the car lurched forward, straight into the metal post with an Employee Parking Only sign. Yanking the e-brake up, she widened her eyes.

Shit, shit, shit. She had been so distracted she hadn't put the car in park. Correcting her error, she turned off the car. She'd maimed her hood, for sure, but she wanted to finish this conversation. It was too important not to.

"But he's already dating, Jen. He had a hookup set up— who knows if he's gone on it by now. And this other date. What if you're wrong, and he doesn't feel the way you think about me?"

"Linds, the only way you'll find out what Travis feels is to *talk to him*. Tell him you don't want him dating, to begin with. It's clearly bothering you. I think that will shake him."

The idea of doing something like that was mind-boggling.

Just talk to him?

As though it's just that easy.

The sight of Maddie and Naomi opening the back door to the Depot, though, caught her attention. They both frowned at her, staring at the hood of her car and the bent post.

"I gotta go. I just ran into a metal post at the parking space at work. Love you. Talk soon." Lindsay hung up and opened the door.

"You can't park there, you know," Maddie said, coming closer.

Lindsay went over to the hood, inspecting the damage. *Great.* A big old dent curled the top of the hood panel back. "I can't park in the employee space?" she asked, baffled.

"No, she means *on* the post," Naomi said with a shake of her head. "It's like her favorite joke each time we drive by a car in a ditch, too. You okay? Someone saw it happen and came and told us."

"I'm fine." Maybe she could use the young, scatterbrained image to her advantage here. "I just got so distracted talking to Jen that I forgot to put the car in park."

"That must have been one hell of a conversation," Naomi said with a lift of her brow.

"You sure it wasn't that mysterious friend of yours from college. Chaz, was it?" Maddie asked with a sly grin.

"Chad." Lindsay started into the Depot, and her sisters followed her. "And no, Jen was just telling me about Ava and Nora."

"How is she? I can't believe she has twins. We should get her flowers or something—even though the orders from the bakery have been all totally messed up the last week, and we've had to tell people we're out of everything," Maddie asked.

"Don't worry, I'm about to send Lindsay over there to straighten things out." Naomi stood straighter. She handed Lindsay an iPad. "The orders for the week are already pulled up. Just talk to Jason or whoever is in charge now and see when they estimate we'll get the full orders and when. We can't have another few days like it's been since Jen went to the hospital. It's been chaos. Thank God for gelato and your brilliant idea of giving browsing customers free tea and hot chocolate."

The compliment was warming, but Lindsay hated to hear Jen's bakery in a negative light.

Jason had offered the job to Travis . . . but had he taken it?

She doubted it, if things were in shambles like this.

And, at the same time, the idea that Jen's business wasn't transitioning smoothly in her absence made her mad. Jen had worked her butt off to build that. "Why not just call?" Lindsay asked, running her palms over the outer edge of the iPad.

"No one picks up. Trust me, I've tried. It's been a mess."

Naomi gave her a reassuring look. "You'll be fine. You're not, like, some girl we just randomly hired to work the register during the holidays or something. You know what to do. You've shown some amazing chops at this."

At least Naomi's confidence in her was comforting.

"And leave your phone so I can go through your texts in the meantime." Maddie winked.

Lindsay gave her a sarcastic smile. "Ha ha." Her palms broke out into a sweat. Teasing or not, she needed to watch Maddie—and make sure she didn't have any damning texts on her phone. She wouldn't put it past her sister to swipe it when she wasn't looking.

Slipping her phone into her coat pocket, Lindsay left the Depot and stepped into the blustery weather outside. It smelled like snow, and from the chill in the air, the storm that had been predicted tomorrow might actually hit. *I'm so ready for spring.* March in Maryland usually meant the arrival of warmer weather but it wouldn't be the first time they'd had a snowstorm this late in the season.

Lindsay hugged her arms to her chest then headed down Main Street. Going to Sweet Escapes was an ordinary enough thing for her—she spent half her afternoons there during the week—but without Jen?

That was strange.

As though Jen knew what she was thinking, Lindsay's phone buzzed with a message.

Jen: *Talk to him.*

Jen: XOXO

Jen: *Here are pictures of the babies to make you smile. If I can nurse two babies at once, you can talk to him.*

Picking up the pace, Lindsay hurried toward the familiar warmth of Sweet Escapes. To her dismay, a sign was hung on the window: *Closed for the Week*. She didn't see anyone inside, though Jen didn't have many employees.

The lights were on.

So she knocked on the glass door.

Nothing.

Knocking again, this time more loudly, Lindsay stamped her feet to keep warm.

Moments later, she saw the back door that led to the kitchen open.

Travis.

He took the job?

He paused when he saw her, removing his earbuds. After a moment, he crossed the space to the door and unlocked it.

"We're closed," he said with a nod toward the door.

"Let me in, smart-ass. I'm freezing out here." Lindsay pushed past him, not waiting for permission.

She flexed her fingers to thaw them, then turned toward him as he locked the door again. The bakery was quiet—none of the life and light that Jen brought to it.

It's silly for me to miss her so much.

Although, when she thought about it, it was as if everything was somehow different at the moment.

And unlike when Jen had Colby, she didn't need Lindsay as much. Her focus is on her husband, her two sons, and now her twin girls. Just as it ought to be.

Why can't I seem to cope with this enormous change?

Especially that Travis was working for Jen. That seemed so . . . strange.

"So I guess you decided to take Jason's job offer."

"Whenever I can take time away from my shop. This week I'm just trying to get caught up on orders, though, until we can hire some transition staff and get fully operational. Jen's ability to get so much done is impressive. She's hard to replace."

His words made her miss Jen even more. "Yeah, she is."

Travis's expression was unusually serious. "I don't really have time to talk today, Lindsay."

"I'm not really here to talk," Lindsay said, peeling her coat away. She set it on the back of a chair. "Naomi and Maddie sent me to find out what's happening with their order." She pulled the iPad out of a large pocket on the inside of her coat.

Travis's lips set to a line as he studied her, as though he was contemplating telling her to go away. Then he said, "Come on back to the kitchen. I'm in the middle of making a crème anglaise."

She followed him to the back, surprised to find they were alone. "Doesn't Jen have assistants who work in the kitchen?"

"Yeah, and we'll bring them back on board once I get my head on straight. I just started a couple of days ago, and I'm trying to figure out what I can handle, what needs to be prioritized, and what will have to get canceled."

Lindsay grinned as he washed his hands and returned to the range. She'd never really watched Travis at work even though she'd seen Jen work her magic a thousand times. Something about seeing him separating egg whites from yolks with an ease that she could never imagine was . . . strangely sexy?

Great. That's what does it for you? A man cooking?

She'd blame it on not having had sex in too long, except that wasn't the case.

Of course, the guy I slept with is also the one cooking.

Travis's gaze darted in her direction, and she realized she'd been staring. "Something the matter?" he asked, raising a brow.

"No—" She cleared her throat and stepped back, then fanned her face. "The kitchen's hot."

"It's a kitchen." Travis chuckled and focused back on his work. "Didn't you ever spend time cooking with your grandfather at his restaurant? He's the famous chef from Brandywood, after all."

His bitter tone was unmistakable.

That source of Wagner resentment she could understand, though. Bunny Wagner was by far the best chef in Brandywood. Jen could give her stiff competition when it came to baking, but Jen had learned everything from Bunny.

"I don't know. Not really. Not that Pops didn't try, but I guess it's more of a thing people do with their grandmothers, and mine was always shooing me out of the kitchen. Then after she died . . . I don't know." Lindsay shrugged and blinked down at the iPad. She'd never really thought about what she might have lost by not having her grandmother around.

Pops had more than filled the hole she'd left. He'd always spoiled her more anyway.

She unlocked the screen of the iPad, not wanting to dwell on anything sad. "So Naomi and Maddie sent me with the order list—"

"I have the list, but if you don't mind reading it aloud to me, I can probably give you an idea of when I can start getting some things to you."

"Macarons are the top one. They're sold out in every flavor."

Travis split a vanilla bean at the workstation beside the range, and the delicious scent filled the air. "Macarons probably won't be until Thursday. I might—and I mean *might*—be able to get vanilla and chocolate out by tomorrow morning if I work all night. The other flavors will have to wait a day. What else?"

"Éclairs and cream puffs."

"Tomorrow."

"Lemon tarts?"

"Probably Thursday, but maybe tomorrow afternoon."

Travis didn't lift his eyes away from the task in front of

him as she continued to rattle down the list and take notes of his responses. It was impressive to see how quickly he worked. He didn't reference a recipe book, either, which surprised Lindsay. He'd walked away from the culinary world. That he had so many things memorized was a testament to his skill.

No wonder his father is mad he doesn't want to take over for Bunny.

Then she remembered Jen's nudge for her to talk to him and his impending date with Hélène, and a jealous stab went through her gut. Having finished with the list, she set the iPad down on a counter. "So does your grandmother plan on importing French models to take over her café?"

Travis lifted the wooden spoon he'd been using to stir the custard and swiped his finger across the back of it. Seeming satisfied with the result, he set the spoon down and grabbed a strainer. "And if she does?"

"Nothing, I guess. I'm just curious. How did your date with Miss Paris go?"

Travis strained the sauce into another container and set the pot down. He wiped his hands on his apron and turned toward Lindsay. "We're going out tomorrow." He dipped his chin. "Which you know. Because you heard the plans. We're going to The Bench."

Lindsay tried to hold her tongue. She didn't want to talk about Hélène or his plans to go out with her. But she didn't really know how to broach this topic. "So is she going to be one of your new hookups?"

Travis's eyes narrowed, and he crossed his arms, stepping closer to her. "Could be." The well-defined muscles of his arms bulged at the movement, and her gaze followed the hard outline of his biceps against the Henley shirt to his rolled sleeves, where the thick, ropey muscles of his forearms flexed.

I really love how strong his arms are. Especially when he's holding himself up over me and—

"What's it to you?"

It's nothing to me. Nothing at all. She tried to keep that same casual tone as she shrugged and said, "Relax, I was just making conversation."

"Who says I'm not relaxed?" Travis's lips twitched in a smile. "You're the one who seems nervous." He shook his head with disbelief. "So you're just genuinely curious about whether I'm going to fuck her? Why?"

"I-I . . ." Lindsay took a step back, feeling the weight of the conversation crashing down on her.

Because I don't want you to.

Because the thought of you going out with her has been driving me crazy.

"If you don't want me to sleep with her, Linds, you might want to say something." Travis stepped closer. "But if you do, you better believe I'll have some questions. Since you're the one calling the shots now."

Her heart hammered in her chest, and she searched his eyes. She wanted to be honest. Wanted to tell him exactly what she barely understood herself.

But how on earth could she tell him she didn't want him to be with anyone else?

. . . especially if I still don't intend to be with him?

I can't ask him not to date just because I don't like it. No matter what Jen says.

When she still didn't answer, Travis let out a short, frustrated sigh. "I should get back to work. I've got enough to keep me busy for days."

As he turned away, Lindsay felt the disappointment at herself burn like acid in the back of her throat. "You know, you can't just put this on me. It's not like you're waiting around for me. You've already moved on. You were even about to go on a date while I was in your apartment with the plague until that other girl canceled on you."

Travis let out a bark of laughter. "Right, Lindsay." He rubbed his eyes, then slid his palm down the length of his face, holding his hand over his mouth for a moment as though he was trying to hold himself back from speaking. "Just so you know, she didn't cancel. I canceled. Why would I go be with some random stranger when I had a fucking goddess in my bedroom —one I happen to care about—and who I wanted to take care of?"

His words stole her breath.

She stared at him, trying to process what he'd said, the synapses of her brain firing way too slowly compared to the fibers of her heart, which were expanding painfully, so that she could barely breathe. She set her hand over her chest, her heart physically hurting as his words sank in.

She didn't know what she wanted.

Except to kiss him.

Not sex.

Not a promise of a thousand tomorrows.

Just to feel the warmth of his lips against hers.

Lindsay closed the gap between them, drawing his head down toward hers.

She stepped onto her tiptoes, and his hand paused at her waist. As her lips brushed his, an electric sizzle went through her body, raw and hungry, intense. He hesitated still, and she drew his lower lip between her own, urging him to kiss her.

Travis drew in a sharp breath, then his body seemed to react to her impulse, and his hand splayed across the small of her back, drawing her in closer as his mouth captured hers.

His breath was warm against her lips, his touch electric as their lips met gently in a kiss, then another. Her pulse sped as he drew her closer, then her lips parted against his, receiving his kiss more fully and deeply.

Her body tingled with anticipation as his tongue swept tenuously against her own, then more boldly, colliding with passion and longing.

I miss this.

I want this.

He pulled her closer to him, and she felt the swell of his erection against her hip, and a soft groan left her lips.

Her phone rang in her pocket, pulling her away from the moment. She drew a sharp breath, then lifted it, her heart still trying to play catch-up. Travis leaned his forehead against hers.

"It's Maddie," she said, swallowing hard.

Maddie, calling me back to the Depot.

"Don't answer it," he whispered, his lips trailing her jaw.

What if she didn't? If she just went on enjoying making out with Travis? Blocking out the world.

The buzzing in her hand made her shoulders bunch.

"I can't ignore her. She'll send a search party."

Lindsay swiped up on the phone and gave a quarter-turn away from Travis. "Hey."

"Did you get lost?" Maddie asked with amusement in her tone.

Sighing, Travis stepped away.

"No, it's just it was closed. Only Travis is in the kitchen, and it took a little bit for him to hear me knocking." Her lips were hot—were they as red and flushed as they felt?

"Travis? Travis Wagner?"

"Yeah, he's helping Jen out while she's on maternity leave." Disappointment started to crest into Lindsay's ribs as Travis turned back to his work.

"Ugh. I don't want anything a Wagner baked. Why would Jen do that?"

Great. Please don't make a deal out this.

"Uh—you know, why don't we talk about it when I get back? I'll be there in like five minutes." Lindsay hung up and then double-checked to be sure the call wasn't somehow still connected.

Travis didn't say anything, his back to her now.

"I have to go," she said. "My sisters are waiting for me."

"Okay." He said nothing more, and she felt that connection she'd forged with him just moments before slipping further away.

"I . . ." *Just say it, Lindsay. I don't want you to go out with Hélène tomorrow.*

But Maddie's reaction to Travis working at the bakery played through her head.

Shame shimmied through her.

Her siblings would never be cool with this.

She didn't know what hurt more—the fact that Maddie's comment had been so mean, or that it had been so second nature. And Maddie fully expected Lindsay to agree with the sentiment, too.

She grabbed the iPad. "Thanks for your help. I'll be in touch soon about the committee stuff. And probably the Depot order."

Then she hightailed it out of the bakery as fast as she could, her heart slamming into her chest.

But, she couldn't get Travis's words out of her mind.

"Why would I go be with some random stranger when I had a fucking goddess in my bedroom—one I happen to care about— and who I wanted to take care of?"

A goddess? Me? That's how he sees me?

But it couldn't matter. She and Travis couldn't ever have anything between them.

If Travis wanted a reason not to sleep with someone else,

she wouldn't be the one to provide it. He might have thought Lindsay was calling the shots, but he couldn't have been more wrong. *It's completely out of my hands.*

I can't even find the words to tell him I don't want him to be with someone else . . . because I know I can't be with him.

She had to forget the attraction she felt toward Travis Wagner, which meant he *was* free to be with any other woman.

Women.

Even if she hated it.

Was it just that Lindsay was feeling discontent? Was that where her focus should lie?

Is it time to move on and focus on myself?

CHAPTER TWENTY-THREE

The fire was just beginning to go out when Lindsay heard a shuffle behind her. Pops, in his pajamas and slippers, stood in the doorway to the living room with a glass of milk in his hands.

He gave her a surprised look. "You still up, or are you sleeping on that old couch?"

She stretched and yawned, shutting the book she'd been reading. "I thought you were asleep."

"I was. But then I woke up and wanted a glass of warm milk." He sipped it and came farther into the room. Sinking down onto the cushion beside her, he smiled. "Your grandma always used to tell me to do that when I'd wake up and couldn't sleep. Works, too."

"Do you miss her a lot?" Lindsay asked, scanning his face. Most of what she knew of her grandmother was through stories she'd heard if she was honest. She'd died when Lindsay had been in first grade.

"I miss her. I miss being married. I miss the company." Pops got a sad look in his blue eyes, then winked at her. "Why I never mind fixing up a room for you."

She sat up, setting both hands on either side of her lap on the couch cushion. Then she scooted back and sat cross-legged beside him. "Why didn't you ever remarry then, Pops? If you liked being married so much. I'm sure you could have found someone to spend the past twenty years with who would have made you happy."

"It wasn't my happiness I was worried about." Pops shrugged, his gaze going to the dying embers in the fireplace. "Besides, it didn't seem fair to your grandma's memory. I married her, and she deserved a whole lot better than me, yet somehow, I outlived her. You know that saying, 'only the good die young'? It's true."

Lindsay laughed, then hugged his arm. "You're crazy, Pops. You're the best person I know."

"You're biased." He winked again, then took another sip. "But what has you up at this late hour? It's after two."

"I couldn't sleep," she confessed, then picked up her book and thumbed through the pages. "I just kept thinking about . . ."

Travis.

And how I should have told him I didn't want him going out with Hélène.

"About what?" Pops nudged her with his elbow.

Lindsay curled the book pages against her thumb. "Did you ever want to do something—something that you knew you'd regret if you didn't do—yet not be able to bring yourself to do it? No matter how much you knew you should?"

Her grandfather took another sip of milk. "I think most of us have done that, Lindsay."

"I know, but I'm not talking about something silly or inconsequential. I mean something big. Something that could change your life."

Pops turned and studied her face. "Do you want to talk about it, little bee?"

If she wished to talk about Travis with anyone, it was her grandfather. He seemed to understand her better than most people. She never felt judged or stupid beside him.

But she wasn't about to talk about sex with her grandfather, either. Not the man who still called her *little bee*.

And she doubted Pops wanted to know—or think about— her sex or dating life that much.

"Not really."

Pops turned his gold wedding band on his fingers, a habit she'd seen him do often. "When I was a very young man, I once, very foolishly, didn't tell someone I cared about something I should have. Changed the whole trajectory of my life, too."

"What didn't you tell them? Or should I say her?" Lindsay raised a brow. "This sounds like a woman."

Pops laughed lightly. "Looking back on it, we were just kids, but that's because I'm an old man now. But yes. I didn't tell her I didn't want her to do something. She asked me not to. My decision came back to haunt me. The details aren't that important, really. It was a long time ago, and from that point on, I made the choice to always, *always*, say whatever I needed to say, when I needed to say it."

Were the details as unimportant as he said? His vagueness was curious. Like he wanted her to learn an important lesson without giving her enough information to figure out if it was worth learning.

He patted her knee, then polished off his milk. "I should go back to bed. Ramblings of an old man aren't good for young girls like you."

"I like hearing them." Lindsay hugged him from the side, then stood with him, curling the toes of her socks against the floorboards. "By the way, I wanted to thank you for going with me to that meeting at the café the other day. I wish I'd been able to accomplish more, but I have a feeling the Wagners aren't going to make anything easy. But I appreciate your support."

Pops touched her cheek lightly. "You made me proud. It's a good idea. All of it. They'll be fools not to consider your proposal more seriously."

Growing more serious, Lindsay felt her throat tighten. "I hope I can bring about a good result for our family, Pops. I'm worried, though. If I don't, I don't want to feel responsible for not being able to keep the Depot on Main where it belongs. And I fear that everyone will blame me."

"There's only so much you can do, little bee. That's just the way of it. No one is going to blame you. I'll make sure of that much."

Anxiety pressed in on her. "And if they do?"

"Then I'll have to take them to task." Pops shuffled back toward the doorway. "Love you, kid. Got to go crawl back into bed before the magic of the warm milk wears off. Then I'll just have to drink more, but I'll be up all night going to the bathroom."

She watched him go, then went over to the fireplace. Grabbing a poker, she balanced it in her palm. With a sigh, she stirred the embers, watching them glow against the soot of the surrounding bricks and send a swirl of gray ash up through the chimney.

Her grandfather's gruff voice came back to her. *"I made the choice to always, always, say whatever I needed to say, when I needed to say it."*

She needed to say so many things—starting with Pops. She should have told him about the situation at the restaurant. And how she wanted to be a contender. But if she failed with the Depot committee, would he even take her seriously? Who would want her running that successful business when she'd failed so spectacularly?

. . . and then there's Travis.

That kiss this afternoon kept playing through her mind on a loop.

The thing was, sharing a kiss with him *was* different from their typical MO. Something about it was weirdly more intimate. Not in a *Pretty Woman* sort of way. But in the sense that that was it. They'd kissed, like couples do. Like boyfriends and girlfriends might. Like excited teenagers who were leading up to hours of making out or dry humping.

The part we skipped when we went right to having sex.

They'd been nothing, then lovers, then nothing again, in a cycle. Sure, they shared Jen's friendship, and they saw each other occasionally, but they avoided getting to know each other or being friends.

Yet they'd gotten to know each other in many ways despite their best efforts.

So they had a history, but not friendship.

Sex, but not intimacy.

They'd fucked—as Travis had put it—but didn't make love because, well, the love thing wasn't part of the equation.

Hot, delicious lust, but none of the tortured buildup of emotions between.

Or, at least, that was what she'd thought.

Maybe she'd been fooling herself. Maybe Travis hadn't spoken up—not that she blamed him. She'd made her feelings clear.

And somewhere in the last few weeks, something had changed for her.

Sure, she didn't love being around him before this—especially when he had a girlfriend or date with him—but now the thought of him going out with Hélène was killing her.

And he'd canceled a damn hookup to spend the weekend taking care of her.

That means something.

Travis cared.

He'd basically told her as much and put the ball in her court.

She set the poker down, glancing back at the doorway, wishing she could have asked Pops for better advice.

But she had a feeling she knew what he'd tell her to do.

CHAPTER TWENTY-FOUR

The Bench was crowded for a Wednesday night, especially considering the snowstorm outside appeared to have no intention of letting up. Travis stamped his shoes on the mat by the front entrance, then turned toward Hélène with a grin. "Does it snow like this in Paris?"

"Sometimes. Not so often." She shook the snow from her hooded parka and looked around. "There's a lot of people here. Where will we sit?"

Travis's gaze swept over the crowded bar, and he paused when he spotted Ben and Grace at the tables. Thankfully, they'd beat him there and nabbed one. "This way."

As he pushed through the crowd, he tried to ignore the headache pounding at the sides of his head. He'd barely slept two hours the night before, trying to fill as many of the back-logged orders from the bakery. This morning, he'd finally broken down and called Jason, asking him to send Jen's assistants in to help. He'd avoided it—mostly as a confidence issue—because he liked to find his way around a kitchen and get back into the groove and mindset necessary to do the work.

Grace had always called him a perfectionist, and maybe that was part of it. But when he did make mistakes, he didn't like there being too many witnesses.

Hélène was surprisingly tall, and she seemed to have no problem keeping up with his long strides. Grace stood as they got to the table. "Hélène!" She gave her a big hug. "I'm so glad we were finally able to get you out." She gave Travis a knowing look. "Nana has been working her to death."

Was I the only one in my family that didn't know Hélène existed?

Hélène laughed. "Oh, it's fine. It's my fault, I keep asking her questions. She knows everything."

Grace grabbed her by the hand and tugged her down beside her. "Hélène, this is Ben Pearson. He's the farmer I told you about a couple of weeks ago." She winked at Ben.

"Oh really!" Hélène's face brightened. She leaned forward toward Ben. "You own all the horses?"

Travis smiled as he sat and tugged out the drink menu from the side of the table, where it was propped between the salt and pepper and the wall. He'd been tempted to tell Lindsay yesterday this wasn't a date with Hélène, but why bother? Her angst about it had been strangely satisfying.

Not that she hadn't turned right back around and left him with blue balls.

He didn't really know what his goal was. She was driving him crazy, and they had to see each other again—sooner rather than later. After that debacle with their grandparents and Brian Pearson at the café the other day, he'd avoided thinking about the Depot issue.

And then his grandmother had pulled him to the side tonight when he'd gone to pick up Hélène.

"I might be willing to consider selling the land that Lindsay Yardley mentioned," Nana had said. "But don't tell anyone in

the family yet. I've given it some thought, and it might be time to finally let it go. Make some money off it, too. I'd rather it go to something that helps the town in the long run than just another development."

Just like that, Nana had proven what a good person she was. How much she cared about Brandywood and the people in it. No matter what the Yardleys might say, his grandmother's reputation for always doing the right thing couldn't be questioned.

Of course, if the offer had ended there, then everything would be simple. Lindsay's plan seemed like enough of an alternative to offer. They could research the logistics, then present it to the committee.

But Nana hadn't stopped there.

"But I'll only sell the land if they agree to move the Depot to it. No tourist center. The land isn't far from Main Street. Peter Yardley wants a place to bring his adoring fans, fine. There aren't a lot of places to build near town that are as suitable as my family farm. But the Depot goes."

Somehow, Travis had a feeling that would never be good enough. Even if it was a logical solution. The farm location was close enough to Main Street for other local businesses to not suffer, there wouldn't be the added expense of creating additional parking lots or buying shuttle buses. The traffic in Main Street would return to normal. *Be safer.* The town stayed the priority, which had been Nana's concern.

Yet . . .

And he was going to have to be the one to break the news to Lindsay.

The server arrived at the table and Travis and Hélène ordered drinks and crabby fries for the table—french fries covered in crab dip. Travis also ordered some buffalo wings, craving nothing but salty food after spending the past few days surrounded by and sampling sugar.

Whereas the smell of motor oil and gasoline and even exhaust appealed to him, he'd quickly remembered how much he disliked being covered in flour all day.

Not that it was all bad.

Despite his exhaustion, he felt more relaxed than he had in years. Losing himself to the process of baking was easy. Just like when he worked on cars, the satisfaction of doing something with his hands—building, creating, fixing—was still there for him in the kitchen. He'd pushed this side of himself away for a long time.

"Do you remember that time we all went horseback riding, and Travis got sprayed by a skunk?" Grace was saying.

Travis lifted his head sharply, realizing he'd zoned out. He groaned, giving Grace a warning look. "Not this story."

Ben threw back his head and laughed. "Let's just say Travis gave a new meaning to the term bareback riding. Poor horse wanted to get away from him, too, though, even though he left his clothes in the middle of a field."

Hélène smiled at Travis. "Poor you. It must have been terrible."

"Nothing a good bath in tomato sauce couldn't fix," Ben said.

"Isn't that your friend from the café the other day?" Hélène said suddenly, gesturing toward the door. "We should invite her and her friends to sit with us. They look like they can't find a table."

Travis nearly groaned again. Lindsay, Maddie, and Jake Yardley were over by the entrance.

What is she doing here?

He could have sworn that before this stupid committee thing, they'd go months at a time, sometimes more, without seeing each other. Now, they could barely go a day without bumping into each other everywhere in town.

Then again, I told her I was coming here tonight. Shit, now she's going to see Grace and Ben here, too. Will she think I was purposely toying with her?

Grace raised a brow and looked in the direction Hélène had pointed. "Oh God, no. Those aren't friends of ours. Remember the people I told you were causing so much trouble in town? That's them."

"Really?" Hélène asked with a frown. "The girl was very nice. Lindsay, yes?"

Lindsay? Travis almost laughed. What about Lindsay had been nice in that interaction?

Then again, he barely remembered much of any interaction Hélène might have had with Lindsay. He'd been preoccupied, thinking about how maddening she was, how frustrated he'd been with her.

She was driving him crazy.

As though she seemed to feel the weight of his stare, she turned just then and her eyes locked with Travis's.

She wasn't close enough for him to see the nuances of her reaction, but she looked away just as abruptly.

He held his breath.

We can be in the same room together. The same bar.

Nothing has changed between us.

Except . . . was that really true?

He knew more about her now. That, even though she'd managed to summon the strength to quit her job at the bar and move out of her house, a few minor setbacks had sent her flying back into a zone of comfort—a job at the Depot and staying at her grandfather's.

He knew she had good ideas but lacked confidence.

That she was so busy caring about what her family thought

about her that she never actually let herself do the things she wanted.

Maybe that was why they'd frequently hooked up after a few drinks. Liquid courage. Just enough to give her the ability to overcome whatever hesitations she had about him.

The heel of Ben's boot squished into Travis's toes, and Ben leaned forward in his seat as though adjusting his posture. "You're staring," he hissed in a low voice that Travis barely heard.

"She's very pretty," Hélène observed, as though she, too, had noticed the direction of Travis's stare. "Yes?"

Grace sipped on her beer, then glanced from Travis to Lindsay. "Yeah, all the Yardleys are so good-looking. A third of the girls in my school had crushes on their older brother, Logan. But our families don't get along."

Travis was spared from responding by the strum of a guitar as the live musical act for the night stepped up to the microphone in the corner of the room and introduced himself. Several minutes later, with music playing loudly enough that lengthy conversation across the table was next to impossible, Travis leaned back in his seat, watching as Hélène and Grace whispered back and forth.

"You've got to get that girl out of your system," Ben said in a low, deep voice, nudging Travis's beer closer to him. "Anyone with two eyes can see you're crushing on her at this point."

"Grace?" Travis took a swig of his beer.

"I don't know. Maybe not. But only because she sees what she wants to see. She's too close. Ever stare at someone from a centimeter away?" Ben shook his head. "It's like she has horse blinders on. But you're playing with fire."

Travis scanned the area near the entrance again, but Lindsay and her siblings appeared to be gone. Maybe they'd gone somewhere else.

But why had Lindsay picked The Bench to come to? If she knew he was going to be here, he would have thought she'd avoid it.

Even though it was for the best, his heart still throbbed at her absence. That absurd excitement, knowing he could look over and see her nearby, wondering if she might be looking at him...

Yeah, I have a crush.

Pathetic, Travis. Really smart, you fucking genius.

Heat flooded his face, and he felt the strange urge to flee. Instead, he stood, desperate for a moment alone. "Gonna go break the seal," he told Ben, then headed toward the bathroom down a dimly lit hallway in the back of the bar.

He'd just walked inside the bathroom when the door flew open behind him and banged into the wall. Lindsay stood there, slightly out of breath, as though she'd rushed to catch up with him. She looked over her shoulder into the dark, empty hallway, then closed the door and turned the lock.

"Yes?" Travis said, raising a brow.

"How's your date going?" Lindsay ran her fingers through her honey-blond hair. She had it down and wore makeup as though she'd taken the time to fix herself up tonight, which was odd, considering it was a random Wednesday.

"Perfect." Travis gritted through his teeth.

What is she trying to do here?

"I don't want you to sleep with her," she blurted out.

Oh...

Then a smile tipped the corner of his lips.

Maybe she did come here on purpose.

"You mean you don't want me to fuck her?" Travis stepped closer to her, crossing his arms. He tried to ignore the fact that they were in a bathroom in the back of The Bench, which might be the least romantic spot he could think of.

Yet here we are.

The significance of Lindsay telling him she didn't want him to be with someone else was . . . monumental, really.

A fool's hope lifted through him.

She shook her head, her eyes wide. "I just . . . I know what I said, and I know we can't be together, but I just . . . I-I can't . . . stand the thought of it."

God, she's so fucking adorable.

He wanted to kiss her.

Wanted so much more.

But he was also enjoying this. Maybe a little too much.

How many times had she told him their trysts meant nothing? That she didn't want him—didn't see her in his future. Whether it was his bruised ego or the fact he enjoyed teasing her, he couldn't help himself and said, "So you want me to give up a perfectly good opportunity for sex with someone who might actually want to be with me for, what, exactly?"

"I-I don't know. Oh God, Travis, I know. I know it's so stupid. I just keep thinking about you and me. Remember that time we hooked up after that concert? When it was like three in the morning, and everyone was asleep in their tents, and I snuck into your sleeping bag?"

He'd remember that until the day he died.

Just thinking about it made him hard all over again.

Or maybe it was the way her full breasts heaved as though she was out of breath or thrilled about their conversation.

She stepped closer to him. "All I kept thinking that night was *what if someone wakes up? Hears us and finds out?* Because it was so fucking risky, and anyone could have. A-and to this day, I regret that no one did." She drew a shaking breath. "Because then it might have all been over. All the hiding and the secrets and being scared that someone might know."

He dropped his chin. "Do you want people to know, Linds?"

"I don't know what I want." She reached out, trailing her fingertips against his jaw. "But when I think about you dating other women, it kills me."

"What if I told you I'm not actually on a date? That we're just hanging out as friends?" Travis asked, his voice softening.

Relief filled her face. She hooked one arm around his neck, her other hand sliding lower against his abs, then lower still.

As she reached the waistband of his jeans, he drew in a dizzying breath. "What're you doing?"

She bit her lip, a tiny, seductive smile on her mouth, then got to her knees in front of him.

Here?

He didn't protest as she unbuttoned him, then zipped his jeans down. Moistening his own lips with the tip of his tongue, he sucked in a shallow gasp as she freed him from his boxer briefs, her warm breath on him.

Oh fuck. She's so good at this.

She made a slow circle with the tip of her tongue around the head of his shaft, and he closed his eyes, digging his hands into her hair.

My God, this woman drives me insane.

"Is this okay?" she asked.

"Are you joking? More than okay." He could barely think straight as she drew him deeper into her mouth.

Every nerve in his body was firing, his brain almost a blank. All he wanted was her.

He wanted to taste her, hold her.

Spend the night fucking her so hard they'd barely be able to stand tomorrow.

And with every twirl of her tongue, he was losing control.

A knock on the door made them both freeze. Her eyes

widened, and she looked up at him. Travis caught sight of them in the bathroom mirror and he nearly came right there, then let a slow breath out from puffed cheeks. "One second," he managed, his voice like gravel.

He almost gasped as she drew her mouth back, then stood. Her cheeks and lips were flushed red. "Are you kidding me right now?" he whispered.

Oh my God.

Oh fuck.

He needed to come so badly that he was going to explode.

He tried not to groan as he tucked himself back into his pants, then zipped them shut.

Lindsay gave an embarrassed laugh, her shoulders shaking as she looked toward the door with alarm. "How the hell do we get out of here?"

There weren't any windows, and the only way out was back into the hallway.

Travis rubbed his neck, trying to still his heartbeat and the rush of his blood. "Leave it to me. I'm going to turn the light out. You hide in the corner and then give it a twenty count and make a run for it."

"Okay." Lindsay nodded again, looking nervous.

The flush on her cheeks was still making him horny as hell. He grabbed her by the waist, then pushed her up against the sink so they were both facing the mirror. Without hesitating, he pushed his hand down the waistband of her jeans.

She was so fucking wet.

He rubbed his fingertip over her clit, and she nearly doubled over, but he held her in place with an arm across her torso. "You see what you're doing to me?" he whispered in her ear.

She gave a shiver of pleasure, her ass backing up against his length.

Then he pushed a finger deep inside her as he continued to rub slow circles with his finger. "Oh *fuck*—" She shuddered, her lips parting. "Please . . ."

He'd intended to tease her, to torture her the way she'd tortured him. But now that he was watching her in the mirror and he felt how deliciously wet she was for him, he found he couldn't stop. Another knock sounded, and he called out, "Hold on. Coming."

She smiled. "Stop teasing," she hissed, pressing against him. "We should hurry . . . oh God. Don't stop . . ."

"There's another bathroom." He turned the sink on for the noise regardless. These walls weren't particularly thick.

"You're wrecking me, sweetheart." He watched her in the mirror, entranced by how fucking beautiful she was right now. He'd give anything to shimmy those pants down and push his length deep inside her. But this would have to do.

For now.

A loud, unmistakable groan left her lips, and she covered her mouth with her hand.

Her volume was louder than she probably intended, but at that moment, Travis didn't care. His eyes locked with hers in the mirror, then he leaned forward and kissed her temple as he withdrew his hand. She gasped at the loss, her knees buckling, but he held her upright. "We're finishing this later. That's not a threat. Come over tonight."

"Okay," she whispered, then pulled away, her eyes looking softer now.

Travis went over to the bathroom light, then flipped it off. Unlocking the door, he headed out into the hallway. "You don't want to go in there, the toilet's completely backed up, I gotta—"

Grace.

She stood in the darkened hallway, arms crossed, her eyes blazing.

Travis froze.

Oh shit.

Instead of saying anything, Grace turned and hurried down the hallway. Travis glanced over his shoulder at the bathroom, then rushed after Grace. Lindsay would be fine. No one else would see them exiting together anyway.

By the time he'd caught up with Grace, she was outside and halfway across the street toward the town square. He grabbed her by the arm. "Hold on, hold on. You don't even have your coat." Snow fell thickly on them, and Grace was already shaking with cold.

They reached the sidewalk, and Grace whirled around. "I'm not leaving. I'm just coming out here so I can murder you without witnesses."

"I don't know what you saw, but—"

"I saw Lindsay Yardley follow you to the bathroom. What I *heard* is a completely . . . I-I can't even begin to wrap my head around—"

"Nothing happened," Travis said, wiping snow from his cheeks.

"For God's sake, Travis! I know what sex sounds like. Don't lie to me. I'm your freaking *older sister!*"

Shit. Fuck.

Lindsay had been loud. But then again, depending on how long Grace had been there, he might have been loud enough, too.

"We didn't have sex—"

Grace held her hands up. "I really, and I mean *really*, don't need details." Then she shook her head, staring at him as though he'd lost his mind. "Okay, never mind, maybe I do. What the hell are you thinking? How long has this been . . . how long have you been messing around with her?"

He didn't want to lie. Lies like this could make or break

family relationships, and the only way to undo any damage he'd done at this point was to be honest.

Travis stuffed his hands in his pockets, the cold seeping through his jeans. "Ten years."

"Ten years? Ten *years?*" Grace gasped. "Is this why Hannah broke it off with you?"

"No!" He should have worded it differently. "No. Nothing like that—"

"Oh my God, my head is going to explode." Grace set her hands on the top of her hair, large snowflakes collecting in her dark curls. Then her eyes filled with tears unexpectedly, and she stepped closer, grabbing his forearm. "Travis, what the hell are you doing? Do you have any idea what Logan—or even Jake—will do to you if they find out you were messing around with their little sister? Because that's how they see her. That's how they will *always* see her. And they *hate* you. They hate us. There is no possible way in which this doesn't end really, really badly for you."

"You think I honestly don't know that?" The words exploded out of his chest as icy air filled his lungs. Relief dripped down through him, strange and wonderful and horrible at the same time, that he could finally talk about this with her. "I have spent years trying to get over the feelings I have for her. Years tortured, trying to make sense of why the only woman I want is the only woman I can't have."

Grace gave a tearful laugh, which broke the tension. "The only woman? Let's not get ahead of ourselves, Trav. There are plenty of women in this town you can't have." She drew a giant sniffle, then wiped her cheeks. "But I understand what you meant."

She turned and glanced around. With the snow, Brandywood looked like a winter wonderland, calm and peaceful. She sniffed again. "Why didn't you tell me?"

He rubbed his jaw. "I didn't know how."

And because I thought your reaction would be much, much worse.

"Plus, Lindsay isn't even sure she wants anything with me. More accurately, she's spent the past ten years telling me nothing can ever happen again."

"So you have had sex with her? Like a lot?" Grace cringed. "You know what, don't answer that." She sighed. "Why did it have to be snowing? This is the worst possible scenario for me having a heart-to-heart with you. We can't even sit down."

"We can always take a snow check. It's pretty damn cold out here."

"Hilarious." Grace nodded. "And we should probably get back to Hélène and Ben. Though from the way she's been flirting with him, they probably don't care." She squeezed Travis's arm. "Just, for now, promise me you won't be stupid. I don't want to hear that you've knocked her up or something in a month. Being an only child wouldn't be my favorite."

Travis barely knew how to respond to her. She seemed to be all over the place with her response, and he was still half amazed she hadn't pummeled him. But he returned her hug as she tucked into him. "Why don't we get you out of the cold?"

Grace smiled, laying her cheek on his chest. "When did you get so much taller than me?"

This time, he laughed, remembering how often they would line up as kids at the measuring wall at home, competing over who was taller. "I'm good at doing things when you aren't looking."

She groaned, shaking her head. "Too soon, Travis, too soon."

Then they trudged back through the snow toward The Bench together.

CHAPTER TWENTY-FIVE

THE JITTERS in Lindsay's stomach hadn't subsided the entire walk over here, which had been through about a foot of snow. She would be sweating and need another shower by the time she stopped.

Her hair was an impossible mess by now, the tips of her ponytail sticking out from under her snow cap.

Only good thing was that the falling snow covered up her tracks almost as quickly as she made them.

She stopped in front of the door and curled her hand into and out of a fist, trying to warm up. Then she knocked.

If this isn't a booty call, I don't know what is.

Maybe she should just go home.

But Travis had asked her to come.

She felt the thrill of excitement bubble through her as Travis opened the door, wearing a fresh black T-shirt and jeans. *Did he shave?*

Everything about him, from the smell of his apartment to the squareness of his jaw, was familiar and unfamiliar at the same time.

The last time she'd come to hook up with him, they'd started tearing each other's clothes off just through the doorway.

This was different, though, and she didn't know how to behave.

Travis grinned, then held the door wider to let her through. "Didn't think you'd actually show up."

"Hoping against hope?" Lindsay asked, stepping inside. She was nearly tackled by Ratchet, who yipped happily at the sight of her, tail wagging at full speed.

"Whoa, dude, I missed you, too." She petted him as Travis ordered him to sit, holding up a dog treat.

Then she sniffed, a new, plastic-like smell reaching her. Travis appeared to be in the middle of assembling what appeared to be . . . a couch?

She laughed as she took off her snowy coat and hat and stepped out of her boots. "Did you get that for me?" Then she set down the backpack she'd carried over onto the console table.

"Hell, no. It was brought to my attention recently that I might need to invest in something more . . . grown-up? So I asked Jason for an advance on my pay for the bakery and used some of it to get a new couch." Travis sailed a dog treat toward the dog bed in the living room and Ratchet went scampering after it. "Can I get you a glass of wine?"

Was this how booty calls went for other people? Not wild *let's hop into bed* frantic scenarios, but calm dates sipping wine but knowing how things were going to probably end?

If so, she should make her own expectations clear, even if she wasn't sure what they should be. "I just wanted to say . . . I sort of want to take things slow. And wine would be great."

"We can take things as slow as you want," Travis said, grabbing a bottle of wine from the counter. "You're going to help me assemble this couch."

She quirked her brows at him. "Wow, you really know how to turn me on."

He uncorked the bottle, then poured them a glass—a cabernet. She should have expected a red wine from him. His family liked French things.

She sipped it, then followed him into the living room and sat on the floor. She didn't really want alcohol influencing her decisions tonight, but the fact was that she had come over here to sleep with him, and she couldn't really deny that, either. Wine would probably help take the edge off at this point.

Travis sat on the other side of the carpet. "Hand me that screwdriver, will you? No pun intended."

"Is there a pun in that?" She laughed and slid the screwdriver beside her toward him. Ratchet padded over toward her, then plopped down at her side, laying his head on her lap.

"Not that I'm aware of, but it sounds like there should be." Travis bent his head, furrowing his brow in concentration as he flipped through the instructions. "I'm sorry this isn't done—I wasn't anticipating you coming tonight—pun completely intended—and didn't do this before I went to The Bench."

"Nice sly one." She ran her fingertips through Ratchet's fur. "I'm offended you didn't think I would come." She choked back a laugh.

"We're devolving into teenagers." Travis cracked a smile at her, turning the screw.

"Maybe it's part of the process. Maybe we need to take it all the way back. Go through all the stuff we skipped." She stretched her legs out in front of her, then crossed her ankles, leaning back against the wall. "Like, what's your favorite color?"

"Red."

"Of course." She rolled her eyes. "I should have known. The Stingray. Anyway, mine is blue."

"You like football, roses, and the beach. And your favorite season is fall—"

"Spring, actually. I like the flowers blooming and the sense of hope. But thanks for making me basic. Also, I like hockey."

"Hockey or hockey players?" He raised a brow, looking oddly impressed.

This time, she chuckled. "The sport, obviously. I maintain that most players don't have half their teeth."

He threw back his head and laughed. "If that's true, it's not hurting their chances with other women."

"I'm not like other women."

"No. You're not." He said it in a way that made her thighs tighten reflexively.

"Why would I go be with some random stranger when I had a fucking goddess in my bedroom—one I happen to care about . . ."

Travis brought out a side in her she didn't completely understand.

But he did make her feel that way.

Beautiful.

Desirable.

Ready.

She wanted to crawl over toward him and kiss him until they were both panting.

Take it slow. Be careful.

"How about this? I tell you what I know about you, and you tell me if I'm wrong." Travis lifted his drill from the floor and tightened a screw.

She sipped the wine again, the butterflies that had taken residence in her stomach fluttering madly now.

Travis pushed the couch back so that the long side of the back was against the floor. It was nearly assembled, just a few screws for the legs. "Hand me that couch leg. When you're nervous, you twirl a strand of hair around your left forefinger."

What?

She frowned, scooting closer to him as she reached out with the part he'd asked for. "What sort of thing is that?"

He shrugged. "I don't know. It's just true. And when you get embarrassed, you bite your lower lip."

I do. I do that.

She gave him a look. "That's an easy one. Everyone does that."

"Yeah, but do they buy a copy of *Anne of Green Gables* every time they go to the bookstore?"

"What?"

How does he know that? "Stalker."

He held up a finger, then went over to a bookshelf. Tugging down a copy of *Anne of Green Gables*, he opened it to the first page, where her handwriting was. *"To all the dreamers who need a smile today."*

"I found this one in a Little Free Library four years ago. Occasionally more show up. Most of the time, I figure I miss them, but I've gotten in the habit of checking every time I pass one. I eventually asked Annie from the bookstore if you buy them a lot and she said every time you visit."

He'd taken a copy of Anne of Green Gables *home?*

And recognized her handwriting.

The thought that he'd done that—and that he visited the Little Free Library—made her heart flop.

He returned the book to its place, then went back to assembling the couch.

She stared at him, amazed. "It's my favorite book," she said after a minute. *And he knows that. He's even kept one here. Why?*

"Mine is *Catch-22*. I don't know why. I just think it's funny. But I like Anne Shirley. She's a little squirrelly and takes way too long to realize that Gilbert is the right man for her, but I like her."

Oh my God. "You've read *Anne of Green Gables?*"

He didn't meet her eyes, moving onto the final leg of the couch. "I've read the whole series. *Rilla of Ingleside*, too."

She shook her head in disbelief. "You're really so much better at this foreplay thing than you know."

"Oh yeah, I get all the girls by hanging out by the library with a stack of classics."

She let out a snicker. "I'm serious. You have no idea how hot it is when a guy reads."

"The caveman thing doesn't do it for you?" The drill sounded as he finished tightening the leg, then he stood. "Want to help me flip this thing back into place?"

She pushed Ratchet from her lap, then went to the opposite side of the couch from him. Together, they put it upright, then pushed it back against the wall.

"Care to take it for a spin?" Travis said, sitting down on it. He leaned back, closing his eyes for a moment. "Oh yeah. This is much better."

The normalcy of the activity wasn't lost on her. She tilted her head, studying him for a moment. If he'd planned to disarm her with his lack of sexual aggressiveness, then it was totally working. She was starting to feel the need to jump him herself if she wanted something to happen tonight.

Sitting beside him, she tucked her back against his chest, crossing her knees. "So much better." He wasn't kidding. Of course, a bean bag would have been an improvement to his old couch, but this was comfortable. Soft. Cozy.

She could practically picture doing this sort of thing with him on a more regular basis.

Watching TV on the couch sleepily with the dog snoring on the floor.

Leaning her head against his shoulder, she let out a slow sigh that released any tension she'd been holding in her chest. "I like this."

His fingers curled against her thigh, and she brought her hand closer to his, brushing the backs of her fingertips against his. Almost tenuously, he stroked against her fingers, and an electric pulse trilled through her.

His touch had a crazy effect on her.

She joined their fingers, interlacing them, then closed her eyes as his thumb trailed against the soft part of her palm. "I like this, too." His voice was low and deep, his lips near her ear.

Is holding hands supposed to be erotic? Not that she was going to tell him that. Every stroke of his thumb turned her core to liquid.

Her heart was beginning to speed up, too, and she struggled to think clearly.

She peeled away from him but didn't let his hand go. Turning to face him, she curled her knees up as she looked at him.

He's so hot.

Why did he have to be so hot?

I could have controlled myself if he wasn't.

Then she laughed at her own thoughts.

No, you crazy woman. You couldn't have.

Because she was much more than attracted to him.

She *liked* him.

She swallowed the fear that came with that idea. "Can I ask you a question?"

"What's that?" He seemed to sense her fears and scooted back some, putting space between them.

"The one-night stands . . ." Heat spread into her face. "I

didn't think that was a normal thing for you. But then you mentioned that hookup app and—"

"No, it's pretty unusual. Limited exclusively to one person, who happens to be seated here with me." Travis's fingers tightened against hers. "Ben convinced me to try the hookup app because last time we were together coincided with Hannah dumping me, and I . . . I don't know. Relationships don't exactly seem to work for me."

They haven't worked for me, either. "Maybe because you haven't been with the right person," she mused out loud.

"I know I haven't been with the right person. But there's not a whole lot you can do about that when the right person keeps telling you she's not it." He searched her eyes, then stopped stroking her palm. "I want you. Only you. And not just for a night."

Her mouth went dry. "But . . . you just broke up with someone else. And not because you broke it off."

He nodded. "I know that. But this thing between us goes back a lot further than Hannah Strickland or any other woman I've ever dated. It was always you. I just didn't think I had a shot with you."

She tore her gaze away, her heart beating wildly. "And you do now?"

"You tell me."

Does he? Does he have a shot with me? Lindsay realized that given she hadn't been interested in another man for some time —*not to mention the outright jealousy she'd felt earlier that night* —that she'd always felt something for Travis, too. Wasn't that obvious, though? Hadn't they kept falling into bed with each other over the years?

"I don't want this to be another hookup, no." Her voice was quiet. "I don't think I'm ready to tell everyone yet. Because I'm terrified about how my family will react, especially my brothers. But I want to be with you. I don't care how we label it. But I am scared."

The corners of his mouth tilted into a soft smile, and he tugged her closer to him. "I'll take you any way I can have you, Linds. It's sort of always been that way for me."

A lump formed in her throat, and she searched his eyes. *Why hadn't he said so?*

Or had she just not been listening?

Leaning forward, she brushed her lips against his, featherlight, her body flushing with warmth. He caught her lips in a kiss, molding their mouths together.

She returned his kiss, desire mounting through her as his lips parted hers, his tongue stroking against hers.

His hand skimmed her thigh, then stopped. Pulling away, Travis stretched back, then stood. "I have a long day tomorrow. Ready to go to bed?"

What?

She drew her brows together, scanning his face.

He wants to go to bed?

As in . . . sleep?

This wasn't at all what she had expected from this night.

She'd gone home and showered, shaved her legs. Then put on her cutest lingerie under her clothes and waited for Pops to go to bed.

And Travis just wants to sleep?

"Okay . . ." Was she supposed to just demand sex now?

How had she gotten this wrong?

"We're finishing this later. That's not a threat. Come over tonight."

She supposed he hadn't said, "we're finishing this tonight," but it was easy to see how she might have jumped to that conclusion.

Then she'd foolishly come in and told him she wanted to take things slow.

Unless this is his way of taking things slow, in which case I don't want to look like I'm throwing a tantrum.

She swallowed her disappointment and stood. "You want me to sleep in your bed with you?"

"Unless you'd prefer the couch."

"No, the bed is good." She went over to the door and grabbed her backpack. "Lead the way."

CHAPTER TWENTY-SIX

TRAVIS SHIFTED in the bed onto his back, not wanting to wake Lindsay. Inviting her over when he'd really needed a long night of sleep was stupid, but he hadn't been able to help himself. He'd told Jen's assistants that he wouldn't be in until after noon today, so he could take care of any business with the shop, but now that over a foot of snow had blanketed the town, he doubted he'd have business at all.

Things were likely to be closed today.

And he had a gorgeous woman in his bed.

One who he hadn't fucked, and now he had the bluest balls imaginable.

It was bad enough that she'd decided to give him head in The Bench's bathroom. Bad enough that she hadn't even brought her pajamas, and he'd lent her one of his T-shirts. Worse that her perfect ass was pressed so close to him. And that he could tell she wanted sex.

Holy fuck.

He was in over his head.

She wanted to take things slow, she said.

And he'd made enough mistakes with her already.

It wasn't that he wanted to withhold sex. Or torment either of them. But these were uncharted waters with someone he cared about. This wasn't just a new girlfriend spending the night. *It's Lindsay.*

For the first time ever, she said she wanted more than sex—even if she didn't seem to know what that *more* really was.

He was terrified.

Relationships weren't exactly his forte. He never knew quite how to keep a woman happy, as he'd proved so spectacularly with Hannah. But a relationship with Lindsay? And one that had to remain a secret?

She wasn't just some girl he'd recently found himself attracted to.

If he messed this up, where would he go from here?

There would be no other dream girl to move on to.

And you're the guy with a knack for disappointing the people you care about the most.

He drew in a deep breath, then turned onto his side, curling his hand around her waist.

Not that anything had changed with their family situations. Grace's support—which he didn't even know if that was what it was—wouldn't do anything to change how his parents or her family would see this. And he still hadn't told Lindsay about his grandmother's counteroffer for the tourist center plan.

This is never going to work, Travis. You're going to completely screw this up, and it's all going to blow up in your face.

He closed his eyes, inhaling the sweet, flowery scent of the shampoo that she must have used the night before. Didn't matter how many times they'd had sex in the past or the fact that she had a wild side that drove him crazy—something about her was endlessly innocent and alluring.

And she wants to be mine.

Feeling the rising tide of panic in his chest, he slipped out of the bed and pulled on a pair of pajama pants, socks, and a sweatshirt. He'd made Ratchet stay out in the living room the night before, just in case the desire for sex was more than he could handle. The last thing he wanted was a cold, wet nose bumping into his ass while he was in the middle of fucking Lindsay.

He slipped out into the hallway, and Ratchet found him before he could reach the kitchen. He patted him, then went to the fridge and grabbed a couple of sticks of butter.

His favorite pot was under the cabinet, and he pulled it out, then set it on the stove. Unwrapping the butter, he turned on the range and the light on the hood. That would be enough light for him to bake with.

When the butter melted, he added a couple of cups of sugar, then the eggs. He stirred them well, the recipe burned into his brain from when he was a kid.

He already felt better.

By the time he scraped the chocolate batter into the pan, the anxiety in his chest had eased. He pushed the pan into the hot oven and straightened.

"What are you making?"

Lindsay's voice broke into the dark silence of the early morning, and he turned to find her leaning against the counter, wearing his T-shirt and barefooted despite the cold.

His heart gave a flip.

So. Fucking. Gorgeous.

When he didn't answer, she tiptoed into the kitchen and found the bowl. Picking up the spatula, she twisted the curves of that kissable mouth in the hint of a smile. "Brownies?"

"I couldn't sleep. Did I wake you up?"

She shook her head. Then she lifted the spatula to her lips and licked it. Slowly. "Mmm . . . this is good, Travis."

An involuntary groan escaped his throat. "Don't . . ."

She feigned an innocent smile. "Don't what?" Dipping her fingertip into the bowl, she swiped it against the side, then brought the tip of her finger against her lips, pushing it into her mouth slowly, seductively.

Fuck me.

She set the bowl to the side, then hopped up on the counter. "Really, really good." She picked up the spatula again.

He watched her, hardening at the sight of her. He doubted his restraint would hold this time. "Stop."

"Or what?" She licked up the side of the spatula. "Why don't you tell me what you'll do to me?"

He went toward her and tugged the spatula out of her hands. "You're supposed to be sleeping," he said, setting his hands on her hips.

"But I'm not. I woke up alone and wet—"

He silenced her with a kiss, his mouth seizing hers hard, drawing her head down so that her lips slanted over his. Their tongues lashed together, and she slipped her hands down and tugged the sweatshirt off him. He returned the favor by pulling the T-shirt up and yanking it away, leaving her there in a bra and panties.

She curved her hands over the muscles of his arms and shoulders. "That's more like it," she whispered against his lips.

He chuckled, his mouth curving down, over her jaw and throat as his hands moved behind her back, finding the hooks of her bra. "This is what you had in mind tonight?"

"My God, yes." She sucked in a breath as he freed her breasts from the bra. Then he cupped them in his hands. Perfect, voluptuous tits that fit into his palms, the pink nipples hardening at his touch. "Touch me, please . . ."

He pinched one nipple in his fingertips, rolling it between his thumb and forefinger while he leaned her back. Then his mouth found the other nipple, drawing into his lips and sucking hard so that she gave a shattered gasp, trembling with pleasure.

"*Please . . . more . . .*"

He pulled his mouth away and grinned at her. "You asked me to go slow, sweetheart."

"I didn't mean with this."

Lindsay scooted closer to the edge of the counter and wrapped her legs around the bare skin of his waist. As her arms followed around his neck, he lifted her from the counter.

"Bed," she ordered, her mouth colliding with his again.

"I like you bossy."

She pulled her tongue out of his mouth, her fingers digging into his hair. "Get used to it."

Ratchet was two steps behind them, and Travis had to use his leg to block him from following into the room. "Sorry, buddy."

Travis closed the door on his face, then carried Lindsay to the edge of the bed. Setting her down, he stood as she sat up and tugged at his waistband. "Travis," she breathed, panting. "I want you now."

She's going to undo me this way.

But he didn't have to pretend this was their first time either.

He tugged his pants down, freeing himself as she reached for him. Her touch was like fire searing through him. He climbed onto the bed with her, then fished a condom out of the nightstand. With that in place, she straddled him, pushing him back against the pillows.

"I'm going to ride you hard," she said, positioning herself perfectly until she dropped down, and he was inside her.

My God.

He had to restrain himself from exploding his full load into her right there.

Fucking her is amazing.

She was slick with wetness, and he raised his hips to thrust deep inside her as she made slow circles, then lifted and lowered herself once again. "Grab me, baby," she groaned, setting his hands on her breasts.

He couldn't remember if she'd ever been this bossy before, but he loved it.

Because she'd wrecked him each time they'd fucked.

Ruined him for any other woman.

Nothing was as good as this.

No one.

She was why he'd been terrible at relationships—they hadn't been Lindsay. Was that what love was? Travis was convinced it was. *It's just always been her.*

She rode against him harder now, and the moans coming from her were feral as she came closer to coming. He released her breasts and held her hips, rocking her so that she hit tight against the ridge of his pubic bone, and she groaned. "Yes, that's perfect . . ."

Then she released, her insides clenching so tight around him that he came in response, a low growl coming from his throat as he pulsed deep inside her.

They were both out of breath, and she continued to twitch from her orgasm as she collapsed against his chest.

His heart pounded, his body relaxing.

"How is this slow?" he asked, chuckling against her temple.

"You have no idea. I spent half the night waiting for you to fuck me, Travis. It was torture."

He wrapped his arms around her. Her words brought a strange mix of pleasure and guilt. "Linds, whenever you want anything from me, all you need to do is ask. I promise."

CHAPTER TWENTY-SEVEN

A morning of sex with Travis and devouring a pan of brownies might be the perfect way to wake up every day, Lindsay decided as she stepped out of the shower. Travis was already out in the bedroom toweling off. She wrapped the towel tight around her, shivering. They'd taken so long in there together that they'd run out of hot water, but Lindsay had needed to finish rinsing her hair.

She rushed toward the bedroom, and Travis snapped her leg with his towel as she reached her backpack. "Hey!" She scrambled away, laughing, trying to keep her towel on. "Are you trying to whip me?"

He raised his brows and a wicked gleam came to his eyes. "That doesn't sound like a half-bad idea."

Dropping the towel to her waist, she flashed him, and his eyes immediately locked on her breasts. With a grin, she went over to him and tugged the towel away. "It's amazing how easy it can be to disarm a man," she teased, wrapping her arms around his neck.

She kissed him, her heart feeling perfectly blissful as he

cradled her head in his hand, the other hand wrapping around her waist.

I love this.

She felt like an idiot for denying herself this man for so long.

Travis's watch buzzed with a text message and he broke away to check it. "Damn, I should probably get going soon. I have so much baking to do to get caught up for a certain Depot."

She left his side and went to her backpack to grab her clothes. "What about your shop? I feel like you haven't been there for days."

A shadow darkened his face, and he looked away. "Yeah, it does feel like that."

But there's something else . . .

"What is it?" She tugged her bra on, then pulled a sweater over her head.

"Nah, nothing."

She gave him a hard look. "Seriously, Travis. What's going on? Everything okay?"

Travis pulled on a pair of jeans and sighed. "I-I don't know. I don't really know what's been going on. Things have just been unusually slow with the shop lately. It's part of why I'm doing this baking gig for Jen. I have bills to pay, but outside of a couple of oil changes here and there a week, I'm not getting any work. I mean, I know it's winter, but that doesn't usually cause *this* much of a slowdown."

No wonder he's been so stressed. She couldn't imagine that was easy to feel so squeezed. At least in her case, her financial problems were from quitting her job at the bar . . .

She stiffened.

"The Wagners won't like it very much once they realize

what it's like to have someone putting the squeeze on their busi-nesses, mark my words."

Logan's words swam in her mind, and she felt her stomach drop.

Could Logan have something to do with the slow down to Travis's business?

She couldn't know for sure and didn't want to add to the animosity between her brother and Travis—there was already more than enough of that to go around. "I'm so sorry. How long have things been slow?"

"Middle of January? Maybe before then. I guess it started to slow after the holidays, but I didn't notice because it was the new year, and everything seemed slow then. But then slow business became a crawl, and a crawl became nonexistent."

Shit.

This sounded like something deliberate.

She had to talk to Logan.

"Hopefully things will pick up once all this snow melts and spring comes," Lindsay said, giving him a quick kiss. "I've got to go poke around my family's place for a bit, but maybe I can come over to the bakery afterward? I don't think anyone would even blink if I'm there, considering they're so used to seeing me. I can help you. And sneak a kiss when no one's looking."

"They'd probably assume you're there because you want to help Jen out," Travis mused, setting his chin on the top of her head. His voice was a rumble in her ear, and she loved how comfortable it was just standing here in his embrace. "Sure. I'll be busy, but it'll make it more fun."

She smiled, then pulled away. "I'm also thinking I'm going to tell Pops I'm going for an impromptu nighttime sledding jaunt with friends tonight and not to wait up for me, if you don't mind me staying over again."

"First of all, I'm never going to turn down the opportunity

to have you spend the night with me. But why don't we do one better and actually go sledding? This is probably going to be the last good snow before spring, so we may as well have some fun. We can go to my grandmother's farm and crash at the hunting cabin."

The idea of stealing away somewhere with Travis for the night was too tempting a proposition to turn down. "I can probably arrange that. My guess is that school will probably be canceled again tomorrow."

"Then it's a date."

"Aw, our first date." She laughed and went back to her backpack, zipping it up. "We do everything so backward."

"What are you talking about? Our first date was at the senior center over meatloaf."

"I'm not counting that one," Lindsay said, then slung the strap of her backpack over her shoulder.

But the mention of the senior center brought other worries to her mind—the damn committee and everything behind it. Things they didn't discuss when they were in the peaceful bubble in Travis's apartment.

Sooner or later, though, that bubble was going to burst. And they would have to figure it all out before it did.

LINDSAY FOUND Logan in the back storeroom of the restaurant, stacking crates of potatoes. She watched him working for a few moments. How many times had they used this very storeroom for hide-and-seek as kids?

The thought made her want to sigh.

That was back when Logan would indulge Jake's and Lindsay's antics and play with them. There wasn't an enormous gap between them—Mom had all her five kids back-to-back, so

Lindsay was only seven years younger than Logan, even though the gap sometimes felt wider now. Funny how most people said the opposite happened. But since Logan had been a teenager, he'd treated Lindsay and Jake like his younger, annoying siblings. Somewhere in the past couple of years, Jake had managed to graduate and become someone Logan wanted to spend time with as friends.

But Lindsay was convinced he still—and always would— see her as the "baby."

She tapped on the doorframe. "Got a second?"

Logan glanced over his shoulder, startled, then straightened. "Hey, kid. Here for your old job?"

She gritted her teeth at the moniker. "I'm working with Maddie and Naomi now. It's been fun."

"I heard that. Yardley women taking over the Depot, eh?" Logan grinned and wiped his hands on his jeans. "Sounds like a good plan." He came a little closer. "Though you could have given me a bit more notice that you were planning to quit. Losing one of our most experienced bartenders when we're short-staffed as it is hasn't been fun."

"Maybe when you treat your bartenders like thieves, they care just a little less about common courtesy." She crossed her arms, regretting the comment immediately. She wasn't here to fight with him, and the more she came across as being salty, the less likely he'd talk plainly with her.

Logan scanned her face. "You're still upset about the drinking comping thing? Linds . . ." He ran his hand through his hair, pausing at the base of his neck. "Look, I'm sorry about that. I wasn't trying to treat you like a thief. You're the best bartender we had. Luis has been struggling to cover your schedule. And I'm pretty sure Jake must have convinced you to give him the seasonal cocktail recipes because he has no clue what the hell he's doing. But also the reason I had to talk to you about comping is because you did it more than anyone."

"Maybe." She shrugged. "But who do you think taught me that? Pops was way worse than I was when he used to bartend."

"Pops had his way of doing things. I have mine. Doesn't mean what he was doing was the best thing for business."

This is a rabbit hole I don't want to go down.

She bit her tongue, then nodded. "It was time for me to shake things up. The Depot is a lot more fun than I expected it to be."

"Right." Logan turned back toward the crates and lifted one. "So how can I help you?"

How in the world could she approach this? She shifted uncomfortably and came farther into the storeroom. "I have a question, and I need an honest answer."

Logan frowned. "That sounds serious."

"It might be." She sat on a crate, the earthy scent of potatoes oddly comforting. She remembered what it felt like to hide between a row of them. One time, she'd spent so long undiscovered that she'd peed herself waiting for Logan to find her. She chuckled to herself. She couldn't have been more than five years old.

She still remembered getting in trouble for peeing in the storeroom, too.

"I'll always give you an honest answer, Linds, even if you don't particularly like it. That's what big brothers are for."

Weren't big brothers supposed to make you feel valued, too?

Sucking in her lower lip, she tried to think about all the ways she'd phrased this on her walk over here. Of course, she'd been distracted by the trudge through the knee-deep snow and the soreness of her thighs. Even thinking about the number of times she'd had sex this morning made her want to shiver with pleasure.

Get ahold of yourself.

"I don't know that there's a good way to put this, but I was talking to Travis Wagner the other day, and he mentioned that work at his shop had been slow. There aren't any less cars in Brandywood these days, and it got me thinking to something you'd said about the Wagners not liking the tables turned on them. So . . . you wouldn't know anything about what's going on, would you?"

If she'd been hoping that Logan would say, *"Nope, don't know a thing,"* that hope was instantly dashed by the flash of contempt in his eyes. "The son of a bitch is finally noticing it, is he? Hope it hurts deep in the pocketbook."

What? Disgust filled her.

"What did you do?" She crossed her arms, trying not to sound as incensed as she felt.

"I might—might—have started a rumor about the shoddy nature of Travis's work."

Asshole.

"And people believed you?" She gave him a skeptical look. "That's like someone taking advice for the best bet to place from a bookie."

He grimaced. "It might be a bit bigger than that."

"What do you mean?"

"Have you checked out Travis's business page on Google recently?"

She whipped her phone out and typed in Travis's business name. Then she gasped. There were dozens of one-star reviews beside his name.

"Worst service of my life."

"Actually made my car worse."

"Expensive garbage 'mechanic.'"

There was no way Travis knew about this. But, then again, he was a small, local business. She doubted he advertised. He probably didn't even think about looking at his Google listing.

"You review bombed him?" She looked up from her phone.

Logan looked pleased with himself. "That took care of out-of-towners. Even someone broken down in Brandywood won't touch his shop with a ten-foot pole."

She hopped down from the crate. "But locals aren't going to him either, Logan."

"That one was somewhat more complicated. But I ended up hiring that private investigator Jason Cavanaugh is friends with. And guess what he found in Travis's apartment?"

Logan had hired a PI?

And he broke into Travis's apartment? Lindsay had no clue her brother was capable of such underhanded behavior. This was . . . unforgivable.

"I can't believe you did that, Logan. That's so not okay."

"Well, we found something real fun. A sex tape."

Lindsay froze. *Oh God.*

"What?" she whispered, as terror went through her.

"Travis and some girl dressed up in a witch costume."

Oh fuck.

Humiliation poured down her as Logan went on. "Once that got out, you know how folks in town are. The straightlaced were horrified, the church folks wanted to burn him at the stake, and the family types all were sufficiently sickened. And everyone else just needed a little encouragement from my friends who were more than happy to make that rumor about the freaky shit Travis is into grow."

Lindsay felt sick.

Oh my God. Did my brother see a sex tape with me in it?

She was going to be sick.

This might be the worst thing that had ever happened to her.

Or anyone.

"Did you watch it?" she asked, her voice trembling despite her best effort.

Logan made a face. "God, no. I don't want to watch that motherfucker doing that. That's disgusting."

Relief, however small, curled in her belly. *Well, there's that at least.*

But who knew who else had seen it?

Oh no, no, no, no . . .

Her brother had used her sex tape to ruin Travis. She was going to murder him.

"Fix it." Her voice was barely audible.

Logan narrowed his eyes at her. "What?"

She drew closer to him, her rage growing. "Fix it, Logan. Fix it now. You undo everything you did to Travis Wagner."

"Hell no. You know how much money I had to pay that PI?"

"I don't care!" She nearly shouted the words. "You don't dox someone because you don't like what his father is doing to your family business. You could face criminal charges. And it's gross. Fix this! Undo it."

"No!" Then Logan stepped forward, scanning her features. "Why do you care so much what happens to Travis Wagner?" Logan's eyes smoldered with fury.

"I care because what you're doing is wrong." Lindsay gritted her teeth, willing herself not to get emotional now. Her tears wouldn't affect her brother anyway. He would only see them as a sign of weakness. "Because you're better than this behavior. It's low and immoral and not at all the way our family has done things. It's disappointing. But I guess I should get used to that from you." She turned to go, her lungs searing for oxygen from the shallow breaths she'd been taking.

"What the fuck is that supposed to mean?" Logan growled

and grabbed her arm, blocking the doorway to the back entrance with his body. "*I'm* disappointing?"

She yanked her arm away. "Yeah, Logan. You. You're not this business hotshot with your fancy degree that you think you are. Pops built this restaurant with a high school diploma. And you know how he did it? By giving a shit about the people in this town. Taking the time to talk to every person who came through that door. Whether or not they like him, every person in this town can tell you Peter Yardley would be the first to hand you money, no questions asked, if you needed it. His bottom line grew because he knew that *people* mattered more than profit."

She stepped closer to him and, for the first time in her life, she saw Logan shrink as she spoke. "You've come in here like the good idea fairy, thinking you can make all these changes to run things better. Wanting to put your own particular brand on this place. Well, your brand smells like shit, Logan, because that's what it is. You don't need to improve the restaurant and bar to be significant. You want to make your mark? Then get creative, bud, because you're not going to win at a head-to-head competition with something Pops already made great. You're going to have to do your own thing somewhere else."

Logan's gaze turned icy. "You think you can do any better, Linds?"

"I do. And I'm coming for you. No one even considered that I might be able to run this business better than you, but I'm going to change their minds. So I'd advise you to look out and get out of my way."

Logan let out a short, frustrated breath but didn't move. "You have no idea how underwater this restaurant was when I took over, Linds. No clue. Because you live in this fairy land and everyone doesn't want to tell you when things are bad because you don't handle bad news well. But Pops spent so much time focusing on the Depot that he basically abandoned the business side of the restaurant. We were bleeding money. Then he spent so much time focusing on the television show that the Depot was being run like monkeys were in charge until Maddie and Naomi straightened it all out. Pops might be brilliant when it comes to personality and ideas, but his execution is unsustainable."

His words slammed her through her core, but she didn't flinch.

Is it possible?

Was she as naive as Logan taunted? Or had she just not paid attention?

Either way, she needed to face the truth. "Get out of my way," she repeated, trying to look as determined as possible. "And undo what you did to Travis. Or I will never forgive you."

To her surprise, Logan stepped to the side. "Fine, run. That's what you do in the face of adult problems anyway. I'm not your enemy, Lindsay. I have no idea what's gotten into you. But I'm going to find out."

CHAPTER TWENTY-EIGHT

ONE LOOK at Lindsay told Travis that something was terribly wrong.

He was halfway through piping a tray of choux pastry for éclairs when he spotted her come into the kitchen, her face pale and hands shaking.

Setting down the pastry bag, he nodded toward Elise, one of Jen's assistants. "Be right back."

He scooted around the workstation, then grabbed Lindsay by the elbow. "Jen doing okay?" he asked, hauling her back toward Jen's office.

Lindsay gave him a startled look, then folded into his arms as he closed the door. "Why? What else happened? Did Jason say something happened to Jen?" She looked like she was on the verge of tears.

"No, you crazy woman." He kissed her temple. "You just came in here looking like someone just kicked your puppy, and I didn't want the workers out there to think you were coming to me for comfort. You know, secret relationship and everything. What happened?"

She sniffed and pulled away, then swallowed hard. "Promise me you won't kill Logan."

Travis drew his brows together slowly.

What?

"Why?" He raised her chin with his thumb and forefinger. "What did he do to you?"

Moistening her lips, she scanned his eyes, looking like a terrified bird. "Technically, he did it to you. Promise me." Her chin trembled.

He hated making promises he didn't know if he could keep. "I promise." Then he leaned forward and pressed a soft kiss to her lips. *That doesn't mean I won't severely maim him if he did hurt you.*

"Well, I know why your business is failing."

Something darker unfurled in him now.

Logan?

God, I should have known.

Travis stepped back from her, his shoulders going rigid. "What'd he do?"

"Check your Google listing." She held her hands over her torso as though she was going to throw up.

With a frown, he pulled out his phone, then googled himself.

The star rating caught his attention before he even saw his name.

What the fuck?

He raised his eyes from the phone, rage clawing at the back of his throat. "He did this?"

"He did."

No fucking wonder my business is dying.

He snapped his gaze at her. "I might have to break my promise to you."

He'd worked so hard. Built the shop in the face of his family's objections.

And now he was on the verge of failing because of Logan fucking Yardley?

"That's not the worst thing he did," Lindsay whispered.

She seemed even paler now, if that was possible. He crossed the space between them, setting his hands on her shoulders. "What'd he do?"

She closed her eyes, tears slipping out of her eyes and onto her cheeks. "You're going to kill him, Travis. Please. Please, I'm begging you. You have to not do anything. I know it's going to seem impossible but—"

"What. Did. He. Do?" Travis was seething now.

He was going to find Logan Yardley and beat him to a pulp.

"Remember the tape we made a few years ago? At Halloween?"

The rest of Lindsay's words seemed to fall away to the ringing that rose sharply in his ears.

Oh, holy fuck, no.

Travis clenched his jaw, his blood pressure rising.

How in the hell had Logan gotten his hands on that? Only one copy had existed, and Travis had kept it closely guarded until he'd given it back to Lindsay a couple of weeks earlier. "Did he steal it from you?"

"No. He hired a PI to get it. He must have broken into your place."

What. The. Fuck? He had someone break into my place?

"Are you fucking kidding me?" Travis's mind spun. *Why the fucking hell would he do that?* "Then I'm going to put that motherfucker's ass in jail."

Tears streaked her face. "You can't. God, Travis, I know. I know you're mad. I'm furious. I want to kill him myself, but that would destroy my family and bring more attention to the tape and—"

"Like he's destroying my life? What the fuck do you expect me to do, Lindsay? Bend over and let him fucking rape me?" Travis's chest heaved. What was he even supposed to do with this information?

Logan Yardley hated him, but breaking into his house? Could he go to the cops? *How the hell can I reverse the damage done to me?* Who the hell had seen it?

"No." She shook her head. "No, I know. I know what he did is illegal and wrong and horrible, and I'm not asking for you to like him or forgive him or anything. I . . . will never forgive him, Travis. Never." She held his face in her hands, and a sob shook her shoulders. "This is why, why things can't go anywhere between us. Because every time, every-*fucking*-time, this stuff gets in the way. I can't expect you to ever want to be around my family. What are we going to do, have the Red freaking Wedding? Have my dad punch your dad over the sweetheart table?"

Her words were somehow equally as endearing as they were depressing. The fact that she thought of him at all in a way that led to wedding bells made him want to grab her and run away with her, hard and fast, away from the town and all the madness.

But she was also right.

He wanted to rip Logan Yardley's heart from his chest.

And it would do nothing but cost him any chance he had with Lindsay.

Strangely calmer, he pulled her into his arms and wiped her tears from her cheeks. "We'll figure it out. It'll be fine."

"How is it going to be fine? I'm never going to be able to look anyone in this town in the eye again. Oh my God, Travis, people have seen that video. They've seen *us. Together.*" She shuddered, then buried her face in his chest. "Why did you keep that video?"

"I don't know." Travis winced, feeling the sting of his share of the blame. He'd thought about getting rid of it more than once, but he couldn't bring himself to do it.

If he couldn't have Lindsay Yardley, he wouldn't force himself to get rid of the memory of her in his arms.

He held her closer. "It's going to be okay. We'll fix this. You and me."

He sounded more confident than he felt.

Because Lindsay was right. How in the hell were they ever going to solve this rift between their families?

CHAPTER TWENTY-NINE

By the time they pulled into the hunting cabin at the Durand farm, Lindsay felt more settled. She nestled against Travis's arm, and Ratchet stuck his nose forward from the back seat of Travis's truck. "It's so dark out here."

"In the summer, it's one of the best places for seeing the stars." Travis killed the engine. "No one in my family ever comes here, though, which will work out nicely for us."

"Ugh, I'm so tired from all that baking that I don't know if I'm even up for sledding tonight," she admitted, pushing open the heavy truck door. "I don't know how you stand it. My back is killing me."

"Yeah, well, I don't really. Not usually. Baking at home is a lot different from baking professionally. I prefer to keep it as a hobby." Travis climbed out of the truck and opened the back door to the cab to let Ratchet out, who bounded into the undisturbed snow. "Besides, I have no idea how *you* do what you do. Eight hours of toddlers?"

"Best birth control out there." She laughed and pulled out

her overnight bag, then helped him with the cooler he'd brought.

"You still want kids, though, right?" Travis asked, almost casually.

She grinned at him. "Are you checking to make sure we want the same things?" Before he could answer, she said, "And yes, I want a big family. I grew up in one. And even though I currently am considering murdering my eldest brother, I usually love it."

"Don't remind me." They took big steps to get to the front door of the cabin. The snow drifts seemed deeper here somehow—maybe because no one was around to clear them. Travis cleared some snow away from the doorknob, then took out a key.

"I'm trying not to think about it. It's almost enough to make me want to switch sides on this whole feud thing if it wouldn't end up completely screwing everyone else in my family." Lindsay blinked as Travis flipped on the light, then stepped over the mound of snow blocking the doorway.

When he'd mentioned his family's hunting cabin, she'd imagined a one-room log cabin with a wood-burning stove in the corner. This was more like a rustic tiny house. The door opened up to a living room with vaulted ceilings, a large window on one side that she imagined let in gorgeous amounts of natural light during the day. No television, but a stone fireplace graced the center of the room, which had cozy sofas and chairs with neatly folded plaid blankets. A small but adequate kitchen was off to one side, divided from the living room by a bar-top counter with stools.

A stairwell led to a large upstairs loft with a balcony—the bedroom.

The whole thing was open air and beautiful.

Why doesn't Travis's family use this place?

"I can't believe your family doesn't come here."

Travis shrugged. "Dad hates it. I don't have time for hunting. And Grace—well, she used to come up here to paint or slip away with a friend or two, but then she stopped coming." He set the cooler down in the kitchen and slid his bag onto the counter. "Mom's probably the one who comes the most, just to dust and vacuum it and clean the bathrooms, but that's maybe every four months."

She peeled off her coat. There weren't any family photos here, nothing overly personal. They could even rent it if they wanted to.

"And your grandmother doesn't come here at all? She inherited the land from her parents, right?"

Travis leaned over and unlaced his boots. "She did. But I don't think she has the fondest memories of her childhood. She doesn't talk about her parents a lot. And when the old farmhouse started to need more upkeep, she chose to tear it down instead of sinking any money into it."

Trying to picture Bunny Wagner as a young woman or a girl was hard enough. But for so long, Lindsay had seen her as a pleasant—though not particularly warm to her family—typical grandmother that she'd never really thought about her past. "It's kind of weird to think about how our grandparents have known each other forever, isn't it? Especially after what Millie said."

A tired look crossed Travis's face, and he came closer. "I've been meaning to try to find out more about that."

"I asked my grandfather, who said your grandmother was one of the girls he dated when he was young. But he made it seem like it wasn't a big deal." Lindsay shrugged, then went to his side and unbuttoned his jacket.

"That's not at all how my mom made it sound." Travis's expression was thoughtful, his eyes darkening. "Why don't we not talk about our families while we're here? Leave the outside world out for a bit?"

She moved closer, trailing her lips along his jaw. "I think I can agree to that. We should probably figure out a time to talk to Brian about the Depot situation again, though. It's already been almost two weeks. We're running out of time to come up with a plan."

"My plan," Travis said and interlaced his hands with hers. He edged her back until her back hit what appeared to be a closet door. "Is to convince you to run away from here with me."

"My family might have something to say about that."

She raised her hands to slip them around his neck when he grabbed her wrists again, pinning her hands above her head on the door with one hand. Pushing his length against her, he slid the other hand down her waist, then over her ass until he had a firm grip on the back of her leg, which he hiked up around his hip.

He lowered his lips to hers with an intense, punishing force. His tongue lashed against hers, his mouth bruising her lips with such raw desire that she groaned. He pulled back just slightly, and whispered, "No family." Then his lips returned to hers, his fingertips deftly moving toward the button of her jeans.

He set her leg down, then unzipped the pants and knelt, tugging them off her legs. His rough palms caressed up her calves, then thighs, hooking on the fabric of her thong, which he gave an appreciative look at. "I've been dying to taste you all day," he growled, pulling it away.

Sweet heaven.

She leaned her head back, her core pooling with slick wetness as he lifted her leg over his shoulder. Every fiber of her body wanted to have his lips on her, feel his tantalizing touch.

He parted her with his fingers, his thumb finding her clit and giving it a swipe that made her buckle against him.

He leaned forward and pressed a kiss to that spot, then trailed his tongue lower.

"You're so delicious."

God, yes.

"Please," she whimpered, and he smiled then rewarded her by returning his mouth to her. Two fingers glided deep inside her, and she tangled her fingers in his hair, gripping his head as electric heat rose in her body.

She wanted him.

All of him. "I want you to fuck me."

"I will, baby. I promise."

"Oh God," she groaned, her hips rising against him. "No, I want—I want you now, Travis. Please fuck me. I want all of you. Nothing between us."

Travis lifted his gaze at her, then pulled back. He sucked his lower lip in, his eyes dark and hot with desire. "Nothing?"

She nodded, and he stood, then stripped her of her remaining clothing. His own came off with ease, and he returned to her. "Flip over." He turned her, grabbing her by the breasts and giving her nipples a pinch. Bringing her hips out from the wall, he leaned her forward and positioned himself behind her. "Hold tight, sweetheart. I'm going to fuck you hard."

She gasped as he drove deep inside her until he was fully buried, and he let out a groan of carnal pleasure. "My God, you're fucking incredible, Lindsay. You're so tight and wet, baby. I could fuck you all day."

"I want you to," she panted as he reached forward and grabbed her breast. He thrust deeply inside her again, and she let out a cry. "I want you to fuck me until we can't stand."

They found a rhythm together, with Travis thrusting

deeply, fucking her so hard that it felt like he wanted to mold their bodies forever, be one with her like never before. When his hand left her breast and reached for her clit again, an intense orgasm exploded from her without warning, but he didn't let go.

"Come for me, baby. Keep coming."

Fuck, yes.

So good . . .

She rose to oblivion, melting in his hands, and he held her upright, then reached for her hands. "I'm going to come inside you, baby."

Still spasming and forfeiting to the pleasure, she reached between her legs and grabbed him. Then he gave a wild moan and pulsed deep inside her, letting go.

They returned to earth together, out of breath, their bodies still joined as she straightened, then pulled away from him. He had a dizzy expression on his face, and she kissed him, smiling. "Being with you like that . . ." He shook his head. "You may have ruined me to anyone else."

"Right back at you." She laughed and then gave the front door a rueful look. "Still want to go sledding?"

"Fuck, no."

A scratch at the door followed by a bark got their attention. Travis's eyes widened. "Holy fuck, Ratchet."

He opened the door, and Ratchet ran inside, his snow jacket and boots encrusted, tail wagging.

"I'm the worst dog parent ever," Travis said with a horrified look on his face.

Lindsay winced and pulled her sweater back on, which was long enough to cover her waist. "I don't know, he looks pretty happy. He couldn't have been out there more than ten minutes."

The guilt didn't leave Travis's expression as he fished his

pants from the pile of their discarded clothes. "You're distracting me, Lindsay Yardley." He shook his head. "Making me think of only one thing. Need something?" He pointed toward the bathroom.

She chuckled and went over to the bathroom, which was off the kitchen and had the door open. Grabbing a wad of toilet paper, she cleaned herself up and glanced in the mirror, saw her messy hair and bare legs.

He's not wrong.

They were distracting each other.

A tiny smile curved her lips.

But when she was with him, she felt like a sex goddess. Like she had some magical power she'd never had before. Travis made her feel whole and competent, like she could do anything.

And he treated her like a woman. Not an irresponsible girl.

Great, now I'm elevating fucking Travis to making it the source of some secret strength.

Then again, other people could make you stronger.

Maybe apart from each other, they couldn't necessarily face the obstacles in their way. But together, they could help each other climb. Lean down and give the other a hand when they needed it.

Together might be a source of strength. She didn't want to do it alone. Alone hadn't been working out for her. Not with her family, not with this committee, and not with the feud situation.

She needed Travis Wagner.

She came out of the bathroom and found him petting Ratchet and building a fire in the fireplace. "Your turn." She grabbed her thong and socks from the clothes. Pants didn't seem necessary, especially considering they'd probably wind up off her again soon enough.

"I cleaned up in the kitchen with a paper towel," he confessed with a smile. "I needed to find Ratchet a treat to apologize."

"He really doesn't seem to be any worse for the wear, but I get it." She sank onto the sofa and covered her legs with a blanket, curling them up on the couch. "You know, those times we were worried about hooking up at your place—you should have just brought me here."

Travis laughed and balled up a piece of newspaper to put under some kindling. "I think I was more worried about just getting you back to my place quick. Didn't want you to change your mind."

"I wasn't going to change my mind. I wanted it just as much as you did." Lindsay stretched, feeling satiated and happy. "You make me happy, Travis. You always have. It was stupid for me not to let myself be happy."

He lit the fire and then joined her. A moment later, Ratchet jumped on the couch beside her and lay his head on her lap. "I think he has a favorite," Travis said, leaning back against the cushions. He rubbed Ratchet's head. "She's my favorite, too, bud. But I'm willing to share."

"So . . ." Lindsay reached over and took his hand, interlacing their fingers. "Are we dating? Is that what this is for you? Because, in some ways, things have happened so fast."

Travis smiled, then kissed the back of her fingers. "Maybe for you. I've been praying you'd come to your senses for a while. But yes, I'd call you my girlfriend if I was allowed."

His girlfriend. The idea warmed her.

"Oh stop. It's not like you were out there pining for me." She scooted over, then leaned against him.

What will the fallout be?

Given the terrible thing Logan did to Travis through the PI —*she would never get over his hateful, unspeakable behavior*—

she couldn't imagine how he'd react to her dating Travis. But since he'd put a personal target on Travis's business and inadvertently involved her, something needed to be done soon. Did Travis even have a plan?

Pressure closed around her heart. "I know I'm not allowed to talk about family, but—"

"Clearly, I didn't do a good job punishing you."

She quirked a brow at him. "If that's how you punish me, I'll probably just be encouraged to do it more."

His chuckle was low. "True. I may have to rethink my punishments."

She pulled the blanket up higher, forcing Ratchet to adjust his head. "I didn't really notice how cold it was in here until you lit that fire," she said, rubbing at the goosebumps on her skin.

"That would be the result of no one staying here. Mom keeps the thermostat set high enough so that the pipes don't freeze in the winter, but not much warmer than that. I'd put it higher, but that's one way she might notice we're here. She had Dad switch it out to a smart thermostat a few years ago so she could monitor the temperature from the comfort of home."

Lindsay tilted her head back on his chest, sleepy. They'd had a crazy night, followed by a long morning in bed. Better to hold off on her question about Logan. *For now*.

"Is all the furniture the same as when your grandfather used this as an actual hunting cabin?" If so, it explained why, though comfortable, it all looked a bit dated.

"No, my grandmother switched it all out years ago. Not sure why, considering she doesn't like to come here." He cleared his throat, then shifted, curling his arm around her. "All right. I know I said no family, but I have something I need to tell you."

That doesn't sound good.

She pushed away slightly and scanned his face. *God, he looks so sexy with a five o'clock shadow.* "What's that?"

"My grandmother said she might be willing to sell the land here."

Lindsay blinked, stunned. *For my tourist center?* "Really?" That had been surprisingly easy. If she could just get Brian to agree to it, even without Travis's agreement, she might be able to put some sort of plan together to present to the town council—

"But there's a catch."

Disappointment stabbed at her. "I should have known. What is it?"

"She says she'll only sell it if your family agrees to move the Depot here. Not a tourist center. And I think she's willing to sell the land directly to your grandfather."

"Oh."

Then it wasn't in support of her plan.

It wasn't even close.

"My family will never agree to that, Travis." She sat up straighter, wishing he hadn't brought the subject up right now. Logan, she could agree with him about, and they could vent and make a plan to take down together.

"And that's her final offer? She won't consider anything else?" Lindsay kept her voice steady, trying to hide her disappointment.

Travis held her gaze. "It's not a bad offer, babe. We may have to think outside the tourist center idea. I'm not putting down your plan, but there are a lot of logistics involved that may not be realistic."

"Because you're being narrow-minded about it." She twisted away and stood, releasing a frustrated breath. *I just want to get away from this whole situation.* "Let's go sledding. Before we end up arguing, and I end up just wanting to leave." And that was when Lindsay heard Logan's voice again.

"*Fine, run. That's what you do in the face of adult problems anyway.*"

Is that what I'm doing here? Running? Escaping the conversation?

If Travis was mad at her, though, he didn't say. If anything, his unreadable expression indicated he was done talking about it, too.

She wasn't going to think or talk about it.

This isn't running.

This is just enjoying a damn night with my boyfriend.

Right?

CHAPTER THIRTY

April 2003

BERNADETTE HADN'T INTENDED to be here.

She didn't really know what she was doing, riding in Peter's car, heading toward the cabin.

But she knew exactly what was waiting in that cabin.

Sex. Infidelity. Broken hearts.

Everything she'd tried to avoid for over thirty years. Tried to stay away from.

It had started innocently enough. She'd never sought Peter out on purpose. Never tried to disrupt his life.

And, in the end, he'd been the only person in this town she knew would get her through this. He'd said he would be there for her if she ever needed him.

She shivered, equally with fear as anticipation, unsure about how she should feel about the whole thing.

If John only knew. Picturing the look on his face was weirdly satisfying.

He deserved everything that was coming for him.

Peter turned down the radio—a Celine Dion song played softly in the background—and reached over, touching her hand gently. "It'll be okay."

He was sweet like that. Always considerate. Kind.

I made the biggest mistake of my life not marrying him.

The jealousy she'd felt toward Marion Yardley through the years was unreasonable. It'd been Bernadette's own doing. She'd been angry and stupid and so devastated when Peter had left. And then, when she'd gotten the news Robbie had died, she'd shattered. She couldn't let herself go through that again. Couldn't let the damn war rob her of one more thing she loved.

In time, John had convinced her he loved her.

The man certainly had known how to show her a good time.

Worthless, sex-addicted good-for-nothing.

She would show him now, though.

Peter released her hand, returning it to the steering wheel.

Maybe all roads led back to Peter Yardley on purpose.

They passed a Red Volkswagen, and Bernadette stiffened, making eye contact with the driver.

Marion Yardley.

Peter hadn't appeared to have noticed her as he was flipping through the radio stations, but Bunny glanced in her passenger side mirror and held her breath.

What if she saw?

Marion had to recognize her own husband's car, didn't she?

Bernadette stared at the brake lights as they turned red . . .

TEARS POOLED IN HER VISION. *How? How did this happen?* She could barely see the wreckage in front of her. It had only been thirty minutes since she and Peter had been on this road. *We weren't at the cabin for more than fifteen minutes.*

Why had Marion been on the road? *Surely she couldn't have known . . .*

It felt as though one second ago, Bernadette had been riding in the passenger seat. Now she was here.

She tried to remember the between.

The violent scene at the cabin. The yelling. The way John had hopped in his car and sped away. *God, he was driving like a maniac. Enraged.*

No wonder he'd hit Marion.

Blinking, Bernadette stared at the mangled brake lights, barely hearing the siren's wail around her. The ambulances loaded both bodies, but the officer said that Marion and John had died on impact. Head-on collision.

How could I have known?

Peter wept beside her, a man bereft.

She should have told Peter she'd seen Marion on the road.

But she hadn't.

She'd been selfish.

Didn't want to worry him.

He'd been happy before this.

She'd ruined his life. Ruined so many things.

CHAPTER THIRTY-ONE

THE HUNTING CABIN had turned out to be the perfect place to have a secret relationship with the girl of his dreams.

Travis turned his truck onto the gated road that led to the cabin and stopped. He hopped out of the cab and walked up to the lock on the metal gate, pulling his key out of his pocket.

The rest of the school week had been canceled, and Lindsay had called out from her new job at the Depot with her sisters, telling them she'd decided to go skiing for a few days with friends for her snow days. She had no desire to be around anyone in town, thanks to Logan's tape distribution, and he didn't blame her, though he tried to comfort her with the fact that, unlike him, no one knew her identity in the video.

Travis still needed to do the work at the bakery, which meant that he'd been forced to drive in every day for about eight hours, but Lindsay just stayed at the cabin, happily reading books.

By Sunday, their routine had become so familiar that it almost felt like they'd moved into the cabin together and were playing house.

But the snow was melting, and fast. The weather had warmed significantly in the past few days, as though March had come, and Mother Nature realized it was no longer time for blizzard-like conditions.

Travis was in the process of unlocking the gate when a car pulled up beside his truck, and he gave a sharp look up. Then his jaw tightened as he saw the driver.

Jake Yardley.

What was that asshole doing here? Even though it had been Logan, and not Jake, who had distributed that video and sank his business, Travis wouldn't be surprised if Jake not only was aware of Logan's efforts but also fully supported them.

Jake got out of the car. "We need to talk, Travis."

Travis stalked toward him, not bothering to offer a greeting. "You've got fucking nerve coming here after what your family did to my business, distributing my private business to the entire fucking town."

"You know about the tape?" Jake grimaced, rubbing his neck. "I swear I didn't have anything to do with it. Logan only told me about it afterward. I swear I'm here in good faith."

Travis stepped closer, menacing. "You have one minute. Or I'm calling the police for trespassing. Maybe even breaking and entering."

Jake's eyes narrowed. "Look, I'm here to do you a favor. Really, to do my sister a favor because I owe her. And I happen to care about what happens to her. Logan has been trying to find out where Lindsay has been the past few days. And he knows she's been at your family cabin. He's on his way here—probably only a few minutes behind me. I've been trying to call and text her, but she hasn't picked up her goddamn phone."

Fuuuuuck.

Travis froze, trying to process what he'd said. "How does he know she's here?"

"We live in a small town, Wagner. People are bound to notice shit. Put two and two together. And you've been coming out here every day after work." Jake's face was red still.

Travis bolted toward the gate and pulled it open. "Get the hell out of here. Unless you want Logan to know you were trying to warn Lindsay."

Jake looked conflicted, as though he thought maybe he should stay, but then nodded and got back into his car and pulled away, going the opposite direction of the town.

Travis didn't know what to think about Jake's actions. For him to come all this way to warn Lindsay, though, meant a couple of things. One, he was truly worried about what might happen. And two, Logan was clearly infuriated.

Travis hopped back into his truck. He considered getting out to close and lock the gate again, but there wasn't time.

He slammed his foot on the pedal, and the tires spun in the mud that had taken the place of melting snow. At last, they stuck on solid ground, and the truck lurched forward.

Shit, shit, shit.

He grabbed his phone and dialed Lindsay, but the call didn't go through, thanks to Brandywood's notoriously terrible reception.

"Come on!" He slapped his hand against the steering wheel.

Just what does Logan know?

He should have asked Jake.

And if he does know anything, do we really want to keep denying things?

He pulled up in front of the cabin a few minutes later and ran inside.

Lindsay was in the kitchen, stirring a pot on the stove, holding a glass of red wine in the other hand. She wore only one of his sweaters, which hung to about mid-thigh, and a pair of socks. The neck of his sweater hung over one shoulder, exposing a black bra strap. Her honey-blond hair was in a pony-tail, and she had light makeup on. Her cheeks were probably flushed from the heat of the stove.

She's so beautiful.

I love this woman.

Ratchet gave a happy bark, getting up from his place at her feet. She grinned when she saw Travis. "Hey, I decided to make—" She stopped short, seeing the alarm on his face. "What's wrong?"

"Logan's on his way here."

The wineglass slipped from her fingers, tumbling to the floor with a crash. A red stain started across the hardwood, and fear crept into her eyes. "What? How?"

"I-I don't know. Jake pulled up as I was unlocking the gate and told me."

"Jake?" Lindsay peered at him as though she was trying to make sense of his words.

"Yeah, exactly."

"Oh my God. Is Jake still here?"

"No, he left. I don't think he wanted Logan to know he came to warn you."

Lindsay reached over and grabbed a wad of paper towels. She dropped it on the floor. "Wh-what are we going to do?" Fear shone in her eyes. "Travis, he's going to kill you. Oh shit, he's going to kill me."

Travis took a calming breath, trying to think clearly. Then he grabbed Ratchet by the collar and shoved him into the bath-room, closing the door. The last thing he wanted was his dog getting hurt, thinking they were being attacked.

He crossed the space toward Lindsay and pulled her into his arms. "It's going to be fine. We'll be okay."

A car door slammed outside.

Lindsay went rigid and he felt her heart pounding against his shirtfront.

She's terrified.

Maybe legitimately so.

Then pounding on the front door. "Lindsay! Open the fucking door. I know you're there." Ratchet barked from the bathroom, right on cue.

She didn't answer, closing her eyes and burying her face in Travis's chest.

Logan pounded on the door again. "Open up!" More barking from Ratchet, this time followed with a scratch on the door.

"Get the fuck out of here, Logan. Before I call the cops," Travis called out, holding Lindsay closer.

"Open the door, Wagner. You think you can just fuck around with my sister and then hide? Open the door. We're going to settle this face-to-face."

Neither of them moved.

Then another voice chimed in. "Lindsay. Sweetie, open the door. It's Dad."

Oh God. Not that.

He had no problem flipping off Logan and telling him to go eat a dick. But Lindsay's dad? Larry Yardley was a surprisingly soft-spoken man—not at all like his father, who was a loud-mouth. Travis guessed he'd inherited that trait from Marion Yardley, who was remembered by most as a kind, quiet woman.

And if he wanted any shot at all with Lindsay after this, pissing off her dad wasn't the best way to go about it.

Travis peeled away from Lindsay and set his hands on her shoulders. "I have to open the door, Linds."

"No—" Her eyes darted back and forth, searching his gaze. "Please don't. They'll go away. What are they going to do, knock down the door?"

"Logan might. And I don't need your dad hating me any more than he already does."

Lindsay's face was pale. After a second, she nodded. "Fine. I'll open it." Her hands trembled. She smoothed back her hair, then looked down at her bare legs.

Her eyes flicked up the stairs to the bedroom, where her clothes were likely scattered on the floor, as though she contemplated getting them.

Then she sighed, her expression more resolute. She moved toward the door and stopped at it, her hand on the knob. "Daddy?"

"That you, Lindsay?"

"I'm only opening the door if Logan promises not to hurt Travis."

"He'll behave himself. We're just worried about you."

Lindsay unlocked it, then turned the knob. She opened the door and stepped aside as her father and Logan entered the doorway.

Larry removed his hat, then glanced at the cabin, taking it in.

On the other hand, Logan locked eyes with Travis, staring at him menacingly.

Lindsay left the doorway and drew closer to Travis. "Daddy, I can explain—"

"Get your things, Lindsay. I'm taking you home," Larry said, little emotion in his voice.

"Dad, I'm not going anywhere. I'm an adult. Who I decide to be with is no one's business but my own."

"Are you an idiot, Linds?" Logan glared at her. "You think Travis Wagner doesn't know exactly what he's doing here? You get tasked by the town council to work together on his family's sabotage of our business, then he convinces you not to speak about it to us. Then because that's not enough and he knows just how he can manipulate you, he decides to fuck you so you feel sympathetic to him and do what he and his family want. He's *using* you, Lindsay."

That would be what Logan would assume.

"You're wrong," Travis said, trying to keep his own anger at bay. "I love her. I've loved her for a long time, Logan. Sorry if that's not convenient for you."

Logan threw back his head and gave a snide, sarcastic laugh. "Are you kidding me, man? You might have deluded my sister with your bullshit, but you're insane if you think I'm buying that. You were just dating Hannah Strickland a few weeks ago. Took her to my restaurant for Valentine's Day."

"I fell in love with her years ago, Logan."

"Did you know he's on some sort of hookup app? Was actively looking for hookups just a couple of weeks ago, Lindsay. I poked around on it to see what I could find out about it. Ended up chatting to a girl who said they were sexting like a week or two ago. *And* he stood her up twice. And this is the sort of guy you want to be with?"

Lindsay's gaze had snapped to him, shock written on her face.

Travis felt his mouth go dry. Lindsay knew about the app, of course, but how to explain Ashley's messages? He couldn't say he hadn't invited them, but then again, he and Lindsay had agreed to stay away from each other. "You still hiring a PI to find dirt on me?"

"You're what, Logan?" Lindsay's dad asked.

Logan crossed his arms, maybe to flex his strength. He also ignored his father completely, his eyes flickering at Lindsay with anger. "You live in a small town, Wagner. You think other people aren't on that app? And once you're spotted, and someone talks . . . let's just say running a bar is an easy way to know everything that's going on in town." *Fucking asshole. It's probably how he found Lindsay.*

He turned toward Lindsay, an apology on his mind. *Logan can go fuck himself.*

"You love me?" Lindsay whispered as though still stuck on that part of Travis's response.

Shit. I never intended for the first time I said I loved her to be like this.

"No, he doesn't love you, Lindsay. I told you about that tape. Even if he weren't a Wagner, I wouldn't want him within a twenty-foot radius of any of my sisters, let alone the most innocent and easiest one to take advantage of."

Travis did look bad. No way around it. Unless they explained the full story to him.

"That's not exactly the way of it," Travis said, narrowing his eyes.

Logan crossed his arms. "Then explain it. Make it make sense."

Travis's gaze met Lindsay's. Was she ready to tell Logan and her father the truth?

He wanted her to say it was okay. To give him the ability to defend himself and not feel like he was exposing her in the process. But he wasn't sure if, by doing so, he would be hurting her, too. "Linds?" He took her hand. "Want me to tell them?"

She swallowed hard, her hands still shaking, then looked at her father. Shame crept into her face.

She's not ready.

Shit.

His chest constricted, not because he feared Logan Yardley or cared what he or Lindsay's father thought of him.

A sharp, shooting pain tore through his chest, and he could hardly breathe.

Because I love her, but she may not love me.

And even if she does care about me . . . she might not care about me enough.

The pain in his chest clouded his vision, and he felt sick.

Larry Yardley folded his hands in front of him. "I'm not sure what you were hoping to accomplish, Lindsay. You said you wanted to prove how responsible you were a few weeks ago, but you quit your job with Logan without giving him reasonable notice, and now you disappeared and lied to Maddie and Naomi about why you were skipping work, lied to your grandfather, and snuck around with Travis?"

He lowered his chin, looking down at her. "I have to say, I was impressed with the work you've been doing at the Depot and with the committee, but I'm worried about Travis's influence on you."

Lindsay's face fell, her eyes filling with shame.

The truth of her father's words had to be killing her. "I'm sorry, Daddy, I just—"

"He's manipulating you," Logan said, his anger brewing hotter.

"That's not true." Lindsay wiped the corners of her eyes with the back of her hand. She sniffed, then raised her chin. "But it doesn't matter what I say. You're never going to believe anything other than what you want to believe. The line in the sand was drawn a long time before we were born, and you're only too happy to stay on one side of it, no matter what. *Nothing* I can do will ever change anything, right? Wagners and Yardleys hate each other. Until forever ends."

"The Wagners will always hate *us*, Lindsay. Facts. Todd Wagner blames Dad for his father's death, on top of a whole host of other things," Lindsay's father said with a frown. "That's never going to change. Travis knows it, too. Even if we didn't have more than enough reason to be suspicious of Travis, I'm sure Travis is aware that his father would never allow you to walk through his front door. I'd personally be worried about his reaction to Travis bringing you here."

What did he say?

"Todd Wagner blames Dad for his father's death?"

As in, Peter Yardley?

His brain spun.

His eyes swiveled to Larry Yardley, whose lips were set to a firm, thin line. "What's that about my dad blaming yours for Grandpa's death?"

Larry frowned, then cleared his throat as though he realized he'd said something he ought not have. "If he hasn't told you, then it's not my place to say anything more. I suggest you talk to your father."

His words made Travis's skin crawl.

What is Dad hiding from me?

"Let's go home, Lindsay. This isn't a good situation for you, sweetheart," Lindsay's father said gently.

Travis was dimly aware of Lindsay releasing his hand and stepping away from him. "I have to go, Travis."

His throat clenched, and he looked her straight in the eye, desperation poking its way through his clouded thoughts. "Don't . . ."

Love me, Lindsay. Love me as much as I love you.

Care more about me than you care about them.

We can face it together.

I need you.

The past few days had been like a dream. Them versus the world in the safety of this cabin.

Laughing as they hopped on a sled and rode down, his legs around hers, her body tucked in close against him, Ratchet running alongside them, barking and eating snow.

Ratchet was barking now, but Travis had grown numb to the noise.

His thoughts swirled with memories of eating cookies he'd brought from the bakery in front of the fireplace. Drinking the French hot chocolate his grandmother had taught him to make in bed. Dancing in the kitchen when she'd found his grandfather's old record player.

"I don't know what to do." Her voice broke, and she wiped her eyes. "My family—"

Is everything to her.

It was an impossible choice.

Her family or us.

Maybe if it had just been Logan, she wouldn't go. But her dad was here. And he wasn't angry or violent. Just worried about her. That had to be killing her.

He was more aware than ever of Logan's watching, distrustful gaze. Given the fact that Logan probably wanted to beat him to a pulp, his restraint couldn't be taken for granted.

Travis stepped closer to her and dropped his voice. *As though we still share any privacy.*

"If you shut the door this time, Lindsay, I can't promise I'll open it again."

I'm not sure I can put myself through this again. Travis didn't feel strong enough for that.

He would lose on every front. His business. His family. *My girl.*

She shook her head, wiping her eyes. "That's not fair. Please don't make me choose all or nothing."

"You know what Logan did, Lindsay. To me. To *us.*" Travis's throat clenched.

"What is going on, Logan?" Lindsay's dad narrowed his eyes at Logan.

Lindsay's face filled with panic. "Nothing, Dad. It's nothing."

"What the fuck, Lindsay? I can't believe you fucking told

him." Logan stalked closer to her, his eyes slits. "You crossed the line this time. Completely betrayed your family in the lowest of ways."

Self-righteous asshole.

Travis felt his own fury mounting uncontrollably. And the sight of Logan encroaching on Lindsay made him snap. "Lower than a brother who distributes his little sister's own sex tape to the entire fucking town?"

Logan stopped, then turned toward Lindsay as she gasped, her eyes flying to her father.

Oh fuck. Why the fuck did I say that?

You idiot, Travis.

Horror filled Logan's eyes slowly as understanding dawned.

He barely had time to brace himself before Logan tackled him. "You son of a fucking bitch," Logan growled, knocking Travis down with such force that Travis had to struggle for air. Logan drew his hand back, his fist connecting with the side of Travis's face, near his left brow bone, sending spots flying through his vision.

Travis scissor-kicked to push Logan off him, then flipped Logan onto his own back. He punched Logan square in the nose. A sickening crunch and a spurt of blood followed.

Then it was chaos. The two men crashed through the living room, furniture breaking, the sound of grunts and groans. Travis stumbled through it, dizzy with pain, adrenaline pumping through his blood and driving him forward out of sheer instinct.

Ratchet was barking nonstop now, the scratching at the door so intense that Travis could picture the splintering wood.

Shit. This is bad.

Footsteps sounded vaguely behind him, then he heard Lindsay cry out. "Stop! Please stop!"

Larry Yardley burst between them. "Logan!" He dragged

Logan off the floor, bleeding, then held him back with an arm securely around his chest as Lindsay got to Travis's side as he struggled to stand.

"Oh my God, you're bleeding. What the hell? What did you do to him?" Lindsay shouted at Logan, supporting Travis with her body weight.

"That's you in that video, Lindsay?" Logan whispered, holding his nose with pinched fingers.

Lindsay stiffened beside Travis, and she caught her breath. Her eyes, wide with betrayal, met Travis's. "I can't believe you told him. *And* my father!"

"I'm sorry, Linds—"

"Oh my God." Lindsay backed away from him. "I can't be here right now."

She ran her fingers through her hair, then saw a trace of blood on her sleeve. Paling, she backed away farther, then ran up the stairs. She returned a minute later, a pair of leggings and UGGs on, her coat draped over her arm, her bag still half opened, then stormed out the door.

Larry Yardley put his arm around Logan's shoulder. "Sorry about the mess, Travis. Let's go, Logan."

And he watched as Larry Yardley walked away with the woman he loved. The woman he'd just lost.

My God. What the fuck did I do?

Lindsay is never going to forgive me.

Travis reached for the couch, nauseated and exhausted. He leaned back and had to catch himself.

The couch had flipped, though, the mesh fabric underneath it, torn.

A stack of neatly bundled letters, yellow with age, lay on the floorboards.

Outside, a truck engine roared to life. Ratchet continued to bark, but Travis didn't have the energy to go over to him.

A couple of drops of blood splattered on the floorboards, and he wiped his brow. Then he numbly reached for the letters.

What the hell is this?

They were all to Bernadette Durand.

From Peter Yardley.

CHAPTER THIRTY-TWO

April 2003

THE BURIAL HAD BEEN in the morning, and by now, most of the attendees had left the cemetery, including Larry with the kids, but Peter couldn't will himself to move. He'd told them he needed just a minute more by himself, thinking that maybe another word, another goodbye might bring him peace.

And now that he was alone with this empty hole in the ground, that was all he felt.

Alone.

Marion wasn't here.

Wasn't at home.

Why was she out on the road that day?

What were the chances?

His brain kept trying to make connections he couldn't be sure about.

Trying to make peace with something that he could never make peace with.

"Peter."

He closed his eyes, not bothering to look. He still knew that voice. Sometimes he still heard it in his dreams.

Bernadette stepped up beside him. He'd seen her at the funeral in the back of the church. Her son wasn't with her, which wasn't surprising. Neither was it surprising or unusual for her to be there in the eyes of others. As much conflict as there had been between their families, most of their peers knew that Bernadette had once been his girl.

They didn't know he'd never stopped loving her, though.

Couldn't know that.

They stood there, side by side, for a while. John's funeral wasn't for another few days, and he wondered if she was dreading it just as much as he'd been dreading this.

"Thank you for coming," he said at last.

"I had to." Bernadette set her hand on his forearm gently. "I'm so sorry, Peter."

When he looked her in the eye, the tears he saw there weren't just misty eyes. She was crying hard, tears cascading onto her cheeks with real emotion.

He turned and tried to hold her, but she stepped back with a shake of her head. She reached into her purse and pulled out a tissue, then wiped her eyes. "You don't understand. I've been trying to find the words to tell you, but I just . . . I haven't known how," she whispered.

What's she talking about?

Peter frowned at her thickly. "What is it?"

She hesitated for another few moments, then lifted her chin, resolutely. "When we were driving out to the cabin, we passed Marion. I thought she might have seen us, but I didn't want to worry you, so I didn't say anything. But she kept going."

Bernadette sucked in a shallow breath. "But she did see. She went home and left a hysterical message on my answering machine—trying to reach John and tell him. Said she was going to the cabin to confront us . . ."

As the meaning of Bernadette's words sunk in, Peter set a hand over his gut, feeling the stab of pain that spread there. *Oh Lord, no.* His mouth dried up.

"She—she saw?"

What must she have thought?

He didn't have to overthink that one. He could still picture her almost thirty years earlier,

shaking his dress shirt in front of him, tears staining her cheeks. Larry crying on the floor beside her, holding on to her shin because he'd never heard his soft-spoken mother yell before.

"But why is her lipstick all over your shirt?"

He'd done a good job for thirty years. Kept his distance from Bernadette. Didn't even look her way to keep his wife happy. He loved Marion, after all, and she was a good wife.

She just didn't know how to handle the fact that he had loved Bernadette first. It had always tormented Marion, no matter how many times he'd reassured her that she was his world now.

But now, his poor, sweet wife had gone to her grave thinking the worst of him.

The guilt rose up his spine. "She never would have been there if it wasn't for me. She wouldn't have been on that road in that car."

Now I really feel sick.

"That's not the worst part." Bernadette wiped her cheeks again. "Todd heard the message on the answering machine. He heard, and now he hates you for it."

Anger curled in his fists. "Then tell him it's not true. If he tells anyone that, you know they'll believe it, B. They knew us as kids."

"He wouldn't do that to me."

Peter turned toward her and narrowed his gaze. "To *you?* You're just going to let him go on thinking—"

"What am I supposed to do? Ruin everything he knows about his father and his childhood?"

Yes. Because he'd been ruining your life. Yet you'd stayed with him.

"Please, Peter. I'm begging you. Only Todd knows anything. It won't go further than that. Please just let the issue die. It'll die eventually."

Peter felt the sting of her betrayal heavy in his mind.

She's asking too much.

I don't want to do this.

Marion deserved better than this.

But he couldn't bring himself to tell her no. To demand she do anything differently.

"If he ever says anything to my family, I'm telling them my version of the events, Bernadette. Understood? You tell your boy whatever you want, but my family is my business."

Bernadette nodded.

His anger tumbled in his mind. *It wasn't right. Marion should be alive by my side.*

Not gone.

He couldn't face Bernadette at that moment. He couldn't face the woman who *might* have been able to stop this senseless death. *His devastating loss.*

"Bernadette . . . please."

"I'm so sorry, Peter. I'm—"

"Leave. And stay away."

CHAPTER THIRTY-THREE

Now

Two weeks later

DAD WAS in his office at his practice when Travis tapped on the door. He looked up and over the frames of his glasses, then frowned with surprise.

Even though it was after hours and no patients were on the schedule, some of the nurses and secretaries remained, which was why Travis had chosen this place and this time to talk to his father. Even his hot-tempered father didn't like making a scene.

He'd waited two weeks, which had felt like torture, to give some time for the bruising on his face to heal. For about four days, he'd walked around with his eye nearly swollen shut, which would have worried him more if the shop had been running like normal. The slow trickle of customers continued, though. Just four days ago, he'd been forced to tell Johnny he couldn't afford him anymore.

Another week of this and he'd be out of business. The only reason he could even pay some of his bills right now was because of the work for Jen's bakery. But she wouldn't be on maternity leave forever. And the rent of the garage and the apartment above it were too expensive for him to continue bleeding money.

And I've missed Lindsay so fucking much.

How had she become my world so quickly?

But she wouldn't answer his texts or calls. Wouldn't respond.

And her silence was loud.

He'd lost her. He'd lost everything.

The only pro had been he'd had the time to keep Jen's Sweet Escapes afloat.

"Got a minute?" Travis stepped into the office, then shut the door behind him.

Dad stood. "What the hell happened to your face?"

Guess I should have waited even longer. Trust his dad to notice that right away.

Not that he had the time. The next town council meeting was quickly approaching. With Lindsay not speaking to him, they were no closer to solving this thing than they'd been when Brian Pearson had suggested the damn idea.

But before he faced anyone, he needed to know why.

Why his father hated Peter Yardley so much.

It had been killing him not knowing.

He *knew* some of the story from the letters he'd found at the cabin. It had felt like betrayal, reading letters written to his nana without her knowledge, but he'd seen their discovery as something he had been meant to find.

But how had a love from over fifty years ago caused such torment to the present?

"Well?" Dad asked impatiently, striding to the front of his desk.

Travis snapped his gaze over at him. "I got into a fight with Logan Yardley."

"Of course, you did." Dad crossed his arms and leaned back against his desktop. "Your temper has always gotten the best of you. Why, may I ask?"

Hi, pot, it's the kettle.

"Because I'm in love with Lindsay, and I took her to spend a few days in the cabin." Travis hooked his thumbs through the belt loops of his jeans, his voice flat. Better to lead with that, he'd decided. Get the worst part of it out of the way.

Dad's face reddened, his eyes bulging. "What?"

"Don't worry, she doesn't love me back, so it's nothing you have to worry yourself about. It's over." He sniffed, then jerked his chin up. "But while we were fighting, Logan—or me— knocked the couch over." He reached into his jacket pocket and pulled out the stack of letters. "And I found these." He held them up.

The astonishment in Dad's eyes was clear as he struggled to keep up with the information Travis was throwing at him at once. Which had also been part of Travis's plan. The less time Dad had to think, the better. The more honest he'd be.

He shook his head as though to clear his thoughts, then narrowed his gaze at the letters. "What are they?"

"Letters from Peter Yardley to Nana. Love letters. I'd give them to you to look at, but they clearly mean something to her, and I'm pretty sure you'd destroy them."

Dad flinched and took an involuntary step forward. "You don't know what the hell you're dealing with, Travis."

Travis gave him a hard look. "No. I don't. Because no one

has bothered to tell me. Which is why I'm here. What do you know about Nana and Peter?"

"Don't mention that son of a bitch's name—"

"I'm going to mention his name. And I'm going to find out what the hell happened that you blame Peter for Grandpa's death. Right now."

Dad tugged at the tie at his collar, loosening it. "What makes you think you can come bursting into my place of work like this and—"

"Now, Dad. I need to understand what Peter Yardley did to make you hate him so much. Why you've been on a witch hunt ever since. Why I can't be with the woman I love because her family hates my guts so much, and she's too afraid of ripping her family apart to consider being with me. Why the *fuck* I should be taking your side in this Depot battle you started and ended up costing me my business"—Travis pointed out the door, in the imaginary direction of his shop—"because that's what happened. Logan Yardley got so furious at what you did, he took what I built and trashed it and wrecked my reputation in this town. He knew you were too well-established to take aim at, but I wasn't."

Now Travis's shoulders were heaving, and his volume had gotten louder than he'd intended.

Because I'm angry.

And I deserve to be.

Either Dad or Peter.

Someone is to blame here, and it's not me.

"Nana had an affair with Peter Yardley," Dad snapped suddenly, his face growing cold. "When you were just a boy. Marion Yardley must have found out about it because she left a message on the answering machine at home for Dad. I guess Dad heard it and then ran out the door to try to catch them in the act—at that fucking cabin, just so you know—and Marion did, too. Except Dad never made it. Or Marion. They crashed and died on impact. All while Mom was being a whore with the man Dad disliked more than anyone else in this town."

Dad's words hit Travis in the diaphragm, and his hands curled into fists.

Fuck.

Me.

He'd taken Lindsay there. To that cabin.

"How do you know?" Travis asked in a whisper, holding his father's eyes.

"Because your grandmother sent me to the house from the hospital, and I found the message on the answering machine. I played it for her eventually, of course. She didn't deny it. Just looked me right in the eye and deleted the message, then went on her way. Didn't even shed a tear."

His grandmother had had an affair with Peter?

The concept was almost impossible to wrap his head around. Maybe because he'd always seen her as being so far above reproach. Almost virginal, in a strange way. Because grandmothers weren't sexual beings and Nana—she was the best of grandmothers.

Travis closed his eyes for a second, every kind word and smile and memory of her disjointed with the concept of an adulteress whose sordid affair had helped to end two lives.

It's not possible.

. . . except. Why would Dad lie?

Dad wouldn't make up something so inflammatory just to appease Travis's curiosity.

And it explains why Dad hates Peter so much.

But if that was the case, why direct so much hatred to Peter but not hold Nana just as responsible?

Dad's eyes were red-veined and watery, as though he might actually tear up, too.

No wonder.

No wonder Dad wanted to destroy Peter Yardley. Why he couldn't stand his success. His grandfather had died, and Peter had gone on to accomplish so much without consequence. No one even knew what he'd done.

A profound sense of sadness filled Travis.

The letters had made him think that Nana continued to carry a torch for Peter—or the other way around—and *that* was what had his father so angry.

But this?

This wasn't fixable, was it?

"Why didn't you ever tell me?" Travis asked wearily, taking a few steps back to the couch in his father's office. He sat, his senses stupefied, too tired to think anymore.

Dad sat beside him, leaning back in the corner of the sofa and undoing his tie completely. "I didn't want to ruin your good opinion of Nana. Lord knows it took me long enough to be able to look her in the eye again after it all happened. Dad wasn't always the best, but he didn't deserve that. Didn't deserve for his last thoughts to be about his wife in the arms of a man he hated."

The two Wagner men sat in silence, staring blankly ahead of them.

Misery crept into Travis's thoughts.

For two weeks now, he'd been thinking about how—if at all —it would be possible to fix things with Lindsay. He'd hurt her deeply by telling Logan about that video, which was clear, but he also was certain she would have answered him if she hadn't felt it was pointless.

And now he understood better.

Maybe it was pointless.

Maybe this feud would never end.

"So we just go on hating them, then? The Yardleys. When

does it end, Dad? When does the cycle of hatred that got so much worse after all this with Nana and Peter get put to rest?"

"I don't know," Dad said, blinking slowly. "But I didn't ever intend for your business to be in the crosshairs."

Travis laughed sardonically. "Don't lie, Dad. If I know you, you probably think it's the only good thing that Logan Yardley has ever done in his life. He did you a favor. Forced me to go back to baking to get by. Just like you wanted."

Dad shook his head, then removed his glasses. He cleared his throat a few times, looking away. "I'm sorry you feel that way, Travis." He took a few deep breaths, then turned to face him. "But that's not true. I'm proud of you, son. I know I haven't always been the best at showing it. And hell, I'm even worse at admitting my mistakes. But it took guts for you to start a business like that, especially without any help or support from the family. And you do good work. That Stingray is the envy of most of my friends."

Travis folded his hands together, leaning forward on his elbows. "You don't have to pretend—"

"I'm not pretending. I swear it. I hate what those Yardleys have done to you. They shouldn't have ever punished you for my petition."

"Can't you just withdraw it, Dad? You stirred a hornet's nest. And it's ruined my life."

Dad turned and met his gaze, his eyes inquisitive. And for the first time in too many years to count, Travis didn't see disappointment—anger—in his father's expression. It felt as though they'd turned a corner. "You really love that girl?"

"I do." Acid burned his throat. "But like I said, it doesn't matter. She doesn't love me."

"How could she not love you? You're a good-looking kid." Dad gave him a teasing, sad smile. "Not to mention she was clearly willing to face her family's wrath if she went off to that cabin with you."

Was she? If she was, then she'd folded to her family's wrath immediately.

She hadn't been ready. She never would be.

"There's just too much bad blood there. Too much to overcome. Starting with that petition for the Depot."

Dad rubbed his eyes, then replaced his glasses. "I wish I could do something to help, Travis, but it's in the hands of the town council now. We got the signatures to move it to a vote—it's not just my petition now. The decision belongs to the town."

"But if you could just convince those people—"

"I can't." Dad's face hardened slightly. "I can't, and honestly, I'm not sure I want to. The Yardleys deserve to have that place booted from Main Street. Now more than ever."

"Dad, I just, I need—"

"Travis, don't ask that of me. I'm begging you. You and I—and our relationship—it's separate from all this. We have work to do. But you're my son, and I love you. I'm willing to do the work. But don't ask me to forgive the son of a bitch whose selfishness killed my father. I'll hate him until the day I die."

He spoke quietly, without obvious rancor, but matter-of-fact conviction.

And, the truth was, knowing what he knew about Nana now, Travis wasn't sure he blamed him anymore.

CHAPTER THIRTY-FOUR

THE FIRST SIGNS of daffodils had started to pop up in the garden, and Lindsay watched them dully from the bench in Pops's garden. She curled her knees into her chest, then lay her cheek against her knees.

Two weeks of not sleeping.

Feeling so awful that she'd been wanting to do nothing but stay in bed all day.

Two weeks of feeling like she'd lost everything.

She was exhausted.

For the hundredth time that hour, she'd checked her phone to see if a message from Travis had come in. She didn't know why she expected it. She hadn't answered his attempts to contact her the week before, but seeing a message come in with his name had been comforting.

Like he was out there, still thinking of her.

Like maybe hope wasn't dead.

But it is.

And when she hadn't responded, he had stopped sending messages.

She called Jen, who had been on the receiving end of way too many sobbing phone calls and texts. But thank God for her. She still picked up. *Every. Time.*

"You doing okay?" Jen asked in a gentle, soothing tone.

"You have a baby sleeping on your chest?"

"Yup. Pretty much twenty-four seven." Jen yawned. "What's going on? Have you talked to your family yet? Maddie has taken to texting me, by the way."

Her family.

They were worried.

And she needed to talk to them. But she was humiliated beyond belief. How could she face them? How could she look her mother in the eye? She'd seen the look on Dad's face when Travis had revealed that his daughter's homemade porno was being distributed through the streets of Brandywood.

But where was the outrage at Logan?

For fighting Travis, for *stealing* Travis's private property, for maligning his name, destroying his business.

For breaking us.

It was all so fucked up.

She couldn't stand the thought of talking to any of them right now. Not yet.

"No, I haven't talked to them."

Jen sighed. "What about Travis?"

"I don't think . . . I don't think it matters, Jen. I keep thinking about how, even if none of it had happened the way it did, we still would have faced a lot of opposition. But this? This was dead on arrival. There's no going back."

She ran her fingertips over her jeans. "What about you? Have you talked to Travis?"

"You know I have, Linds."

But she won't tell me more because she doesn't want to lose either of us.

Jen cleared her throat. "You're going to have to see him soon, you know. The council won't let you off the hook. Can't you find a way to talk to him, Linds? I know how much he loves you. I think he's been in love with you for a while. He's so sorry."

She knew that. He'd texted it. If she gave him the chance to talk to her, he'd probably say it, too.

But it wasn't that she didn't forgive him.

"It just doesn't matter if I forgive him."

"You keep saying that, but it's not true, Linds. It matters. Forgiveness matters. It matters to him. And it'll matter to you, too." Jen cleared her throat. "Look, I wasn't going to tell you this, and I probably shouldn't because I owe my business staying afloat to Travis right now. But he's planning on leaving town. He put his car up for sale on eBay and will start liquidating his inventory so he can get out before he's completely bankrupt."

Goddamn Logan.

Travis . . . not in Brandywood?

It was incomprehensible.

The squeak of the garden gate made her look up, and she saw Pops standing there, blocking the glare of the setting sun with his body. He held a mug of steaming hot tea in his hands.

"I gotta go. I'll call you soon," Lindsay said before hanging up and looking up at Pops.

Thank God for Pops.

He'd taken her in, no questions asked.

Didn't force her to talk about it when she didn't want to.

Didn't tell her she should shower or go to work or anything.

Listened to her when she cried but didn't offer unwanted advice.

He pushed the gate open and came down the garden path toward her, walking carefully to not spill the tea. When he reached her, he set it down on the bench, then sat on the other side of her. "How're you doing, little bee?"

She sighed, then picked up the tea and sipped it. Lemon, with a slice of lemon and honey, which was her favorite. "Surviving. Barely."

"You up for a visitor?"

She squinted at him. "What sort of visitor?"

"Jake."

Ugh. She didn't want to see Jake. Even though he'd texted and called and then shown up to warn Travis, and she was grateful for that, he could have done more. *Like stick around and stand up for me against Logan.*

"Can I tell you what I think?"

Lindsay blew a stream of air through the steam, watching it dissipate from the top of the mug. "What's that?"

"You should talk to your siblings. They're not perfect. None of us are. But they love you. And they're worried about you just as much as your mom and dad."

She knew Mom and Dad were worried. Both had tried reaching her as often as her siblings—except Logan—had. But without Logan showing any remorse for what he'd done, she wasn't even sure she knew how to have a conversation with her parents. From now on, it was going to have to be either him or her.

She hated feeling like an outsider in her family. Hated that they were all probably talking about her. "Yeah, okay," she mumbled. "I'll talk to Jake."

Pops squeezed her shoulder. "I'll be a holler away if you need it." With an affectionate wink, he stood, then went back down the path.

A minute later, Jake came toward her, hands in his pockets. He gave her a sheepish grin. "Hey, Linds."

Somehow, despite the fact that she hadn't wanted him

there, Jake's presence made tears bubble to the surface. She stood and folded into one of his bear hugs immediately.

"Hey—" He stroked her hair softly. "Lindsay. It's okay. It's all going to be okay."

She sniffled and held him close. Since he'd started working with Logan, she'd felt a rift between them, and she hadn't realized how much she missed her brother. "You don't hate me?" she managed, sniffling as she stepped back.

"Hate you?" He took her hands. "Linds, you're crazy. How could anyone hate you? You're sweet and funny. And smart. And the only one who knows how to give it right back to Logan when he's being a dick. Which he is most of the time. And— don't tell the other ones—but you're my favorite sister."

"I heard that, douche," Maddie said from a few feet away.

Lindsay turned and saw her sister standing on the path. Naomi was only a few feet behind her.

What are they doing there?

They had ambushed her.

And, until that moment, she hadn't realized how much she'd needed that.

"What'd he say?" Naomi asked Maddie.

"He said Lindsay's his favorite."

Naomi rolled her eyes. "She's everyone's favorite, Maddie. Goes with the territory. Baby of the family—the favorite. Oldest —bossy, crotchety, and mean. Birth order never lies."

"And you?" Maddie asked, crossing her arms.

"I'm the second of five, so I'm the *actual* overlooked one, even though the middle child always complains it's them. I also have better chances at being the peacemaker, make better friends, or be a fantastic criminal."

Lindsay released a tearful laugh, overwhelmed by the fact that they'd decided to visit all at once like this. *Why have I been pushing them away?*

Because I couldn't handle talking about Travis with anyone who I know hates Travis.

I'm devastated over him.

They'll never understand.

But she was glad they were here, regardless.

Naomi and Maddie joined Jake. Maddie bit her lip when she saw Lindsay. "Girl, not going to lie, but you need a shower and a facial. Have you been at least talking to Jen while you've been busy ignoring all of us?"

Scrunching her nose, Lindsay gave a regretful glance at her overturned cell phone on the bench.

"Some. On the phone." She didn't want them to feel bad at the extent to which she'd picked discussing her troubles with Jen over them. "She's really busy with the twins, and I don't want to bother her."

"What an inconsiderate time for your best friend to have twins," Maddie said, setting her hands on her hips. "I tell ya. Best friends just aren't made like they used to be."

"Guess she'll have to settle for sisters. And a smelly older brother," Naomi said, winking at Jake.

Lindsay's lower lip trembled. "You all aren't mad at me?"

"For what? Sleeping with a super-hot guy or making a now infamous Brandywood porno?" Maddie asked with a mischievous grin.

Oh God.

"I thought I wasn't allowed to mention that," Jake said with mock outrage. "How come she gets to mention it, and I don't?"

Lindsay buried her face in her hands. "Oh God, I'm so embarrassed."

"I mean. Don't worry, none of us have seen it. To be honest, my guess is that fewer people have seen it than have talked about it. And we're still the only ones who know it was you and that's only because Older-Brother-Who-Shall-Not-Be-Named told Big Mouth over here," Naomi said with a pointed look at Jake.

This is so embarrassing.

"She's turning so red," Maddie whispered loudly.

"Sweetie, if you're going to have the confidence to make a sex tape, then you may as well own it. So you're a secret nympho who has a thing for cosplay? We're not judging," Maddie said, then sat on the bench, accidentally upsetting the mug of tea. "Shit. Sorry. I'll have to ask Pops to make his favorite some more tea."

"I love you, Maddie," Lindsay managed with a tearful laugh.

"Serious question, Linds. What was up with the witch costume?" Jake quirked a brow at her. "I mean, good for you and all, but it's a little kinky."

She would never be able to look her parents in the eyes if they knew this.

"It was Halloween."

"Oooo, makes sense. I've totally had Halloween sex before. It's a very underrated sex holiday, given the fact that half the costumes for women barely cover the goods." Maddie flipped her hair over her shoulder. "But it's a good thing you had a costume because it kept your identity safe, Batman."

"I cannot believe we are still discussing this," Lindsay said. "Does Mom know, too?"

Naomi gave her a sympathetic side hug. "Your secret is safe with us—from Mom, anyway. Dad is currently looking at legal recourses to get any copies out there, but I don't think he's told Mom. You know how they are with talking about sex. Mom still uses the term 'intimacy,' and it creeps me out. She won't actually say the word sex."

She had a flashback to her awkward encounter with her

parents a few weeks earlier. *I wonder if Jake told them about me walking in on Mom and Dad.*

Jake laughed. "I think the extent of the sex talk I got was 'keep it in your pants.'"

"That's more than I got. I had to learn about sex from Naomi!" Maddie shook her head. "Who did me the favor of handing me a historical romance novel set in Scotland and saying, 'here, read this.'"

Lindsay's jaw dropped open at the revelation, a strange relief pouring through her at her siblings' lack of judgment toward her. "Hey, that's what you did with me!" she said to Maddie. "You got that from Naomi?"

"Well, I wasn't about to sit down and explain penis, vagina, or fellatio to you three." Naomi shrugged it off with a wave of her hand. "I was an awkward teenager. I had to do my best."

"You three?" Maddie's gaze swiveled around to Jake, then a delighted look crossed her face. "Did you get the romance novel, too?"

"Hey, I'll have you know that *Taming the Wild Laird* is still one of the best books I've read," Jake said with a cackle.

Lindsay was unable to help herself from joining in their laughter. "Did Naomi really just say penis, vagina, and fellatio in one sentence? The mom in this group?"

"Well, obviously she's not a prude since she and Jeremy are popping out babies all the time. I guess it runs in the family, right, Linds?" Maddie gave her a knowing wink. "You know, on a more serious note, the only thing I'm mad about is that here we were thinking we were sending you off to Sweet Escapes and saving us a giant headache, when you were probably over there getting lucky and having the time of your life laughing at what dummies we were."

"I think I've done enough thinking about my sisters' sex lives for one night." Jake shook his head. "She looks like she's eating, even if she's unemployed and not showering. I think our work here is done."

Naomi reached for Lindsay's hand and squeezed it. "Listen, Lindsay, we love you. You can always come back and work at the Depot if you want to. Even though you weren't there long, it's just as much yours as it is ours. But at the end of the day, I think all of us just want you to be happy and feel valued."

You have no idea how much I needed to hear that.

Naomi's words made Lindsay want to tear up again.

"I thought you all would hate me for being with Travis."

Maddie gave her a sad pout. "I'm so sorry you felt that. I think we all are."

Jake cleared his throat, then looked from Maddie to Naomi. "Speaking of people who are sorry . . ."

An awkward silence fell between them, and Lindsay's gaze snapped past them. A cold, clammy feeling encapsulated her. "Is Logan here, too?"

Naomi nodded, her lips drawing to a taut line.

No.

I don't want to see him.

Her heart throbbed painfully. "I don't know that I'm ready to talk to him."

"Will you consider just hearing him out? We can stay if you want. Or you can talk alone. Whatever you prefer. But he is sorry and wants to tell you that, at least." Naomi's fingers tightened against Lindsay's.

"If you don't feel safe with him—"

"No, that's not it." Lindsay twisted the toe of her shoe into the gravel pathway. It was Logan. He'd never hurt her. Even if he was furious, he'd always been protective. Sometimes annoyingly so.

She hated that it now felt like he'd sent in a warm-up crew

ahead of him, but that was also her hurt feelings talking. Logan had messed up, big time.

"I'll talk to him alone."

"We'll be right around the corner if you need us," Maddie said comfortingly. Then they left, and Lindsay sat, jiggling her knees nervously.

She raised her head at the sound of footsteps. Logan still had tape across his broken nose, bruises and scrapes on his face. Travis had gotten some good punches in, and the sight of Logan made Lindsay's stomach twist, her mind revisiting the scene.

Logan nodded toward the bench. "Mind if I sit?"

She shook her head but scooted over to have more space between them.

He didn't say anything for a while, then leaned forward. "Linds, I don't know where to start."

"You can just start with *I'm sorry* if that's what you're here for. Otherwise, I'm not sure I want to hear it."

"I'm sorry." Logan's eyes were mournful. "I really am. I'm an asshole. And I got so focused on taking Travis Wagner down that I lost sight of . . . well, everything. The family. The values I was taught. Right and wrong. But, I swear to God, if I had known it was you in that video—"

"It doesn't matter who it was, Logan. That was something personal that belonged to Travis. The fact that you thought you could go there just shows how low you sank. I mean, the fact that you hired someone to find dirt on someone was just so, so wrong. He'd done nothing wrong." Her tone reflected her bitterness.

Can I ever forgive him?

Worse still, could she ever forgive Travis for telling Logan it was her?

"I know," he whispered the words. "I know that now. And for what it's worth, I've spent the last couple of weeks trying to scrub any trace of it. The damage is done, and I can't promise it'll never be seen, but I'm doing my best. And I was able to get all the negative reviews taken down."

It was all he could say. And sadly, it was definitely much too little too late.

He'd ruined Travis's business. *For what.*

"I think I'm in love with him." Lindsay stared at her hands, curled in her lap. "I think I've been half in love with him my whole life, Logan. I keep thinking about how and why I always had such bad luck dating in the past—and the only thing I can come up with is that I always compared every guy to him. I started sleeping with him when I was sixteen."

Wow. Did I really just admit that to Logan, of all people?

"I . . . I didn't know."

This time, she let out a slow, depressed sigh. "Yeah, how could you have? I barely knew it. And I wasn't about to tell you about it. You always hated the Wagners so much."

"Actually, I had a crush on Grace Wagner for years," Logan admitted with a wry twist of his mouth. "Not anymore. Don't worry, I know that would be weird now anyway. But definitely when we were in school."

Lindsay expected to have tears, but somehow, she didn't. A breeze rustled through the buds on the tree branches as they swayed. "I'm tired of this feud, Logan. And not just because of Travis. I know the situation with him looked really bad, but we had a long history together. One I wasn't sure if I was ready to tell anyone about when you showed up at the cabin. And now he probably hates me for not speaking up on his behalf and forcing him to tell you about the damage you'd done to both of us. Because that broke us."

Logan's face filled with remorse. "I'm so sorry, Lindsay. I wish I could take it all back."

But it was all just words now. The damage was irreversible.

Like he'd intended it to be. "By the way, I knew about the dating app. I'd told him I didn't want to be with him when he joined. And while it looked like everything happened so fast to you, that's far from the truth."

"So you would be with him if it wasn't for what I did?" Logan shifted in his seat and studied her. "You can see why it's hard for me to trust him, given everything that's happened with his dad and the town council."

"I can. But you've proven that it doesn't take much to take something too far, Logan. What you did to Travis—it's just as unforgivable."

Unforgivable.

The word had slipped out before she could catch herself. Logan noticed it immediately, and his face fell with a look of defeat.

"I didn't mean for it to go so far." He sank his head into his hands. "But you're right."

She stared at his bowed head, her heart tugging at her.

I don't want to hate my brother.

"I want you to know that I told Pops I think you should be running the bar."

She choked out a skeptical laugh. *Talk about an olive branch.* "I don't know if that's what I should be doing right now. I'm barely hanging on to my preschool work by my fingernails."

A gentle smile tipped Logan's split lip. "You had a really busy month, didn't you?"

She chuckled, despite the circumstance. "Yeah, you're not kidding."

He shifted and shrugged. "Well, Pops agreed with me. Nothing happened in a vacuum, Linds. That's not the way things work. Circumstances have to be taken into consideration. Everything good you've done in the past doesn't disappear because of one bad month."

Pops agreed?

They both must be crazy.

But how was she supposed to run the restaurant when she couldn't even get one foot in front of the other right now?

"I don't know that I want to have my name in contention for that job right now." Lindsay's voice broke. "I think I've lost the confidence in myself. In two days, I have to show up to a town council meeting and tell the whole town of Brandywood that I failed them . . ."

Logan slipped off the bench and knelt in front of her, then took her hands. "I love you, Linds. And I fucked up. Really badly. I'm so sorry. Seeing you so torn up like this and knowing that I'm to blame for so much of your pain. It's—it's killing me. I want you to be happy. To love anyone you want to love. I'm hesitant about Travis because I love you so much, and I don't want to see anyone hurt you. And it might take time for me to get over that, but for you, I'm willing to do anything."

Lindsay pulled her hands away and wiped her eyes. "I don't think I can fix things with Travis at this point, Logan. I think it's all so screwed up that he might even have given up this time."

"Then he doesn't deserve you," Logan said earnestly. "He—"

"He's a human, Logan. What's he supposed to be, my doormat? He got seriously dicked over by our family, including me in the end. Maybe I don't deserve him. Did you consider that possibility? There's a good chance we could be completely toxic together."

"You're not toxic." Logan sank back onto his heels. "But this situation with our families—it's pretty damned bad. The question is, what are we going to do to fix it?"

Lindsay reached for her mug, then remembered that Maddie had knocked it over. She wrinkled her nose. "I don't know if there's much we can do. I think Travis and I were the only ones who didn't hate each other. And with the Depot still being threatened and the town council meeting in a couple of days . . ." She shook her head. "We have no plan. I tried to make one, but our relationship and everything that happened—it all got in the way."

"I don't think that's true." Logan stood, towering over her.

She squinted up at him. "What's not true?"

"All of it. Pops told me all about the plan you came up with —for a tourist center. And he told me something else, too. But maybe I'm not the best person to tell you about it." Logan cleared his throat, then looked over his shoulder and called, "Pops, you want to come over here for a few minutes?"

Lindsay couldn't help but shake her head at the situation. Had they all planned this ambush together?

Pops returned to the garden a minute later, and her spirit lifted at the sight of him. *My wonderful, reliable grandfather. What would I do without you?*

He stopped beside Logan, clasping his hands together. "Yes, Logan?"

"I want you to tell her," Logan said, dipping his chin. "Tell her what you told me about Bunny Wagner."

CHAPTER THIRTY-FIVE

BERNADETTE HUNG UP THE PHONE, her gut roiling.

She looked around the familiar, soothing sight of her café, now emptied of its patrons for the night.

That was one phone call I wasn't expecting.

Maybe she should have been.

When Brian had shown up here a few weeks ago with Peter, Lindsay, and Travis in tow, she should have been suspicious.

Brian Pearson had been up to something. She'd been sure of that.

And after a few minutes of watching the way her grandson looked at Lindsay, she'd known. Maybe she should have paid more attention before, but if he'd been hiding his feelings when he was younger, he hadn't been anymore.

Travis was in love with the girl.

Her, though?

Bernadette hadn't been so sure about her. So she'd dangled Hélène in front of her, just to see her reaction.

And then she'd realized the extent of it.

History had a funny way of repeating itself, it seemed.

Bernadette removed her apron and smoothed her hands over her skirt. She never felt afraid here. This was her café. The one place that had always been her refuge. And in the dark days after John's death, she'd lost herself here. His life insurance policy had saved her from her financial woes and throwing herself into making it even better had become her sole purpose.

But it didn't give my life meaning.

Didn't restore her relationship with Todd, that was for sure. Only the truth could do that.

And that was what Peter wanted from her now.

The truth.

Twenty years too late.

. . . and my family's land, apparently.

She'd gone along with Todd's petition for the same reason she went along with most things Todd asked of her. He already thought the worst of his mother. She didn't need to give him any more things to hold against her.

But that had been foolish, too. It had only perpetuated the idea that she really disliked Peter Yardley.

Tears pricked her eyes.

That's the furthest thing from the truth.

He is, and always has been, the best man I've known. A good man.

She loved her family, she did. Loved Todd fiercely. Todd had given her a reason to breathe when things had been the worst with John. She was thankful for Todd.

But she'd never regretted anything as much as the fact that she hadn't waited for Peter Yardley to come home from the war. That she'd closed herself off to his love after Robbie's death.

Instead, I married a man who hurt me over and over again.

What she wouldn't do to go back to Paris, find her younger self, and shake her by the shoulders. Peter had gone *because*

Robbie had been captured. He'd signed up, admirably, to show his loyalty to his friend. Because he'd always been loyal. To her, to Robbie . . . *and to Marion.*

Folding her hands on the table, Bernadette bowed her head, praying for strength.

I know what I need to do.

But what if it's too late to make a difference?

CHAPTER THIRTY-SIX

GRACE WAITED in front of the town hall, right where she had said she would be, and Travis crossed the street toward her. He'd felt a little foolish, calling his big sister and asking her to go into the town council meeting with him, but he also needed someone on his side. Jen, God love her, would never be fully just on his side. And even though he knew he could count on people like Ben and the Pearsons, they all had split loyalties over this issue, too.

As he drew closer, Grace waved and then came over, giving him a hug. She'd dyed the tips of her dark hair purple recently and wore a sundress, even though it was barely sixty-five degrees out. If that. Spring was in the air, and Grace had apparently decided it was already summer weather.

"I should have brought concealer for your face," Grace said with a shake of her head. "Remind me to spit on Logan when I see him."

"Yeah, that's what this meeting needs. More spit."

Grace took his hand and squeezed it. "You ready?"

Travis surveyed the front of the town hall facade. He

nodded, the sadness he'd been carrying around settling heavily on his shoulders.

My last town hall meeting.

He'd put the Stingray up for sale on eBay after his meeting with Dad, and—shockingly—it had sold to an online buyer within minutes. The buyer would be picking it up in three days. Then Travis would liquidate his assets in the shop, turn over his keys, and he'd be gone.

It might take a few weeks, but hopefully, he could do it sooner.

Brandywood couldn't handle both Wagners and Yardleys. He and Lindsay had proven that.

So he was going to remove one Wagner from the equation.

He hadn't told his family yet. He'd only told Jen, but they'd barely talked, which felt so weird. She'd asked him to visit a few times, but he just hadn't been strong enough to face her—hear everything she had to say about his situation. And was he ready to face Lindsay? Not even a little.

He frowned and then met Grace's awaiting stare. "No. I'm not ready, but there's nothing to be done about that now."

"She's already there. With her posse," Grace said without emotion. "They got there early."

Travis nodded absentmindedly as they went up the steps. The thought of facing Lindsay here was too much to think about. He felt like a kid in school who'd just realized they had a term project due and had forgotten to do his homework.

Actually, that would be preferable to this.

He could do this. Show up at this meeting he was required to attend. Even if he planned on not being a member of this town after this.

Even if he'd been the worst of the Wagners, it didn't mean he couldn't leave on a high note.

They went inside and Travis kept his gaze unfocused, unsure if he could really stand to look Lindsay's way.

He hadn't gone far inside the foyer when Ben caught up with him. "Hey, I was wondering when you'd get here. Grandad's been on a rampage all this morning. Made me drive him at the ass crack of dawn so he could be the first one here."

Ben had barely gotten the words out when Brian came out of nowhere. He glowered at Travis. "Now listen here, sonny. You've been damn near impossible to reach. I even went to your shop. Doors shuttered. Lights out. And your girlfriend— just as bad. What sort of committee is this?"

"She's not my girlfriend." Travis's tone was flat.

Brian shook his head. "I saw the cow eyes you all made at each other. I'm too old a man and been too many times around the sun to be lied to—"

"What did Lindsay say?" Travis cut in, crossing his arms.

Brian frowned, looking at him in bafflement. "Whad'ya mean? She didn't say anything. That's the point! We have nothing to tell the town council—"

Travis gave him a skeptical look. "That's not what I remember. I'm fairly certain she told you the plan at that lovely dinner at the café."

Grace snickered beside him.

Travis kept his tone even, but his voice low.

Only Grace knew what he intended. Only Grace would stand beside him after this anyway.

Brian stepped back, scratching the top of his head and Travis reached over, clapping him on the back. "Just let Lindsay and I handle it. We've got it covered." Then he winked at Brian and kept walking into the hall, his shoulders thrown back with a confidence he didn't feel in the slightest.

Time to be brave.

His parents were in their usual spots, along with Nana,

though Travis wasn't sure if he could really look at her right now. He nodded toward his mother then went to the front of the hall, to the chairs reserved for individuals presenting at the meeting.

That was when he saw her.

His heart lurched, his body still reacting viscerally to her.

He wouldn't ever stop loving her.

A lump formed in his throat.

That's why I have to leave.

He knew that now.

As though she sensed him looking at her, Lindsay turned his way. She didn't smile, didn't look stricken, but her gaze clouded.

Just nothing.

He looked away. Was she going to come sit with him or stay with her family?

He took his own seat, Grace sitting beside him. Thankfully, Ben accompanied his grandfather up at the front with him, making Travis feel slightly more supported. Ben would be on his side. He had been through the years.

Bill MacKintosh kicked the meeting off less than a minute later with a bang of his gavel.

"Alrighty, folks. I think we're all anxious to get the matter before the town council settled today. So I won't take a long time to get right to it. Brian, Lindsay, and Travis, why don't you go ahead and tell us what you've come up with for the Depot dilemma?"

Brian stood and Travis looked at him more closely for the first time. He'd clearly dressed up and slicked his gray hair over in a combover, a flower pinned to his lapel. Holding back a smile, Travis leaned back in his seat, intrigued by what he might say. "Well, folks, I think that it's better to leave matters like this to the young folks. So I'll let them fill in the details." He sat back down, nodding toward Travis.

Travis held back a smile and glanced at Lindsay. He didn't bother to stand. "Actually, Mr. MacKintosh, it's Lindsay Yardley who came up with the plan."

Lindsay shot up onto her feet. "Um, I'm not sure—"

"Tell them about the tourist center, Linds." Travis held her gaze.

Whatever you tell them, I'll do.

I'm not going to fight with you.

Not here, not ever.

Then Lindsay blinked at him, words seeming to fail her.

Shit. I'm going to have to help.

Travis crossed his arms and looked around the town hall. It appeared even more crowded than the meeting a month ago. Was everyone in town here?

Ignoring the gazes from his family, Travis cleared his throat and stood, slowly. "Lindsay came up with a brilliant plan to build a tourist center. We don't want to relocate the Depot at all."

A murmur broke out in the crowd.

"The Yardleys are right. There have been a lot of benefits to the town and there are too many small businesses in town that have come to rely on the foot traffic from tourism to consider moving the Depot, including Bunny's Café and Strickland Ice Cream." He took the opportunity to give Hannah and her father a severe look, because he could. "Hannah Strickland even admitted it to me a few times."

Hannah sank low in her seat.

"What sort of tourist center?" Fred Strickland asked in a rude tone.

Travis turned and looked over his shoulder at Lindsay, who

continued to watch him with an astonished look on her face. He smiled gently at her. "Lindsay?"

She took a few seconds, then a bolder demeanor took over. Leaving her seat, Lindsay came toward the front of the hall, stopping in front of Bill MacKintosh's podium. "It would be a center for all of Brandywood. A place for people from out of town to explore what's here—not just on Main Street, but everywhere. And we could build a large parking lot for tour buses. Have shuttles running regularly to Main. Even consider revitalizing the old streetcar line."

The hubbub in the town hall started to grow. "Where?" Dad asked, standing from his seat. "Where would we build something like that?"

Trust Dad to get involved. But the look he gave Travis wasn't entirely unsupportive, either.

Is it possible he might not fight this?

"We were thinking the old Durand farm," Lindsay said with a resolute expression. "It's a great location, with a lot of the necessary infrastructure already in place."

The noise in the hall doubled.

Then Peter Yardley stood. He walked to the front of the hall and patted Lindsay's shoulder, then kept going, up to the podium. Waving Bill MacKintosh to the side, he stepped in front of the microphone.

He cleared his throat. "If I may."

The hall went completely silent.

Peter turned toward his family. "Todd. I need you to know something."

Nana's eyes widened and she stood. "Peter, no."

With a sigh, Peter looked around at the town. "I think some of you are old enough to remember when Bernadette and I were kids. We were in love. Then I got called off to war and well, life had something else in store for us."

Dad rose to his feet and put his arm around Nana. "Just stop right there, Peter. No one in town needs to hear about this."

Peter gave him a skeptical look. "But they do because, they—and you—need to understand why this is all happening. I won't go into the details but—"

"You son of a bitch. Just shut up." Dad's voice was threatening.

Travis sought out Lindsay's eyes. She looked oddly emotionless. *Does she know?*

"The thing is, folks, Todd thinks I'm to blame for his father's death."

Rage seemed to burst from Dad's body. "Because you are! And your own wife's. You had an affair with my mother. They died while trying to confront you both."

The town hall was so silent that Travis swore he could almost hear his heart pounding outside of his chest.

"No." Peter's normally kind eyes became like flint. "No, that's not true. I was never unfaithful to my wife."

"Oh, stop lying, Yardley. You know what you did. You destroyed my family's life and your own family's because you couldn't stand the fact that Dad married my mom and not you."

Peter looked directly at Bernadette, appealing to her with his gaze. "Bernadette? It's time."

Nana appeared torn. She took a few deep breaths, then turned toward Dad. "Peter's telling the truth, Todd."

What?

Now Travis stared at Nana, riveted.

What is she saying?

Nana looked down, then seemed to settle her conflicting emotions. She reached for Dad's hand. "Your father—he was . . . he'd been having affairs almost from the moment we'd gotten married. I'm sure I'm not the only one in town who knew about it. He wasn't entirely discreet. But he'd taken a second mortgage on the house and put a lien against the business. I would have lost everything if I left. So I stayed. Until I found out he was planning on leaving me."

His grandfather? Travis didn't remember him well enough to have any true idea of what he'd been like. But this sounded so foreign to the image Dad had always presented.

"So I decided to confront him, turn the tables on him and leave him, first. My lawyer said it would be beneficial if I had concrete evidence of his betrayal, so I decided to catch him in the act. I was afraid of what he might do to me, though, so I went to Peter and asked him to come with me. He was the only person I thought I could trust with something so sensitive. But on the way, Marion saw us and thought we were the ones carrying on."

Oh no . . . oh God, poor Nana. Poor Peter . . .

Nana gave a sad smile. "She must have decided to come to the cabin and see what was going on, but in the meantime, John fled after we got there. He was a man possessed, driving with fury, and we think he must have crashed into Marion as a result."

Dad's face blanched. Taking a dizzy step back, away from his mother, he looked for the comfort of Mom's hand. "What?"

"I—I didn't tell you because I didn't want to destroy your image of your father," Nana said tearfully. She glanced over at Peter. "And in the end, I destroyed so much more."

Grace sidled up to him. "Holy shit," she whispered. "Did you know any of this?"

Travis shook his head.

No wonder.

Oh my God, no wonder.

He had never expected this. Never thought it was possible.

How could he blame Nana? She'd wanted to preserve Grandpa's image for her son?

But if she'd just told the truth, so much could have been so different.

Lindsay's eyes shone with tears and Travis's throat clenched. Funny how history had an odd way of repeating itself. Nana had cared about Peter in much the same way that Lindsay cared about him—*not quite enough.*

"I'm proud of you, B." Peter wiped his eyes and then Travis realized—there wasn't a dry eye in the town hall. "Thank you."

Even Brian Pearson looked teary-eyed.

"Will you sell the town the land for the tourist center, Mrs. Wagner?" Lindsay asked, her voice sounding unusually clear. "Put this to rest once and for all?"

And even though she wasn't his, Travis's heart swelled with pride at her.

Fuck, I'm going to miss you. I have no idea how I'm going to walk through this life without you in it.

Nana nodded and the town hall burst into applause.

Everyone was on their feet now, cheering, and Travis looked at Grace, who beamed at him.

Then he turned and slipped out of the town hall through the back door.

Maybe now, this town could start to heal, even if he never would. *Not without Lindsay.*

But she didn't want to talk to him.

Time to go.

CHAPTER THIRTY-SEVEN

BERNADETTE HADN'T COMPLETELY LOST the tremor to her hands as she left the town hall. Todd had several questions for her, which had taken time to answer, and she'd made a point to go and apologize to Larry Yardley, too.

But Peter was nowhere to be found.

She sighed and started down the sidewalk, toward her café. Embarrassed.

But free.

She was finally free of it.

Free of that damned, noxious lie that had festered for so long.

She should have told Todd years ago. But time had turned into fear. Fear that he wouldn't believe her. Fear that he would think she was trying to rewrite the history he was so certain of, to suit her own purposes.

And because of it, she'd hurt her family and Peter's.

She tightened her sweater around her shoulders, catching a glimpse of her reflection in the window of Jen's bakery. She could still picture it when it had been Price's Hardware. What

Jen had built was amazing. Someday, she'd do a wonderful job taking over the café, too.

Now she just needed to find the courage to break that news to Todd in the future.

The image of herself was so different than it had been fifty years ago when she and Peter Yardley had huddled under that awning during that rainstorm. Her dark hair was all gray now, her shoulders and body rounded and soft, her skin wrinkled. The thought of red lipstick made her laugh.

She'd never been particularly courageous, never been good at fighting for the things she wanted.

Today is a new day, filled with opportunity.

Her mother used to tell her that as a girl. Who knew she'd still need that advice at her age?

She sighed and turned the corner toward the café, then stopped short.

Peter stood in front of the locked door, holding a bouquet of daffodils.

She stared at him with astonishment.

"What are you doing here?"

With a smile, Peter held out the flowers. "I came for my girl."

Tears welled in her eyes. "Oh, you old crazy loon."

It's been such a long time since he's called me that. So many years of sadness. Of loss.

Peter stepped closer, then swiped away one of her tears with his thumb. "I loved Marion as much as I could, and we had a good marriage. I grieved her loss. I grieved what it did to our families, and then our town. But, I never stopped loving you."

Bernadette tried to talk but he placed a finger over her lips. "It's been long enough, Bernadette. We've punished each other long enough, don't you think?"

We did punish each other. She, because he'd left. Him, because she'd refused to tell Todd the truth.

Could they really move forward now? After all this time?

Tearfully, she nodded, then accepted his embrace, the daffodils taking the brunt of it. She didn't care about that right now, though.

"I'm so glad you came back, Peter."

CHAPTER THIRTY-EIGHT

LINDSAY PULLED into the parking lot at the top of Main Street, her heart pounding wildly in her chest. No matter how many times she'd played this scene over in her mind, it never quite went the way she wanted it to.

Travis would get mad, then leave.

Call her ridiculous.

Tell her it was too late.

But Pops was right. She had to try.

If she'd learned anything from this feud with their families, it was that waiting to speak the truth was never a good idea.

The sun shone down on the hood of her car and she basked in the warmth of the coming spring for a few minutes. Then she saw him, pulling into the parking lot with the Stingray.

Here goes nothing.

She got out of the car, then closed the door watching as he pulled into the far corner of the lot, like she'd instructed him to do in the email.

Crossing the parking lot toward him, she shoved her hands

into the pockets of her vest. Travis met her gaze as she drew closer, then he frowned and killed the engine.

She got to the car just as he was opening the door. "Hey." She stopped and gave him a timid smile. "You're here."

Travis rubbed the back of his neck, glancing back at the interior of the car. "Hey . . . uh, listen, this isn't really a good time right now. I'm meeting someone here."

"A girl?" She quirked a brow.

"Yeah, but not like that." He closed the door gently. "I sold the Corvette. I'm meeting the buyer here."

"I know." She held his gaze and her heart ticked up a notch. "I'm the one who bought it."

Travis's brows drew together in confusion, and he did a double take. "What?"

"Yeah. The Stingray. I bought it. You sold it on eBay, right? To LittleBee26?"

Travis's eyes widened. "A-are you kidding me?"

"Little bee is my pops nickname for me." Lindsay held out her hand for the keys. "Thanks for doing such a good job restoring it, Travis. I'm so excited to give it to him. He's going to love it."

Okay, I might be enjoying this a little too much.

She didn't know if this was going according to plan or not, but Travis's bafflement was delightful.

Slowly, Travis straightened, then handed her the keys on a ring. "Who did you—how did you?"

"Logan gave me the money, actually." She shrugged and her lips tickled with a smile she could barely hold back. "He owed me so he took out a loan for it."

Travis blinked, as though impressed. "He does owe you."

"Yeah." She dangled the keys in front of him. "I bought it for my boyfriend. As an apology. For my brother wrecking his business. And for not being brave enough to tell my family I loved him when he was willing to take on the world for me." She took a step closer to him. "If he'll forgive me, that is. Take me back."

I don't want to cry.

Oh God, please forgive me, Travis.

The meaning of her words became clearer to him, and his jaw dropped open. "What? Are you crazy? I-I don't—"

"I am kind of crazy. Mostly about this car mechanic who lives on the wrong side of the tracks. And I'm begging him, right here, right now, to please forgive me for not coming to my senses long ago."

Travis glanced back at the car, then at the outstretched key. Ignoring it, he set his hands on either side of her face and pulled her in for a kiss.

Lindsay's heart raced as she returned his kiss. When he pulled away, she searched his gaze. "I love you, Travis. I love you so much. I don't know why I was so afraid, but I promise I'm not afraid anymore—"

"I'm the one that owes you an apology. I shouldn't have told Logan about the video. I know it hurt you and—"

"It doesn't matter." She sniffled and kissed him again.

"All that matters is that we finally get *our* chance. It's our time."

Travis nodded and kissed her again, this time starting with her forehead, then her closed eyelids, then her lips. "I love you so much, you beautiful, crazy woman." Then he scanned her eyes. "You didn't really buy my car for me, did you?"

She laughed tearfully. "I did. Or Logan did, really. I mean, it's sort of a toss-up. He gave me the money because—let's face it—what he did to you is immeasurable financially. And I knew you'd never actually *take* the money from me otherwise. By the way, there's no need to transfer the title to me. I'm not actually taking possession of it."

"But I'm—I'm closing up shop, selling my business."

Lindsay gave him a sharp look. "Then where the hell am I going to live?"

Travis laughed out loud. "Are you planning on moving in?"

She gave him a shy smile. "I mean, if you don't mind a new roommate. I figure the walk to the restaurant is a whole lot closer from your place than anywhere else. And the sex is infinitely better than—"

"Don't even finish that statement." Travis cut her off with a kiss. "I love you, Lindsay."

"I love you, too. Until forever ends. You're going to have a hard time getting rid of me."

"Good. Because I don't plan to. Ever."

EPILOGUE

Planning a wedding in less than a month had been a unique challenge, but with all the Yardley sisters and Grace Wagner taking over the affair, it had somehow gotten done.

Now, sitting at the edge of the dance floor under the gorgeous tent that they'd set up on the field, Lindsay leaned back while still in her chair into Travis's arms. "I think I'm a little drunk," she murmured, holding her glass of champagne.

"That's my favorite type of Lindsay," he said, kissing her temple.

"Also my favorite type of Lindsay," Jen piped up from her other side, then gave a mischievous waggle to her eyebrows. "But for a totally different reason."

"Let's hope so," Jason chimed in from beside Travis. The two women had insisted on sitting next to each other during the reception and now Jason was on duty holding one of the twins, though Lindsay didn't know which one. They were identical, after all. Jen's mom was showing off the other twin to Lindsay's mother at the parent table.

Lindsay tipped her head at Jason. "Ava or Nora?"

Jason snuck a look at Jen, then whispered loudly, "I'm not really sure. But don't tell Jen that."

"I heard that," Jen said with a frown. "That's Ava. Mom has Nora, you terrible father, you. You can't even tell your own daughters apart?"

"Just kidding, darling," Jason said sweetly, kissing the top of the infant's head. As soon as Jen glanced away, he gave an exaggerated shrug.

Lindsay shared a laugh with him, then cozied closer to Travis. The ceremony had been absolutely perfect—right next to the peach tree, which had been the reason for the rushed wedding. Bunny wanted it blooming when they said their vows.

The DJ announced, then Lindsay straightened as Pops and Bunny walked hand in hand toward the wedding cake Jen had come out of maternity leave to make.

"They're the cutest bride and groom ever," Lindsay whispered to Travis. Then she hiccuped and he laughed.

"You really are drunk." Travis reached for her hand. "Why don't we grab a bottle of water and go for a little walk? Walk it off a bit before your parents notice and blame me."

"Fine." Lindsay nodded at Jen. "Make sure I get a piece of cake, though. I haven't had a Jen Cavanaugh baked good for over two months and I'm starting to get cranky. I need my quota for the year."

"I'll guard it with my life."

Lindsay blew her a kiss, then let Travis help her stand. He slipped his arm around her, and they started through the tent to get to the outside. As they reached the edge, all the guests cheered and they glanced back. Bunny and Pops were feeding each other a piece of cake.

It was perfect.

Just as it should be.

The band started back up again, and Lindsay let her gaze rove over the crowd under the tent. So many faces from Brandywood—friends, regulars at the bar, Yardleys and Wagners. Brian Pearson had served as Pops's best man and Millie Price had been the matron of honor. Lindsay didn't know if she'd ever seen two people who looked happier at their friends' wedding.

In her own olive branch, Lindsay asked Logan to co-manage the bar with her. He did know more about running a business than she did, after all, even if she knew the ins and outs of the restaurant in a different way. So far it had been smooth sailing, and Logan and Travis were even on speaking terms.

One slow step at a time.

Which was really what she needed to concentrate on now. She leaned against Travis, blinking at the starlit sky above them as they got farther away from the tent. "It's sort of a shame that we're building the tourist center here, don't you think? I kind of like this place."

"I do, too. But I think tearing down the cabin will be cathartic to a lot of people. And we can always find new places and new adventures."

"Only if they're dog friendly." Lindsay gave Travis a stern look. "My puppy needs to go anywhere I go for a while. You think he's okay? We've been gone for so long today."

"You know, I think there's a chance you love Ratchet more than me."

She grinned and stopped, grabbing him by the tie. "Guess we'll never know, will we? Now how on earth could I prove my love to you?" Biting her tongue slightly, she edged toward him, slipping her hand down the waistband of his pants.

"That's not fair," he growled in her ear, pulling her closer.

She gave a throaty laugh and kissed his neck. "And why not?"

"I mean, unless you're planning on doing something about it." He ran his hand over her ass, tugging her against him.

"I've had a couple of drinks and Travis Wagner is in my vicinity. I'm a victim of circumstance unable to steer away from this collision course." She trailed her lips up his neck toward his mouth. "And I plan on colliding . . . and colliding . . ."

He groaned against her lips. "Here?"

"Here, there, anywhere you are. I'm yours. I love you."

He chuckled as she pulled him down toward the ground. "And I love you, especially when you—"

She silenced him with a kiss. In the distance, the band struck up a lively rendition of *I Think We're Alone Now*, and Lindsay smiled as she kissed Travis.

Perfect.

THANKS SO MUCH FOR READING! If you enjoyed this book, please consider leaving a rating or review. I'd really appreciate it so much and ratings help me to continue bringing you new books. To keep up with all my current releases and grab bonus material (bonus scenes for all series are coming soon) sign up for my newsletter!

And don't miss the next book in the *Brandywood Small Town Romance Series*, Ever With Me, available now!

NEWSLETTER AND NEXT BOOK

Want to keep up with me and hear what's going on in my world? Join my newsletter on my website! I have freebies and giveaways, exclusive content and, of course, you get to hear all about upcoming book news, my life, and my small army of children.

I hope you enjoyed Lindsay and Travis's story (and Bunny and Peter's, too). Thank you so much for reading; my readers really are what make this possible and I am so grateful for you! If you enjoyed this book, I'd love it if you took the time to leave a rating or review at your favorite book retailer. It truly goes a long way.

And if you'd like to stick around and see more of the world of Brandywood, you can! The next Brandywood story continues with Maddie Yardley's story in Ever With Me. Or, check out the Winnick Contemporary Romance series, in See You Next Fall.

ACKNOWLEDGMENTS

There were two main factors that contributed to the finishing of this book: my husband being crazy generous with the time he took from his work schedule to let me write and an indecent amount of coffee. (Also, probably that terrible cold I got that knocked me off my feet and forced me to sit in bed for a few days helped. 10/10 do not recommend.)

But *once* I had a shell of a book to deliver to my incredible editor, Marion Archer, she was able to help me bring it from its pitiable state into something that was worth reading and, for that, I'm extremely grateful. I also couldn't do this without Julie Simms, Amanda Coleman, and Julie Deaton who are my A-team with edits and proofreading.

And speaking of that crew of little rascals (who were ironically very into that movie while I was writing this), I'm so blessed to have their humor and antics to inspire me daily.

Last, but not least, to anyone who has ever written me a good review or sent me a note of encouragement or popped a few words of praise into an ad or even just bought my books (even if you have no intention of reading them, haha!)—thank YOU. Everything that my readers do to support me has made the biggest difference in the world.

Writing for readers has been the biggest dream come true.

ALSO BY ANNABELLE MCCORMACK

The Windswept WWI Saga:

A Zephyr Rising: A Windswept Prequel Novella

Windswept: The Windswept Saga Book 1

Sands of Sirocco: The Windswept Saga Book 2

Whisper in the Tempest: The Windswept Saga Book 3

The Brandywood Small Town Romance Series:

All This Time

I'll Carry You

Once We Met

Until Forever Ends

Ever With Me

Winnick Contemporary Romances

See You Next Fall

He Loves Me Knot

Don't Forget to Write (Coming Soon)

To find out the latest about my new releases, please sign up for my newsletter or Facebook Reader's group! I love hearing from readers and have some great offers lined up for my subscribers.

ABOUT THE AUTHOR

Annabelle McCormack writes about timeless love and unforgettable journeys. She is a graduate of the Johns Hopkins University's M.A. in Writing Program. She lives in Maryland with her husband and five children. When she's not busy writing, she's probably overwhelmed by laundry and . . . *let's be honest*. She's always busy writing. But she wouldn't have it any other way, either.

Visit her at www.annabellemccormack.com or http://instagram.com/annabellemccormack to follow her daily adventures.